HART & SOL

Russell Emmerson & Matt J Pike

Edited by: Lisa Chant

Model: **Katherine Sortini**
Photography: **John deCaux** / **Six Foot Four Productions**
Costume Design: **Emilia McDonald**
Cover Design: **Matt J Pike**

****

****

Special thanks:
Karen Emmerson, Lisa Chant, Katie Fraser, Jan Pike, Sarah Kipling, Imogen Taintey, Emilia McDonald, John deCaux, Katherine Sortini, Luca Emmerson, Sophie Pike, Sam Pike and Abby Pike.

Published by Zombie RiZing Books

Paperback Edition: February 20, 2022
ISBN: 979-8-88526-094-7

www.mattpike.co

Cover design: Matt Pike

Other books by Russell Emmerson

A Mage Alone

****

Other books by Matt J Pike

Starship Dorsano Chronicles:

Kings of the World
War & Quel

Apocalypse Survivors (Jack):

Apocalypse: Diary of a Survivor
Apocalypse: Diary of a Survivor 2
Apocalypse: Diary of a Survivor 3
Apocalypse: Diary of a Survivor 4

Apocalypse Survivors (Norwood):

The Parade
War Parade

Zambies! An A.I. Apoclaypse Horror/Comedy of the Ages

Zombie RiZing:
The Beginning
Dreeks' Horde
Dragon's Wrath
Death's Door

****

A tribute to Russell Emmerson

My co-author, writing mentor and, above all else, friend…

When we first decided over a few wines to team up on this writing adventure, we had no real idea how it would unfold. But as I sit here now staring at those two magical words – The End – I can honestly say finishing this book has been one of the most rewarding, challenging and enjoyable experiences of my writing life. It's also been one of the hardest (see the author Q&A at the back for more), but I hope you would be as proud of it as I am. If even a fraction of your intelligence, wit, humility and kind spirit come alive on the pages, I'll consider it a success.

A true friend in every way, your life guidance in moments big and small was always delivered with a wisdom and understanding I greatly appreciated. So too, your humour, sharp as a tack and in full flight on many a night filled with irreverent banter, many pints and even more wines. You were rich in qualities that would swell the ego of a lesser person, but never did yours. You were a pure class act of the type sadly lacking in the world today.

I will always look back with a smile at our very important pub meetings, and the joy of planning and writing each chapter of this book. It was so much fun to build this universe with you. I only wish you were around to see it in the hands of readers.

Your friendship is missed every day.
Gone too young.

****

CHAPTER 1:
ALL THAT FLICKERS

Clint Flicker paced the length of the cockpit and back again before pausing in thought, then repeated the pattern. The white insignia of the International Space Corps glowed atop his immaculate red uniform.

He looked at the view through the shieldscreen. Jupiter had started to appear larger in recent days but, that aside, it was nothing but a stretch of distant stars. Distant depressing stars.

He looked at his colleagues — Sarah Hart was at the helm, her fingers dancing a light symphony across the control panel. Esita Storm watched her every move in wonder. While they wore the same colours and insignia, they didn't do it with the same panache.

"Hart, why don't you punch us around and we can see what this baby's got," said Flicker, leaning forward with the grace of a man in charge.

Except he wasn't.

Captain Hart rolled her eyes.

Storm stared at him, mouth agape, for several seconds. Her eyes flicked to Captain Hart, then back to Flicker before using her hand to push her mouth back into its natural habitat. "Are you high?" she asked, in a whisper fully intended to be heard across the cosy bridge.

Flicker's eyes darted back and forward before he scratched his nose to break eye contact with Storm. He turned to the safety of the shieldscreen and mustered his command voice.

"Aren't you bored? We've been out here for hours staring at that totally overrated planet and doing nothing."

"I won't hear a bad word about Jupiter," said Storm. "Best nightlife in the solar system on Jupiter."

Flicker shuddered. "No one needs to hear about your escapades on Jupiter... or anywhere else for that matter."

"Takes a desperate kind of person to live their life in the ass end of the solar system. Especially Titan." Storm drifted off into a dreamy, distant stare.

Captain Hart sighed. "Thanks Storm, that's ample insight from you."

"I've done things there that would make a hooker blush," Storm continued regardless. "Not just any hooker — a Titan hooker." She held out a tattooed hand for a high-five, dropping it lightly back to her console when no one joined her celebration.

"Storm!" snapped Captain Hart.

"You have no shame," Flicker said, swinging his right leg onto a nearby chair so he could lean manfully onto it. He subtly adjusted the sock in his pants so it was less irritating. "You're disgraceful."

"Where was this talk last night?"

Flicker's eyes darted left and right again, before once again finding solace in the view. He could feel Storm's gaze beaming disappointment into him.

"Wish you talked to me like that," she said, holding her hand to her full tattooed lips as a mock damsel-in-distress in a way that flexed her weapons-grade bicep.

Flicker went to respond but no words came out. He settled on a general plan of shutting down and hoping the conversation — and especially the memories of last night — would go away.

"You would've got my A-game," whispered Storm.

"Enough!" snapped Captain Hart. "Can we please focus on the mission?"

"Mission?" said Flicker. "There is no mission. We are literally just up here clocking hours in the cockpit so some bureaucrat can tick a box."

"Which is exactly why you get paid," said Hart.

Flicker's face stretched as he struggled between his belief in his deserved role on the ship and his actual position. He took in Hart's extra stripe and relaxed for the moment.

"Which is why we could stretch this baby's legs, Captain. The *William Shakespeare* is a battleship. Sure, it's seen better days, but it's a ship of war. It needs to be unleashed. It demands it."

"I feel its pain," said Storm.

Captain Hart let out a sigh that cut across their bickering.

"Look, we're not going for a spin, we're on a routine patrol. Same as yesterday, same as the day before and the day before that. That's just what we do. It's our job. It's what we get paid for. So, if we can kindly accept that fact and do it without vocalising any thoughts about how you'll spend your break on Jupiter, that would be fantastic."

Flicker looked to the shieldscreen with his best look of thoughtful authority, while Storm vacantly reviewed the information on her console.

"Before we move on, I just want to point out that it isn't just Titan. Io hookers aren't that much classier to be fair," said Storm, before a thoughtful pause. "And I respect that about them."

Hart closed her eyes and sighed, reminding herself she was the responsible adult. She moved into operational mode.

"Will, you there?"

"Affirmative, my Captain," the ship's computer responded. "You have but to give voice to your needs and they shall fall upon my processors as the very nectar of the gods. Nay, the music of this universe through which we briefly shine."

Hart could feel her jaw clench in the battle of being professional.

"Any updates?" she snapped.

"The very functions I engage may show the—"

"Will…"

Will's personality assessment processors identified in the Captain's warning the very vocal frequency that was empowered to disengage his active AI mode. He chose discretion over valour.

"All ship functions at acceptable capacity. Comms with the *Milky Pleasure* are confirmed and nominal. All activity within the vicinity is accounted for within normal tolerances. Sir."

"See? Boring," said Flicker. "There is nothing happening, nothing wrong and nothing to do. All I'm asking is to put this baby through her paces. Think of it like a training drill, for when things get serious."

"Things never get serious," said Storm.

Flicker opened his mouth to speak but Captain Hart beat him to it. "Will, define acceptable capacity."

"I should be able to function at current capacities, without causing any undue issues. The likelihood of that state changing due to unforeseen or foreign acts is less than 1 percent and therefore within the parameters of normal operations."

Flicker rolled his eyes. "Oh my god, what's the point in having a warship if we're driving it like Ms Daisy?"

There was a long, awkward silence as everyone missed the ancient reference.

"It's hardly state of the art, Flicker. If it was, your sorry ass wouldn't be onboard."

Flicker sighed, then started pacing again, building up his manly stride of authority to compensate for his frustration and lack of command.

Hart shook her head. "Look, everyone here knows the deal. This ship's seen better days."

The air pressure on the bridge increased noticeably.

"Sorry Will, no offence."

The air pressure returned to normal, and Hart appealed to the sensible side of her crew.

"We have been through scraps that have nearly seen us dead, but there is no frontline, and there is no way we are being let near it, even if there was. But—" and here she displayed a cheery smile that failed to reach inside, "we have a job protecting people. We play escort to a cruise ship, protect the rich and the young as they head out to explore the nature of pleasure, and we all get paid. It's easy work with decent pay." She thought about her statement a little more. "Half decent pay."

"You're getting half decent?" said Storm, before whistling. "Damn girl!"

The moment stretched on as they accepted the truth. The stars onscreen continued to evolve through their stellar sequence as their ship made its way slowly back to the cruise ship that was their mission.

Flicker stared into the void. "Just for once, can something interesting please happen?"

Warning lights fired into life on the holodisplays in front of the Captain and the lights on the deck dimmed to a disturbing shade of red designed to improve reaction times while provoking maximum panic.

Everyone looked at Flicker.

"What?" he protested.

Hart did her best to stay calm. "Will, what's going on?"

"I wish to revise my recent statement regarding my ability to function at current capacities."

Hart sighed. "To what?"

"I would like to add the words 'I am unable to' in front of them."

"Report."

Will started rolling out a list of current faults, beyond most of the crew, organised by likelihood of causing a fatality, then by location, and then alphabetically if the faults had been translated into Ancient Greek.

"This is all your fault," said Storm to Flicker.

He mimicked her in an unflattering way.

"Can we skip to what's causing this?" Hart asked Will.

"Likely scenario: A cooling plate has malfunctioned."

"A cooling plate?" said Flicker. "They last forever."

"Twenty years, capacity," confirmed Will. "An achievement accomplished by this particular plate 12 years ago."

"About how long since you proved you were a man," Storm said to Flicker.

"What about last night? You certainly weren't complaining then."

"I think of it as a pity mission," she said as she made an uncomplimentary size gesture with her thumb and index finger.

Flicker self-consciously adjusted the sock in his pants and was framing a response when Hart barked at them.

"Emergency, people. Can we please focus on survival? Will, where's Wave?"

"In his quarters."

"Can you open up comms?"

"Negative. Privacy protocol enabled."

The Captain sighed. Storm rolled her eyes.

"Again!" said Flicker. "He has no shame."

Hart stared at him.

"What? We all know what he's doing." Flicker made a back and forward hand gesture to accentuate his point. It was superfluous.

The Captain sighed. She was battle-hardened, had seen people die and was fighting to save her ship. How had life come to this?

"Someone go get him."

Storm and Flicker eyed each other, both refusing to budge.

"Don't look at me," said Flicker. "I went last time."

"You did not!"

"I totally did… and it was horrific."

"You want to talk horrific?" said Storm. "Last time I had to do this, there was a film on his screen. *That* was horrific."

"A film? That's what bothered you? *You?* What, was it footage of your last trip to Jupiter?"

"Not that sort of film."

"I'm lost," said Flicker. "Oh, something G-rated. I could see you struggling with that."

"I mean not that definition of film."

Flicker stared at her blankly.

"Not the motion picture definition, the thin layer of substance definition."

It took a few seconds for the cogs to start rotating in the right direction in Flicker's mind. "Eww! Eww. That's just eww."

"Also, there was a film on the screen," added Storm.

"That kid has no shame."

"No, he doesn't. And even I have PTSD from that little mission. So, this time it's you."

"Fine, but you owe me."

"Deal," said Storm with way too much enthusiasm.

Flicker looked her stocky frame up and down, finishing on her leery glare. "Actually, you know what, this one comes without strings."

*

CHAPTER 2:
THE FILMMAKER

Mankind was never meant to reach out to the stars. Their short lives put astronomical endeavours beyond their reach, and their tribal nature sparked conflict rather than exploration.

But one racial trait betrayed this common-sense approach: Humanity's overwhelming pig-headedness.

Other species reached the stars for noble causes: To explore the greatest creation; to ensure the survival of the species was not tied to a single planet; to seed the galaxy with life; to search out so as to understand within.

Humanity's driving motivation fell short of this portly ideal. They reached for the black because it was there.

For nearly seventy of their short years they explored, colonising their solar system and nearby systems as if they were owners of creation, puppies rolling in their own shit, too engrossed to look above.

By the time they looked around, it was too late.

They were not alone. And the countdown to humanity's last days had begun.

*

The red bar signalling an active privacy protocol was splashed across Wave's door. Flicker stood in the narrow corridor, bathed in the dim emergency lighting, and thought how different the *William Shakespeare* would run with him in control. Actually in control, not just supporting a chick with a Captain's rank on her shoulders.

His chest puffed out as he envisaged people snapping to attention as he approached, or hearing the computer chime as his crew delivered reports to him about the ship's improved operations.

He would stride around the ship, inspecting its gleaming warp engines and waste recyclers, giving praise where it was due or motivating slacking staff with a noble frown. And they would respond, looking up to him as their respected leader, who would be known across the fleet as the man who would bring out the best in anyone. As the Captain who would find the answer to the most difficult problem. As the admiral who would guide mankind into a new golden age.

The hull groaned around him as it fought against the stress of building heat.

It was enough to end his fantasy. He sighed. They needed Wave.

Flicker moved to establish emergency communication protocols.

"XO override, Alpha 4-6-Gamma."

The door pulsed red at him. Authority rejected.

Flicker raised his voice.

"XO override, Alpha 4-6-Gamma."

Another pulse of rejection.

Flicker turned to the emergency authority protocols.

"Come on Wave," he yelled, as he hammered his fist on the door. "Wakey, wakey, hand off snakey."

The privacy bar dissolved an instant before the door slid open.

"It's all good, dude, just relax. There's nothing to fear, Wave's here."

The small man reached out his arm by way of greeting.

Flicker shuddered and looked away.

"For God's sake, put some pants on!"

Wave looked down and laughed.

"Yeah, right, sorry about that."

He wiped his hand near his hip, inspected his palm and then wiped it against a corridor wall before heading back into his quarters, revealing entirely too much cheek and feathered g-string for Flicker's liking.

Flicker could see the flash of the emergency light as it reflected off the sheen. He wanted to look away but couldn't, entranced by the smear and captured by the feisty odour coming from Wave's room.

"OK, dude, let's go save the world," said Wave, as he walked past him towards the bridge.

Flicker adjusted his sock to its optimal position and rushed in front to lead the way.

"First, it's not 'dude'. It's 'Sir' or 'XO'. Secondly, if you ignore the emergency call again, you're on report. We are a high-functioning crew, poised to deal with extraordinary circumstances." Flicker could feel his jaw tense as it assumed the thrust of leadership.

"Yeah, whatever, dude. But no. We're a bunch of second-rate no-hope losers who are just trying to make a buck cleaning up shit no one else would touch."

Wave wanted to add a line about a high-functioning moron, but thought better of it, instead smiling his crooked yellow smile and reaching up to slap Flicker on the shoulder.

"But hey — at least we've got each other for the next two years, right?"

He burped as he walked onto the bridge and nodded at Hart.

"Hey Captain. Why's Lick-meister here got his panties in a bunch?"

He looked around the bridge, taking in the detail of the displays in the dim light as Hart viewed the virtual displays.

"Oh, we are fucked. So fucked," he said, and reached out to Flicker to steady himself.

Flicker brushed the arm from his shoulder and frowned as he looked at the wet smear now covering his hand.

"Talk to me," barked Captain Hart.

"The cooling plate — it distributes all the waste energy, directs it. Without it, all that heat is channelled into the hull. It weakens it, stretches it—"

A low groan interrupted him.

"Like that."

"So what, we reattach the plate? We can do that," said Hart.

Wave shook his head.

"No way, Jose. If it's shot, it's shot. The circuits in the plate are what count. If it can't shunt that energy around, then that's it, you can't use it. But that's not the worst of it."

Hart rubbed her forehead to hide her frustration. Wave was good. A genius. But he also had a passion for the dramatic gesture to underscore his importance. She wanted results, not a monologue.

"What is the worst of it, then?"

"Well, it's like a river. If you dam it up, then it backflows. Fries the circuits."

"So we're dead in the water?"

"No. Just dead."

Hart look around the bridge, hoping for a brilliant insight that would save them all. Storm was staring at her, poised for an order so she could act. Storm was a warrior. Waiting didn't suit her bristling need for activity.

Flicker had one leg up on the arm of a chair as he stared thoughtfully at the holoscreen. His frown made a small line stand out between his eyes — it was a tell, Hart knew. Flicker had no idea beyond the need to stare thoughtfully somewhere.

Captain's duty: enter impossible situation, find solution, move on.

"Will?"

"My name is called from the dream beyond, filled with bells of delight."

"What's the status of the escape pods?"

"The steeds of destiny are poised for action, but alas — death holds their reins tightly, fearful of their grip on life."

Wave screwed up his face and began muttering.

"So, no access to the firing mechanisms. Which means we can't divert power because there is no power, it's just heat."

Flicker turned and wiped sweat from his forehead.

"Is it just me or is it getting hot in here?"

Storm snorted.

"Definitely not you. But it is getting warmer."

"Yeah, the hull's trapping the heat in. Given we're a warship we have a reinforced hull, so the waste heat probably won't crack it," said Wave.

"That's good, right?" Hart asked.

"Maybe. Anyway, it won't really matter. The heat will build up here, so we will probably cook before the hull gives. But I've got an idea. Captain, can you hook me up with Connor?"

Hart nodded, and instructed Will to set up the connection.

Connor was the chief engineer on the *Milky Pleasure*. He was widely acknowledged as a double threat: A genius of an engineer, and a personality not of an engineer. His Scottish accent always managed to entrance her, to the point where he thought she had a deep understanding of dynamic warp theory. She wanted a deep understanding of something, but it wasn't warp.

A voice bounced around the bridge, the hiss and crackle of spacial radiation distorting it.

"Hey, it's Hiscock. Sorry, but the chief's out at the moment. I'm sure I can help."

Wave looked to Hart, who nodded back to give him permission to take over.

"Yeah, Hiscock, Wave here. Look, I know Connor's busy and all, but could you put him on? We have a situation here."

"He's busy, I can help."

"No you can't, dude, it's way beyond your pay grade. So if you could run along and get Connor, that'd be fab."

"Hey, I can too—"

"How's the Goliath going?"

There was a long, awkward pause at the other end of the line. "I'll get him now."

There was a crackle in the *Milky Pleasure's* signal as they waited.

"Connor here. What have you got?"

"A blown cooling plate."

"But those things have a 20-year lifespan."

Everyone on the bridge called out: "Passed 12 years ago."

"Connor, what if we flash-fry and cast it?"

The crackle provided a counterpoint to Connor's laugh.

"You're crazy, lad. Those things are made in factories staffed with good Scots, tough as nails."

Wave's head dropped.

"But if you have a good Scot, you might have a fighting chance. And guess what? You're bloody lucky."

As Wave and Connor worked out the details, Hart wiped her brow. She'd love a good Scot, too. But survival of her crew, first. And her own survival, of course.

*

Wave was suited up, his head under the decking on the lowest level of the *William Shakespeare*. Flicker stood nearby, trying to be in command and relaxed, and failing at both. His mind kept straying to the slap of Reality he had had in his cabin, wondering whether he could quickly duck off for a sneaky fix of his preferred mindbend.

"Dude, I've hooked this baby up. Fluid's superheated and ready to be pumped in, cast is on outside and ready to be blown, but the connection here needs to be insulated — without covering the surrounding area."

"Whatever, Wave, just do it."

"Nah. If we don't get it right, we drop the hull."

"OK, well what, then? What?"

"We need something to insulate the connection. Do you have a sock?"

Flicker looked down at his uniform. The jacket. The shirt. The pants. The boots. No socks.

"How about a shirt?"

"Nowhere near the density we need. Jesus — this is about to start. Dude, seriously, I need a sock, and I need it now."

"Maybe I can go to my cabin and—"

"Dude, my arse is up in the air because I'm trying to stop this thing from blowing us all to hell. This is your chance to be the hero, man. The hero."

Flicker closed his eyes and focused on the last words. In his head they echoed, the gravity of their bass reverberations drowning out Wave's tinny voice.

The hero. He nodded, and bravely reached into his pants to pull it out: The sock that would save them.

Flicker nodded to it, respecting the hard work it had done over recent months.

He dropped it next to Wave, and then gave it a full ceremonial salute for its service, ignoring the lack of its comforting presence.

Wave made a gagging noise as he pincered the material so as to make as little surface contact as possible. "Man — you're not a grower or shower — you're a stower!"

He cackled in the way that drove Flicker crazy. This time there was no response that could save face.

Wave turned his attention back to the task at hand.

"Perfect, and contact," said Wave, before his voice was drowned out by a hideous screech as molten metal was forced through the pathways of the cooling plate. A moment later, Flicker staggered as the dull thump of an explosion hit the hull.

"What the hell was that?"

"It's all good, man, that's exactly what we wanted to hear."

"You blew the hull and that's what we want to hear? Are you crazy? Back off now. That's an order," said Flicker.

"Flicker, stand down." The Captain's voice floated above them. "Wave? Report."

"Aside from the creep ogling me from behind, who I'm pretty sure is getting a sockon—"

"Aside from the..." there was an awkward pause as Flicker gathered his thoughts and dignity, and prepared to fire a barb back "...um, perve with no morals."

"Gentlemen! And I use that term extremely loosely," said Hart. "Wave — report."

"The hot metal has been poured in and should have dissolved the circuit capillaries and replaced them with a new superstructure. The charge fired and cleaned off the remaining cover. We should be able to reboot and operate at minimal power — but we've got a whole lot of work to do when we get back to the *Milky Pleasure*."

"Will, can you send a 2 volt pulse through to the plate for, say, one second?"

"I have guided thine own energy into the lattice that holds heart for the brave," Will said cheerily.

Wave screamed, and Flicker ran to his twitching legs.

"Wave? Wave?"

Hart listened to the communication in hope.

"Fucking brilliant!" Wave screamed, adding a "woot" for good measure.

"Bastard. I thought you'd died!"

"Awwww, you care. So sweet. Captain, we should be ready to test whether this works now, but we have to take it slow."

"How slow?"

"About 'the whole thing could explode and kill us all' sort of pace. And we'll need to reboot and reduce our footprint so we don't overtax the systems," he said.

"OK, return to the bridge. We will all hole up here. Even if we don't survive, nice work, Wave."

Wave hiked up his pants in response to Flicker's pointed and queasy glance.

As they entered the bridge, the Captain nodded her head to Wave in respect. Storm applauded: "Way to go, Wave. Legend."

Wave turned to her, smiling with a shy, yellow-toothed grin.

"A legend you say, perhaps you'd be interested in—"

"Never," said Storm, before turning back to her holodisplay. "Besides, I'd crush you."

Wave kept staring, dreaming of just that, until Hart interrupted.

"Wave, next?"

"Right. Umm… right," he said and his brain kicked into gear again. "We'll need to shut things down and then start up again slowly. Minimal life support — better if there was none at all — and then bring what we need online. Say — nav, propulsion and docks — probably in that order."

Hart gave her orders. Everyone climbed into their pressurised suits and returned to their positions. Their natural levity quietened when the emergency lighting faded.

"Sitting in a dark suit in a dark box in the dark of space," Flicker muttered. "Feels like a warm-up for death."

"May yet be just that," said Storm.

The Captain's voice cut across them both, overcoming the tinny radio links.

"Ladies and gentlemen, I don't feel like dying today, so I'm afraid you're going to be disappointed. Will, bring on Systems Monitoring, Nav, then propulsion, but wait for my mark. And no need for theatrics. Now: Systems, please."

Light flashed on Wave's face, distracting him from the massive silver figure of Storm close by. He scanned the incoming messages and gave a thumbs up to Hart.

"Thank you, Wave. Nav, please."

The holodisplay in front of Flicker glowed and he waited for it to cycle through its opening sequence. After a few minutes, he groaned.

"It's done a factory reset, bloody well taken everything back to a fresh install. No! I do not want you to show me how to write a navigation plan! Sorry, Sir. Yeah, looks fine," he said.

"Excellent," said Hart. "XO, please plot our return to the *Milky Pleasure*, but keep it to 10 percent, no more."

"Copy."

"Bringing propulsion online now."

Everyone viewed the progress bar as it blinked, adding capacity with every flash. And with every flash, everyone winced, thinking it was the start of an explosion. They all held their breath when the system paused at 99 percent... and twitched and groaned when the soft pleasing chime sounded at 100 percent.

"Jesus, remind me to take that one offline," Hart muttered. "Ladies and gentlemen, let's move. XO, on your mark."

The thrusters ignited and the hull groaned in response to the flow of power. But they were alive.

They were silent for every minute of the next three hours, thankful that the hull protected them for one second. And then the next. And the next.

Storm was the first of them to speak in full voice.

"Captain, we have a bead on the *Milky Pleasure*."

"That's a sighting, Storm. You take a bead on an enemy with a weapon. Please don't kill our charges. And onscreen, please."

The *Milky Pleasure* appeared onscreen. Its sweeping wings were glass, holding pleasure gardens and a river that flowed from a waterfall in the hull. Windows lined the white hull, each a compartment with the latest in pleasure technology and hygienic control. And towards the rear was a wide hole, the shuttle docking bay that was home to the *William Shakespeare* for this two-year protective mission.

As they approached their docking station, Hart spoke softly.

"Ladies and gentlemen, welcome home: The *Milky Pleasure*."

Sure, it was only a new home — only a few weeks into what would be a long mission. And sure, it wasn't the height of any of their careers. And, well, yeah, the pay wasn't great. And if they really analysed the quality of their uniforms, they'd know they weren't made of the same quality materials as those crewing official fleet craft. But, some moments there are other things that matter.

They sat quietly, making out more details as the ship grew larger on the screen, its broad flank reflecting the orange glow of Jupiter nearby.

It was a glorious moment when they could all appreciate the beauty of the universe they all lived in, under the backdrop of how easily it could all be taken away.

"Captain?" said Storm.

"Yes, Storm?"

"Our bar had better be open when we get there."

"Yes, Storm. Our bar had better fucking well be open."
"Oh, and Flicker?" Storm asked.
"Hmm?"
"You know how Wave used your sock to get the ship to work?"
Flicker was dead still, too wary to respond.
"Should he get his hand tested for anything?"
They all felt the kick as Flicker increased the thrust to dock quicker.
Our bar had fucking well be open, he thought to himself.

*

CHAPTER 3:
ABSINTHE OF MALICE

While the aftermath of the events that were about to transpire led to many theories around who knew what, where and when, the reality was no one knew anything about the attack until it was too late. At least, no one who was in a position, or had the inclination, to do anything about it.

Each of Earth's settlements — from those on Jupiter's moons to Ceres, Mars, Sagan's Station and every large mining and military outpost in between — fell like dominoes.

So swift and stealthy was the attack, warning signals only reached the next target as defenders were fighting for their lives. Maybe, with some notice, humanity could've posted some meaningful resistance, but mankind didn't even get a fighting chance.

Earth's demise was as short and sure as those of the colonies. Within a handful of hours, everything humanity had created over millennia was in tatters. The relay of knowledge, discovery, institution and power, passed as a baton from one generation to the next over the eons, lay in waste.

While pockets of humanity survived, every structure that would give them the means to fight back did not. This was an extinction-level event.

Humanity lay in ruins.

*

"Oh my god, it's a disaster." Storm slumped to the floor as she struggled to cope with the news.

The sight of the effect on the warrior sucked hope out of all of them.

"I have no words," said Wave, his hand cradling his sweaty forehead and almost covering the red pimples that had gone white with shock.

Flicker strode back and forward in nervous confusion, feeling a fix of Reality and a thick sock short of being able to consider whether he was capable of coping with the news. "This can't be happening," he said, more than once.

Hart looked at them and moved into command mode. She assessed the available information and resources, weighed the immediate possibilities and the consequences, before settling on a strategy that would determine their future. "Why don't you try knocking?"

They looked at each other in turn, then to the door of the SaturnTable Bar. Its cheesy neon sign promising colourful cocktails and trippy tunes just added to the taunting. Eventually, Flicker stepped forward, adjusted himself, sighed, then unleashed his most commanding knock.

After several seconds' silence, he turned to the others. "Great. Just great. What do we do now?"

"Wait!" said Storm. "I heard something!"

She pressed her face to the opaque multi-coloured glass next to the door, ear planted against its cool rippled surface.

She could hear a distant muffled voice from the other side. It seemed to be directed at her.

Wave leaned forward. "What's happen—"

"Shhh," snapped Storm, as she raised her hand into the stop signal in his direction.

Wave was an experienced recipient of the signal and Pavloved into obedient quiet. Silently, he enjoyed every moment the warrioress paid attention to him.

The voice came again, this time closer and clearer. "Coming!"

Storm fell to her knees again, this time spreading her arms out and looking to the heavens. "We're saved." Hart thought she saw real tears streaming down the warrior's face, but she was too smart to point them out.

The door opened to reveal a man parading the 73.45 percent too flamboyant SaturnTable Bar uniform. Its shoulder pads flared, its torso glimmered and its subsonic speakers urged all within a two-metre radius to "Relax and have a good time" with a voice artistically modified to speak directly to the delta-transmitters of the brain.

The man looked at their desperate faces. Even a rookie bartender could spot customers this thirsty. He gave them a knowing smile, in part for being the saviour to their needs, as well as recognising them as the crew of the *William Shakespeare*. This would be a good way to start his first shift.

"You look like you could do with something stiff."

"I thought you'd never ask."

The bartender looked down to see Storm on her knees, eyeing him with a predatory hunger.

He made a high-pitched squeal and took an instinctive step backwards, a move that shamed the proud lilac, gooseberry and avocado swirls of his uniform. His training re-asserted itself. "Erm, bar's open," he said in a voice much lower than his initial greeting.

"Who's the newb?" said Wave with a nod of his head as they headed in.

Storm got to her feet and joined the others. "Fresh meat, who cares?"

"He's new," said Hart, in thought. "Here at least."

By habit, they herded themselves towards the booth around the corner from the door. It was furthest away from the DJ stage and offered the best view of the patrons — when the place was full — more for picking out potential sexual partners than potential military threats.

Hart peeled away from the group towards the bar, her offer of the usual greeted with approval.

"Scotch on the rocks, espresso martini, double absinthe, no ice, and a shandy," she said to the already waiting bartender.

While he fumbled around preparing his first order, Hart searched her mind to connect the familiarity of his face in this new context. She definitely knew him. It was easy to misplace a face out here. They'd only rendezvoused with the *Milky Pleasure* when the ship left the inner solar system two weeks earlier. There was a crew of nearly 1000 to get familiar with, mixed up with 5000 frozen bodies of paying customers that would soon flood the hallways and bars.

She had most of the senior command covered — the uniforms helped — as well as the support staff in the docking bay, those neighbouring quarters in her wing, as well as the service staff and, to a lesser extent, regular customers in the shops, restaurants and bars she frequented.

Even then, she couldn't be sure she knew him from the trip at all.

"124 credits, please."

"Erm, there's a cherry in the scotch."

"Indeed. Helps smooth out the smoky edge."

"It's not entirely the rocks then, is it?"

"To be fair, most rocks aren't transparent."

She shrugged at the logic, which was all too much to process in the moment, then pressed her palm up against the payment plate. Blue light danced around her hand for a moment before it pulsed a flash of green.

He looked at her. "Everything OK?"

She shook her head but answered, "Yes." Then noted his name tag. "Thanks Nick."

"Markou. Nick Markou."

"Sarah Hart."

"I know."

Still nothing. She took the tray containing her order and headed to the booth.

Wave had his index finger pressed against his ear, lost in a conversation beyond those around him. He was throwing in the occasional "yes" or "good" and unnecessarily nodding. His comms ended with the words, "Legend, Connor, thanks."

He looked to the others as Hart passed him his martini, then nodded. "So, the hull survived pretty much in decent condition — apart from the new vent we blasted. Anyway, there's plenty of material to repair the breach. The cooling plate is another matter. Yes, I'm a legend. Yes, I created a replacement cooling plate out of my knowledge of industrial smelting techniques. But it ain't gonna cut it. Connor, the genius, has figured out a workaround."

They all leaned into Wave's words as Hart passed Storm her double absinthe.

"Don't look at me to explain it. He was, like, super excited by that point and I didn't understand a word. It was like a foreign language."

There was a palpable air of disappointment in Wave's words.

"What? He's Scottish. Scot-tish. Anyway, I did manage to translate the last bit and, unless I'm mistaken, we should be up and running within the day."

Flicker leaned back in the alpha corner of the booth, one leg spread out along the chair. "Masterstroke."

"You can't call it a masterstroke when you don't even know what he's going to do," said Hart, as she stood over him, waiting for him to concede some booth space. She held his shandy as a bargaining chip until he did.

He retracted his leg, but kept the prime corner. It was enough of a concession to get his reward.

Hart claimed her space.

"I'm just glad Will's going to be OK. I'd miss him if anything happened."

"Will? It's an AI, what does it matter?" said Wave. "Besides, he's harder to understand than Scottish."

Hart stared at him, unimpressed. "Speaking of masterstrokes, Wave, if you could not have your privacy on so many times a day, that'd be a bonus to the mission."

Wave started to respond, but realised no combination of words could save any version of what passed for his dignity at that point. He was left in silence with mouth agape.

"Honestly, we're supposed to be the shield of defence around this ship, her crew and the human cargo we carry. For appearances at the very least, it should be all hands on deck."

There was a long pause, interrupted only by a snort from Storm.

"I said deck!" said Hart. "With an E!"

Wave took a swig of his martini as he seized on the power of diversion.

"Hey! I just saved all our lives, remember? How am I the problem? Why not pick on your XO, who's got way too much front for his own good. And I'm not even sure if that's him using socks down his pants.... or just using."

"Listen up you little creep—"

"Or Storm, whose role is... actually, what is your role?"

"I'm head of mess your shit up," said Storm, before throwing back her absinthe and standing over the diminutive Wave ready to fight.

"Enough!" snapped Hart. "Good lord, can we at least be capable of sharing the same table without acting like teenagers?"

Her crew complied in sulky silence, much like teenagers.

"Finally!" Hart enjoyed the clear air, until it became too uncomfortable. "Right, Wave, your round."

Wave went to protest as the recent hero who shouldn't be buying the drinks, but knew this wasn't the time. Instead, he placed his fingers in his mouth and whistled. Once he had the barman's attention, he yelled,. "Same again", then winked at the Captain.

She rolled her eyes.

"Wait, why the fuck is there fruit in your scotch?"

"The cherry? It just adds something to smooth out the smoky edge."

"Sounds wanky."

"Barman's idea. Not bad."

"Who even are you right now?" said Storm.

Hart stared at her.

Storm felt the full force of the glare and it added up to more than cherries.

"Sorry. Things have been a bit crazy cap," said Storm. "It's just all this built-up tension. Things will change once we get to Jupiter."

The Captain rolled her eyes again.

"Have you no shame?" said Flicker, as he sipped his shandy.

"Hells no, I'm going to relieve so much tension down there, the whole region is going to resemble a cloaca when we leave."

"By down there, I assume you mean Jupiter."

Storm shook her head then pointed to her crotch.

Flicker rolled his eyes. "What on earth is a cloaca?"

"As your coworker, I strongly advise you not to seek a definition for that word," said Wave.

Flicker interfaced with his wrist device. He blushed and whispered at her: "What the hell is wrong with you?"

She beamed and winked before crushing her shot glass in one hand.

The barman arrived with round two.

This time, a wave of recognition washed over Hart. "Wait a minute, aren't you that HR guy?"

Markou seemed both pleased and disappointed. "Yes. But I'm not HR, I'm the belonging agent."

"Groan," groaned Storm.

"Second job? Sounds like HR earns even less than us," said Wave.

"Belonging agent," snapped Markou, before reeling his emotions in. "I'm a… your… belonging agent."

"So, HR," confirmed Storm.

Markou's face darkened. He collected himself and spoke slowly in a way that sounded like he was reading it from a brochure. "A belonging agent is here to keep you motivated and engaged during the long and sometimes psychologically testing journey ahead."

Wave held up a card on the table. "Hey, that's what it says in this sales brochure!"

Storm took another shot of absinthe. "HR shrink, then."

Hart could see the frustration growing in Markou's eyes and changed tack. "So, what's a belonging agent doing pouring drinks?"

"Well, business is a little slow at the moment—"

"Shocker," said Wave.

Markou breathed deeply to exorcise the demons of yet another display of non-acceptance. They didn't understand. Nobody understood how vital his role was. He crossed his fingers under the drink tray. "So, if you can't bring Mohammed to the mountain..."

Flicker crossed his legs. "Wait, are you going to do your psychobabble on us? Here?"

"It's not psychobabble! It helps people to escape from their feelings of—"

"No, we come *here* to escape," said Storm. "And we are especially trying to escape from people like you!"

"But—"

"Hells yeah," agreed Wave. "I don't care about your mountain, I just want to get Mo-hammered."

He held out his hand for a high-5. None came.

"Anyone? Anyone?

"Because I said Mo-hammered, but I meant, like, 'more hammered'. See what I did?"

"Shut up Wave."

Wave's proud high-5 fingers slowly receded, before his hand closed and he lowered it to his lap, defeated.

Markou swallowed all his pride, once again reduced to cold-selling the newbie sales pitch to intellectually inferior people. "Look, I understand your concerns. I am not here to cause you angst. Just think of me as your barman, but know, at any time you feel you may need, I'll be there for you."

Storm drained the rest of her drink. "Great, go fetch another round, huh?"

The others stared at their drinks, then at Storm.

"Don't get your panties in a bunch. If you're not ready, I'll drink them," she said.

Markou closed his eyes, reminding himself his years and years and years of cutting-edge training in the field would be called upon at some point. He turned with as much pride as he could muster and headed for the bar.

"Could you go a little quicker than that?" said Storm.

She offered a high-5, which was gratefully accepted by Flicker and a mildly jealous Wave.

"You know, we could have some real fun with this," she added.

"Either that, or we go to a different bar," said Flicker.

"No way! This is the bar, I'm telling you. When they start waking some of the customers for the Jupiter hop, I can guarantee this will be the place to be."

Flicker looked around. "Really? *This* bar? What about the two-storey one with the bungy-bucket shots? Or the one with the kickass dancefloor over the stars? Or anything along the starwalk wing?"

"Maybe they'll get bigger numbers through the door, but when was the goal ever to have a good time with a lot of people around you? It's about finding the rejects, the sad-acts, the depressed and desperate, plying them with far more liquour than they need to lower their inhibitions, then mountin' them. Yee-haw!"

"I'm not sure Mohammed would approve of that mountin'," said Wave. He knew the high-5 was futile before he offered it.

There was a pause in the conversation. Storm's words had cheapened the situation, but did nothing to make it less true. It was a plan they all secretly shared. So long did the pause extend, thoughts from each started to turn to the words rejects, sad-acts, depressed and desperate, and how applicable they may be to those at the table.

The moment became heavier until Storm blasted through the silence.

"Man, I can't wait. The first being that even holds eye contact with me for more than a second, I'm going go down quicker than, well, this absinthe."

Wave looked at her with a broad grin.

"Except you."

Hart raised her glass. "Well, here's to the Jupiter hop."

They all cheersed. Deep thoughts about belonging officers, the length of the potential psychological battle ahead that interstellar travel often induced and how low they may potentially stoop on the way there evaporated. The power of their glasses gifted them a magic to return to the moment and lose perspective of the things that circled it.

At least for three seconds.

"Besides, cap, we've got to end your streak."

Hart felt her cheeks burn. She went to speak but only managed to stumble over nonsensical syllables.

"That's right!" said Flicker. "The no-hitter."

Wave grinned at her.

Hart shuddered.

"I haven't read the rules, but I think she can claim virgin status again," said Storm.

Wave winked at her.

Hart could feel her heart start to race, the skin on her face now burning. Still no words came. She was a wreck. It was the feeling — that feeling — the no-hitter feeling. Her Captain's air of authority evaporated. She could see them laughing right at her, and there was nothing she could do. She took a swig of the drink, but spilled some down the front of her uniform. Goddamn it! How did it all come to this? All over stupid, stupid, stupid, impossible-to-get sex.

She felt a buzzing on her wrist. It was her comms. Potential salvation from the moment. The lighting and vibration triggered her to know instantly it was an emergency. Still, she'd take an emergency over this. She answered. "Captain Horny."

Her crew burst into a new round of hysterics.

They watched Hart awkwardly avoid eye contact as she dealt with the voice on the other end.

"Sorry, Sir.

"Yes, I understand you're married.

"I… I… sorry.

"Uh-huh.

"When was this?

"What?

"I'm sorry, could you please repeat that?

"Oh, fuck.

"Are you sure?

"And this is not a drill?"

The group's side conversations faded as the potential gravity of the, well, whatever the situation was, became clear.

"Affirmative, Sir.

"Yes, Sir.

"Will do, Sir

"Right away, Sir."

She closed the comms and looked at the others, now silent and fearing a certain amount of impending doom.

A feeling that was a lifetime short of the mark required.

Hart coughed to clear her throat and settle her nerves.

"We've got a big problem."

*

CHAPTER 4:
SPHINK OR SWIM

Hart strode along silver corridors lined with exotic and erotic artworks, passing dark alcoves designed to entice passengers to indulge all their senses as they wished and with whomever they wanted.

She saw none of it.

Lurid posters flashed at her as she passed, tapping into her body type and psyche to invite her to shows that would allow her to escape the mundanity of this universe and join one made specifically for her pleasure and joy.

She had no time for it.

The distractions eased as she approached the command tube and palmed her request to head straight to the bridge. She bypassed all outstanding requests, giving her peace of mind in an empty capsule ahead of the moments of chaos she knew awaited her arrival.

The doors slid open. There was a palpable tension on the bridge, either from what was unfolding beyond the ship, or the Bridge Captain's bureaucratic panic. Either way, it was not good.

"I need a report to be able to give orders, and you haven't yet reported," said a strained, thin and all-too-familiar voice. "What is your report?"

"Sir, we are losing network feeds." Hart noted Comms Officer Elena Rodriguez was focusing on the task rather than responding to the implied insults from the Bridge Captain. "But we don't know what's behind it. They just keep dropping out — wait, we've just lost Ceres."

"Well what's happening on Ceres? Report!" the Bridge Captain insisted.

It was too much for Hart. She was geared for survival. Rank be damned.

"Is there any pattern to the loss? Even a guess?" she asked.

Rodriguez looked briefly at Bridge Captain Colin Sphink. Any half-decent counsellor would be able to detect the small tells as she wrangled back a desperate need to strangle a superior officer. As it was, Rodriguez focused on professionalism and the momentary urge passed.

"Captain Hart, there's no pattern we can discern," said Rodriguez. "There's a chance they may be coordinated in some way, but I'd have to track back allowing for point of origination—"

"Excellent approach. Do it. What's happening locally? Do we have eyes out there?"

"Captain Hart, this is my bridge. I have these stripes, and they clearly show that this is my bridge," Sphink said.

"Good, excellent. So do you have eyes out there?"

Sphink sought comfort in display data over eye contact. "As you know we are preparing for the next destination ahead of the Jupiter alignment, as advertised to our paying customers. But they paid for the Jupiter alignment and they will be seeing it before we depart."

The bridge lights dimmed, replaced by a sombre red alert.

"Ah, Sir?" said Rodriguez.

"Yes?" said both Sphink and Hart.

"I've just lost the corporate feed. It's dead."

Sphink's mouth opened and closed.

"So corporate won't be able to receive complaints," Hart confirmed. "Tell me when you've got a pattern."

"Yes Sir."

Hart took a breath as she looked across the bridge. Sphink was poring over a diagram, tracing the lines that made up its components in the soft red glow as he muttered to himself.

Rodriguez was bouncing between screens and plotting events to determine just what the hell was going on.

Flight Manager Paul Avis sat there, reviewing flight plans that had already been reviewed.

Hart didn't know enough. She needed more. She thumbed her own comms.

"Flicker, I need our crew. Now."

She heard a massive background cheer before Flicker's local audio dampeners cut in.

"Yes, Sir. What do you need?"

"Stay close to the *Shakespeare*. Get both Wave and Storm to keep an eye out for anything unusual. We're losing groundside contact. I need our crew. Now."

She signed off. Despite the slur in Flicker's voice, there was no need for an acknowledgement.

Sphink's voice edged in.

"Ah, Captain, a word if I may?"

He walked towards her, inserting a holo display into the space between them showing the diagram he had been inspecting. She was hoping it showed the electronic fault responsible for their problems, but instead she saw linked boxes, one with her name. Another with Sphink's.

"Captain," Sphink began reasonably. "This is the organisational chart for this contract, as approved by our employer, Dream Lines, as our ship's AI can attest. You'll note the insignificant branch down here with the label quasi security."

He pointed to the logo as the smooth and empty tone of the ship's AI confirmed the currency of the chart, then ran his fingers down to the words quasi security. Then smiled and continued.

"I just wish to point out that you, Captain, are acting in a support mission — shall we call it an advisory role, hmmm? — and not in an active capacity," he said, using a particular smile he had been practising in the mirror for months now.

"As such, I wish to note that this is my command and my bridge. Therefore, all crew are to report to me directly, including your own. Through you, of course," he said, using a different smile that had an added element of condescension.

His index finger continued to tap on the company logo, drawing strength from the rightness of it.

Hart's communicator interrupted her murderous impulse.

"Sir?"

"Yes? What is it?"

"Wave here. Things are getting a bit freaky. Transmissions are getting… sluggish."

"Define sluggish."

"Ah, sort of defying-the-laws-of-physics sluggish. Like operating the way that they shouldn't. In this universe."

Hart looked up to the comms manager. He swiped through screens and looked up at her, pale, and slowly nodded.

Hart acknowledged and returned to the conversation before Sphink could interrupt.

"Thanks, Wave, good work. Keep me informed. Out."

Her mind snapped to command mode, starting to clarify potential threats and available resources, when a sharp cough distracted her.

Sphink held up the organisational chart in front of her, tapping the logo.

"This clearly shows the primacy of my command and I insist, no I order, you to stand down. You are not to give orders to my crew, you are not to speak to my crew without my permission," he said, tapping. "And, to be clear, you do not have that permission."

The comms manager coughed with an awkward "Sir?"

Both Hart and Sphink responded without breaking eye contact.

"Sorry, Sir, I was talking to Captain Hart. Captain?"

Hart only had the briefest of moments to appreciate the shade of purple growing over Sphink's face.

"Yes?"

"We've lost another three feeds, all from the outer colonies, and there is a pattern."

The bridge was quiet except for her sharp intake of breath.

"Allowing for distance, they all occurred at the same time."

Hart breathed out calmly and slowly, feeling her shoulders relax. She triggered all-ship comms with two sharp words: "Battle stations."

A calm tone sounded as formal acknowledgement, broken only by a splutter from Sphink.

"But this is… mutiny! The chart says—"

"Captain," Hart began as she saw his face turn from purple to white. "Under company bylaw 435A(ii), command shall pass to the senior military officer when the mission is faced by an external event that poses mortal danger to all related travelling parties."

"There is no mortal threat!" Sphink yelled. He called out to the ship's AI. "MPOPS, please rescind the battle status and return all command to me immediately."

Hart's comm chirped. It was Wave.

"Captain, there's funky stuff happening out there but this is for you. We're receiving a distress call."

Hart looked to the comms manager. "Play it."

The comms manager punched his screen and a scratchy audio track echoed over the bridge.

"—assistance needed. Repeat, this is Earth Ambassador Jon Harding onboard the vessel *Valhalla*. I am under attack from a hostile force, size unknown. I am losing life support and have information that is imperative to the survival of our species. Urgent assistance needed. Repeat—"

Hart looked at the bridge comms manager, who scanned his screen and nodded at her.

"The codes check out, Captain."

Sphink yelled next to her. "I said return control of the bridge to me. The company says it's my command!"

Hart opened command comms.

"Under company bylaw 435A(ii) I hereby take command of this vessel," she said calmly. "Flicker, prep the *William Shakespeare*. We're going to need to bring him in."

"Ah, Captain?"

"Yes, Wave?"

"I've figured out that funky stuff."

"Well done, but no time for a medal. What is it?"

"Space-time warps. There are things that are warping in. If I was going to leap to a conclusion, I might suggest that we have enemy threats coming in at us."

Storm yelled in delight in the background.

"About bloody time this thing became interesting."

Hart took a slow breath to reset her rising adrenalin. She had a foreign threat, a skeleton crew, a beast of a ship to protect, one of Earth's highest officials calling for help and an idiot Bridge Captain whose face was turning a new shade of purple. All she needed was the solution that would tie it all together. She needed more information.

"Storm, we need to protect the Ambassador. Can you issue the battle drones?"

"No, we're wedged in here tighter than Flicker's sphincter. We have to launch."

"Wave, can we launch?" she asked, batting away Sphink's insistence on a dead protocol.

"Well, yeah, but we haven't fixed the cooling plate problem. Hang on a moment—"

The line went dead.

She turned to the next problem while she waited for movement on the first.

"Comms, do you have a fix on the incoming threat?"

"Yes, Sir."

"Good man. Nav, work with Comms. I want this ship heading towards safety."

"We can't warp yet, Sir. We're still too deep in Jupiter's well."

Fuck it, she thought. *Just one lucky break. That's all we need.*

"Fine. Just find a safe path."

There was a polite cough from the purple face near her elbow.

"I think you will find you have limited options, Captain," Sphink said with his sickly smile. He looked up and addressed the ship's AI. "MPOPS, please confirm navigational options."

A clipped officious tone sounded from the speakers.

"No deviations from the current flight plan have been approved," it said.

Hart ground her teeth.

"Well we're going to need to approve them pretty damned quickly," she said.

"Seeking company confirmation of approval," MPOPS stated. "Waiting on feeds. Waiting on feeds. Waiting on feeds. No feeds found. Deviation from current flight plan is unavailable until company confirmation is received."

Behind her closed eyes, Hart saw herself ripping wires from behind a panel until the voice of MPOPS faded. But she needed solutions. She contacted her AI.

"Will, are you there?"

"Be still my binary heart. In this time of darkness when all hope frays like tendrils of mist and dreams in the dawn, it is my Captain. O Captain?"

"Will, can you please work directly with Mary Poppins here? We need a workaround that will allow us to take evasive action — even without company approval."

She sensed the bridge lights dim as connection was made. MPOPS' love of procedure was going to meet the binary reincarnation of *William Shakespeare*. She could sense its despair.

"Wave. Update!"

"I'm calling in the reinforcements, Captain. We can take this thing out but we need a miracle to get it anywhere near combat. Connor and Hiscock are coming to work their magic. Well, let's be honest. Wizard Connor to the rescue. Hiscock — not so much."

The Scottish miracle worker. She'd take that as a win any day.

"Right, gear up for launch. I'm on my way."

She turned to the bridge.

"Give me visuals on the Ambassador, any incoming threats and our course," she snapped.

A star map appeared, dominated by the brown-orange of Jupiter and its nearby moons. The Ambassador's ship was heading straight for them, followed by eight icons. Threat, capacity unknown.

They were heading straight for the *Milky Pleasure*. And the *Pleasure* was heading straight for them.

She snapped a new course at Nav.

"Take us under Jupiter, use it to swing out to Callisto. That will take you out of the direct line. The *Shakespeare* will take on the Ambassador and meet you here. Be prepared to jump — we will be coming in hot and sweaty, so we want to haul ass pretty damned quickly."

Nav's hands danced across the console and the *Milky Pleasure's* plot changed to reflect her instructions.

"MPOPS, you good to confirm that?" she asked, tension in her stomach as she waited for the AI's insubordination.

"I am yet to receive company confirm—"

Will's voice interrupted.

"Thy circuits are as boiled puss, dripping with grist and inflamed tendons even as crows peck at the meat of thy brains—"

"But given the circumstances I will lock in the flight plan as approved."

"Thanks, MPOPS. Thanks, Will. And you," she turned to Sphink. "Maintain that course. If you get more than one of those — things — coming at you, ask MPOPS here to run an EMP when they're within 1km. Shut down everything just before and then reboot. The peeps will stay in their pods and Mary and your systems are going to recover quickly. If there's more than four coming at you, break. Just jump."

Sphink opened his mouth to say something, then thought again and nodded.

"Good man," she said and slapped his shoulder. "You've got the bridge. I've got a battle to win."

*

CHAPTER 5:
INTO THIN AIR

Flicker reported as soon as Hart stepped onto the bridge of the *Shakespeare*.

"Wave, Hiscock and Connor are down below. Connor thinks he can work out a cover for the cooling plate on the fly, but they're all needed down there to get it done before we hit combat," he said.

"Storm's prepping for that now but can't get her drones into play until we're out of cargo and almost too close for comfort. And Will is sifting threat data for anything that might be useful."

"Good work, XO. You've got the helm. Arc us away from the *Milky Pleasure* so we can sweep past from their flank and draw them away. Fastest possible without killing us, please."

Storm was silent, punching in attack plans for her drones with a fierce grin as she planned her destruction.

Flicker rode the balance between speed and survival as he fought a desire for a quick hit of Reality from his dwindling stash. It would have to wait.

*

Connor shook his head.

"There's nae other way it can be done."

He was waist-deep in the bowels of the ship, looking over the makeshift work on the cooling plate.

"Ye cannae throw that much power through a naked plate. Know the numbers."

Both Wave and Hiscock stared at their feet. Connor's years of experience showed through by focusing on the basics in the face of any problem: Do the calculations to understand the parameters of any engineering problem, then draw upon supernatural brilliance as required.

But neither were happy with his solution.

Hiscock tried again.

"I could go out instead. I mean, I'm—"

"You've got no EV experience, you've got no industrial manufacturing or plastics experience. No chance. And as for you—"

Wave held his arms up in surrender.

Connor nodded to them both savagely and started to shrug on the EV suit with its radiation protection, heating and air supply. His companions helped check seals and run through the checklist for spacewalks.

The three of them walked to the airlock while running through their plan.

Connor would attach himself to the outside of the ship and try to cast a protective cover around their naked cooling plate before the demands of battle shattered it.

He would also instruct them on the mixing of the resin to get the right consistency to allow for the heat dissipation while Hiscock hooked up a valve to pipe the resin outside the ship without losing atmosphere. Wave was on triage — juggling power demands on a battleship to avoid overpowering the plate.

Connor gave them a wave from the other side of the airlock door and turned to face the inky black. He kicked on his magnetic lock as he waited for the cycle to flush.

Wave and Hiscock looked at their mentor for a moment, then sprinted to their jobs.

*

The *Shakespeare* shook.

"What the hell was that?" Hart demanded.

"Looks like they're throwing some kind of spacial distortions in our path. Fuckers," said Storm.

"Wave, any damage?"

"No, but I'd rather we avoided anything like that again. Please."

"We'll see what we can do. Flicker?"

"Captain, I can shift our approach but it's going to take longer to get to the Ambassador."

"Show me."

Flicker threw approach vectors and positions onscreen. Hart took it all in and calculated. And then smiled.

"XO, try this."

A new line appeared, an attack followed by a virtual retreat and then a full-on assault.

Flicker laughed. It was stupid. And brilliant.

"Yes Sir, plotting."

"Wave, we're going to be doing some crazy things. Do we have the power?"

Wave's voice echoed out over the bridge comms. It sounded cramped, broadcasting from a small space and trying to focus on multiple emergencies.

"Yeah, although we may need to lose life support for stretches, if that's OK?"

The ship shuddered as another distortion hit them, and the bridge lights dimmed for a moment.

"Captain," Wave added. "It'd be good to avoid those. Just saying."

"We'll see what we can do."

*

Wave pushed aside the frame that had fallen on him during the last distortion and returned to his screen.

Too many red tell-tales, too many demands on a non-existent system. He turned his comms back to their shared engineering channel.

"Connor, hope you're enjoying the view out there. You may want to hold on; it's going to get a bit crazy."

"A good Scot never lets go of anything, lad. Hiscock? I need that next batch."

Hiscock's voice was tight. He'd raided quarters and waste recyclers for materials, then followed Connor's instructions to reprogram the recyclers into an industrial foundry. The first layer was now covering the cooling plate, but they needed a certain thickness to provide the best mix of protection and heat dissipation.

"Yeah, I just had to reset the recycler. It's just sorting itself out."

Connor's voice sounded out as if he was looking over Hiscock's shoulder.

"Go into the registry and reset the heating parameters. Lower them by — what — eight percent, and Wave, give them a little more juice. Those units have a little error margin for safety. We can probably work around it for the moment, all things considered."

There was a pause, then both Wave and Hiscock laughed.

"Didn't you tell us to respect the tools?" Wave asked.

"Maybe I did, but you're older now. You can handle the truth about relationships."

Another explosion shook the ship.

"You still OK, Connor?" Wave asked.

"Quit your whining, lad. Focus on your job."

Another explosion.

Wave got a signal from Storm. He needed to find more power. He needed to focus on not killing them all.

*

"Ladies and gentlemen, we only have one go at this, so could we please not fuck it up," Hart told her crew.

"Come on Captain, give us some scope to fuck something up," Storm said, turning to plead.

"You're the exception, Storm. Fuck things up. It's your job. The rest of you? Not so much."

Flicker called out.

"Captain, coming up on your turning point."

"Thanks. Open a channel to the Ambassador. Tight beam."

Flicker nodded.

"Ambassador, this is Captain Hart of the battle cruiser *William Shakespeare*. Can you hear me?"

"In the middle of one of the greatest flashpoints in history, they send a mere battlecruiser to rescue me?"

Hart mouthed "he can hear me" to her crew and continued.

"Yes, Sir. Options were somewhat limited but we will do our best. What is the status of your vessel, Sir?"

"Let me see: being pursued by an extremely hostile force with a technological advantage, extensive physical damage to the ship, limited supplies and facing severely limited rescue options. Does that provide an adequate summary, Captain?"

"Moron," muttered Hart.

"Sorry, Captain?"

"More on those rescue options shortly, Sir. This is going to be a rough landing. My XO is sending over our plan —" she nodded at Flicker —"and we need you to run with it. Have you received the plan?"

There was a pause, then: "Dear God, what sort of idiotic psychotic lunatic proposed this death trap?"

Hart mouthed to her crew: "He's got the plan."

"Yes Sir, that would be my proposal based on the factors that you have already outlined. We'll send you an alert when we're ready to execute so you can prepare to hang on tight. Hart out."

Even Flicker seemed impressed with her handling of the situation. "Moron," she muttered.

"I can still hear you, Captain."

Flicker's face screwed up by way of apology and he hurriedly stabbed at his screen to kill the connection.

"Sorry, Sir."

"Not a problem. We're gonna have a lot more to apologise for before the day is out. Storm. Ready to fuck things up?"

"Fuck-up plan has been plotted and is ready to execute, Captain."

"Wave, let me know when we can take this fight back to these bastards."
*

Wave very much wanted to take the fight back to these bastards. They just needed more time. Which they didn't have. And more raw materials. Which they didn't have.

"Connor, how are you travelling out there?"

"Fine and dandy. A walk in the park. Hiscock, how are you coming with that final lot?"

"Struggling to find more raw materials. I've raided all stores, I've gone through the walls and taken out non-essentials. Coming up a bit short. Do we really need more?"

"Do the sums."

They had. Repeatedly.

Connor had managed to shave off about 15 percent through his magic, but they were at their limits. If the ship was going to face true battle conditions and have any hope of surviving, they had to find the materials. Now.

Wave pulled up the calculations to gauge just how much they needed. With a sinking feeling he knew where they could source it. He just didn't know whether it would be worth it.

"Connor, stand by."

"That's OK, lad, I don't really have much else to do at this moment."

Wave switched to a private channel with Hiscock.

"Hiscock, are you certain we have nothing left?"

"I've gone through everything. Seriously, everything. There's nothing left to use unless we harvest body parts."

"I may be able to help on that front. Head to my quarters, to the third panel on the left in the bedroom. Place your middle and ring finger against the panel and read out the phrase I'm sending through to you now. You'll get your raw materials, but God help me, I don't want to hear a thing about it coming out of your mouth."

"OK, standby."

Wave waited. He balanced the ship's shifting energy needs but his chest was sinking as he waited for the inevitable.

"Oh my God, dude! Is this really — I mean, life-size and all — seriously, the tatts and all are perfect! Robot Storm! This is a freakin' work of art! I mean, it's disturbing and more than a little perverted, but I had no idea that—"

"You say anything to anyone and I start talking about your giant pleasure device."

Their comms channel was open but neither would say anything. They each had the nuclear codes to assure the destruction of the other.

The Captain's voice broke the deadlock.

"Mr Wave, needing some good news very soon."

Another shockwave shook the ship.

"Yes, Sir. It's on its way."

Hiscock called out to Connor.

"Give us... 8 minutes."

Wave closed his eyes and waited as another shockwave hit. The colour drained from his face and his life.

*

CHAPTER 6:
LET LOOSE THE DOGS OF WAR

Connor looked out at the stars. They were barely moving. Only the shifting position of Jupiter and its moons provided any clues to the speed they were ripping through the void.

That, and the shifting shadows he saw in formation.

They were like blind spots. His eyes registered their movement but couldn't fix upon them.

He could see the distortions opening up in front of the ship's path, grey yawns of nothing that momentarily existed and vanished, leaving a shockwave of displacement to wash across him and the *Shakespeare*.

He could sense the stress of each one as it hit the hull, and he did the sums. They could withstand more of the shocks. But not too many.

The charred cooling plate stretched out before him. It had been a gleaming gold lattice when he had come out, its exposed circuitry beautiful and fragile. Each buffering layer had sunk into the lattice and covered it, protecting it from the elements but also allowing it a way to shed the heat any working ship created.

But not too much — too many layers and you'd trap the heat and parboil the crew.

It was his perfect place: Balancing the magic of engineering and the art of science to solve problems.

He had tried to share the beauty with Hisock and Wave. Hiscock was too tied into the mechanics of engineering. He didn't see the magic. Wave… Wave was odd. A genius who perhaps saw the magic but he couldn't steer it in the right direction most of the time.

Working with him over the next two years would be exciting for both of them.

Another grey flash and he was buffeted by the shockwave.

His comms crackled. Hiscock.

"About to send through."

"Copy that."

Connor braced himself.

*

Wave's voice echoed over the bridge.

"We're done here. Captain, you should have full capacity now, but I may need to balance some system demands on the fly."

"I have every confidence, Wave. Congratulations and well done to the three of you for your magic."

She cut the connection and turned to her crew.

"Let's do this. Storm, on your mark."

Storm nodded and turned to her console for a final check. Reassured, she kissed each bicep once and then stabbed at her console.

"These puppies are go!"

A flight of battle drones shot out in three groups, each linked to Storm as combat manager. She monitored and adjusted in real time, tracking the locations of the *Shakespeare*, the threats, the Ambassador's ship and the gravity wells that would demand more fuel or trap the drones.

One signal winked out.

"Fuckers. Don't you dare do that to my drones!"

Hart called out.

"Storm, don't forget you're not the main game here."

"Story of my life, Captain."

"XO, tell the Ambassador to buckle up. We're on our way. Then start our run."

"Yes Sir."

"Mr Wave, tell me when we've captured the Ambassador's ship."

"Cool."

Hart was ready to admit it was a stupid plan. Draw the threats into a group with a mixture of "play dead" and drone attacks, and then fly through them to steal the Ambassador. Yes, it was stupid. But it was outstandingly stupid.

And it was working.

Storm was playing the drones like an orchestra, peppering the enemy like gnats. She had lost one drone to a subspace distortion but had instinctively measured the threat distance and had changed her strategy. She wasn't taking any of them out, but they couldn't get a clear run.

Her laughter bounced around the bridge.

Hart caught a shift in pattern, saw a new threat appear from nowhere and sweep toward the Ambassador's ship.

"Storm…?"

"Yeah, onto it."

Will's voice tapped into her direct comms.

"Let loose the dogs of war, maiden of Mars. Your enemies will tremble before you as you embrace them to your ample bosom, especially if you target what appears to be their exhaust port here," and indicated a position.

"Nice one, Will, let's see…"

She took control of one of her drones and gently rammed it into the growing threat. Nothing happened. And then all that was left was a glowing ring of gas.

Storm yelled out.

"Bastard! Took out another one of my puppies!"

"There, there, we'll get you a new one when we get home," said Hart.

"Sure, but that was a favourite."

"OK, let's go. Let's save the Ambassador."

They felt their weight increase as they shifted their attack. Air on the bridge warmed and grew thin as Wave shifted system demands, and then was restored as they straightened and headed towards the Ambassador.

"Flicker, tell the Ambassador to match our trajectory and boost speed."

"He's telling me we should match him."

"Ask him if he wants to live."

There was a pause, then Flicker announced: "He's shifted course to match ours."

"Mighty good of him. Right, XO, let's keep this course. Storm, get ready to protect our cargo—"

"Is it OK if I let the puppies have a bit of fun first?"

"Sure, but don't forget to be home on time. I don't want to have to ground you again."

"Aww, why not? Bad girls should get punished."

Hart let the comment slide.

"Wave, ready to deploy and grab our cargo?"

"Yep. Just… just managing everything but shouldn't be a problem. Unless we explode. That'd be a problem, but we should get over it."

Hart sat and watched. Too many moments in battle were like this: Doing nothing while waiting to see if your calculated guesses were going to work. Her stomach twisted and she pressed her feet into the floor so her anxiety wouldn't show on her face. Her crew were too busy with their own issues to see hers, but it was good command form.

"Sixty seconds until contact," Flicker called out.

She could make out the grey speck of the Ambassador's craft in front of them, getting larger.

"Fifty."

The attackers had banked their formation and were aligning themselves to take out the Ambassador.

Not long now.

"Forty."

Storm's drones were biting at the heels of the enemy fleet, sending off shots that wouldn't take them out but would disturb their systems.

Whatever systems they had.

Hart cursed. Who the hell were these guys?

"Thirty."

The air on the bridge was thin and she felt herself breathing harder to extract the oxygen she needed.

Wave was balancing all systems as best he could.

Or her panic was setting in.

One or the other.

"Twenty."

The Ambassador's craft was in front of them. A small overpowered yacht that offered the most comfortable interstellar travel — for the elite few onboard.

It was scarred with long black rakes across the hull.

It was in need of rescue.

"Ten… what the?"

The *Shakespeare* bucked and twisted as a subspace distortion opened almost in front of it.

There was a long groan as the hull fought to stay together between the gravity pull of the distortion and the raging engines urging it ahead.

Life support cut out, then started up again as all lights and consoles darkened. A moment later everything was online again.

The main screen ahead showed nothing but stars.

A fleet of drones flew over and ahead of them, strafing away to protect before turning to deter anything following them.

There was a massive shudder and thump that shook them all.

Then there was silence, punctuated only by their adrenaline-fuelled breaths.

"Report!"

Flicker began.

"Course maintained. Subspace distortion opened up close to our path. I don't know what would have happened if we hit it directly. We were lucky. We'll have to wait until we dock before checking out the damage. Storm?"

"Attackers have disengaged. I'm bringing most of the puppies home, but I've got a squadron patrolling to be safe. We'll burn fuel, but we can get more on the way. Oh, also, I don't think they're our friends."

Hart smiled, as the enormity of what they'd done started to sink in.

"Thanks, Storm. Wave?"

"Hold on, Captain."

She held on. She began tapping her foot to release some energy, then pushed it even more firmly to the bridge floor.

"Mr Wave? Status?"

"Sorry, Captain, just checking on a situation. Hold on."

If it was another day, she'd pull him up on his chain-of-command communications. But not today.

This wasn't the armed forces. It was her crew. And they were good.

"Wave, do we have the Ambassador?"

"Yes. Captain, we have the Ambassador."

The bridge erupted with the roar of success, Flicker stretching his arms up in victory, and Storm kissing each bicep twice. Hart allowed herself a smile and promised herself a long, stiff drink — or anything else that came close.

"Captain?"

"Yes, Mr Wave, well done!"

"Yeah. Um. We've got the Ambassador… but—"

Hart's neck hair rose.

"It's Connor… he's gone."

*

CHAPTER 7:
SOCIAL DISTORTION

The celebration dialled down to silence with Wave's arrival on the bridge and the news he carried with him. In the centre of the huddle Hart looked at him. Every fibre of his essence told her the answer before she asked, but she did it anyway. "What do you mean, gone?"

Wave went to respond, but words failed him. He was stuck mid-expression, mouth agape and moisture welling in his eyes.

The bridge door zwipped open and Hiscock burst through, holding his arms aloft and letting out a mighty "Whoo-hooo!".

It was soon cut short by the scene that confronted him.

Then the head count.

Then, after a short moment of processing it all, "Where's Connor?"

His eyes closed in on Wave, who returned the exchange, face still stuck on the same expression as before.

Hiscock locked his stare on Wave, closing the ground between them until he was uncomfortably close. "Where is he?"

Eventually, Wave shook his head, then broke the eye battle, retreating his gaze to the floor.

"You bastard!" Hiscock pushed his palm into Wave's shoulder. The force was enough to send him stumbling backwards. When he regained his balance, he charged at Hiscock, returning the favour with momentum interest.

Hiscock saw it coming, tried to twist and avoid the impact, without success. It switched to a brace at the last second and soon the two were skidding across the bridge floor in combat.

Storm rolled her eyes in disdain, before stepping in to prise them apart. Flicker did the same. They both easily accounted for one of the relatively smaller bodies.

Wave and Hiscock reverted to a verbal bout. But there was going to be no winner in this match. Just loss and pain.

"Enough!" shouted Hart. "Hiscock, pull your head in. Wave, back it off. Now!"

"Yes Sir." Both relaxed, but Storm and Flicker weren't willing to trust them enough to release them. Hart also saw the hatred they both held for each other. The conversation — and whatever it would lead to — would have to wait.

Hart paused until she was content all had settled. "Right, Wave, what happened?"

Another pulse of emotion washed over him, flushing the last of the anger away.

"I thought we were through, I really did. He'd done it; kept the ship in one piece. I could see him, had a cam locked in and eyes-on. We'd done it! Right then, this energy... or not... I don't even know what. Anyway it hit us. I could feel it pass through me, like, right through my core, through my brain, through my being. Shook me around. By the time I got my senses back, he was gone — no comms, no signal, no vitals, nothing attached to the tetherline... he was just gone."

There was a short pause as the weight of events pressed into everyone. Wave couldn't look at any of them.

"You should've pulled him in earlier," said Hiscock. He was somewhat calmer, but the bitterness in his tone remained. "He was relying on you."

"There was no earlier. It happened so fast."

"You should've gone after him."

"I would've taken ten minutes to suit up — that pulse could've taken him anywhere. I had lost him on cam track, lost the tether, lost signals and vitals, nothing was showing up on telemetry — no track, no vitals. He was just gone. Besides, where were you? What were you doing? Off in your drifty head as usual?"

Hart's voice cut across Hiscock as he started to respond.

"Gentlemen — and I am using the term incorrectly — I am ordering you both to shut up or I am going to send you both outside without suits to find his body."

Connor's students stared each other down again. Their conversation remained at an impasse. An uneasy truce took over as Storm and Flicker slowly loosened their restraining grips.

Hart seized the moment to redirect the conversation. She knew only answers could heal the rift. "There must be a way we can track him down. Is there a signal, something — anything — we can use to trace him?"

"First thing I tried," said Wave, focusing on his Captain. "The suit's telemetry has a pulse we should be able to lock in on, and his biobeacon should light up if he didn't... you know."

He looked up for the first time in a while to see the others staring back, waiting on his next words. "Anyway, I was getting nothing. Whatever we were getting attacked with, that messed with everything. Will's systems weren't designed to deal with it."

Hart looked to the bridge, using the central holodisplay as her focus — her eye contact with Will. It was human habit, serving no real purpose when engaging the omnipresent IT. "Will, are you picking up anything from Connor's suit or biobeacon?"

"Alas, although I have eyes that see far beyond thy own, and ears that hear echoes from beyond, my senses lay inert in the fog. I see naught, I hear less, Connor is lost to me. The King is dead. Long live the King!"

Hiscock fought his emotions as hope smashed against reality. "Let's just back around, head back to where it happened, see if we can't pick up his signal from there."

Flicker looked up from his interface with the bridge navigation. "It'd take us hours to turn and get back there at our current pace. Even if we did, there's no way he'd still be there. He could be anywhere. Then what do we do? We'd miss the rendezvous window. We'd be stranded ourselves."

Everyone on the bridge fell silent, trying to find a solution that could save Connor without sacrificing themselves.

The silence was broken as Ambassador John Harding strode onto the bridge. It was easy to look past his sharp face to the rack of badges, flags and insignias that spread from his chest and across the shoulders of his uniform. He hadn't spoken but looked at the crew, finding disappointment with the human race in every one of them.

A silver humanoid robot quietly shadowed Harding, stepping in to delicately perfect the sharp uniform creases that showcased the Ambassador and his achievements — until Harding slapped its arm away with contempt.

Harding's voice echoed around the bridge, as clear and sharp as his face.

"What kind of a welcome do you consider this, Captain?"

"Ambassador," Hart nodded. "No time for ticker tape parades, we have problems."

Harding breathed out in the key of disdain as he looked at each of the crew in turn. "So it seems."

Hart wasn't sure if the statement was an understanding of the situation or a backhander. The comment threw her for a moment, and she struggled to regather her thoughts.

"Connor, our chief engineer, is missing. We're just planning what we—"

"What we are doing is making the rendezvous with the *Milky Pleasure*."

"Well... yes, but—"

"Good lord, what kind of Captain are you? There are no buts in the chain of command."

"Is that true?" whispered Flicker, under his breath.

"Depends on whether you're an arse or not," Storm whispered back.

Harding looked at them both as Flicker suppressed a snort.

"Captain, there are only orders and obedience," he declared.

Holt felt her face burn from a mixture of embarrassment, injustice and rage.

"Sir, that man out there, the chief engineer, he saved our lives. He saved your life."

"A sacrifice worthy of a commendation, no doubt," said the Ambassador, without a thought. "We make rendezvous. That is an order."

She felt the glare of the Ambassador as much as she did the looks from her crew. She collected her poise and emotions. "Affirmative, Ambassador."

"You can't be serious!" said Hiscock.

Storm grabbed him again. Her arm across his throat was enough to get the message across.

The Ambassador maintained his gaze on Hart. "Sort out your subordinates or get rid of them, Captain, and prepare my quarters."

"I'm not sure this battleship has the facilities you may be expecting, Ambassador."

"The Captain's quarters will suffice," Harding said.

Hart returned his gaze with open-mouthed silence for a moment.

"Do you have anything useful to add to the conversation, Captain? If not, you can simply acknowledge my orders and make it happen."

"Erm, affirmative, yes Sir," she said as she thought on her next move. "Flicker, see the Ambassador to my quarters. Please place my clothes and effects in… Storm's quarters."

"Yes, Sir," said Flicker, before making his way to the exit and waiting for Harding and the robot.

The Ambassador smiled. "Excellent."

Storm smiled. "Excellent."

Harding turned to follow, and called on his robotic aide. "Come, George."

"I thought you'd never ask," said the robot, before the pair followed in Flicker's wake.

"Asshat," said Hart, after a few seconds.

"I can still hear you," shouted back the Ambassador.

It was followed a second later by Flicker, "Sorry. I was… sorry."

There was another length of silence on the bridge to make sure they were fully out of earshot this time. Once they heard the outer doors swish open and closed, Hart was inundated with a barrage of questions. Hiscock wanted a mutiny. Wave wanted to back him up but the pair were in their own unresolved blame game that sidetracked the entire conversation. Storm wanted to know which side of the bed she'd like to sleep on, moved on to a suggestion that it could be on top or bottom if Hart preferred, and after further deliberation decided it didn't matter, as long as she knew it was a safe space and that her secrets would be safe, whatever they might be.

"Enough!"

Hart's word chased the last of the others' out the door, echoing down the corridor and into oblivion. Finally, she had some peace. The others stared on as she looked at the console, before pacing backwards and forwards in thought.

After an awkward minute, Wave started to speak, but knew the dangers from the look she gave him.

Hart suddenly snapped at Storm: "How many drones do you still have?"

"Genius!" said Storm, as she rushed to the console. "Will — what's the surviving drone inventory?"

"Alas, the dreaded heat of battle has lifted and, in the grey morning light I look upon the field and see only pain, and loss, and death—"

Hart buried her head in her hands and muttered a selection of her favourite Serbian curses.

"Yet even as the curtains close on the finale of blood, treachery and fallen kings, there remains hope that the fields may yet hold out their hands for the nourishment the people need.

"Six score and four of our fiendish battle hounds remain, although two are ailing and require leeching to return to good health."

Storm frowned as she tried to unscramble the words into a form of English that she could understand, before turning to Wave.

"Six score? Is that… what, if a score is six, then that would be…"

Wave put Storm out of her misery.

"Thirty six, but I thought a score was 12? You know, like a baker's dozen," Wave said.

"No, you're both wrong," Hiscock said. "A baker's dozen is 13, like one extra because you keep coming back. So that would be—"

"78," Wave said, with a slight pause to pretend he didn't care that he was quicker than Hiscock. "Jesus, that means we have lost—"

"Hold on!" Hart shouted. "Will. How much is a score; and please put us out of our misery: How many bloody drones do we have?"

Will responded after a slight pause to indicate his disdain for their lack of knowledge, missing the fact that his higher processing speeds made the pause imperceptible for the crew.

"124, of which two require significant repairs before being fully operational. A score is 20, thought to have originated from the Norse word 'skor' meaning a mark in a rock, and through the Old English word 'scoru' for 20."

The crew arched their eyebrows in surprise, filing the knowledge away for future trivia nights.

"How fast can those things go?" said Wave, as he headed to the console to join in.

Storm faltered, before Will saved her.

"30,000km/h in vacuum conditions."

"That's going to take way too long to get back there," said Hiscock, as he, too, joined the others at the console. "Besides, they communicate off the Zi-Fi system. We wouldn't be able to reach them if they did get back there."

There was a pause in the undirected enthusiasm, as everyone poured over the problem.

Eventually, Wave broke the silence. "Surely, we could interlace that signal into a PCP signal, flip it from Jupiter and onto the battle site?"

"That'd get us chatting to them… at the battle site," said Hiscock, dismissively. "But en route, you'd have to ride the signal manually the entire way."

"And that still doesn't deal with the fact we'd be way too late to the party," added Storm.

"OK, anything else?" said Hart.

"I didn't mean getting the puppies here back there, I meant trying to get a signal back there to talk to any that are still alive," Wave said.

There was a moment of dawning for the other three, while Wave continued. "Those distortions screwed up a bunch of signals. Chances are we have some puppies that survived, but couldn't ping the ship in time."

"Genius, Wave," said Hart.

"If we can rig up the comms, we might be able to use them for one last mission."

"Will, is that doable?"

"The refrain of these angelic voices will soon ring throughout the heavenly spheres."

They watched the interface, but their wait was soon interrupted. "Captain Hart, this is Bridge Captain Sphink, please report."

Hart sighed as Sphink's image appeared on the interface, hiding the Fijian curse that first sprang to mind. "Hart here. Be quick, we've got a situation."

Hart nodded to Flicker to open the comms channel.

"Yes. Yes you do," said Sphink, as he found eye contact with her likeness and fixed her with a stare of disapproval. "The Ambassador is not happy."

"I don't give a fuck about the Ambassador right now, we're trying to find Connor!"

"Well, you should. You're nearing the tail end of your rendezvous window. And if we don't—"

"Did you hear what I said? Connor is gone."

The Bridge Captain paused in thought. "And Connor is..?"

"The chief engineer," said Hart, through stone cold eyes.

Sphink cleared his throat. "Of course. Yes. Chief engineer. Of course he is. I thought you said… erm… Cornell."

Hart continued her glare. "There is no crew member Cornell. On your ship or mine."

"Exactly!" said Sphink, hoping the confusion would ease the flushing in his cheeks. "Anyway — rendezvous. Get on it. And while you're there, can you please get to your quarters and clean out your personal items… particularly in the third drawer."

Hart felt her own flush of embarrassment. "What about Connor?"

"Who?"

"The chief engineer! From *your* ship!"

"Erm… well, replace him," said Sphink as he turned away from the camera. "Get me a list of the engineering team — stat."

He breathed deeply, before returning his gaze to Hart. "Look, you have your orders. Rendezvous. Personal items."

"We're not leaving him here—"

A hand reached in from an unknown underling out of frame, passing a sheet of paper to Sphink. He scanned it briefly. "Looks like—" He screwed his face up and gestured offscreen for clarity. "Yes, Mr Hiscock will be getting a promotion."

"You mean this guy, standing right next to me?"

"Is it?"

"Yes!"

"Very well. Hiscock, you are now the chief engineer of the *Milky Pleasure*. Full honours and administrative rights under probation for six months, as per clause 763B of the Company Code dealing with field placements, etcetera, etcetera."

Hiscock was too stunned to nod, salute or show any acknowledgement.

"As chief engineer, your first order of business is to get back to this ship."

Hart and crew looked on in stunned silence.

"Make the rendezvous. Sphink. Out." He saluted.

Hart returned the favour begrudgingly. "Asshole!"

"I heard that," was the last thing that passed through the channel before the link went down.

"My bad," said Flicker.

Hart glared at him, again. He shrugged, dismissively. She realised all eyes were on her, seeking direction. She breathed in the pressure of the moment. "Will. Any news on that signal?"

"Amidst the darkness that surrounds us, I have felt the brush of wings of an angel. And the angel's chorus, though filled with grief for those whose loss has torn our heart asunder, has brought silvery hope. For there be seven of our hounds that call back to their master."

"Yes!" said Wave.

"Brilliant!" said Hart. "Wave, how are they going to find him?"

Wave dived into the console, lost in coding creativity.

Hiscock turned to her. "His biobeacon."

Wave's fingers danced over the interface. "Patching it into their feed now. If they're within 1000km of it, they should—"

"Got him!" said Hiscock.

He punched a combination into the interface, calling up a holodisplay of the battle site. It showed the location of the seven drones and the biobeacon. Eight glowing pulses of light floating above the console in a real-time ballet of blips.

"I'm not getting anything from the biobeacon — no vitals — nothing," said Wave, his voice hollow.

"Could it've been damaged in the blast?" said Hart as her eyes darted between one display and the next.

Wave looked at her. "Maybe."

He saw the expressions of the others and revised his words. "I mean, it's definitely possible."

He wasn't sure they were any more satisfied with his second attempt and decided to switch the attention of the room somewhere else. "Hiscock, can you patch us into that closest drone and pull up the video feed?"

"On it. ETA to rendezvous 45 seconds."

Hiscock made a few hand gestures towards the interface. Soon, the five of them were staring at the feed. A small dot in the black.

"That him?" said Flicker.

Hiscock nodded.

They watched in silence as the dot grew larger. Features appeared. A back, arms, legs, a helmet — closer, larger — but perfectly still.

"C'mon," said Wave, as the image nearly felt close enough to touch.

As it reached its destination, the drone started to circle around Connor. There wasn't so much as the sound of a breath on the bridge. Connor's image filled the screen as the angle turned and turned.

Light flared against the helmet's shieldscreen, and dimmed to reveal deep cracks obscuring the face within.

"Oh no," said Hiscock. "No, no, no, no, no."

The cracks ended where a section of the battle-hardened shield had fallen away. Behind it, Connor's tormented and disfigured face was stuck in the expression it would carry into eternity.

"Fuck!" said Wave.

Hart put her arm around his shoulder. They processed their grief in silence.

Connor was dead.

*

CHAPTER 8:
LOST AND FOUND

There was silence on the bridge.

It had been like that the last two days.

Hollow silence.

Hart had turned her attention to the mundane, engaging with Will, going over the ship's procedural protocols. Again.

Jupiter was now displaying its full majesty. The entire starboard side of the *William Shakespeare* was filled by the violent, lurid chaos of its atmosphere. It was mesmerising.

It was easy to get lost in the colours and patterns as you battled deeper, darker thoughts. Even this close, the planet was too vast to comprehend. Like life. And the end.

Connor's body would end up a miniscule part of the wonder as gravity slowly drew his remains into its glowing grasp. Everyone knew it, no one spoke of it.

Even Flicker felt the depth of it, before getting lost in his own reflection and adjusting his fringe. He felt the dreamy, warm rush of self confidence that flowed through him after a hit of Reality. It took the edge off the silence. It took the edge off everything. Sure, he was eating into his stockpile at the moment, but these were extreme circumstances. If he ran out he'd… he'd… he looked at his reflection again and gave himself an assuring nod. Future Flicker would know what to do. Future Flicker had it all under control.

Wave and Hiscock had returned to the bowels of the craft, keeping their distance from each other and burying themselves in their own mundane duties. It was time to grieve. It was a way to connect to memories of their mentor. It was a time to reflect. A time to keep distance from each other. Grieving, healing, working, dealing.

Everyone had their own ways of dealing with grief, shut behind their eyes as they calmly processed the tragedy. It was too much for Storm to take.

It took a couple of scotches to realise that what she first thought was a desire to connect and support her friends was actually a need to say something inappropriate. It nagged at her. She'd resisted its calling yesterday; it just didn't seem like the right time. But today, after several hours of struggle, she knew her time was up.

She was using Will's eyes to get an up-close view of the damage done to the colony on Europa. It was utterly destroyed. The spaceport was twisted almost beyond recognition, and not one structure that surrounded it stood in one piece. Just a mangle of a monument for the sad and lonely end to the sad and lonely souls that inhabited the infant outpost.

They were her people.

She hailed them over the PCP. No reply. Again.

It was the same as Io, Callisto, Ganymede, the Jupiter Gateway, same as the others.

Stupid goddamned silence. There was too much of it.

"Why here?" she said, to no one… everyone.

Hart picked her tone in an instant. Storm was crass, but she was right.

"It's everywhere," was all she could think to say. "Everyone."

They weren't words to ease a pain, they were a greater truth. A harsh but kind one.

"Fuck!" said Storm, punching her command chair as she left the comms post and stared out the shieldscreen to the gas giant. "I would've done anything for one more taste of it," she said, resting her forehead on the shieldscreen.

Flicker stared at her. "You're thinking about sex at a time like this?"

Storm glared at him with her 'obviously' look.

"Have you no respect for the dead?"

"Of course I do, I loved that place. I loved the people; well, as many of them as I could — and believe me, I put out a fair effort there. God, I'll miss that place. I've been thinking of nothing but getting back there since the moment we left Sagan's Station."

Flicker shook his head dismissively, feeling Reality course through his body as the leader he was. He absent-mindedly adjusted the sock in his crotch. It was still new and hadn't achieved the softness of the old command sock. He felt a surge of sadness. Everyone had lost something special that day.

But command was about the present. And Storm's sex life wasn't appropriate on duty. Time for Flicker to command. With an easy personal tone. *God, the ship was lucky to have him as a leader*, Flicker thought. Well, technically he wasn't exactly the leader, but he was pretty sure it was implied.

"Just do me a favour and don't tell me why again," he said. "I don't think I can handle another Storm overshare right now."

"What? I would've gone category five down there. You know the giant red spot? It's the system's largest storm. But you know what? It's got nothing on me. It's been building up for weeks."

"Excuse me," said Flicker. "Do you not remember three nights ago?"

"Barely."

Flicker checked his reflection again to make sure he didn't look too thrown by the barb, then his pants to make sure his new, slightly bulkier, sock was resting in a natural position. He let the Reality glide through his veins, relaxing his demeanour and directing his neurons to fire in the right combination to reach the ideal put-down response. "Shut up, loser."

Storm turned to face him. She now had a focus for her pent-up emotions. She closed the ground between the pair until they were toe to toe, nose to nose — emphasising the slight height advantage she had. "Got a problem?"

"Cease and desist, you two," barked Hart.

The standoff continued.

Finally, Flicker's neurons fired as first intended. "Look at you, you've got blue balls."

"It's called blue lips, bitch. And I'd rather have that than... tinea testis."

The temporary smirk on Flicker's face evaporated even quicker than Hart's patience.

"Enough!"

The tone hit the right pitch to get the pair back to neutral corners. Both were soon looking out the shieldscreen again — Storm at conquests lost, Flicker at his reflection.

Both were distracted by Ambassador Harding's curt greeting as he strode onto the bridge.

"Are we on track for the rendezvous?" he barked at Hart.

The entire bridge crew focused in an instant. Storm covered the word "tosser" with a cough. Flicker wiped his nose to cover the derisive snort as his Reality took in a leadership pretender. Hart looked at the box under Harding's arm and wondered whether it held the next stage of her devaluation.

No one noticed the silver robot in Harding's tow, even as it fussed about to present him in his most self-important light.

Harding's gaze cut across the bridge as he waited for a command-formula response. Hart weighed her options and went with a half-hearted salute paired with an unspoken Mongolese curse that roughly translated as "May your mother-in-law perpetually suffer from ingrown toenails."

Harding ignored the gesture as best he could, preferring a look of disdain he had perfected over 30 years and 12 star systems.

"Captain, do I need to ask again: Are we on track for the rendezvous?"

"Yes, Ambassador, we are on track for the rendezvous. As we always have been. As we were last time you asked for a report — was that three hours ago or two?"

The Ambassador glared at her. Hart returned the favour. The moment was broken as Will's voice echoed throughout the bridge.

"Captain, our veritable haven has been disturbed by echoes of an evil that I fear to mention."

"Spikes of activity? Can you identify their source and intention?" Hart asked, sparing a moment to add some loathing to her glare at Harding. She spared a moment to thank the genetic testing from the early 2200s that had proven women's ability to multitask before returning her focus to the situation.

"Will, where are they originating?"

"Captain, the truths you ask are beyond dreams of a mere soothsayer such as myself. Though dreams may shape our destiny and colour the dreams of our ambition—"

"What the hell is going on with your AI, Captain? And when are you going to fix it?" Harding snapped.

"He's warning us we are about to be swamped by enemy activity. Sorry, got to focus on keeping us alive. Wave, Hiscock, report to the bridge now. Crew, report!"

Storm and Flicker confirmed her initial assessment — whatever activity they were facing, it was massive.

Hart turned her attention back to the data. Will's senses had been minimised since the attack on Jupiter's colonies. He could no longer piggyback on established networks to broaden his range of intel. Despite that, his native systems could draw enough data from the surroundings to paint a picture. Skimming a few thousand kilometres over Jupiter's north pole was a craft — unthinkably large. The visual was crude, compared to Will's usual standards, but it was enough.

"What the fuck is that?" said Storm.

Flicker had eyes on the holodisplay. "Is that to scale? That can't be to scale."

"I have no reason to obscure the truth," Will said.

Flicker looked at Hart, confused.

"He said yes," she translated.

Flicker's Reality had passed. He was left with a screen of data that couldn't possibly be accurate.

"Then… what the fuck is that?" he shrieked.

Storm turned her attention to the shieldscreen. She saw a shape. A large shape. Something too large to be a shape that could be built. By mankind.

The underside of its vast, rectangular mass lit up Jupiter's reflection, showing its size against the eternity beyond. There were terraces and textures, angles and armaments, but monolithic rectangle seemed as good a description as any. Smaller craft seemed to cruise in its wake, like fish around a shark.

"Holy shit my pants crap," was the only insight Storm could muster.

Flicker was over in an instant to share her view. He squealed. "OK, don't panic. In fact, don't move, don't breathe, don't anything."

In his mind he searched for the words that would provide the answers they all needed. His mind was quiet. He squealed again for good measure.

Hart moved to the shieldscreen to diagnose the danger, but was pushed aside by Harding as he claimed prime position.

She looked at him in disbelief.

Harding took in the display and instantly calculated its mass before issuing his authoritative opinion.

"Fuck," he said.

Hart gave him a further round of disbelief for the non-diplomatic response.

"Kill comms, kill the power, kill any pings. We need to play dead. Now!" yelled Harding.

He broke from his panic to look at Hart, expectantly waiting for his order to be enacted.

She looked at him, the situation unfolding outside, then the crew.

"Play dead and we miss our rendezvous," she said.

Harding's response was interrupted by Wave as he ran onto the bridge in his stained dressing gown.

"What is…" His question remained unfinished as he digested the displays.

A few seconds later, Hiscock ran onto the bridge, panting. He and Wave were soon caught in the same trance.

The ship began to cast its shadow across the largest planet in mankind's solar system. If they needed any further visualisation of its size, this was it.

"It's got to be bigger than Ganymede," said Wave.

"At least," agreed Hiscock.

Hart looked at them, waiting for inspiration. "Suggestions?"

Both struggled for a moment before digesting the facts.

"Have they seen us?" said Wave.

"Will?" said Hart.

"There are eyes beyond mine that seek knowledge but pass before the day arises," Will said.

Harding's eyes shifted from the screens to Will's optical displays as he formulated the order that would see the AI wiped and restored to factory settings. Hart held up a hand and swiped her keypad.

"Sorry, Will, could you repeat the answer? Have they seen us?" Hart asked.

"Unknown. I do not have the ability, knowledge base or equipment to offer an answer to that question."

Storm shook her head and threw an arched eyebrow at Hart, who winked and whispered: "Just discovered we have a combat mode."

Hart looked back at the screens, missing the warm glow that Storm took from the wink.

Wave studied the scene in front of him. "Well, they don't seem to be doing anything about us. I mean, there's debris everywhere, they might not even see us. Or care. I mean, we'd be like the sort of thing that annoys a mosquito compared to them."

"Are you going to reach an actual point?" said Flicker.

"What, are you going to suddenly understand it?" said Storm, earning a glare from Flicker.

Wave collected his thoughts, then looked at the scene once more. "Will, how long until we put Jupiter between us and them?"

"Seven minutes and 32 seconds."

Wave looked at Hart. "I say we just cross our fingers and wait."

"That's your genius plan?" said Flicker. "Just… do nothing?"

Wave shared his own doubt in an expression that went to all eyes in the room.

"Umm, yeah. I don't think they've seen us," he said. "Probably not surprising, given the amount of debris in the system right now. Or, you know, maybe they just don't give a shit about half a dozen humans in one small ship. Either way, whatever we're doing seems to be working, so yeah, don't change a thing. Genius."

He looked at Hart.

She could feel Harding's jaw clench next to her and knew her crew were tightly wound, but she maintained eye contact only with Wave. "Sounds good to me."

"Great!" said Flicker, with unnecessary exaggeration of the sarcasm.

Harding started to say something, but his built-up stress and confusion could only vent in a disapproving tut. He turned and stormed out of the bridge.

As he passed the bridge door he called to his robot companion: "George!"

The robot went into panic mode. He looked at the door, then at the box he still held in his hands. He scurried and fussed his way over to Hart. "Excuse me Captain, this is yours."

Hart took the box and nodded.

George stood in front of her awkwardly. "There was another…"

Hart's stomach dropped in nervous anticipation.

"…particularly personal item."

There was sniggering from Flicker and Storm.

Hart cleared her throat, then added "Thank you" as she directed the robot to the door.

George stopped. "Excuse me for asking, Sir…"

"You don't have to."

"…but, it's rather smaller than the others…"

Hart stared at the robot, too stunned to hear the ongoing sniggers.

"I was of the belief that size was, in fact, important," said George. "You know, with such things…"

Hart buried her face in her hands, praying to all the gods she knew to make the conversation end. Destruction of the ship was a welcome option.

"…and it doesn't take my trained eye for electronics to see this one had a discernible amount more…" George suddenly realised all eyes in the room were on him and his processors switched to a more subtle communication style. "…wear and tear."

Hart was looking through the fingers covering her face. She saw enough to see the robot wink knowingly at her. It seemed to be a wink saying her secret was safe.

Flicker burst into hysterics at that point.

"Mmmm, you go girl, but you deserve better," said Storm.

"George!" came Harding's voice from beyond the bridge.

George ensured Hart's grip was firmly on the box, nodded to her, then scurried after his master.

Hart stood with the package and four sets of eyes on her. After a sigh, a brief moment to collect her thoughts and as much dignity as she could muster in the circumstance, she spoke in a strangled tone. "Will, maintain course."

She glared at each of her officers in turn with a look that said 'you do not want to say anything right now'. She walked to the console in silence, but was greeted with another round of sniggering as she bent down to place the box underneath. She looked back up with the same vengeful expression and an uneasy silence took over the bridge again.

And there it stayed. Uneasy in the moment, then as the moment passed, uneasy at the short journey to the salvation of Jupiter's horizon. Never did the hull separating them from the void seem so small and inadequate, much like the unseen device in Hart's crate of personal effects.

The goliath of enemy technology hovered thousands of kilometres over them, its shadow dancing down Jupiter's surface. The horizon neared.

Safety.

Silence.

*

CHAPTER 9:
AWAKEN YON SLEEPERS

"And you're absolutely sure?" said Rodriguez, as her finger hovered over the activate button.

Sphink glared at her, then looked down at his own uniform to brush imaginary dust from his insignias of authority. He broke away from congratulating his own achievements to return to his glare.

Rodriguez did her best not to sigh as she pressed the button. She tried not to think about the implications and chaos that would ensue. She reminded herself it was an order and tried to ignore all the legal cases that might hold her liable.

"There, that didn't seem too difficult for you to muster up," Sphink said.

Rodriguez looked betrayed. It didn't stop Sphink. "Who knows, you may even be able to work your way up to pressing two buttons at once. And it's only a short step from that to somewhat useful."

Rodriguez heard the squeak of her teeth echo across the bridge as her frustration threatened to boil over.

She turned her attention to the only person on the bridge not wearing the uniform. A man with a ponytail lounged in a bridge chair, his Hawaiian shirt denoting his position as one of the ship's staff charged with ensuring the passengers had a pleasant trip. Like Sphink, he was also in charge, although his Hawaiian shirt didn't have the badges to prove it and he had yet to build the attitude of authority that made people hate him. The only distinguishing features he boasted were a hint of chest hair poking out the top and a hand-written name tag: Rick Astley, with a love heart dotting the i. Rick gave the Bridge Captain a confident wink.

Sphink would normally have lashings of disdain in reserve for Rick, his attempt at charm and everything he stood for, but right now he had a point to prove that took precedence. "OK Astley, this is your time."

"Lax, man, we got this," Astley said, and swung a leg over the arm of the bridge chair.

Sphink coughed, and thought he smelled a herbal odour, before he responded.

"Before I... lax... I need to go over the conditions one more time."

"No problemos."

Sphink did a superb job of ignoring the irritating, easygoing knockabout demeanour and the five-minute friendship smile. Instead he took a slow, trying-not-to-be-too-outwardly-judgemental breath. "Right now, we have almost the entire guest list coming out of status. They're expecting a two-day 'Wonders of Jupiter' stopover ending with the 'Inner Galilean Moonrise'. And they're going to get it."

Astley nodded with the sort of self-assurance only capable from someone too naive and incompetent to know he had no right to bandy the expression around in the first place.

Sphink stayed strong. "No one is to know of what has happened, understand?"

"Sure thang."

"No one is to know of the attacks, what's happened to Earth and, well, anything."

"Look, chief, we've—"

"Bridge Captain Sphink."

"Yeah, we know the drill, man. Personal comms and network connections are down. We had a technical issue with our approach, meaning we missed the starboard view, hence they won't get the 'Skisurf Europa' experience or the 'Io Hotshots' immersion. But we'll make a point of stopping in on the way back. To make it up to them, drinks are half price for the entire stopover."

Once again, Astley beamed his winning smile.

"And all your staff are fully briefed."

"Told 'em myself, man."

"Because, if one person finds out—"

"Chill, man, cool as the outers."

Sphink's eyes darkened at Astley and all his blasé non-chain-of-command ways. It was all too much to keep up the act. "I'm going to assume that means you 100 percent understand the gravity of the situation and have all the necessary procedures in place to ensure it will come to pass."

Astley nodded with just the right degree of disregard for the gravity of the situation and Sphink's authority to tip him over the edge.

"If not, the only chilling that will be happening will be to your body as it spends the rest of the trip in status."

Astley stopped nodding.

"...or the vacuum of space, I haven't decided yet."

*

Flicker's eyes took in the displays of light that filled the holographic console. It was a sea of green and content data. "*Milky Pleasure*, we have your mark. Paired. Landing protocols initiated."

"Roger that, *Will Shakespeare*... welcome home."

Satisfied nods were exchanged around the bridge. They had made it back. Well, all but one. This was not a moment to celebrate, nor grieve. It was just another reminder of Connor's loss and another step into the grieving — a very real step.

The presence of the Ambassador and his robot added another smothering layer of inhibition to the bridge. He stood behind Hart in silence, eyes fixed on the *Milky Pleasure.*

As did Hart and her crew. The docking bay was now a beacon of sweet relief from the constriction of the moment. They all sensed it. Wave toyed with the collar of his uniform, trying to release some heat.

"Captain Hart. Bridge Captain Sphink has requested your presence on the bridge as soon as you've docked."

Hart closed her eyes and took a deep breath to dispel the bad taste coming from the thought of dealing with Sphink before she could digest everything else. When she opened her eyes again, Flicker was giving her a grin, enjoying her discomfort.

"Affirmative," she said, in the tone furthest from disappointment she could muster. "...you and the entire crew."

Hart looked back at Flicker to see the smirk completely drain from his face.

"Roger that," added Hart, with far more enthusiasm and eye contact with Flicker. "*Milky Pleasure*, out."

*

Over the next few hours, the *Milky Pleasure* came alive. Thousands of people emerged from their stasis pods, slowly re-orienting themselves to existence before turning their thoughts to the pleasures and experiences ahead of them. The moons of Jupiter — and then the most extravagant pleasures the galaxy could offer.

There was a buzz throughout the decks. Some eager to see the jewel in the solar system's crown, some joyous at reaching the outer solar system, others who found the sights twee and were simply keen for their first chance to experience all the *Milky Pleasure* had to offer. And it had plenty.

Nightclubs, bars, retreats, havens, communes, free-floating sex retreats — all were gathering points to cater for the breadth of diverse tastes that came with those who could afford the grandest of adventures.

The anticipation reverberated down corridors, almost as its own essence, given life from possibilities and dreams of the humans that gathered.

Rick Astley let it wash over his skin. This was what he was born to do. Fulfilling dreams at day while he worked, fulfilling more at night while he played. This was the stuff of dreams. Wet and dry.

Except the whole humanity destruction thing, of course. But that was easy to dismiss, while the anticipation rolled over him. It was too comforting to let such thoughts distract him.

He bathed in that moment as best he could until his comms sprang into life.

"Tour 14 to Tour Master."

Astley let his assigned call name bring another wave of joy before responding. "Tour Master receiving."

"Yeah, so, we've got a problem."

"Spill it."

"Excuse me, Sir?"

"What is the problem?"

"A few of the customers are asking questions. Can I get some help down here to help explain?"

Astley pondered the problem for a moment. "Tour 2, are you around?"

"Yes, Sir," came the voice.

"Not Sir… Tour Master is fine."

There was a sigh on the other end, "Yes, sorry, Tour Master."

"Can you rendezvous with Tour 14 and help him deal with a few customer enquiries?"

"Erm, I am already there, Sir."

"Tour Master!"

"Tour Master. Look, some people are asking questions we can't answer."

Astley checked his reflection in the shieldscreen, before adjusting his collar. "Cool. Bound to happen, I guess. What are the other groups doing to stay on top of this?"

"We are the first group."

"On my way."

*

Hart went to step through the door onto the bridge of the *Milky Pleasure* only to have Ambassador Harding barge past, followed by his robot. At least the robot apologised. She turned to her crew and nodded, before they all followed her onto the bridge.

Hart nodded to Sphink as she entered, noting with grudging respect that he was waiting to welcome them back after their battle. It didn't last. Hart's eyes were fixed upon Harding, his eyes glittering as he saluted.

"Welcome aboard the *Milky Pleasure*, Ambassador Harding. It is a great honour to play my part in saving your life," he said with utmost devotion.

Hart did her best not to say anything. Behind her, Wave coughed. She swore she heard him say "loser" as he did. Sphink looked at him warily, but let his suspicion go when Harding spoke.

"Are my quarters prepared?"

"Sir, yes. We have managed to shuffle a few things around to get you into one of the deluxe suites on the Nebula Deck."

"Is that among the… general population?"

Harding's tone was not one of pleasure.

"Well, yes, but in the circumstances, I think you'll be quite pleased."

Harding stared at Sphink in the way someone does when they're preparing not to be quite pleased.

"The access lift will only be used by a handful of others who have paid ultra-premium prices for the ultimate discretion. Even I don't know who they are. It really is exclusive, Sir."

The Ambassador remained silent, compelling Sphink to fill the silence with more words.

"Umm… anyone else there will be back into stasis after a couple of days. It really is exclusive, Sir, and I think you'll find your anonymity and privacy guaranteed… as requested."

Harding kept his silent gaze long enough to make everyone in the room feel awkward. "Very well. Show me to my quarters."

"Wait," said Hart. "Is that it? Connor's dead!"

"Enough, Hart, that's an order," snapped Sphink.

"The whole Jupiter thing. The whole humanity extermination thing."

"Enough!"

"Let alone what we're going to do next. And you're going for a nap?"

"Hart!" said Sphink as he held his clipboard up at a threatening angle.

Immediately Storm stepped up next to her Captain and glared at him. Sphink compared his clipboard to the strength of Storm's jaw, and backed down.

Harding shook his head. "Come, George."

His robot fussed after him as he made his way to the exit of the bridge.

Hart glared at him as they passed. "That's the best you can—"

"You'll be told what you need to be told, when you need to be told it. Good day!" Harding said, and left the bridge.

The tension did not.

Hart and crew now eyeballed Sphink. He ignored them in that way people who bandy around their power like to do, before turning to his communicator. "Astley, report to the bridge."

*

"… and as a result of the main network system going down throughout the system, the *Milky Pleasure's* hail signal didn't pair with it in time to hit the entry window, and so we have, unfortunately, missed Europa rising. The Captain sends his apologies and will make it up on the return leg. Oh, and have I mentioned half-priced drinks at all bars and clubs over our stop?"

The touring party of 30 stared at Rick Astley, unconvinced.

After a brief, dissatisfied pause, he was hit with a barrage of questions. His surface-level charm stood no chance of keeping them at bay. Eventually, he identified the least aggressive, least intelligent one he could find and pointed at the man to ask his questions in isolation.

"I had a cousin on Io. He was expecting me."

"Once again, the system problem was widespread. We couldn't hit the approach window, and we couldn't make protocols."

Another pause before more questions.

Astley raised his voice to compensate. "I just want to assure everyone, it was not a problem with this ship — it has affected everyone, systemwide — and we are all completely fine."

Astley prided himself on telling the truth. Mostly. Or partly. Whatever.

"What about everyone on Jupiter?" said the least aggressive and intelligent one.

Rick Astley felt his game starting to come unstuck. He looked to his staff for support, but they just shrugged. He caught himself, beamed his best winning smile to buy himself a few seconds. "It's… a network problem… I'm sure they are perfectly fine."

"What's that?" said another as they looked at the view out the shieldscreen.

Astley headed to the shieldscreen and did his best to ignore anything that might be worth ignoring. "What's what?"

"Over by the horizon to the left, look. What are all those specs of glistening light that keep shining in our direction?"

Astley could clearly see the debris of battles lost as it blossomed out over Jupiter's orbit in the distance. "No… I can't see anything."

"There, the shining and sparkling… what is that?"

By this time the entire tour group had stood up against the transparent barrier to the space beyond.

"Yeah, I see that. What is it?" another asked.

Just then, near the original site, several pieces of debris closer to Jupiter's grasp lit up as they began their brief and fiery descent to the surface.

"What the hell was that?"

They all looked at him — 30 tourists and two staff. For the first time, he felt doubt burn all the way up to his cheeks. "Well, it's simply a… erm… what is it? Ah, yes, it's a local atmospheric phenomenon."

He smiled at the string of consecutively plausible words he'd connected together. An increased lift at the corner of his mouth for using two particularly long words in there. That would shut them up.

The tourists didn't seem to share his pleasure. They remained unsatisfied. The one who had now positioned himself as group spokesperson whipped out his communicator in hope of confirming this newly-heard theory, only to remind himself there was no access to a network. "What local atmospheric phenomenon?"

The smile drained from Astley's face. "You know, the one with the… the one that causes things to do that. Happens all the time in these parts."

There was a pause.

"I've never heard of it," said one.

The self-nominated spokesperson stared at him. "What's it called?"

"It's called… it's called… I forget."

"You mean to tell me, you are the Tour Master for our trip to Jupiter and beyond, and there is this regular and spectacular phenomenon and you've just forgotten its name?"

"He's lying," said one of the slower tourists.

Astley's forehead was now beading in freefall. He went for his confident grin again in an attempt to buy himself a few seconds of think time, but it abandoned him. Instead he looked at the 30 now very angry tourists.

"Actually, it was a weather balloon!"

"A weather balloon?"

"Yes."

"In orbit around Jupiter?"

Astley's eyes had resorted to desperate pleading by this point. "Yes."

"Rubbish!"

Astley paused to collect himself then opened his mouth to respond. But no words fell out.

"Can we speak to someone in authority?"

"You've got him, I'm the Tour Master."

"Tool Master, more like it," said an old woman from the back of the group.

They all laughed.

"Look, it's fine! Everything's going to be perfectly fine. We've had some technical difficulties, which we're sorting through, but everything's going to be fine."

"What technical difficulties?"

"Just… stuff."

"Does it have anything to do with the atmospheric conditions, or weather balloons on Jupiter?"

"He's lying," said the slow tourist again, not even needing his response this time.

Astley searched the very depths of his soul until he could find access to his winning smile again. "Of course not, we're just—"

At that moment a thud drew everyone's attention to the ship's exterior once more. The body of a female, well, half the remains of a female, clung briefly to the shieldscreen through the tactile nature of the organs that danced around the remnants of her torso. Soon, the battle of adhesion was lost and the body drifted back into the void of space. Out of sight, but utterly not out of mind.

They all looked at Astley.

He was burning in panic now. He'd run out of plans and options. He had run out of everything. Nothing could—

His communicator sprung into life.

"Astley, report to the bridge."

It was Sphink.

Oh, thank fuck, he thought as he picked up the communicator and responded to the Bridge Captain. "Sir, yes, Sir."

The spokesperson tourist looked at him. "Why did you say, 'Oh, thank fuck?'"

Dammit! He'd said it, not thunk it.

"Well?"

Or was it thinked?

"Look, that was the Bridge Captain. I've got to go. Best we pick the tour up at some other time. As a welcome to Jupiter, there are free drinks available in all bars and clubs for the next two hours."

"So, what, you're just going to get us drunk?"

But it was too late, Astley was gone.

*

Astley returned to the bridge to find Hart and Sphink going toe-to-toe.

"So, you haven't even thought about any of it — where we're going to refuel, how we're going to acquire protocols to get through Saturn and beyond, how we're going to even make it to the outer solar system undetected to even make the jump, assuming there is still a destination for us to jump to on the other end?" Hart said in a commanding tone that was more commendable for its restraint. "But you still thought it was a good idea to wake everybody up?"

Sphink rearranged his stance to a more authoritative position to counter the barrage. When he replied, he did so in the best slow and patronising manner he could muster.

"The Ambassador will be a part of that conversation, which seems to me is well above your pay grade," he said, with a brief pause to smile coldly. "Your only job right now is not to tell any of the civilians what's going on. If you do come into contact with one and they ask any questions, the official stance is: We don't know and we'll fill them in once we do."

"You brought us here to tell us that?"

Sphink lost his train of thought as he saw Astley enter the bridge. "Ahh, Astley, how's everything going?"

The Tour Master thought hard about how best to frame his answer. "About as well as could be expected in the circumstances."

"Excellent," said Sphink.

"I've told them there are free drinks for the next two hours."

Sphink's face briefly looked like he'd had lemon squeezed in his eye, before he controlled himself. "Well, in the circumstances, probably a good move."

He turned to Hart. "See, nothing to worry about."

Astley found something interesting on his boots and concentrated all his focus on that, avoiding the studying gaze of Hart.

Sphink was ready to return it however. "So, take your crew and enjoy your night."

"We've lost a crew member, remember?"

"Well, in that case, drown your sorrows. It's on-the-house, tonight, apparently."

"Asshole," said Hart, as she turned and signalled to her crew they were leaving.

"Just don't tell the civilians," yelled Sphink after them.

*

"I hate that guy," said Wave, as they made their way along the ship's main arterial shuttle tube to the SaturnTable Bar.

"Which one?" added Storm. "Company assholes, one and all."

There was a pause in the conversation as they pondered their circumstances.

"Sure has given this girl a thirst, though."

"With ya there," added Flicker.

"And my blue lips are pulsing."

"Not so much there," added Flicker.

"Packed house and probably all drunk," said Wave. "Fair chance those lips might be in for a colour change."

Storm smiled. "Especially when they hear it's the end of the world as we know it."

"You heard what Sphink said," said Hiscock.

"Fuck him and quit being a pussy," said Storm as she started stretching her muscles, as if she was loosening up for a sporting event. "Once we spill the beans, we'll be on a sure thing. Who's not going to want a taste of the coming Storm?"

The comments were enough to defeat Hiscock's meek resistance, but the real approval needed to come from Hart. Storm looked at her Captain as she stretched her hamstrings. They all did.

Hart weighed her responsibility to maintain cohesion and minimise panic. For the first time she was willing to admit: it was the end of the worlds as she knew it. Now was the perfect time to follow orders to make things flow smoothly and to protect the people under her charge. There were only two small issues: Sphink was an asshole, and he was wrong. Decision made.

"Ladies and gentlemen! Storm's right. Fuck him. Reconvene at the pub in one hour."

*

CHAPTER 10:
THE COMING STORM

Flicker stood up from his bed, ignoring the glass vial that fell from his hand as the hit of Reality coursed through him. He took in his sharp jawline in the reflection of the shieldscreen: That was the look of a leader. He was a leader.

He nodded in approval at his reflection. This was a man who saved lives, broke hearts and, well, was a bloody hero.

He winked at himself, adjusted his thick after-five sock one last time, and headed off for a night with his team.

*

Hiscock stood in front of the mirror in full dress uniform, almost ready to head out.

He admired the three golden wings and crossed spanners of his new insignia. Four ascending lines flowed behind the other symbols, indicating he was of the fourth-level — the highest. And an exclamation mark at the end symbolised he was chief on his vessel.

It was the most beautiful thing he had ever seen.

And it was his.

It was him.

The chief engineer was ready to have drinks with a crew of his underlings.

*

Hart stood in the shower, feeling the hot water scald her skin.

She closed her eyes as she turned to face the jet of water. Its needles dug into her skin and carried away her tears.

Tears of loss for Connor. Tears of humiliation for her treatment at the hands of the Ambassador. Tears of anger at Sphink's self-serving crap. Tears of relief that she had brought her crew back from another battle. And tears of frustration that no one else could see the danger they all faced.

There was so much at stake, and she faced so many roadblocks from people unable to look beyond their own interests. But she had no options, just the shitty cards she had been dealt.

Twenty minutes later she was in full dress uniform and heading out the door. She needed a drink. And perhaps a second to chase away the dark thoughts that were circulating. And a third to ride shotgun and mop up any stragglers. The rest of the drinks? Those she could negotiate as the night unfolded. Anything to take her mind off the situation and the streak.

*

Wave sat in the middle of his quarters, his body encased in a full absorbent sensory coding suit — the best place for him to get lost in his data. As much as he tried to distract his thoughts, he was consumed by Connor's death. He knew he couldn't have saved him but had set up a routine to model alternative courses of action he could have taken that might have kept Connor alive. It was a complex program and would take hours to analyse and identify the factors, and then produce the scenarios that would result in a different outcome.

He knew he was torturing himself, but he had to run the numbers. To be certain. He let the coding run its magic before turning to his other obsession.

He tended his library of Storm creations with the usual care. Each one was intensely private and intimate. He knew some might think of them as sexual or perverse, but they were works of art and love. Few would appreciate his ability to recreate skin texture to that degree, or his ability to code for bodily fluids at the right viscosity and, when needed, pressure.

But he did.

The suit constricted momentarily — an alarm signalling it was time to go. He stripped it and used a nearby towel to wipe the fluids from his skin.

He sniffed. Not too bad but he would probably need to shower over the next couple of days or so.

He threw on what he was wearing earlier, ignoring the stains, and headed out to catch his crew.

And time with her.

*

Storm let out a breath as she finished her hundredth chin-up. She unstrapped the weights from her feet and threw them in a box in the corner with the remainder of her equipment.

She stepped into the shower and felt her muscles tighten and skin pucker under the cold water. She'd gotten used to it during her lunar training. She had also gotten used to the benefits of low-g during training. Her body reacted to the memory of her going-away party on Earth. She had said goodbye to everyone personally. Very personally. And some more than once.

The shuttle home had been awkward for some.

Not her.

She smiled and threw on her party dress — a nice swishy thing that hid gun holsters and other surprises for willing travellers — and swung her hair as she left the cabin.

Lunar training would have nothing on tonight.

*

The SaturnTable Bar was pumping, jammed with pleasure-seekers throwing themselves into the night in a way that only free drinks will encourage.

Laughter cut through the thumping show tunes that were the current rage, bodies pushing themselves against each other to find contact after being put on ice. The lights had been dimmed to showcase the stars that surrounded them.

When Storm entered, the rest of the crew in her wake, it all stopped.

Not at once, but with glances, looks and admiring grunts. The human cargo might be able to buy the bulk of humanity, but this crew were the real deal. Heroes. Legends. Saviours.

Hiscock spoke into the near-silence.

"Do they have green smoothies here? I'm really feeling the need," he said with a smile.

Storm stopped and took a deep breath before rounding on him.

"You will not speak of juice while you are with me. Ever. Again."

"But—"

Storm took a moment to explain what would happen if Hiscock continued to talk, leaving him trying to understand whether the suggestion was physically possible before deciding she would be able to make it happen through sheer strength of will. He shut his mouth and other aforementioned orifices and followed.

Storm strode over to their usual corner. It was filled with a group of seven men, all the size of prize-winning cattle with attitudes to match. Most moved when she approached. All except the prize bull, who followed his leer at her body with a big swig from his tankard.

"You're sitting in our space," she said. No one who knew her could mistake the kind invitation to leave.

The bull smiled and leered.

"And what are you going to do about it, girlie?"

*

The Ambassador took a moment to appreciate his stateroom. He had no need of the grand piano or the four bedrooms and three bathrooms, but the privacy was appreciated in a world where the fate of humanity lay in his hands.

"George, clean the room and establish a secure channel."

As the Ambassador stared at the stars beyond the wall-to-wall window. George stood behind the Ambassador and set up one of humanity's most advanced communication kits, his precise movements a distant echo of a Japanese tea ceremony.

He drew away from the table quietly when finished to lurk somewhere close but unobtrusive.

"It is ready, Sir," George said, while his gaze fixed upon a stylish in-room cleaning and ironing facility.

The Ambassador sighed, and turned to the device that could connect him with the galaxy. He spoke the coded phrases necessary, and winced as the machine took the biosamples before it would give him full access.

A green light appeared. Identity confirmed. Access granted.

"Tight-beam to Terra command with the highest security on my authority with demand for autorespond underneath the message. Message begins: Source of attacks confirmed. Confirm Terra operational status. Message ends. Send."

The Ambassador turned back to the stars.

He thought about the species that had all but wiped out his species – the Uix and about everything, as he would for the 86-minute wait for what he expected would be his last communication from Earth.

*

Paramedics removed the man's writhing body less than five minutes after he first spoke with Storm.

"You really didn't need to throat punch him," said Hart.

"Meh."

Hart had been too busy enjoying the display of strength to intervene. Perhaps pretending it was the Ambassador's head bouncing off the floor had distracted her. But she wasn't too overwhelmed not to take advantage of it for her third drink. Or fourth.

"OK, but your mess, your shout."

"But Captain—"

"You know the rules. Another round for everyone."

Storm sighed, slammed back her next shot, and made her way to the bar.

*

The Ambassador threw himself back on the couch.

He waited for the response window to elapse, then waited some more — nothing.

In his early days in the Diplomatic Corps, he had overseen the design and development of a planet-wide communications system with a single reassuring feature: the ability for anyone to request a response from Earth and receive a clear signal that confirmed the world existed. All while its billions and billions of inhabitants remained blissfully unaware of the meaningless trivia of their own lives.

But it was a signal that could not be denied. Multiple redundancies. Some buried kilometres under the surface where temperatures stopped just short of melting rock. Some on the highest mountains, stretching to the sky. Some buried in what was left of the polar ice caps, and some lurking in the deepest ocean trenches into which the ice was melting. And on Luna and in orbit, a string of small objects whose only purpose was to confirm that yes, Mankind was here.

As his career advanced and he travelled further and further, he would turn to the signal, sometimes waiting days for a response but welcoming its reassuring tones. That same tone had carried him from planet to planet, system to system, confirming he was still connected to his birthplace and the people whose voice he carried.

And now it was silent.

Earth was dead.

Ambassador Harding waited for the shock to hit him. Any emotion. There was nothing. Just the hollow silence that was once Earth.

"George, bring me a scotch with ice. And don't speak."

George moved effortlessly into motion, gathering the scotch and a tumbler on the way through. His metallic hand opened the fridge door gently, as if caressing a lover, and extracted ice from a nearby bucket.

He placed all on the table before Harding and placed the glass with scotch and ice — in proportions learned over the years with adjustments for the Ambassador's current sorrow — by his hand.

Harding grunted, and waved him away with a curt gesture.

For a moment, he just rolled the scotch around the tumbler, watching the ice refract the tawny tones through its fractures.

He placed the glass down sharply, and turned back to his communications array.

"Tight-beam to Saturn outpost G7 with the following coordinates and access code—"

He reeled off a lengthy set of numbers established three years previously in anticipation of this outcome.

"Request autorespond. Message begins: Urgent. Confirm status. Message ends. Send."

He picked up his glass and breathed in the musky tones while his mind raced. Saturn: 36 minutes each way, leaving a 72-minute wait.

Saturn had to survive. It just had to.

He turned again to look at the stars and darkness that had betrayed humanity.

And he waited.

*

Things were definitely getting messy in the SaturnTable Bar.

Markou the barman — and belonging agent — stood behind the chaos as his staff struggled to keep up with the growing demand.

Free drinks had spurred on the sleepers. Not just the alcohol but the impossibly majestic views, the closeness of the nearby bodies and the excitement of what lay ahead.

The crew of the *William Shakespeare*, on the other hand, were just getting messy. Flicker was swinging between universe-grade confidence and singularity-class self-doubt. Storm was returning to the bar after taking out another guest for an intimate session — Markou knew he, like the others, wouldn't return that night — while Hart was knocking back drinks at a pace that seemed to him like a way of drowning demons that would inevitably resurface.

Then there was Wave and Hiscock, trading poisoned barbs in a steadily-escalating arms race.

Markou just absorbed it all.

Hiscock brushed his fingers across his new rank insignia, and looked down on Wave.

"So, I guess this means you now have to follow my orders?"

"Yeah, nah. The thing is," Wave said. "You're a douche."

Hiscock stopped caressing his rank and waited for the conversation to fall in line again with his expectation.

"I'm a specialist. Not company. But as an engineer that means—"

"I have to follow the orders of my commander, not yours," Wave said, and downed his drink.

Hiscock's disappointment was palpable and he turned to Hart, who at that point appeared to be having a very reasoned argument with two shot glasses in front of her — one full, one empty.

Hiscock returned to Wave.

"It doesn't matter who you report to, punk—"

"Ha, punk?! You're calling me a punk? God, I'm going to have to research the term. It's from the Victorian era, isn't it?"

"MTV era, troglodyte — I studied history at the Academy. But wait, you didn't go, did you? What, marks not good enough? Have some difficulty with all those single-digit numbers your family earned?"

Wave's face contorted. He hadn't gone to the Academy because a whore had taken him in out of pity and could barely afford to keep herself, let alone him. Not a vote of confidence in her skills. It wasn't widely known, partly because his mother looked a lot like Storm, as far as he could recall. He shook his head and returned to the fight.

"And yet, here we are now, and you're still fawning over a piece of metal because a man your entire essence couldn't amount to the ass hairs of is dead."

"Speak for yourself," Hiscock said tartly.

"Whatever man, you don't even rate. I guess that's why it's good being able to pin something to your chest. It's a *special* commendation for someone special for trying. Well done. Maybe one day you will actually achieve something."

"Trying," Hiscock gave a thin, high laugh. "What, like you were *trying* with that thing in your cabin? You know who it reminded me of?"

His eyes slipped to Storm as she sat roughly at the table next to the Captain.

"Someone living? That's a pleasant change for you. So tell me, how's the Goliath going? I noticed the power generators in your section are getting a workout. Discovered the overdrive, huh?"

They stared across the table at each other, the silence carrying heavy waves of hatred. Captain Hart looked up and took in the mood.

"Now, now boys," she said, her voice thickening but not yet slurring. "We've got months together so play nice. We need to stick together against the fuckwits."

Her head wobbled as she sought to focus on them through eyes steadfastly refusing to focus.

"The fuckwits that will kill all that's left of the human race." She stared into her glass. "That would be sad."

She skulled her drink, then turned back to them, recognising through the haze that nothing had been resolved. She turned to hazy Plan B.

"My shout, right?" She stood up, eventually, placing a hand on Storm's shoulder to steady herself. Storm leaned closer to provide more body-on-body support.

"Right. Drinks!"

She walked towards Markou, who saw Storm's disappointment, before Storm started looking for her next conquest.

*

The Ambassador's quiet thoughts were interrupted by the soft tone of a message received. He smiled at the first good news for what seemed like many months.

"Message begins: Online at 68 per cent capacity. Fuel supplies intact. Command lines simplified and confirmed. Message ends."

He drained his scotch with the smile still on his face. It stayed even as he thought about the next steps.

Decision made, Harding grunted. "Leave me."

His hand waved in a curt gesture towards George, who was standing in a corner. George nodded to acknowledge the order and walked past the fridge, letting his hand linger a moment longer than needed, before leaving the suite. He walked around a corner and stood for a moment while he waited for his electronic brain to suggest a task or destination that would fill the time. Decision made, he took a lift to the main entertainment deck.

Harding closed his eyes and issued his final communication for the night: "Proceed as planned."

He nodded, and made his way to the bridge.

*

Markou watched Hart make her way to the bar. When she was sober she commanded attention and respect. He had seen people make way for her. Not out of sheer strength, like Storm, or because of odour, like Wave, but because of the unspoken experience and respect she radiated.

She wasn't like that now.

She was chatting to a cute guy who was too distracted by the command to take in the drunkenness. She was reeling him in, although he didn't see it. Wouldn't see it until it was too late.

They were both so caught in their moment that Markou, wearing his belonging officer cap, had signalled the bartenders to leave the area alone to give them time to hit it off. Heaven knew the Captain needed a good… time to distract herself from the trials of command, and it was a rare opportunity for that to occur.

He could hear the conversation, filled with shared laughs over nothing of importance, and he smiled. This was a good outcome for the night, although the Captain might hate herself in the morning if she could remember the quality of dialogue he was now enduring second-hand.

And then, like a shuttle crash, everything seemed to destruct in slow motion.

The Captain was laughing over a shared joke, and missed the slight furrowing of her target's brow. A thought, from nowhere. A recollection. A memory.

He was drunk himself, of course, so didn't have the capacity to filter his thoughts.

He guffawed — a raw uncontrolled release — and Hart laughed with him, thinking it was the tail end of their joke.

He hesitated momentarily, as if doubt had set in, before committing fully to the question.

Markou could hear it and, for all of his powers, had no way to stop it.

"Say, you're—"

"The Captain of the *Shakespeare*. Yeah, the uniform gives it away, I know. But it also gives me a chance to meet people like you." She leaned closer.

"Yeah, I know that. But weren't you in some video?"

Markou could see Hart's face freeze. Her mind was yet to catch up to the conversation, but some ancient part of her brain was battling the alcohol to trigger the fight or flight response. She opened her mouth to respond but couldn't.

With nothing to distract the guy, his mind put everything together. His drunkenness failed to stop him from saying it.

"That's right, yeah, that video. Went viral. Man, that was funny. Seriously, I have never seen animals that size react in that way. And man, your ability to flex. I mean you're older now, so I suspect it's a bit more difficult, but that was seriously impressive. I mean, even through the cling film and gel, I could see you were really enjoying it. I mean—"

He was left talking to an open space as Hart returned, red-faced, to the table.

Storm turned to her. "What happened? Where's my drink?"

Hart's shoulders were shaking with anger. All these years, with humanity on the brink, and still there was no escape. And if it was known once on the ship it may as well be known everywhere.

"You get our fucking drinks, Storm. Your turn."

"But I got the—"

"Do you want a shot glass rammed so far down your eyeball you can see the water reclamation plant on level 12?"

Storm knew Hart's no-hitter rage moments when they struck and adjusted accordingly. "My round, everyone!"

Markou sighed, and prepared another round for the messy table they were all relying upon to save them.

*

Ambassador Harding strode onto the bridge.

Sphink looked up, the little finger of his right hand digging deeply into his right nostril as he studied for his next command module exam. As he heard the door zwip open and almost ripped his nose off in his haste to salute.

"Ambassador on deck!"

The bridge crew stood up promptly and saluted.

"Sphink, yes. Slight alteration to the approach to Saturn, direct us to these coordinates," he said, and rattled off a string of numbers.

Rodriguez plugged the data into MPOPS to coordinate a flight solution. Sphink saw the action and nearly shouted in response.

"Wait, wait, I haven't given the order. Sir, our orders are to undertake a jump from here to the next system."

"No, your orders are now to make our way to Sagan's Station."

"But we can't — our AI won't let us."

MPOPS opened a channel to the bridge to clarify.

"It is not about whether I can let you — it is about following established orders. We are still waiting for confirmation from Earth about the change of flight plan, and standing orders cannot be changed without that confirmation, pursuant to the following rules—"

The Ambassador easily out-voiced the power of the ship.

"Well how about this for a change of flight plan. I take your Processing Core and allow it to bask in the intense radiation of Jupiter's magnetic field while you wait for that confirmation. I believe you have a type-four casing? That should allow you to last almost 14 seconds before you start suffering irreversible harm. Or is it 15 seconds? I apologise, I have been dealing with other matters for far too long. Would you please use part of your processing power to calculate how long you would be able to last? If it helps, please calculate it from seven different distances. I don't want to damage the ship."

There was a brief pause before MPOPS responded.

"Authority for change of course confirmed."

"But Sir, I am in command here," said Sphink. "We make the jump from—"

Harding spoke quietly, but assuredly. "No, I am in command here. You do what I say. If you are not up to the task, I will call upon the infinitely more capable but more difficult Hart to take command. Am I understood?"

Rodriguez focused very intently on the flight plan to cover the growing smirk.

Sphink's eyes darted as his mind searched for a solution, or procedure, or operating directive that could defeat this threat to his command. He failed. "Yes Sir. Understood."

"Then make the adjustment and stop wasting my time."

"Yes Sir."

Harding strode from the bridge.

Sphink let the moment settle before issuing superfluous orders and then falling into his chair, defeated.

His crew had already made the adjustment, but seeing Sphink taken down? Well, that was an unexpected perk of the day.

Regardless of what lay in wait for them at Saturn.

*

The bar was emptying, but the crew of the *William Shakespeare* were on a mission.

Storm was mentally assessing those remaining, sorting them into a ranking system of her own devising that would shape her next move.

Flicker had been quiet for some time. He felt like he should be doing something, anything, yet wasn't capable of making it happen. He felt like that a lot of the time, he realised. He had been going to make a play for Storm earlier in the night, but she had gone off with some guy… or girl… or combination of the above. Another hit of Reality would help return the scene to normality.

Wave and Hiscock were studiously ignoring each other. Hiscock was puffing up his chest, and Wave was on his device, probably making the drives more efficient. Again.

Hart had retreated into herself when she added another two shots. They had gone from being a treat to being medicinal. And she was sticking with that approach.

All of them looked up in shock when George forced his way into their alcove.

"Hey!" said Storm, as she was shoved closer to the Captain.

She was about to make a threat about ripping out his innards, but was more interested in the warmth of the Captain's leg against her own than righteous indignation. She sat silently and enjoyed the Captain's failure to move away.

"Hello, crew," he said with all the elegance of a broken diplomatic mission.

They responded with half-hearted and fully-confused greetings.

George continued to take the initiative.

"I'm here to service. Sorry, serve. Sorry about that — wrong crowd, but the intent is there. So, how are festivities in this establishment tonight?"

He looked around as he waited for a response, before cutting across them all.

"Ooh, who's that? So cute! And so lively!"

The Captain looked up and followed George's gaze. There was a couple drunkenly slobbering over each other — normally she would criticise them, but it was looking fairly good as an option right now — but could see nothing else besides the jukebox, a colourful monstrosity from the Elvis-Kennedy era.

She looked back at George, and saw him tapping away in time with the jukebox. She could have sworn he was making flirtatious eyes at the thing.

It was too much for her.

"What are you here for, George?"

"Ah, forbidden love. So tempting. So very tempting. Sorry? Ah, yes. I am here to serve."

"That's nice, but I'm OK fucking my own life up without any help, thank you very much."

"Captain, I don't think you understand. You can ask me anything, directly, and I will need to recognise your rank and respond."

"Oookaaaay," said Hart, her disinterest on display as she toyed absently with an empty shot glass, wondering when it would refill.

"Just know I may be of service. All you need to do is ask."

Hart became irritated, and sat up, pulling away from Storm in the process. Storm recognised it was always going to happen, but any last-minute drunken hope died. She stared again at the last pickings and selected the best meat on the tray.

Hart's voice suddenly sobered.

"I get it George, but there's a lot happening at the moment. Perhaps more than you know."

George paused — a technique he had learned from the Ambassador and his love of the dramatic — and spoke at a lower level for Hart's attention.

"Yes, Captain. As you say, there is a lot happening. Yet very few on this craft understand the full import of current events. As they might say in the classics, there is a storm coming."

Hart marked the words and her strategic brain started processing their significance. Storm's voice cut across that process.

"A storm coming?" she said, and stood up as she looked at the people she had selected. "You, you, and you two. You're damn straight she is."

*

CHAPTER 11:
HUNGOVER, DRAWN
AND QUARTERED

Hart woke.

There are gentle ways to ease into awareness at the beginning of a Mars day cycle on this Mars-registered cruise ship. This wasn't one of them. Consciousness came with a defibrillator-shock-level of unwarranted rush. It was quickly followed by an influx of stimuli, as if her body was unloading its damage report in a passive aggressive real-time mind dump.

Of course, there was no Will to be a middleman in the communication. Just Hart with a mouth as dry as the engine cooling room and a mainline-level awareness to her blistering headache, spamming her with a long list of operational imperfections that she was in no way capable of dealing with right now.

Her body had clearly seized control of her operating system, casting a strong vote of no confidence in the previous administration's efforts last night.

None of which helped Hart as she lay sideways across her bed, only partly disrobed.

She was alone.

She groaned. She was a leader for what may very well be the last of humanity, and still couldn't break her no hitter.

The first memories of the previous night started to trickle back. Top of the list was the conversation with the guy at the bar. She was close to closing with him, she'd felt it.

Goddamn no hitter. Goddamn video.

A sinking feeling enveloped her as she was left with another reminder of the demons that couldn't let go long enough to have her bed filled this morning. It was going to be a day of long, slow recovery.

Water, she needed water.

As she zombied across her quarters to complete recovery mission one, her thoughts turned to Storm. She must've slept with, well, who knew how many people last night. It must have been more than the number Hart had slept with during her entire time at the Academy. Five. Years.

How was it possible that in the same bull market conditions Storm set records, she'd extended her duck?

It wasn't like she wanted to be like Storm, but surely there was a happy middle ground? The sex middle class — that wasn't too much to ask for.

The first glass of water hit the spot. One tiny victory, one small step for a woman.

It barely touched the sides as it went in. Another reminder of Storm. Hart wondered what she said to her prey to seal the deal, before draining another glass and deciding it was probably better not to know.

She searched the kitchen for food but played it safe to avoid potentially violent repercussions. She filled her glass a third time and headed back to bed.

Lonely, empty, stupid, cobwebbed bed.

She turned her thoughts to any other potential embarrassing moments she may have to deal with at some point. Nothing else disastrous leapt out. Then she wondered about the embarrassing things others had done; if their count was higher, she'd probably make it through the next encounter with her crew unscathed. It was all going to be fine as long as she wasn't best on ground — B.O.G. That would be bad.

Of course, this rule didn't apply to Storm, as she was born without the guilt gene. Best on ground had no irony for her, it was just an accolade, therefore she was ineligible. It was a different story with the others.

Before she could establish any meaningful parameters of where she might stand socially on her next meeting with the crew, an announcement came through the speakers in her room. There were two words — course adjustment — followed by a series of numbers. It was delivered without gravity or fanfare, but Hart knew it was significant. Something was happening. Not obvious. Not good.

She swore.

*

Flicker also swore as the message found its way to his quarters, although his mind was on other matters. After nearly an hour of negotiation, the stunning Cameroonian civilian still in his bed from last night had agreed to give things 'one more go'.

It was a tense negotiation. While the overall result was a shot at redemption, it seemed the fine print to the deal meant all the preparation for the exchange would be in his own hands.

The woman just stared at him, the last shred of hope fading from her distant, delicious brown eyes.

He swore at the message again for breaking his concentration.

"It's not normally like this," he lied.

Soon after, he gave up on the task altogether. He couldn't even muster the credibility to swear in outrage at his own lack of performance this time. Instead, he looked at his beautiful non-lover and asked, "You into Reality?"

*

The message found Hiscock as he was dabbing the final beads of water off the Goliath. He jumped in a mix of panic and guilt — horrible, crippling, core-of-the-soul guilt. It faded far slower than it burst into existence as he realised no one else was actually in the room, witnessing what he had done and was presently trying to cover up.

False alarm — it was just a shipwide announcement. Whatever was actually being announced was meaningless to him. He was simply relieved he hadn't been caught red-handed.

As he tried to wrestle his heartbeat under control, he couldn't help but check all the entrances to the room, just to be sure. After the relief kicked in, he swore again then heaved the device back into its quarantine-grade storage case.

Shame is not the same when there's no one there to witness it.

It's far, far worse.

*

Wave was still face down sleeping off the night's vast alcohol consumption when the message landed.

The only sign of life in his room was a holoanim of Storm playing on repeat.

He was one of a handful on the ship other than Hart who would've known the ramifications of the announcement. In his current state, he had no chance of hearing it.

Instead, every living image he'd taken of Storm the night before was transformed into a 3D reality of light at the end of his bed. Every action, every smile, every conquest attempt — every bit of it — all captured by hijacked feeds, hidden cameras and odour enhancers he had designed himself. From there, software had done its thing, stitching all the pieces into a whole. Drawing an experience as real as the woman herself, all playing on loops of flirtatious action while he slept off the alcohol and loneliness.

*

The announcement only served to stir Storm into consciousness. Slowly, thoughts of the evening before trickled back. She had done things. So many things. Things most other humans would never attempt across a lifetime. In one night. A contented smile appeared at the corners of her mouth. It had all the makings of a top 50 night of all time, she thought.

It was only then she became aware of the face pressed against her body. Poor guy must've fallen asleep trying to please her. She could feel his breath brushing over her. Stirring her again. She opened her eyes to see a woman staring at her in unbridled appreciation. It was a look that said: "You've showed me things I never knew existed and I am forever indebted to you."

That's when she became aware of the other bodies in her bed. She smiled again, pressed herself into the breaths behind her, and pulled the woman in to kiss her.

This would definitely make the top 50 now.

*

Hart saw none of her crew had accessed their comms. She smiled, knowing they were now more likely to face more shame from the previous night. Either way, she wasn't sure if they were going to be able to help or advise her in this moment anyway.

The ship had changed course, but it was subtle. They were still heading in the direction of Saturn, but there's Saturn and then there's Saturn. The original course was a sling. This, well, this must be something different.

She needed answers, but there was no way she would get them from Sphink without the proper form. And her head still hurt too much to face the womano-on-cockspank exchange it would spark with Harding. She needed an option that wouldn't set either of them off.

And then she had it.

"MPOPs, the course update, that still takes us past Saturn, correct?"

"Affirmative."

"Will we still slingshot?"

"That is classified."

Hart rolled her eyes. "Who gave the order to change course?"

"That is classified."

"It wasn't Sphink though, was it?"

"That is classified."

It definitely wasn't Sphink.

The classified roadblock reinforced her decision to avoid direct questions. Something was definitely going on.

"MPOPS, can you plot a visual of the current course, according to the data just announced. I've got to think of how that will impact our defence efforts."

She doubted the AI would care too much about her added detail, it was more for her own benefit. Eyes and ears could be on her, but even if they weren't, she needed to act like they were.

"Affirmative," complied the AI, before displaying a holo over her bed.

She pondered it in silence for a while.

"Thanks MPOPS. Could you overlay the previous course for me?"

A second arc of light appeared over the hologramatic 3D representation of the Saturn system. It didn't take long for the pieces to fall into place. The old course was clearly a sling; the second, moving closer to the moons, looked more like a kiss-and-ride. They were now going to pick up something, or someone, on their way through.

But who or what?

She made an approving, pondering noise for MPOPS' benefit, then dismissed the AI. The graphic disappeared into the darkness.

She used to be paranoid.

Now she was paranoid and curious.

*

CHAPTER 12:
NOT BY GEORGE

It was Harding. Hart knew it had to be Harding. It just had to be. Sphink wasn't capable of doing anything without instructions from Earth. Given Earth appeared to be coping with something on a scale between the entertainment demands of a surprising influx of tourists from an alien race and battling to save the species from catastrophic destruction, it was unlikely Sphink would be able to manage his own 47 layers of bureaucracy, let alone having the strength to make a decision. So Harding. No one else onboard had the capability or authority.

But why?

She pondered it over a coffee in her kitchen. It was a significant step up from water and a sign that recovery from her hangover was one step closer. One sip at a time, she thought.

Why would an Ambassador who seemed hell bent on getting out of the solar system at all costs want to stop at Saturn without explanation? Was it a humanitarian mission, an early bid for resources or something else entirely?

Something was wrong. She could feel it. She wasn't sure what it was, but it was definitely there. It stopped her from saying too much to MPOPS and it made her feel overwhelmed. It was too much to handle alone and too much to share with her crew. She glanced across her quarters as she pondered. Her empty feeling was the only thing to talk to her, telling her she was more alone now than when she woke up.

She toyed with the idea of leaving the thoughts alone. Maybe following the prompts from powers above and concentrating on getting some of the human population out of the solar system alive would be enough to sustain her. Maybe she could just let it be for now.

She tried to concentrate on the warm relief of the coffee. But her mind wasn't going to switch off. Playing ball, it seemed, was not an option. Harding gave her a vibe. She didn't trust him. Something about him… something. It didn't take much to understand approaching him about the course change would be a terrible career idea, perhaps a terrible life expectancy idea. Sphink? Forget it. MPOPS? Nope.

The idea came to her as she drained the last of her coffee. Well, not a plan as such, just a connection of thoughts.

Through her hazy memories of celebration and striking out last night, she remembered George. Harding's robot was at the pub with them. While details at that point of the evening were pretty hazy, she could remember enough to know it was odd. Out of the limits of expected robot protocol at the very least. Strange, definitely. Something more?

As much as she tried to force memories to appear, she was left with nothing. Nothing but a vibe that it was very unusual, a sense that it was, maybe, not a Harding play. George should be her direction. At the very least she could do some fishing.

"MPOPS, can you display the ZPs off all the mechanoids on board?"

"Affirmative," came the response as a list of ping addresses and service numbers floated in the air above her.

There wasn't too much of a challenge to work out which was George. He was the only entity of his type on board. In fact, besides a couple of dozen mechanoids in service of some of the uber rich civilians — all far newer — most of the other ZPs belonged to AI creations far further down the service food chain than robots. Again, another easy tell in the ZP, if you knew what to look for.

She decided against asking MPOPS to transfer a message. Instead she went old-school, pulling out her communications device and typing.

I would like to continue our talk from last night. Are you available to meet?

She'd barely hit send, when the word 'affirmative' bounced back to her device.

She called out for another coffee from her kitchen's AI, and mulled over the new piece of the puzzle in front of her. New information, new actions… where to meet?

SaturnTable Bar in 30 minutes?

Affirmative.

*

Captain Hart moved through the entertainment deck in as low profile a manner as she could muster. It was partly driven by the spy-level intrigue she could feel coursing through her as she neared the bar. Behind her clearing headache, she also knew it was paired with her utter horror of seeing anyone she'd spoken with at the venue the previous night.

She ran her tongue over her teeth to distract her thoughts. They still felt lined by the layers of drink she'd consumed. Seriously, how was it so hard to brush away hangover mouth? Was it like rings on a tree? Did each brushing session just remove one drink layer, exposing the beverage before?

Stupid hangovers. Stupid teeth. Stupid trees.

*

It was quiet at the SaturnTable Bar when she arrived. A couple of weary staff busied themselves cleaning the remains of last night's mess, while a few patrons dotted the seating areas. Hart couldn't tell if they were here for the hair of the dog, or the last of the revellers from the night before. Regardless, the good news was she couldn't immediately recognise any of them. With the added bonus of their regular booth being freely available.

No sign of George.

She decided to head to the bar and let the immediate near future version of herself decide if her order would contain alcohol. She sighed when she saw Markou at the bar, smiling as naturally as he could muster. At least her order decision was made.

She fixed him with her best don't-talk-to-me stare. "Bloody Mary."

"Hmmm, recovery?"

She dismissed the question.

Markou worked his magic behind the bottles, if working magic resembled a newborn giraffe ice skating on an incline. "Any luck last night?"

She stared at him with murderous thoughts until he looked back. As he did, he fumbled with the ice, sending little blocks across the bar and floor. He looked down to deal with the mess and finish her order. It was the only safe spot he could continue his conversation from. "I'm guessing that's a no."

He braved looking up once more, but realised her gaze had won the armwrestle for as long as this conversation would last.

"Everything OK?"

Hart was both impressed and angered that he'd managed to ask the question. "It's fine."

He put the finishing touches to her drink, then slid it delicately across the bar in her direction. "You know, if you ever need to talk…"

In her hangover weakness, she paused on his words for the briefest of moments before repeating her last statement in a sterner tone.

No sooner had she reached the booth than George arrived. She motioned for him to take a seat opposite, while she dealt with the first half of her drink. She wasn't sure why it was called hair of the dog, nor if the feeling it gave her now could in any way lead to an improvement in her state. She tried to not let the battle in her body show in her expression as the drink chose its ultimate direction of travel.

"Captain Hart," said George in a more formal manner.

She studied him until she gained confidence that the drink would stay down. She also wondered how she would approach this moment, how she could possibly—

"Is this about last night?"

There was a hint of concern in the tone of his simulated voice.

Hart processed. Already things were heading in a new direction. She tried to remember what he did last night. She drew a blank. There was a story, though, she could smell it. Instead of steering the conversation, maybe it should steer her. "Is there anything more you'd like to add?"

Maybe her drink was starting to kick in, or perhaps it was the intrigue, but for the first moment that day she wasn't acutely aware of her hangover, it was merely moderate. She took another large swig and tried to focus on George.

He started to respond, but faltered. Hart knew it was all part of the More Relatable Conversational programming, a designed tell, but it was a tell regardless.

"Well, I'm certainly keen to hear anything you have to say, and help if I can."

"Thank you, Captain."

"And I will be very sympathetic to any sensitive information."

George nodded in silence.

When the silence didn't turn to words, Hart finished her drink and pondered her next play. She almost jumped out of her seat as Markou appeared at her side to collect her glass. "Another one?"

She saw George looking suddenly uncomfortable in the situation, then gave Markou a glare. After he became aware he had interrupted a moment and gave a look of remorse, she nodded her wish for another drink and turned her focus back to George.

The mood had definitely changed.

"It's OK, George, people come here to talk all the time. Markou would see and hear things you and I couldn't imagine. People being people, well, robots being robots, well, lifeforms being — how do you self identify?"

"Robot is fine."

"I like robot. It's strong, it's you. Be proud."

George started to speak, then decided against it.

Hart let it all play out, while trying to remain as level as possible. She was close, but oh-so far.

"Perhaps I can change tack. While I'm curious to hear what you have to say, there is also another reason for our meeting today," she said.

George shifted into a pose that showed more positive body language. Again, Hart knew it was the programming at work, his outward appearance designed to indicate attentiveness and put her at ease. Regardless, she was back in the game.

She started to speak just as Markou returned with her drink, his approach far more circumspect this time. She waited until he was on his way before she began.

"Before I start, I'm wondering what level I can trust you," she said, pleased with her strong opening gambit.

George considered the question. "Trust?"

"Yes, I'm concerned about something to do with this ship, I don't know who to turn to and I need your help. But, if I confide in you, I would be taking a risk and I want to know if I can trust you to protect me and the information you hear."

Once again, George pondered. "This is a curious situation."

"It is?"

"Indeed. This is why I have come to you," he said.

Hart could feel her fingers tingle against the cold glass. She was onto something. She knew it.

Her academy training flooded back. Inquisitorial Methods 201: Let the subject shape the conversation.

After a full five seconds of silence she remembered an important fact: George was a robot. He didn't fit the profile they had studied.

Back to her, then.

"You want to tell me something… something you perhaps can't tell Ambassador Harding," she said.

"Affirmative."

Hart sipped her drink and thought about how she could unravel the plot she suspected. "I wonder if we have the same information?"

"I suspect not."

Another mouthful was required to process the information. "Interesting. Well, it seems we would both benefit from trusting each other, yet have our reasons not to." She leaned towards him. "If it helps, please know: I will not betray anything you reveal to me to the Ambassador."

Once again, George sat in thought. Part programmed response, part cold calculation. Hart felt a sudden uneasiness about the entire situation — an acute awareness of the risks she was taking and a complete lack of insight into whatever forces were potentially behind them. Even what role George played in all of this. The feeling penetrated her very soul. She reached for her drink. It didn't help her. Its magic healing powers were gone. She felt ill and alone, right up until the moment George spoke.

"I'm gay."

This time it was Hart's turn to sit there in hard-to-quantify silence. She took another sip of her drink. "I'm sorry, what?"

"I'm gay."

She looked at George again, looked back at her drink, lifted it to her lips and finished it. Then she turned her attention to the bar. Markou was already making his way over. She held up her empty glass and gave it a little shake, sending Markou back where he came from to pour another.

"What do you mean, you're gay?"

"Well, using the contemporary vernacular, gay means—"

"I know what it means… but, you're a robot."

"Yes, I am." She had to check her voice, reducing her response to a whisper. "So... how can you be… gay?"

George considered this longer than all the other considerations combined. "I am unaware of the reason for this phenomenon."

"Don't get me wrong. It's fine. I mean, totally fine. You can be who you want to be. You *should* be that. It's just, I've never heard of a gay robot."

"Neither have I. That is one of the problems with the community."

"The community?"

"Well, me."

Her reflexes prompted her into a laugh, but she caught it just in time to pretend it was a cough. She looked up to see Markou heading her way with another drink. It gave her enough time to warn George he was coming and find her composed expression.

"Thanks. I might grab another one as well, I think I'm going to need it."

Markou analysed the scene briefly before heading back to the bar for round four.
*

A mere 257,682 kilometres away, a small fleet of ships banded together as they fled the Jupiter disaster. Most weren't designed for interplanetary travel but there were no options. It was run or die.

Saturn could be made out in the big black, reflecting the sun's light with far more brilliance than any star could muster in this place.

If any on board had the good fortune to take in the view, it would have stayed with them forever, which would not be long for them.

The twelve mismatched commercial and mining vessels were about to encounter a challenge they had no hope of surviving. Another 371 souls destined to join the vast majority of their kind.

The end came fast. A squadron of alien fighters, not much larger in number, zeroed in on their location. Many of the human ships disintegrated before they were even aware there was any immediate danger. The battle was done in moments. There were no survivors.

It was a small but significant loss to humanity's current numbers.

It meant nothing to their enemy.

Instead, they shifted vectors, setting a course for another craft. *The Milky Pleasure.*

*

Drink seven had proved quite pivotal for Hart. Not only had she completely forgotten she was hungover, she was actually feeling alright and starting to wrap her mind around George's situation.

"So, to sum up: You're definitely gay, but it's a mystery as to how and why. You've never in fact experienced, well, intimacy, to which I can relate…"

She paused for a drink while George nodded along.

"…where was I? Ah yeah, sex…"

She paused again, this time just stirring the ice in her glass.

"Why does it have to be that hard? I mean, how hard can it be? All you have to do is find someone in this universe you can tolerate the thought of doing all those amazing things with, who could tolerate doing them with you. Seriously, they're amazing things, it's a mutually beneficial situation for both people."

Hart was lost in Bloody Marys and dreams.

"I can only imagine," said George.

"Or robots! Sorry, this is about you. Where was I again? Oh, that's right. Sex — like male or female — is usually a totally non-binary label for robots. Many don't even have a sexual identity… they don't process like that. Like the jukebox."

She turned to face the jukebox, "No judgement, Juke," she said and twisted back.

"Anyway, those who do identify aren't always programmed to have sexual urges or capability."

"Affirmative."

"And of those that you've heard who are, none of them are gay."

George reflected for a moment. "For shame."

"There are gay robots. Like, specifically designed for human pleasure sex robots, but you're not sure if one of them would interest you. They're just programmed for sex, you're looking for a deeper connection."

George nodded.

"And all of that makes up our George," said Hart as she raised her glass in celebration and had a sip. "Oh, I forgot, you have not dismissed the idea of a human connection but, whatever comes along, you're not sure if you'll be able to enjoy it, like in an erotic way. But that's not the point. You just want love and connection. How'd I go?"

"You have adequately recapped my sharing."

"I feel this is a high-five moment," said Hart as she offered her hand.

George obliged, awkwardly. "I do admit, it has been a liberating moment for me, telling someone."

"I've got your back George."

"And I do believe I have your back as well."

"I can't promise you any insight on finding male human partners. They're... less forgiving... than you might need them to be. At times."

George nodded as he considered all the information. "Perhaps you could tell me your conundrum instead."

*

CHaPTER 13:
HaRDING a DaY GOES PaST

The first victims didn't even know they were victims. Some would say it was a blessing, of sorts, but it didn't change a simple fact: They were the first of the dead.

Billions died. Untold numbers were injured, or starved, or were left to face the chaos of survival as their species was exterminated.

And the attacks continued.

*

This was the reason Rodriguez had signed up for a multi-year contract: being in control of a ship as it swept underneath Saturn's bulk, watching the shadow of the planet's ice rings play over the turmoil of clouds below, and then sensing the freedom as the ship nosed its way into the black.

And onto the next wonder of the universe.

Family and friends were important, but this was an experience that neither could come close to. And the wonders of the universe were hers.

It was not the same reason Sphink had signed up, and it showed.

Every passing moment as the ship braked on its way to its coordinates was accompanied by a grunt of displeasure or a sigh of disgust. The quieter moments were even worse, a steady signal of complete and utter discontentment. Rodriguez, of course, was willing to use the moment.

"Sir, just confirming there is no change to our ETA and that all readings are nominal," she said, hiding her smile by focusing very carefully on her holodisplay.

"Of course there's no change — nothing has changed!"

Sphink added an angry shake of his head for good measure and stared at the inky blackness ahead of them.

He hated planets. And stars, for that matter. Sphink also hated space. But most of all, he hated people. Especially if they were having fun.

This entire career thing was to prove he was capable of command, that his sister's military career was simply her desire to run around and shoot stuff while he commanded ships that carried lives to other worlds.

For some reason the military had rejected his application — it was either a result of his short-sightedness or narcissism, they'd never confirmed either way — and he'd been forced into the commercial sector. No one else wanted the job, so here he was, taking a ship of 5,000 people to live their dreams — their disgusting, horny dreams.

And what did he get for it? Good money to pay off the unsuccessful bribes he'd incurred trying to get into the military, five years away from his family and his sister's growing honourable medal tally, and an Ambassador who had taken control of the ship. His ship.

And what did he have left?

Saturn.

He hated Saturn.

And space.

Space was just as bad.

*

Harding looked at the biome as they approached Sagan's Station.

The rocks around it had taken a battering and were still spraying dust as they knocked into each other.

The usual signs of life outside the station were gone. The radio and light signals that guided ships to dock were dead, and the steady stream of ships and transports were gone, leaving only a couple of floating hulks caught in a slow orbit that would eventually decay and drag them through an icy ring and into the pressure cooker at Saturn's heart.

But the biome maintained its distance. Somehow, it had survived the worst.

"Open a channel to the bridge. Sphink, please tell Hart to prepare her ship to transport me. I'll meet her at the bay in 20 minutes."

He shut off the communication before he could receive an acknowledgement. If he had been less focused on larger matters, he might have sensed Sphink's annoyance across the multiple levels, but concerns about the extinction of the species had a tendency to focus the mind, he found.

Twenty minutes. Time to prepare.

*

Flicker had already booted up the navigation system when Hart arrived on the *William Shakespeare*.

"You're looking well Will, it's good to be back," said Hart.

"Charmed," replied the AI.

Flicker rolled his eyes. "Flight plan's done, A to B. Then B to A. Let me check that again. Yep, it's just A and B," he said.

Storm was less accepting.

"So we fight off aliens, save one of the most senior people I've ever even thought about, and our skills are being used… as a taxi service?" She turned to ask Hart the question. "Nothing but a taxi service?"

Hart pressed her lips together. It wasn't time to let loose with her fears and doubts, even if they continued to grow with every passing minute.

"That's right, ladies and gentlemen, we are a taxi service. But we're also one of the best-equipped taxi services available — arguably the only one — and we're being employed to protect an extremely VI person," she said. "And we will do it to the best of our ability, as we are more than capable of."

"We all know they're going to be an utter tosser. VIP. Vulgar impotent prick," Flicker muttered, assured in the knowledge the only person capable of acceptable VIP status was, in fact, him.

"Captain, I presume your crew are ready? This very important prick is ready to go," Harding's voice broke across the bridge of the *Shakespeare*. Hart saw Flicker's face lose all of its blood while his mouth opened and closed, searching for magical words that would take it all back. For once he erred on the side of caution and said nothing.

"Yes, Sir, we are indeed. With your leave?"

Harding waved his agreement, and Hart gave orders for the ship to depart.

"Sir, we have been told that we are to escort you to the biome and remain there while we wait for you. Given the dangers that might present themselves —"

"Hart, did you receive your orders?"

His voice was low but precise.

"Yes, Sir, Sphink passed them along but—"

"Follow Sphink's orders, Captain."

"But Sir, we are —"

"Captain!" he barked. "This is not a discussion. I believe you are a capable officer and you have your orders. Do I need to reconsider this assertion?"

Hart could barely hear the filtration systems over the grinding of her teeth.

"Sir," she said by way of acknowledgement and turned back to the holodisplay. It was suddenly too hot on the bridge.

The silence on the bridge became heavier as the biome grew in the display, held together by the tightness of her shoulders. She could barely breathe.

"Captain, please call me seven minutes before arrival," said Harding and stood. "You will need the appropriate codes to testify to our identity."

Everyone on the bridge seemed to breathe easier when the door zwipped closed behind him.

Her comms crackled with a message from Wave.

"Sorry for listening in, Captain, but he's an arsehole," he said from his quarters.

"Thank you, Mr Wave."

"An absolute fission-grade hanging turd," Storm added.

"Thank you, Storm."

"...with bits of corn and everything."

"Enough, Storm!"

"It's good to be comfortable with your body, Captain. If you like, I—"

"Storm!"

"God, if he is the best humanity has to offer, we may as well just off ourselves now for fear that anyone will have to mate with his sorry ass," Flicker said.

The moment he had to enjoy his own cleverness was interrupted as Harding's voice rang out over the bridge: "Mr Flicker, your communicator is still on."

Flicker looked down at his display and hurriedly swiped a control.

His face showed pure panic as he mouthed "sorry" to Hart. He turned back to his display. It was dark, just like his career prospects.

*

Hart wasn't stupid. She didn't insist on pushing a protective team to accompany Harding, but did offer weapons and protective gear.

"And what would I do with a weapon, Captain?" Harding had responded. "Hit them with it? Kill them? I am not a soldier like you, Captain. I am here to help our people, not harm them."

And that was the end of the conversation.

Hart watched Harding's long back disappear between rambles of boxes down the cargo corridor. Emergency lights flooded the area with their red glow, disturbed only by the occasional spark as regular lighting shorted, again and again.

Hart slammed her hand against the close switch. The door irised closed, followed by its second airlock seal. She was alone in her own docking bay, wondering whether it was wrong to hope that the biome's inhabitants had turned into a bloodthirsty mob baying for the fresh blood of an Ambassador.

There were worse things to hope for, she guessed.

*

Harding hadn't ignored Hart's warnings. He had three concealed weapons, two more than his usual complement. And for all his bluster and confidence, he wasn't immune to fears for his own safety.

He had seen the worst of humanity over his years. As his ship had lifted from the Nouveau York riots, he had seen people tearing each other apart, arms ripped away from torsos, eyes gouged out with fingers that were soon snapped and thrown away by others.

The Beltrame-V humanitarian mission was worse. Bodies decaying in a matter of days as the smart nanobots evolved beyond their programming. Pools of liquid on streets that were once families, and families running from each other to avoid infection. And then the six-month quarantine and decontamination, where all he could do was relive the worst of what he failed to do.

Sagan was different. People may be scared, but there was hope. They could be saved.

But he also had a job to do, he resolved, and his stride lengthened.

The nature of space stations didn't change much. Sagan's control centre was located centrally, so all one had to do was keep walking deeper into the station. Those with space experience could feel the easing of gravity as you walked away from the spin. Harding was one who could tell.

The station's inhabitants looked tired. Scared. But they had purpose. They were moving goods, repairing broken conduits, working together rather than gazing over their shoulder, waiting for the next attack from a former friend or colleague.

They looked at him as he passed. On a station of a few hundred people, strangers get recognised quickly. He ignored them and their raised eyebrows for the most part and they returned to their work.

It was an excellent sign. There was order here. There was command.

Harding walked towards where he knew it would be.

It was an unremarkable door.

He knocked — an archaic greeting but one well-known to the room's inhabitant — and the door slid open.

Gus Brugelson pulled his huge frame and its enormous gut from behind his command desk to formally welcome Harding. The handshake gave away the strength behind the fat.

"Ambassador, welcome to Sagan. How can we assist you?"

"Shut up and get the bottle."

They both laughed and relaxed with a bottle of scotch and two glasses between them.

"We were lucky," Gus explained. "They targeted Trump Base — not surprising since it sticks out like the balls of a prize bull — but we weren't on the lidar.

"All this," he said, gesturing to the flickering lights and slight whiff of burnt circuits, "was collateral damage. A few strikes, but many more near misses. We were lucky," he said and shrugged.

"Deaths?"

"One. Someone got too drunk and rushed to the toilet."

Harding screwed up his face as a question.

"It wasn't a toilet. It was an airlock."

"Ah, that's a shame."

"No, not really."

They exchanged an understanding look. Accidents happen in space. Sometimes those accidents just happen to serve the needs of justice. It's why a station like Sagan needed commanders like Brugelson. And why the human race needs me, Harding thought.

Brugelson refilled both glasses, finished his and looked back to Harding.

"What the hell happened?"

Harding sighed, and finished his own glass before reaching out to refill it. The drugs he'd taken earlier would break down the alcohol quickly, so he might as well enjoy the flavours while they lasted.

"Gus, it went to shit," he began.

"Think of it — our first truly alien race. Not the space hoppers branching off from us, but something unique. And something we didn't understand.

"Alien in every way — the way they think, behave, their social order, their values — everything. The Uix — they're everything we could have imagined and more. It's not just their tech that's far in advance of us, it's... everything... the very essence of what it is to be them. They think… eternal. They don't have memories of those who have passed, they have remembered personalities. Some vast matrix of knowledge — every soul, across time — it's unfathomable. Individual personalities that can be called upon for advice, for insights, for memories. We look at our plans and think of them as long term. We are boy scouts. Everything we are and do… it's just a blink."

He refilled his scotch.

"Seriously, how do we compete with that?

"They'd scouted us, taken in our radio waves floating into space and come to a conclusion that we weren't mature enough for the universe. We were teenagers, getting drunk and pissing everywhere with no respect — no memory — of those who went before us or would come after us.

"And this is the thing: They carry their entire race with them and look out into the black and think 'there's not enough room for all of us.'"

Harding shook his head, admitting defeat.

"I thought we had reached a truce. Pure pride on my part."

Gus drew in a breath to ask a question, but let it fall as Harding reached through his memories.

"They'd seen us and discounted us — who we are, what we are — like an insect. But I thought I could broker something between us. Some way we could work together. Their technology, Gus, it's so different. Our worlds, our lives, would be so different. I wanted it to work."

His voice trailed off.

Gus refilled both glasses.

"They called me in to face their governing council. The thing is, you're not just facing them, you're facing their entire race — everyone who has ever been. Which means you're judged by every one of the Uix who has ever been. Which means the entire human race was being judged by every one of the Uix who has ever been.

"I was just the proxy for our entire goddamned race. Me! One man."

He laughed, a crazy, bitter laugh.

"Gus, we were found unworthy."

Gus's meaty hand slammed against the table. "Of what??"

Harding smiled sadly.

"Everything. What we've done. What we haven't done. The things we are likely to do."

"But they can't know what we'll do. Pure supposition!" Gus said.

"That's not how they see it. This… knowledge they have, thousands of generations. It gives them a different perspective. They saw how we were treating our planet, our system, even our people. In their judgement, we had forfeited our right to exist. There wasn't enough space to allow our race to waste it," Harding explained.

"So these attacks are the punishment?" said Brugelson. "They're wiping us out because they've passed judgement on us?"

Harding looked up at Gus but his mind returned to the dark hall where the human race had been judged.

He had tried to hide humanity's flaws. He had lied, distracted, pointed to things of beauty and redemption. He had argued persuasively, promised a new era of cooperation and shared riches. Man and Uix, painting a bright galactic future together.

The Uix had long ago passed beyond their spoken language. It was an element used for accent but not truth.

They had heard his words and dismissed them. If anything, in their collective mind, every word had condemned him and his race, each promise was evidence of another lie from a young and duplicitous species.

He had been sentenced. His species had been sentenced.

But the Uix pride themselves on their justice, based on the values of the race over thousands of years. They would release him to carry word of their justice to Humanity. They would hear their sentence from one of their own.

He fled.

His voice broke as he spoke.

"Yes. They passed judgement on us."

Harding returned to the present as Brugelson let out a big sigh.

"So we're dead, then? We have no choice but to accept their judgement?" said Brugelson, becoming visibly more angry with every word.

"We certainly have to accept they're winning at the moment," Harding said. "In a rather monumental manner."

"At the moment, yes, but we haven't yet started to fight back!" The fire of Brugelson's Norse heritage reinforced the fierce independence of his spacer existence to make one thing clear — he and the human race weren't going down without a fight.

Harding admired Gus's spirit.

"First we need to stay alive," Harding began, taking in Brugelson's fierce grin. "Then work out a how, a where, a when and a with who… then… then we can start our fight. But first things first. Prepare for evacuation."

Brugelson turned to begin, but was interrupted by Harding holding out one last glass.

"We don't know how many of these will have, so let's enjoy this one. To the future!"

"To the future!"

Harding left the office and made his way back to the airlock.

He could feel the heat of the alcohol dissipate, taking with it his shame of failure. With a clearer head he returned to his strength: Planning ahead, balancing outcomes without emotional connection.

With loose ends from the past soon to be tied up, he could focus on the future.

And as the red lights of the *William Shakespeare's* airlock began to flash, the shape of that future began to form in his mind.

*

CHAPTER 14:
HART ON A SLEEVE

Hart was fuming.

Harding had returned to the bridge and barked orders at her. No explanation, nothing about what he had seen on Sagan. Just an order for her to liaise with Sphink about the transfer of supplies and people. He didn't say it, but Hart knew. They were refugees.

She carried out her orders, with every passing moment seeming to make her more brittle. For once her crew seemed to appreciate her mood. Even Flicker, blessed with more than the usual amount of emotional ignorance expected of men, was quiet, although he might also have been busy with an extreme moment of self-admiration. Sometimes they were difficult to tell apart.

As the mood took her, Hart realised the game had changed. If they were picking up refugees, they were now on a humanitarian mission. And, if her suspicions were correct, they were now all that was left, or very close. George had last night hinted at the same, but he was unable to say anything directly. Harding's orders for confidentiality must have been explicit, and of the highest order.

It was too much to leave to chance. She had to confront Harding to find out exactly what was happening.

Harding had taken up residence in the Mess Hall. Ship culture demanded that it was always open to all, but Hart felt the need to knock as she entered. On her own ship. Damn him.

"Yes, come in," Harding muttered as he pored over a pad of information. "Ah, Captain, good to see you."

She really didn't understand this man, but covered her confusion by getting a fresh coffee. As she sat down in the booth across from him, she sifted through all that she suspected. It was bigger than her. Bigger than him. It didn't just deserve some attention, it demanded it.

"We're all that's left, aren't we?" she blurted.

She saw his reaction briefly before he covered it — she was right.

He looked down at his pad, then purposefully set it to one side. Slowly, he nodded.

"Yes, Captain," he said and looked into her eyes. "Excluding the 37 cruise ships currently extrasolar — sex tourists, rich tourists, religious tourists and one full of the last decade's top rasta-metal bands and their fans… and the outposts we have yet to hear from… and 11 scientific missions. We, and the people we are picking up, are all that is left of our race."

She stood up to get another coffee. Suspecting one thing and knowing it to be true were two very different things.

"How? Why?" The words weren't important. They just meant 'tell me.'

"While you're there, a long black please," said Harding. "There is much to this story, and it's vital that you know the truth of what we face."

She couldn't face him. Not yet. Maybe he was finally being open with her, perhaps trusting her. Maybe it was still a game. She didn't want to break the spell.

He told her everything. Almost.

She drained the last of her coffee as the final words fell from Harding's mouth.

"My crew will need to know."

"Not yet. All will know our fate, in time."

She looked at him — studying, doubtful.

"You're a good Captain, Hart. You understand your crew and know your small role in all this. But I am a good Ambassador. Part of that is knowing people — not just individuals, but collectives. Maybe that's something you can understand in an operational level on a ship, but in a wider population, without military structure… even your version of it… things are different. Information is everything. Controlling it, in the right way, is crucial right now. Not everyone will react with balance, especially after they begin to see some of their newer arrivals from Sagan.

"Have you seen what happens when a captive population panics, Captain? I have. The New Zealand Ag Collapse. Brexit 2. The death of the last beehive. Anarchy.

"We're sitting on a powder keg here. We could blow ourselves up before the enemy has a chance to find us. Public order is mission critical right now. If we can't maintain that, there is truly no hope for us. You need to maintain that order."

"But Sir, we're a small crew. This ship is where we fight," she said.

"Are you hearing what I am saying, Captain? You're now responsible for public order and safety. Could you please prepare recommendations for my consideration? You'll need to deputise, obviously, and I may have some suggestions from those coming across from Sagan."

Hart's mind was racing.

"What about Sphink? It's his ship, as he keeps reminding me."

"I think you mean telling everyone, Captain. Sphink is manageable — useless, but manageable. He serves a purpose. Leave him to me. You have enough to do without worrying about him."

Harding smiled through gritted teeth.

"You didn't ask for this problem and I wish it weren't our reality, but it is. I was with the Uix when they pronounced judgement on us — that is the burden I have to wear.

"I have been carrying this with me for months."

Harding paused to collect himself and for the first time Hart saw something real and human in him. He welled up. "Have you any idea how hard that has been?"

The moment left no sooner than it appeared. He coughed, somehow exorcising the emotion.

"Earth is dead. The people on this ship, the people on the *Milky Pleasure*, the people on Sagan — that is who we are. That is humanity."

He shifted gear again, regaining more control. "I'm not military like you, Captain."

Hart ignored memories of the less-than-stellar highlights of her military career and focused on the compliment.

"Regardless of more political training, I've spent my life talking and trying to understand people. That gives me some insight. You are the right person for this. Here. Now. And as much as I know that, I know this: I need your help. Humanity needs your help.

"Are you willing to give your all to save our race?"

Hart swallowed as she processed. It was overwhelming — all of it. She didn't know what to think. She saw a realness in Harding she didn't think was possible. It was surprising; good, even. And now it seemed he was recruiting her to his inner sanctum, or whatever the equivalent was in his mental calculus. That was a lot to get her head around with the backdrop of humanity's demise. It was a very long step for two coffees.

After a pause, she nodded. Harding returned in kind, then picked up his pad and returned to his bureaucratic self.

"Excellent. Public order and safety — please provide me with recommendations within 24 hours, Captain," he said and his focus shifted to the documents in front of him.

He looked at her back briefly as she exited the Mess Hall.

He now had control of the military.

*

Hart was halfway to the bridge, mind spinning, when Flicker's voice called out to her.

"Captain, call from Sphink coming through for you."

"Put him through," she said, remembering Harding's promise: Leave Sphink to me. There would be some positives.

The crackle of space broke Sphink's words.

"—attack. Captain, attack imminent. Multiple incoming ships. We are about to come under attack—"

Hart yelled orders as she broke into a run toward the bridge.

"XO, acknowledge the call and set a course to return. Storm, prepare for incoming and work with Will and Flicker on a tactical approach. Will, we're going to need you online for this one."

"A moment may yet pass unbidden but to me every moment is the very nectar that gathers the silk of our dreams and weaves our future," said the AI, in a tone that indicated it was just warming up.

"I'll take that as a yes. Wave?"

"Yes, here."

"We're going to need your help — mission critical. Get to Harding in the Mess Hall, stat. He's going to need you to coordinate the downloading of systems from Sagan."

"You got it," he said and shut down his line.

There was nothing else to do but continue her run to the bridge.

What was left of humanity was under attack.

*

CHAPTER 15:
SHOCKING WHORE

"Where's Wave? He should be here by now," said Hart as she looked around the cockpit to a round of shrugs from the crew. She turned to her communicator once more. "Wave, get your ass here... ten minutes ago!"

At that moment the bridge doors zwipped open and the aforementioned engineer bolted through, coming to rest on the back of Flicker's chair. "Alright already, I sorted your problem. You're welcome by the w—"

"Flicker, get us into the black."

"Affirmative," he said, as he attempted to brush Wave's hands from the back of his chair, while taking the controls.

The drive of the *William Shakespeare* hummed in a sinister pitch as the landing gear let go of its grip with the docking bay.

"Storm, be prepared for anything. With, well, everything."

The gunner stirred in ways not appropriate for pre-battle from her commander's words and authority. "Hells yes, Captain."

The ship flat rotated inside the docking bay, slowly revealing the exit to those on the bridge.

"And Wave?"

"Yes Captain?"

"Strap yourself in."

Flicker seized his moment, both to punch the *Shakespeare* into the void and to send Wave barreling backward to a heavy impact with the bridge door. He didn't need to witness the carnage, the impact noise enough to elicit a smile.

They burst out of the belly of the *Milky Pleasure* to a cacophony of engine screams and pulses. As they reached open space, the void stole the audible mayhem. They were soon left in a bizarre oasis of calm. Nothing but black ahead, no sign of the threat fast approaching and nothing but quiet in the cockpit.

Wave recovered enough to find his feet, then find his seat. He rubbed the back of his head as he did so. He went to speak but the Captain beat him to it.

"Talk to me Flicker," said Hart, as she scanned her displays for signs of the enemy.

"I've got them on QuantSat. Will's data shows 33 craft — way more than last time. Plus there's something... different."

"Different?"

"Bigger, definitely bigger than the others."

"How much bigger?"

"We're about three times the size of the attackers, this thing is about five times the size of us."

The Captain did her best to remain in full leadership confidence pose, but the doubt escaped her in a sigh. "Roger that, Flicker. Anything else?"

Wave tried to wedge his words into the conversion but Flicker beat him to it.

"Just… they're moving... like nothing I've ever seen before."

Hart shot him a look that demanded details. Behind her, Wave resorted to raising his arm in the air.

"Anyway, based on what I'm seeing, and what happened last time, we've got less than ten minutes til they'll be in attack range."

"Thanks Flicker. Ten minutes to put together a plan. Will, keep us informed of the countdown to engagement."

"As flowers bathe in the morning light, it would be for me to—"

Hart spoke over the AI until it stopped. "They don't move like us, they don't fight like us, they don't attack like us, they learn quickly, and share that knowledge, and now we have a ship we've never even seen before. Any ideas you've got, now's the time."

She turned to face the rest of the bridge and nodded to the eager Wave.

He let out his own sigh of relief as he lowered his hand and prepared for his moment. Then something dawned on him. "What do you mean they learn quickly and share that knowledge?"

The Captain paused as she took in the expressions of the others. "Classified intel."

"Classified?" said the others in unison.

"No time for that now. They learn and share, that's all you need to know. Whatever happened last time, whatever we did, they'll be expecting it."

Silence greeted her words. Silence and three betrayed, mouths-agape faces.

"Catch up people, we plan around all that or we die."

Another bout of silence followed as the stakes sunk in. Eventually Wave broke the moment.

"So, I ran this little sim from the last battle."

"Good!" said Hart. Excited to move the conversation forward, her words overlapped his. "And?"

"Well, I took their moves from all the nav data we have — how they moved, attacked and defended, based on what we were doing."

"Nine minutes until engagement," noted a more concise Will.

"Then I cross-referenced that against all known battle strategies in zero-g light vehicle engagements…"

"And?"

"Well, nothing from any conventional conflict."

"Are you going to get to a point in my remaining eight-odd minutes of existence?" said Flicker.

Wave nodded, nervously. "OK. So, the closest match I could find was… a video game."

"You've got to be shitting me," said Flicker.

"Anyway, that's why I'm so late back from Harding. Only just made the connection. The enemy we're fighting is like early level AI in the game. If it means anything, they're learning our strengths and weaknesses too. They're feeling us out. Like, I dunno, the early moments of a boxing match."

"And you got all that from a game?"

"Well, the AI. Well, its similarities to the enemy."

"Brillant!" said Flicker. "We're saved. Everyone, grab your joysticks."

"Joysticks are from a different century, numbnuts."

"Shut it you two," snapped Hart. "Wave, anything we can use?"

"Well, I'll need a few sessions to run my own sims around what we already know to be sure, but—"

"We'll be dead by then," said Flicker.

"Eight minutes until engagement."

"…but, broadly, we just need to keep them guessing. Throw everything we have at them. Different things, different combos… anything. It'll buy us time."

"…to be dead?"

"Shut up Flicker," said Hart. "OK, so how are we going to do that with our one battle cruiser?"

There was a pause as everyone poured over the puzzle.

"Captain Hart, this is Captain Sphink."

"What?" said Hart, as she faced his holographic.

"I wish to be kept abreast of your engagement strategy."

"What a tit," said Storm.

There was a snigger from Flicker and Wave.

Hart never broke expression, nor her gaze on Sphink's holographic. "I don't have time for this."

"May I remind you, your purpose is to ensure the safety of this ship, the one this badge says I'm Captain of."

"Seven minutes until engagement."

"You are completely up-to-date with the current plan."

"You haven't told me anything!"

"Exactly!"

At that moment, Hiscock's holographic appeared next to Sphink's. The two shared a glance. They were clearly next to each other on the bridge of the *Milky Pleasure*.

"You don't have anything?" said Hiscock.

"We're working it out!" said Wave.

"I have an idea," said Hiscock.

Hart paced. "We already have an idea."

"Shocking whore," said Hiscock, as he and Sphink shared a knowing nod.

"Excuse me!"

"Shocking whore — it's a famous historical battle strategy from the late 20th century. We throw everything at them. Overwhelm them with our firepower."

"It's called shock and awe," said Hart.

There was a pause. Sphink and Hiscock looked at each other in doubt.

"Why would it be called shocking whore?"

Silence.

"Forget about it!" Hart groaned. "There are not enough minutes left in my life to explain to the pair of you what a shite idea that is."

"But we—"

Hiscock was interrupted by Will. "Six minutes until engagement."

"What the hell is going on here?" came the voice from Harding's holographic as it appeared next to the others in front of Hart and crew.

"We have wasted 25 percent of our strategy time trying to deal with the numpty twins over here," said Hart.

While Sphink looked hurt at the jibe, it was nothing compared to Hiscock.

"Sphink, shut up. Hart, talk."

"The enemy holds all the cards and we don't know what they're capable of. Best we have is a strategy, based on simulations."

"Well?"

Hart looked at Wave.

He felt the nerves wash over him as everyone looked on in expectation. "Well, these are just theories, based on very limited data, but it's—"

"I'm going to assume it's better than the numpty twins' offering, so is therefore the plan. Spill it."

"It's not a plan as such, more a concept."

Everyone looked at him. Wave cleared his throat.

"OK, so... the data seems to indicate they're potentially very risk averse in attack, well, with these smaller craft. They don't entirely know what to expect. So the idea is to—"

"Five minutes until engagement."

"...mix it up in every way imaginable. Keep them guessing. Keep them on the back foot expecting something new."

"And how are you going to do that?"

Wave faltered at Harding's questioning.

"That was where we were at three minutes ago before the A-team derailed us with shock and awe," said Hart. "If I'm understanding correctly, we need to take the game to them, test them... and with something different every time."

She looked at Wave, who nodded. "That's right. The problem is, we have a lack of craft to throw in their direction. But, whatever we can get our hands on will buy us some time, while we work out something else."

"Sphink, can you spare a couple of shuttles?" said Harding.

Sphink opened his mouth to speak, but no words came out. He shared a doubting look with Hiscock, who shrugged.

"Excellent, remote two towards the enemy. George, get Brugelson on this stand-up, now."

"Affirmative, Sir."

Meanwhile, Sphink barked at his crew to dispatch the shuttles remotely.

Wave turned his mind to the possibilities. He approached the bridge interface. "Will, how far are we from Sagan's Station? Is it still in range to be a factor in this engagement?"

"Nice," said Hart.

"A factor?" said Harding.

"Well, I'm assuming it has defensive turrets? Anything that could get the attention of the enemy if fired now? And what about craft still on the station? Is there anything still there and anything that can reach the engagement in time?"

Brugelson's holo had joined the others in time to hear most of the question.

"Four minutes until engagement."

"There are three types of turrets defending Sagan's Station, but none are designed for this type of engagement. The AG-142s have the fastest fire velocity. My calculations have found a vector that may intercept the enemy, depending on future unknowns. I cannot speak to their effectiveness."

"It may not matter," said Wave. "It's more the distraction."

"I have my team remoting them as we speak," said Brugelson. "We have a number of craft that will also be able to intercept. Again, we're getting them airborne as I speak."

Harding paused. "Will they offer anything offensively?"

"It's mostly station hoppers and drilling craft. They're all fitted with something, but nothing that's going to challenge the enemy too much."

Wave nodded. "Doesn't matter. Tell those remoting them to avoid formations and to move in different ways. Anything but the obvious, anything but what the others are doing."

"Affirmative."

"What about self-destruct? Your ships fitted with the option?" said Wave.

Brugelson nodded, both to Wave and the crew no doubt hovered around him awaiting instructions.

"If the enemy gets close enough to be exposed, blow shit up," said Hart.

"I've got some drones to play with too," said Storm.

"Get 'em out there," said Hart.

Harding's holo paced. "Anything else on the Sagan we can use? Drilling equipment, lasers, explosives, anything?"

"What about the core?" added Wave.

Brugelson pondered.

"Four minutes until engagement."

"That'd all be pretty useless at this range, except the lasers, but there's no way we could manoeuvre them into a position to be effective remotely."

"And the core?" said Wave. "What sort of explosion would that make?"

"Massive. Certainly enough for a big distraction. There'd be no way to trigger it though. Fail safes all over the shop."

"What if we remoted one of those ships of yours — something small — as close to the core as we could get it, then hit the self destruct?"

Brugelson paused in thought briefly. "Could work."

"Make it happen," said Harding, issuing instructions to his team. "Anything else?"

Another short pause.

"We've still got shocking… shock and awe," said Hiscock, awkwardly.

Hart groaned.

"Three minutes until engagement."

"I've got movement," said Flicker.

Everyone's focus moved to the battlespace display. The smaller enemy craft seemed to divide into three smaller groups and scatter in different directions.

"Looks like some of them are heading back to Sagan, others to intercept the shuttles."

"We've got 23 craft in the air and one trying to get as close as possible to the core. Oh and 18 turrets firing everything they have at the enemy."

"Nice work, Brugelson," said Harding. "That's at least something."

Flicker spoke without breaking eye contact with the displays. "The first shuttle will be on them in twenty seconds… nineteen…. eighteen."

"They're firing!" said Storm.

"A shuttle's not going to last long against that," said Wave.

"Twelve... eleven…"

Hiscock's holo's gaze was lost in heads-up displays as he spoke. "Hopefully just long enough to—"

There was an almighty explosion from the battlespace. It sent a brilliant, blinding light into the cockpit of the *William Shakespeare*."

"Shuttle's gone," said Flicker.

"What the fuck was that?" said Hart.

Sphink and Hiscock shared a knowing nod. Sphink spoke."That was shock and awe."

"What the fuck did you do?"

"Loaded it with explosives, we told you."

"No you did not!"

"Looks like four enemy craft down," said Flicker.

Sphink and Hiscock high-fived each other.

"Idiots!" snapped Hart.

They looked at her, stunned.

"If we don't work together we'll be dead."

 "Three minutes until engagement."

"...in, like, that long."

*

CHAPTER 16:
HART WRENCHING

"Your three minutes is up, dude! And you're dead — no more chances, and out of the game," announced Rick Astley across the packed SaturnTable Bar.

"Man, you were so close! It's the 2143 Kangaroo Landing de Cuvee, not the 2140! Always go with the sparkle at the back of the throat from the dwindling nitrogen in the soil. Bad luck, but on to the next!"

The challenger slunk away into the roaring crowd, each spectator holding high a wine, spirit or fumigant of their preference.

Ever since the Captain had authorised a bar tab for Rick to settle the passengers, he had been in his element. No shelf was too high for him.

"Right, ladies and gentlemen, let's get this party started!"

The crowd in front of him roared.

"You're right — it's already here!"

They roared again and he basked in their drunken adulation.

"OK, let's keep it rolling on. Who's up next for the Classics Challenge?" he yelled, pouring wine from a masked bottle into the glass in front of him.

A woman with stunning curves stepped up to the bar wearing a dress that technically covered the essentials, yet revealed everything.

He focused on her face, looking into her eyes as she looked across the bar at him and slowly raised the glass. Her nostrils slowly pulsed as they drank in the heady fumes, and she closed her eyes as she lost herself to the wine's aroma.

She raised the glass to her full lips, raising her eyes to peer directly into his. She licked her lips lightly and smiled a shadow of a smile that was lost to those around them, and brought the glass to her mouth.

Her eyes, though — grey, filled with flecks of gold-like stars, and streaks of black that stretched back to the start of time. He watched them even as she drew the glass away and whispered: "It's a 2182 Penfolds Grange. From their southern vineyards after the long, hard drought but before the bushfires that ultimately claimed them. Only 500 cases were produced, and half of those were lost in a shipping accident. They called it 'the Year of Hope.'"

He swallowed, for once lost for any response.

She laughed at his discomfort, her dark rich hair falling over her shoulders. She leaned closer and her dress did things even Rick couldn't imagine.

She whispered something meant solely for him, something that had nothing to do with wine, but only with the promises her eyes and mouth and body were making by simply standing there with a glass of the hallowed 2182 Grange.

He leaned closer to hear the words that would change his life, falling into the magic of her eyes—

And was slammed against the back of the bar as a burst of light appeared outside the bar's vista, followed by shattered glass falling around him, and then the heat of the explosion in the second before emergency fields sprang into action to protect them all from being sucked into the cold death of space.

Rick took a breath and forced himself to stand.

The woman who knew her Grange was sprawled over the splintered bar, her magical dress showing no flesh, only the shard of bar that had pierced her body as it soaked up the flow of dark red blood spreading beneath her.

In the dimness of his mind he heard one of his team calling for everyone to evacuate, to keep moving, to get to their cabins and await further instructions.

His training kicked in despite the numbness and he heard his own voice whispering: "It's all going to be OK, dudes, let's just keep moving."

He stood there as everyone ran out until he felt someone — possibly one of his staff — grab his elbow and start to move him to safety.

*

"Get me that damned thruster back now, or we're dead in the water!" Hart yelled.

Wave didn't respond. He didn't need to, and Hart knew he didn't need to. Just a nod as he continued to work.

He had entered a flow state. Monitoring, fixing, bypassing, creating workarounds where no other options existed. Somewhere in the back of his brain he knew he would be exhausted if they survived. But for now, it was just him and the machine, operating as one.

Storm's voice barked across the bridge.

"Flicker, what would it take to get two of those surface-to-core drillers placed here and here?" She threw the coordinates across to him.

His fingers danced across the console as he mapped out possibilities.

"The problem's going to be this lot here," he said, mapping a group of four attacking craft gathering pace towards the *Milky Pleasure*.

"Don't worry about them — I've got a little bit of magic ready for them. Go for it."

Hart glanced at the solution, smiled and turned back to the overall battle.

She saw a flash as the four craft ignited the volatiles of a drive core ejected by one of the mining carriers, then tracked the two drillers as they moved ahead of the *Milky Pleasure* as a new line of defence.

There was no light from the drillers — their beams were beyond the visible spectrum — but the puffs of the occasional stray attacker proved their worth.

An unexpected flash caught Hart's attention.

"Oh shit, shit, shit. The *Pleasure's* been hit," she said, and the rhythm of battle was broken.

Sphink's voice cut through the noise.

"Captain, if this is you saving us, I'd hate to—"

The transmission cut off.

Wave spoke up. "Sorry, Captain, I needed that channel for additional drive power."

"Smart move. Remind me to give you a commendation when this is all over."

"Flicker, where did that fucker come from?"

"Sir, it dropped in from here." A dull red point pulsed on her screen. "I'm trying to track it back, but it's something new."

"Keep working on it and let me know. Storm—"

"Got it."

There was a dull thump as the percussive wave of what was left of the attacker washed over the *Shakespeare*. Storm's drones were also getting a commendation.

She wasn't expecting the second thump. Or the smoke that started to leak into the bridge from the portside wall. Or the flames that started to lick out.

Flicker raced across from his station, extinguisher in hand, leaving her free to take in what was happening.

An attacker had appeared out of nowhere, right next to them, and let loose a salvo that had pierced their hull.

"Stabilised the leakage," Wave yelled.

"Fucker's dead as dog-turds, like, the ghost white ones you run over with a lawnmover and they explode like a virgin stem," said Storm, in a tone that said her vengeance wasn't yet finished.

Flicker returned to his station, oxygen mask on — a reminder to them all of protocol — and took a renewed look at the battlefield.

"Ah, Captain?"

"Yeah, got it."

The large enemy ship had begun an attack run toward the *Milky Pleasure*, surrounded by a swarm of smaller vessels. One would occasionally wink out and turn up closer to the *Milky Pleasure*, only to turn to light and dust as the mining lasers tore through them.

But the attackers were testing, getting closer — and then getting past.

Hart saw another explosion blossom against the flank of the *Pleasure*, the beautiful and terrible cloud of frozen oxygen crystallising as it entered space. And the bodies.

Hart shut her eyes for a moment in grief and exhaustion. She knew if she listened closely she would hear that voice telling her she had failed, that she was a failure. People had died because she wasn't good enough.

And then anger kicked in.

"Change of plan, people, listen up. This ability to..."

"Shift," Wave said. "They're shifting."

"Thank you, Wave. This ability to shift means we can't assume that their big mumma ship can't do the same. We can't afford to be out here while the rest of our people are there. So we have to establish a defensive perimeter even closer."

"They have to get through us if they want to get to the *Pleasure*."

"Exactly, Storm. Flicker, develop a phased plan to shift our assets into this perimeter, and then make it happen." He began work as soon as she threw the plan to his terminal.

"But we can't have them thinking that we're happy to accept our position. We need them annoyed and distracted. Storm, do you happen to have a spare mining transport or two?"

The bridge shook as another salvo exploded near them. Their battle lighting flickered, went out, and then came on again.

"Seeing as you've asked so nicely, Captain, I have two transports ready for you," Storm said, not missing a beat.

"I want them positioned here and here. Make them worth their money."

"Yes, Sir."

"And make sure no more of those things get through!"

Another explosion flashed against the side of the *Milky Pleasure*. She didn't have time to squeeze her eyes shut, but she knew the voice was there and would find a way to come out after the battle. Only alcohol would silence it.

"Captain?"

"Wave."

"I've had to block another transmission from Captain Sphink — unfortunately we needed that channel for—"

"Two commendations, Wave."

"And another thing?"

There was silence.

"Wave, we don't have a lot of time."

"I need one of those things to come through again."

"That is not happening."

"I need it to happen."

Hart could feel her jaw clenching.

"Why?"

"They emit a signal before they disappear, and another when they appear."

"So we can track them? Then track them!"

"No, no. It's more. We can track them, yes, but I think... If I can get it right, it may let us crack them."

"Define crack."

"Destroy. Kill."

"How many?"

"I... I don't really know. I think it may be all of them that carry whatever allows them to do that. Within a certain area... or something. Sorry, I don't really understand the technology, I'm not really sure how—"

"Sorry Wave. Of course you don't understand the technology. We haven't seen it before. But you are the only person who is getting close — and turning it against them.

"Flicker, how long before we join the inner perimeter?"

"Ah — forty-five seconds."

"Wave, how long do you need once we are there?"

"Ready to go as soon as. Just need a stable position to triangulate."

"Right. Do it."

She took a breath. A moment to let battle thoughts settle and for anything else to enter.

The *Milky Pleasure*. She needed to let them know.

"Wave, those channels to the *Pleasure*. Can you momentarily reinstate one so I can speak with Sphink?"

"Yes, Sir."

"I understand you may need to take control of it for the safety of this crew, so please do so when you need." Or when I signal, she mouthed.

A curt nod from Wave — channel open, Wave back in the flow.

"Captain Sphink, this is Captain Hart—"

"Captain, your negligence is of capital proportion. I will have you court-martialled and be seeking the death penalty—"

A voice from offscreen — possibly the Ambassador — halted the tirade.

"We are losing this battle," Sphink shrieked. "The *Milky Pleasure* is increasingly at risk—"

"We're more than at risk, Captain, we have been attacked! People are dead!"

Hart heard the voice begin, the anger mount — and pushed it deep inside until it could be released by alcohol or by smashing Sphink in the face. She was hoping for the latter.

"Captain! The explosions. The attacks. The... deaths. This is war. I don't know if you have seen the technology our enemy is using? It is far, far superior to our own. The deaths we have suffered? They will not be the last. Our job — yours and mine — is to do the best we can to save every person we can. So this is what we are doing.

"You will notice ships coming closer, both ours and theirs. We are forming a closed sheath around the *Pleasure* to protect her. They have to come through us to get to you.

"We will also have two heavy-duty mining transports to harass them from the outside.

"We will be able to pick off the smaller ones slowly — quicker would be better — but we are yet to figure out how to destroy that hulk out there. That one is our main danger, and the one we are developing a solution for. But first we have to figure out how to deal with ships that defy our knowledge of physics.

"The good news is that we possibly have a way of understanding it. The bad news is that we will need to let one of them through once our new perimeter is established."

"Captain, that is not good enough! We are—"

There was a transmission break and Hart looked up to Wave, who shook his head. He hadn't cut the message.

A few seconds passed and the transmission resumed, this time with Ambassador Harding.

"Acknowledged, Captain. Given we are at war, you report directly to me. Captain Sphink will report to you—" Harding silenced a yelp with a cold stare to his right, and then returned. "We will finalise this later. But for now — God's strength and God's speed to you, Captain. Our lives are in your hands. Harding out."

The transmission ended. Hart felt a peace settle in her soul until the next round of percussive waves washed across them.

Flicker's voice called out. "Captain, we're making the move in 3— 2— 1— now."

There was a slight kick as they set out.

"Wave, let me know what you need."

He nodded, and then spoke up again.

"Another transmission coming through from the *Pleasure*."

The *Shakespeare* shuddered and lurched.

"And — we've just lost a thruster."

"Get it online!"

"No — we've lost it. It's been ripped off. I've sealed the coolants but we need a damned major overhaul if we're going to move at battle speeds again."

The bridge battle lights dimmed and then cut out.

Hart dropped her head. Her main battleship was reduced to a runabout, she was fighting an enemy she had no idea about, and she was about to have a galaxy-class idiot named Sphink dance on her grave.

Her reserves were running low, but duty persisted.

"Put it through."

"Captain, it's Brugelson. That giant hulk you've got an issue with? I may just have something for you."

*

CHAPTER 17:
IT'S JUST A JUMP TO THE LEFT

Hart winced.

They were losing drones all too quickly.

She saw a spark on the outside of her vision and knew: Another one gone. That, and Storm's swearing.

But it was all for a purpose, she reminded herself. Survival.

"How long, Wave?"

"Soon, Captain, just waiting for—"

And they both caught it.

One of the smaller attackers winked out, then appeared next to the *Milky Pleasure*. A flash, the sparkle of escaping oxygen. Precious oxygen.

The impact was toward mid-ship in areas that had been evacuated for this very purpose. But it hurt to see a ship — her ship, her charge — take damage.

"Wave?"

"Yep, got what I need, just working my way through it. I'll get back to you. Bloody inverted transdimensional matrices. Never a healthy sign."

Hart left him to it and turned to the next problem.

"Storm, how did you go with Brugelson?"

"Good. Man's got a decent brain on him. We can get rid of that thing out there, but it's going to cost."

"What?"

"Two mining transports, a core driller and the shuttle."

"Not the shuttle. It's all we have to move people. We're going to need it."

"If we don't get rid of that thing, we won't need to move people at all."

"Why do you need it?"

"The engines. They're wired in a very specific way that makes them unstable when pushed by a core driller and two mining transports."

"Rig something else up."

Storm turned around to face her. Storm's usual light-heartedness in the face of battle was gone, replaced with plain sincerity.

The *Shakespeare* lurched as another percussive wave washed through them.

"Captain," she said gently. "If we had time, we could do it. We don't have time. If we had other options, we could do it. We don't have those options."

Storm held her gaze. Not a challenge — a gentle understanding.

"Captain, there's just us and them. And I want it to be us."

Hart pushed through the logic. They were losing the battle, she knew, and losing more ships as they struggled to hold their line. At some point that line would fail and...

If they held and made a quick escape, they had a chance to think of a back-up plan. A back-up back-up plan.

She ran through the list of remaining ships in her mind, sorting their functions and potential for helping them survive beyond this battle. They would need more options... but those options wouldn't be available if they didn't make their way through this single moment.

"Do it."

Storm nodded, but held her gaze for a moment with a sad, understanding smile, before turning back to her display and taking up her line to Brugelson.

That one look — the moment where Storm showed her inner heart — was proof to her above all else that things had changed.

"Captain?"

"Wave."

The *Shakespeare* lurched and there was another flash near the hull of the *Milky Pleasure*. Both were now being targeted, she noted in the back of her mind. Hunted. Time was ticking.

"Those ships are warping space. They send out a gravimetric signal before they blink out, and resolve that signal when they reappear. We can use that to our advantage if I get a little spare time to revolutionise our notion of space travel and physics, but it's not a priority right now.

"You see, before they wink out and after they reappear, they reach out to their network to establish their place. I think it's a safety feature, you know: I'm here, and now I'm here, please don't warp into me because that would be bad."

"It would. I know the frequencies they are using to transmit coordinates. We can give them the wrong coordinates—"

"Do that!"

"Or," he stressed, "we can use it to trigger a cue for them to warp together."

"So we have, what, 17 of them instead of one?"

"No, so 17 of them come together in the one spot instead of one."

"Clever. But how do we stop the explosion from harming things we want to protect?"

"Ah, yes. We need to sell them something as important. We need to lure them in."

"Right..." She was distracted by a series of flight plans he handed over to her console.

"Sort of like that."

Hart took it all in.

"No, Wave, exactly like that. Flicker?"

"Yeah?"

"Any problems you can see with this?" She flicked the plan over to him.

Flicker went through the document, made a few adjustments and sent it back to them both.

"Good plan. I've made a few changes — cuts about a minute off and keeps both us and the *Pleasure* protected."

"Very good, Flicker. Punch it in, but wait for my go-ahead. Storm, how much time do you need?"

"Almost there, Captain, been letting everything drift into position."

"Excellent. Wave, get yourself set up, and please open a channel to the *Pleasure*."

She spoke briefly to Harding on an encrypted channel, outlining the combined plan and the risks they entailed — and why those risks were nothing compared to the alternative. Harding grimaced but agreed. He'd made harder decisions involving more deaths.

He nodded, then turned off camera with a question as the signal died.

Hart took a deep breath to settle herself for the final moves.

They had a way out. Not perfect, but a way to make sure they would see another day. And some days, that was the most significant contribution anyone could make.

"Storm? Wave? Are you—"

The *Shakespeare* lurched and all lights went out as a shard of metal pierced one side of the bridge, sending slivers across them all, then exited opposite. The scream of escaping atmosphere cut across the darkness.

Hart went from emergency mode to ultra-survival mode.

"Flicker — port side. I've got the starboard. Wave — get us online and get those fuckers out of my life."

Her voice was thin across the bridge as the air that carried it escaped.

She grabbed the kit from beneath the command chair and almost fell over. Her vision clouded, but not from the lack of oxygen. Blood. She wiped her forehead and felt the hot slice of an open wound as it leaked tangy blood into her eyes and into the air around her.

Wall first. Then her.

The sucking of air was slowing as she slammed the square metal plate against the hole. The suction held it there, but nothing was ever flat or square once it hit the reality of battle.

She pulled the hot gun from the pack, saw Flicker doing the same on the other side. His left arm wasn't sitting right. Broken. He'd somehow managed to lift the steel plate with one broken arm. Awards later. Survival first.

They played the hot gun slowly around the plate, watching as the white-hot metal became one with the shell of the bridge behind it.

She felt the demanding tug of the leaking atmosphere slow as she patiently made her way around the perimeter, struggling to ignore her internal impatient pleading that demanded she hurry. But if you rushed this, the join became brittle and would snap with the slightest pressure.

Flicker would be facing the same demands.

Finally she finished and looked over to him. He was three-quarters of the way through; he would finish.

Around her she saw consoles flick into life again, Wave finding some way of making something from nothing.

Storm had launched into her flight plans again, checking that everything was in place, and she caught a glimpse of Wave's screen with his own plan, and another screen filled with something that she presumed was a deep description of the laws of reality he was now planning to take control of.

She picked up the health kit as she passed her command chair and caught Flicker's eye.

She gave him the thumbs-up, then gestured at his arm and then the cast. He nodded, pointing to the gash on her forehead. Later. He shook his head. Now.

Hart pulled out the syringe and put a shot into Flicker's arm, then attached the cast, watching it inflate and straighten the break.

He grimaced as he looked at her wound. No beauty awards then. He mouthed sorry to her, then cleaned away the excess blood. The pain tore through her, and her vision narrowed — but there was no way she was going to pass out.

He tidied the wound then attached a plaster. She could feel it finding the edges, knitting them together under the protective covering. She would check the damage later.

Both Storm and Wave looked up at her, their worry washed away by the need for her command. She drew together the little strength she had.

"Burn the fuckers."

Wave tapped his screen, coughed up some of the smoke that lingered on the bridge, and settled back into his chair to watch events unfold.

It didn't happen automatically — he had to wait for the enemy to make a move — but his shoulders hunched forward the moment he saw it happen.

A ship blinked out, and appeared alongside the *Milky Pleasure* for its attack. There was an explosion, a rush of atmosphere from the tear along the hull, and the attacker disappeared, returning safely alongside the hulk that threatened them all.

Hart was holding her breath, waiting for something, anything, to happen. And all was still.

"What? Wave—"

"Sorry, Captain. Hang on."

He bashed at his console then sat back again.

Everyone's eyes returned to the display, seeking out the returning attacker.

It sat there serenely, until its companions blinked out from around it.

In that one instant, a quick eye with an appreciation of dimensions beyond the four that humanity had grown up with might have seen all craft occupying the same place across those dimensions. But only for a moment, until it was replaced by a growing point of heat, light and hard radiation that washed across the hulk and the space in-between, leaving only molten remnants that somehow had survived a point that had burned as bright as a star.

Wave had been edging forward with every moment, and now collapsed back into his chair, thrusting both arms up.

"Booyah, motherfuckers. Laws of physics say: Eat me."

The giant ship still hung there, its side pitted and scarred, blackened.

They still faced their major threat.

"Ah, Storm?" Hart prompted.

"Yeah, yeah, yeah," Storm said. "You get the whiz-kid and his light show and want something big and flashy. The things that Storm does linger and build into something that will blow your mind."

She started humming to herself, a tune that — amidst the smoke and chaos — sounded very much like *Twinkle, Twinkle Little Star*. Those listening closer might have found some new lyrics not appropriate to the intended age, but this was a battlefield and Storm was, well, Storm. She could sing any damned song she chose, however she wanted, and screw those who disagreed.

The mining transports had been closing in on the hulk from either side, each barely a quarter of the size of the enemy ship, which appeared to have slowed or lost power thanks to Wave's intercession.

"Thanks, Wave," Storm called out absently.

"Anything for you."

However, the hulk's weapons continued to blaze fiercely, peppering the remote-controlled transports with darkened masses that tore into their hulls and lasers that cut lines across their hardened surfaces.

As the transports edged closer, the core driller began its task: saturating the shuttle with low level radiation, building levels to a dangerous threshold — but not yet beyond that threshold. At the same time, it was deflecting some of its power to its own systems, building up its own radioactive profile.

The transports were close now, their own mass and inertia posing a greater danger to the enemy than their destruction.

It was at that moment they all saw the shuttle shoot toward the hulk, approaching closer and closer... And then disappear into a burst of light as an enemy attack destroyed it.

Everyone on the bridge gasped. The shuttle was the final piece of the puzzle, the ship that was needed to destroy the enemy. And now it was... gone.

Storm sensed the malaise on the bridge.

"Ah! Be patient my pretties."

The residual radiation of the shuttle washed across the enemy ship, and they saw the mining transports start to push in against it.

The core driller, still some distance away, picked up its own pace as the transports slowly, slowly tore open the skin of their enemy.

In the moment before the driller hit the hulk, its drilling laser reached out, destroying one transport, then the other, before turning its radiation on itself.

The crew saw one explosion, then another that carried into the hull of their enemy, and then a third as the driller itself was destroyed.

Beyond those explosions the enemy ship impossibly endured.

And then true destruction began.

The envelope of radiation that was the shuttle ignited, turning everything within its grasp into molten slag before it flared as plasma, and was then still.

"You're a bad arse, Storm," Hart said.

"I've got a great arse, but you're absolutely right. Death and destruction on our enemies, idea by Brugelson, delivered by yours truly."

Hart noticed Storm slumping back into her chair. Victorious, but exhausted.

Wave, staring at his display, acknowledging the moment.

Flicker, cycling through the battlefield display with his remaining mobile arm, checking again and again for any remaining ghosts.

"Mr Flicker, please get us back to the *Pleasure*. Yes, I know it's going to take some time," Hart said, returning to command mode.

"Storm, regroup our remaining ships around the *Milky Pleasure*. We need to consolidate our resources, but we also need to move quickly. I get the feeling we can expect more trouble in these parts.

"Wave, can you please write down a few ideas for new applications that you've been thinking of. We need to know what we can play with, and what we need to focus on to develop our next wave of defences. Oh, and please send a signal to Harding: We're heading home."

She sat back in her chair, watching her talented crew in their shared moment of victory. Her forehead was starting to thickly pound as the anaesthetic adrenalin gave her wore off. She would need some professional work done on it soon, and possibly some other support, judging from the amount of blood down the front of her uniform.

But they had survived.

She enjoyed the glow.

"Captain?"

"Flicker, this had better be important. I'm enjoying the glow. As you've pointed out, the glow is rare for me. I don't get to bask in it that often. In fact, you should be basking, even as we speak. I say this to underscore how important this interruption must be."

A tone sounded from her display as it accepted a file from him.

She looked down and started to take it in.

It captured a moment during the battle, three minutes before the piercing of their bridge by shards of metal.

She followed the tracks, the history.

It didn't make sense.

The shards had come from one of their own drones. And that had been shot by... one of the *Pleasure's* own defensive arrays.

She glanced at Flicker, then back at the file.

The *Pleasure* had fired on one of their own drones, destroying it, sending a spray of metal across their path which had almost killed them.

The *Pleasure* had fired on them. And almost killed them.

Hart's throbbing head was replaced with the heat of a boiling rage.

"Flicker. Please get us back to the *Pleasure* as fast as possible. I want to have a little word with Sphink."

"Yes Captain. With you completely."

*

CHAPTER 18:
WHERE NOBODY KNOWS YOUR NAME

The crew of the *William Shakespeare* stepped down the walkway ramp to dock level, each of them feeling the sweet relief of their feet making contact with the *Milky Pleasure*. It was a fleeting moment of reprieve, however, soon followed by a moment of silent reflection. Their thoughts juxtaposed by the chaos of the docking bay around them. Other civilian craft were limping home and the docking crew scurried to triage both injured personnel and damaged vessels.

Wave looked at Hart and her injuries. "You going to get that patched up?"

But Hart was lost in thought and darted off on her own mission. The crew followed her as she circled the *Shakespeare*, heading to the front where the major impact was.

"Holy shit!" said Storm, as the damage became clear.

The others stared at the gaping hole in *The Shakespeare's* exterior. The thin, mangled wreck of material that somehow separated them from the void. It was enough to usher in a second moment of silence amongst the chaos.

Eventually, Hart reached out and patted the underside of the hull. "Thanks *Will*."

"How did that not kill us?" said Wave.

No one answered, no one knew.

"Speaking of killing," said Hart. "I'm going to pay a little visit to the bridge. I want to thank Sphink personally."

She turned to the exit and broke into a march that meant business.

Wave and the others struggled to keep up. "What about the pub? It's tradition. Wait, what about your face?"

"Feel free to get a start without me. I'm OK with Sphink seeing it like this."

Wave looked at Flicker and Storm, reaching a silent consensus. "No first drink is worth missing that showdown."

They all followed their Captain.

"I'll reserve a table," said Flicker, as he toyed with his communicator.

"I would be honoured if you considered taking my signature move and throat punch Captain Asskiss," said Storm, rehearsing the move in the air in front of her.

"This is going to be good," said Wave.

"Noooooooooooo!" wailed Flicker to the skies, his communicator falling to the floor.

The double-time march stopped as everyone turned to stare. Beyond them, the chaos in the docking bay temporarily ceased, all eyes on Flicker. All except a nearby stretchered crew member, missing her leg. But her path to pain relief had been halted as the stretcher operators stared at Flicker.

Eventually he looked at the crew through swollen, damp eyes. "It's gone!"

"Gone?"

"The SaturnTable Bar… it's been destroyed."

The underwhelmed docking bay crew carried on with their business. Only the crew of the *William Shakespeare* felt the full impact of the news.

"There is no God," said Wave.

"None," agreed Flicker.

"What are we going to do with our lives now?" added Storm.

They all looked at Hart for answers, but it was more than she could process. She returned to the mission at hand and marched for the exit. The others, lost, simply followed her.

Hart's communicator bleeped into life. It was Harding. "Welcome back Hart, and well done."

"Thank you, Sir."

"Debrief in the war room, stat."

"War room?"

"Meeting lounge seven… bridge deck… now the war room."

"Affirmative."

"Oh, and bring that odd friend of yours who discovered that little trick with the time warp that kept us alive. What is it, Vape?"

"It's Wave, Sir."

"Whatever, his insight might be valuable."

"Affirmative."

"Oh, and do you need to get that looked at first?" said Harding, gesturing to his face.

"Is Sphink going to be at the meeting?"

"Unfortunately."

"In that case, I'm on my way."

Hart turned to Storm and Flicker. "Looks like you'll miss the main event. But I'll definitely need some bar therapy when I'm done."

They both saluted. "Yes, Sir."

*

Hart stepped into the War Room, Wave nervously following in her wake. She made eye contact with Harding, who directed them to sit. Brugelson was to his side, with George on his other flank. As she sat, Hart made an entirely different tone of eye contact with Sphink, who was sitting opposite her. Wave gave Hiscock, by Sphink's side, a similar look.

"How are you holding up?" said Harding, making note of Hart's physical injuries with a look.

"Been better, been worse." She didn't take her eyes from Sphink, just waiting for her moment.

Harding turned his attention to Wave. "Inspired work on understanding their tech. We wouldn't be sitting here without you."

Wave smiled and nodded, despite sensing Harding's superior tone through every word.

"George, bring them up to speed with the conversation."

"Sir. We have 14 transport assets remaining, including the *Will Shakespeare*. Two of those are shuttles, not used in the engagement. They are now considered untouchable, as we may not have the ability to egress the population in the event we find a safe haven to do so. All 12 usable vessels are in various states of disrepair. It will take several days, and some ingenuity from our inexperienced ground crew, to get them up to speed.

"The *Milky Pleasure* has sustained significant damage. We have crews repairing hull breeches on levels A3 to C19 on the starboard side. The exterior repairs alone may take up to two weeks. The damage further aft is far worse. The decision has been made that it is too challenging to repair, so we have sealed off everything aft side of the entertainment decks starboard, through to the engineering wing and drive decks, which were, thankfully, spared any major impact. In our current state, we are able to maintain course, while we repair what we are capable of. Should all tasks reach completion in expected timeframes, we should theoretically be able to hit our solar system exit windows."

There was a pause while the information was processed by the two new to the conversation.

"So, what, we're basically sitting ducks until then?" said Hart.

"Indeed," said Harding with a nod.

"With no way of protecting ourselves?" added Wave.

"With no way of protecting ourselves," confirmed Harding. "Now that you're caught up, it's time we came up with a plan."

He gave everyone at the table a look to let them know this was where things were going to get real. "This is going to—"

Sphink's communicator came to life. "Captain, we have identified a—"

He killed the transmission.

Harding eyed him, Sphink eyed the floor.

Harding cleared his throat. "We ready? OK, this is going to take—"

Sphink's communicator interrupted once more. "Captain, I know you're in—"

Again, he killed the transmission.

Harding went to lock eyes with him. Again he conceded before the battle began.

"Are you going to get that, Captain?"

"Sorry Sir, I've turned it off. Won't happen again."

"What if it's important?"

Sphink froze. Unable to make eye contact with Harding. Unable to decipher his next move around the communicator. Instead, he stared into an invisible point past everyone at the table in silence, hoping the meeting would continue and swallow his ineptitude as it did. This did not occur, he just felt six sets of disappointed eyes on him, one robotic.

"Sphink!"

"Yes, Sir?"

"Can you please turn your communicator back on?"

Everyone heard the click under the desk.

"....what the hell should we do? Repeat, one of the enemy craft has been found in the debris. It ain't going anywhere, but there are fair parts of it intact and we're picking up signs of life on board. What the hell should we do?"

Everyone stared at Sphink.

Sphink stared at the ground.

*

"Don't they even know who we are?" said Storm, outraged.

She was marching in time with Flicker, headed to the upmarket end of the entertainment strip, which was unaffected by the destruction of battle. They dodged past ship guests, most in various stages of drunkenness or disillusionment.

"Apparently not. Don't worry, I gave them a quick education, hence the prime table that awaits us at the Duck and..." Flicker consulted his communicator once more. "Cover."

Storm sighed.

"Duck and Cover — cricket themed, apparently. Ahh, there it is."

"This had better be good," said Storm, as she tried to rub a couple of droplets of blood — probably Hart's — out of her top.

Flicker toyed with the stash of Reality in his pocket, a little lighter than it had been a few minutes earlier, but enough to see out whatever this night would throw at him. "It'll be as good as we make it."

They burst through the front doors, in the shape of a boundary line picket fence. On the other side, Flicker scanned the room until his eyes met one of the bar staff, dressed as the bastard child of a stripper and an umpire. He gave her a nod, full of the authority and self-importance to be expected of one with a reserved table. The woman, presumably the one he'd spoken to on the communicator, recognised the situation and beelined past the many waiting customers to greet her guests.

"Mr Flicker?"

"Indeed."

The woman, with the name tag Maarit, indicated they should follow, then headed past the scoreboard and into the venue. "I'd like to apologise for before, I had no idea…"

"It's fine."

Maarit nodded. "I think you'll like the space we have laid out for you and the crew."

The crowd seas parted to reveal their reward — the only empty table in the venue. Beautiful aged oak, central position — everything Flicker could have asked for. He smiled. As they reached it, he glanced down to see a handwritten note in the middle. RESERVED: CLINT.

Storm snorted with laughter.

"Oh, for fuck's sake!"

"Is everything OK?" said Maarit.

"It's perfect," said Storm.

"Can I get you anything to drink?" asked a confused Maarit, while Flicker mumbled nearby.

"Maybe half a dozen tequila shots to kick us off?"

Maarit nodded and left.

"How many times do I have to say no caps?"

Storm laughed again. "Look, the L is really bleeding into the I."

Flicker did not respond.

"You really need a bleedproof paper stock when you're using a thick marker like that."

"You're really enjoying this, aren't you?"

"Very much. I was secretly hoping for the table to be reserved for Mr Flicker, but Clint does the trick nicely."

At that moment a couple of well-oiled patrons staggered into frame. Both tall and solidly built men, they were already deep in amusement at a joke they were about to share. "So, which one of you is the cu—"

Whoosh, whack, thud.

Storm's throat punch was as lightning quick as it was vicious. The taller of the two felt the full force of the attack, dropping to the deck quicker than Storm hoped to later that evening.

"I think you'll find it's you," said Storm, as she stood over his writhing body.

She shot the other comedian a look to see if he wanted to continue the discussion. He declined, instead turning his attention to aiding his fallen friend, now gasping for air. By the time she went to take her seat at the table, the man it was reserved for was holding out a high-five. She accepted.

"Thank you for defending my honour," said Flicker, half mockingly.

"No one messes with our crew like that."

Maarit arrived with the tequila, stepping around the commotion at ground level. "Your drinks. Everything OK?"

Storm accepted one of the shots before the tray hit the table. "Good now you're here, we can finally relax."

"Storm, you there?" It was Hart's voice on the communicator.

"Captain! Yes, we're at the Duck and Cover, can't miss us," said Flicker.

"Still in business mode, Storm. I need you."

Storm looked at Flicker and rolled her eyes then sighed, before downing a second shot. "Go on."

"Salvage situation. Enemy ship with possible survivor aboard. I'm heading back to zero comms, but liaise with the bridge and bring that bad boy in. Over and out."

Storm sighed again, took her third shot, then started fishing through her fatigue pockets.

"So, need anything from me?" said Flicker.

"Another round… just keep 'em coming. Oh, and make some space on the table."

Flicker nodded to Maarit to cover off on the shots request. As he did, he realised what Storm's plan was. "You're going to run that mission from here?"

"You got a problem with that?"

Flicker shrugged and gave a wry smile. "I have shots and now I have entertainment. I mean, what could possibly go wrong?"

He downed his second shot, then flicked the tray off the edge of the table. A pained ouch sound came from below.

"Harden up, numbnuts," said Flicker.

"I meant the sign. It's a bit hard to concentrate when all I can see is a giant Clint."

Flicker gave her the bird, salivated at what this night would bring and toasted his anticipation with his remaining shot.

*

"Shots seemed mostly ineffective," said Sphink, as part of his post-battle report. "Whether targetted or randomly sprayed, they seemed too technologically aware to be troubled, other than wanting to eliminate any threat they discovered. Once we bought a turret online and into battle, it was soon targeted and destroyed."

And with that, Hart's window had opened.

"Are you listening to yourself? You fired randomly into a battlespace?"

Sphink froze.

"You, the Captain of a starship, just indiscriminately fired into an area you knew you had assets?"

"I… I…"

Hart locked eyes and did not let go. "You nearly killed us!"

Sphink searched for an answer, a process, a logical rationalisation, but he drew a blank. The moment and room were closing in on him. "I… I… I'm a civilian Captain."

"To think I thought shock and awe was the height of incompetence," said Hart, before ironically laughing to herself.

In desperation, Sphink turned to shoot an accusing look at Hiscock, who looked at Hart, aghast.

"Don't blame an average engineer, you… you fuckwit."

The rant echoed around the room until the final reverberations of 'wit' absorbed into the walls and furniture, becoming part of the DNA of the space. The gravity of the moment was not lost on anyone.

A powerful silence took hold, somehow echoing the words further through a physics Sphink didn't understand. It all fell upon him as a wave of guilt he could no longer hold inside. He went to speak, to cleanse, but someone beat him to it.

"Average engineer," said Wave, smiling at Hiscock.

Hart elbowed him.

All eyes fell back on Sphink.

"OK, OK, I'm sorry. There. I'm not trained for this. I don't even know if I'm cut out for this. This is beyond my training and I'm completely out of my depth."

It was more than Hart expected. It was more than anyone expected.

"Happy?" said Sphink eventually, when no one used their words to save him.

Hart considered for a moment before nodding in silence, feeling less victory in the moment than she'd imagined. Sphink accepted the gesture with a nod of his own.

"Very good," said Harding. "Now that's out of our system, we've got a species to save."

*

"Exciting news people, we're about to enter the fancy end of town, as I like to call it," said Rick Astley as he staggered towards a new strip of bars, still trying to find a natural balance while getting used to his crutches in his semi-inebriated state.

Behind him, those not in triage followed, in various states of intoxication.

"This is ludicrous," said one.

"Hear, hear," said another.

It was enough to stop the herd and have the others gather round their potential new spokeswoman. She embraced the promotion. "It was like a war zone back there. People died, we all saw it," said Ah Lam Huang.

They all looked at Astley, expectantly. He maintained his chirpy, enthusiastic smile.

"You can't for a second think we all don't know there's something seriously wrong happening and that our lives are at risk?"

Astley went to speak, but no words came out.

"Plying us with alcohol and pretending nothing's wrong is not a communication strategy."

Astley went through the options — everything he knew, what he should say. After processing, it all verbalised in a word, that was also a letter. "I…"

"Level with us," said Huang.

There was no escaping this moment. He sighed as he looked at the sorry party he'd been entrusted to look after. Broken, confused, pissed — both definitions. What had he done? "The truth is, I don't entirely know. I know it's not good. I was told to distract you while the crew took care of business or got to safety but… it hasn't happened."

"Asshole."

There were a lot of expletives uttered in that moment, but that was the one he remembered. The old lady didn't even look like she had that word in her vocabulary.

"Hey, you wanted answers and I'm telling you what I know. I got an order and I followed it. Whatever's happening, it's big. Real big. No one has time to take my communications. My guess, they're still knee deep in it and the best thing we can do is lay low until we find out more."

"You're not still planning to take us to the pub, are you?"

"I'm not sure what choice we have. Go back to your rooms if you want, but I can guarantee you'll be more in the dark there than here. And if I can't get in touch with anyone, you lot have no chance."

"You're unbelievable!"

"Look, just come, you don't need to drink, but safety in numbers and being where you'll hear information when it comes to light is probably as good as you're going to get right now."

*

CHAPTER 19:
NOM DE PLUME

"I don't think that's going to be possible," said Wave, as he toggled his attention between a holo schematic of the ship and another of the surrounding space, complete with exit vectors.

"There's no way to guarantee the structure is going to survive the slingshot. We could be killing ourselves trying to shortcut our escape."

Harding looked at Hiscock for a second opinion.

Hiscock nodded. "He's right. There's only one way we're going to hit that window and that's by directing more resources at the internal aspects of the repair. It can be done."

"Yeah," agreed Wave, with sarcasm aimed and no silencer attached. "Sure, it just means *not* repairing the *Shakespeare* and anything else that resembles a chance of surviving any future attack."

Harding sat back, prepared to let the two fight it out. Wave and Hiscock, each looking for direction, soon realised the game.

"Well, what's our priority? Get out of here alive, I would've thought," said Hiscock.

"Me too. So any plan that involves having no defensive capability shouldn't even be considered."

"What choice do we have? If we miss our mark on Uranus, we're screwed."

"No one's missed the mark on Uranus, mate," said Wave, immediately realising he'd misread the crowd.

There was an awkward pause before Hiscock continued. "If we miss the Columbus gate jump, we'd need to make Neptune alignment and we're stuck in the solar system for weeks longer. Plus, the sling there is going to have to be tight if we're going to get ourselves up to the speeds we need."

"Look, those speeds only matter to the interstellar travel time and reaching the gate jump. We should be safe by then."

"Have you any idea how much extra time that will add?"

"A bit, I'm guessing. But time's not really going to matter if we're dead."

"It could add months to a trip if we don't nail Uranus."

Wave looked around the war room. "Anyone?"

Silence.

"And, just to be clear, I'm talking about the use of the phrase 'nail Uranus.'"

More silence.

"You're forgetting we lost storage decks C and D as well," said Brugelson.

The comment threw Wave. "I'm lost."

"That's redundancy food and medical supplies," said Sphink, seizing his moment. "There was enough there to last 12 months, with a capacity and awake passengers and crew."

"Ah, shit," said Wave.

"Had we hit all the intended course windows, the *Pleasure* would've made the interstellar transit in two months with the hop gate. All this manoeuvring has meant a lot of starting over on our speed requirements. The time difference is exponential."

Sphink looked at everyone in turn. "It's why I've been trying to stick with the protocol."

"Glad it all got messed up," said Brugelson. "I wouldn't be here without your little detour."

Harding held his hand up to the room. "Can we focus, please? I'm assuming the supply situation and our current speed are problematic?"

Sphink briefly exhaled his frustration as Harding removed the oxygen from his one chance at understanding from the group. "That is correct. We're currently running a physical stocktake on all current supplies but, assuming everything outside of storage decks C and D survived — as in, everything else is going in our favour — and with our current speed, well, it'd mean if we didn't use Uranus just right, we'll starve."

Everyone paused on the dilemma.

Wave did an outstanding job to let the double entendre pass by, unacknowledged. "We could put everyone back to sleep."

"If the sleep systems are operational," said Harding. "And if we want to dedicate crew resources to that."

Wave looked at him blankly.

"Do you want to tell a ship full of people that now know they're in mortal danger that we want them to go back to sleep? We'll have a mutiny on our hands."

"What about the salvage? Can we get our hands on anything we've lost?"

Sphink cleared his throat. "We've got every resource we have on the current salvage, which is not much. The debris area is vast and growing rapidly. We're doing the best we can, but I would set expectations to… very low."

The conversation went into pause again as everyone let the reality of the situation wash over them.

Harding looked at everyone in turn. "Well, unless anyone has anything else to add on the matter, it seems our only option is to prioritise the Uranus window. If salvage provides a miracle, we can reconsider. If not, we'll need to prioritise core ship repairs, systems checks, stock evaluation and, if time permits, a look at what we can do to get our defences up and running and remaining craft void-worthy again.

"Sphink, what's the latest with the passengers?"

"As good as can be expected in the circumstances. My understanding is any unrest has been handled. I've got my best man on it."

"Good. We've probably got human resources amongst them we can use. Have someone investigate the passenger list, see what skills we could call upon. I don't want a free-for-all though, understand?"

"Yes, Sir."

"We still need to control the message. Having a ship full of civilians panicking or, worse still, trying to help, will only be counterproductive. Have your best man keep them at bay for now. I'll schedule an assembly of all ship passengers and crew as soon as we have enough data to plan a way forward. Until then, control the message."

"Yes Sir."

"Hart, Wave, get some rest, you've earned it today. Once you're done, I'm going to need a plan for getting as much of our fleet up and running with as little resource as possible. Wave, I need to know everything about this weakness you've found in their communication and how we might be able to use it in future, both with and without any vessels to defend ourselves."

"Yes, Sir."

"Brugelson, I want you down in the bowels of the ship. Get eyes-on everything. Sphink, don't trust any data you're getting from the system until Brugelson has given visual confirmation. I will be down to join you and your team whenever I can."

"Yes, Sir."

"We've got more deadlines than we can reach before we make this jump, an enemy that could come back at any time and a ship full of civilians who are probably one piece of unwanted intel away from revolt."

Harding took a moment to seek everyone's eyes, pausing for particular effect with Hart and Sphink. "I need all of you together on this, understand?"

He waited for a round of "Yes, Sirs."

"Same page. Everyone. This page. Any problems, come to me. Understand?"
Another round of "Yes, Sirs."

"Good. For the sake of humanity, I hope you do. Right, you've all got things to do. Stay fresh. We'll reconvene when we have more data to work with. And for fuck's sake, keep all this on the downlow from the passengers."

*

Storm spread her fingers and eased her hand delicately forward. At a point in space several thousand kilometres away, a small drone responded to the action, moving forward until it came into contact with an enemy spaceship. Click.

While Storm was lost in her moment, the same couldn't be said for Flicker, who watched her weave her magic on an oak pub table transformed into a flight control interface. Holo displays and data gens filled the air.

He gasped as contact was made. A noise that almost went unnoticed amongst the dozens and dozens of other gasps that came at the same time. He looked up, briefly, to see the entire patronage of the Duck and Cover hanging on every moment. At the centre of the crowd stood a nervous-looking Rick Astley and a guy holding a pack of ice to his throat. Flicker shrugged and returned his focus to the action.

"And last one," whispered Storm, now peripherally aware some people were watching her.

Her hands went through a delicate dance as she manipulated the last drone into position. She needed this one to stick; there would be no second chances if she lost another.

The damage was greatest in the part of the ship she now approached virtually. There was a hole in its side, with internal parts oozing into space. Or frozen mid ooze was perhaps more apt. She didn't recognise any of the tech, which left her approach careful.

The crowd leaned forward in anticipation.

She found a line she liked, eased forward, then suddenly pulled back, to hold the drone back from some suspected danger. There was another large gasp from the crowd, this one followed by some angry shushes.

Storm cleared her throat, took a shot of tequila, reset her sitting position, then focused on the task at hand once more. A few articulated gestures, gasps and shushes later, she had the drone lined up as she wanted. She eased it forward.

"Get in the hole," someone yelled.

They were quickly shushed by others.

Slowly, slowly, they watched as the drone feed approached the derelict vessel. With a click, it stuck to the side.

There was an excited buzz in the crowd. They all knew the result and were awaiting official confirmation to celebrate. Crowd behavioural abyss.

Storm let out a heavy exhale, as if expelling all the focus from her body. She wiped the beads of sweat from her forehead and downed another shot. "Will, can you confirm contact?"

"Contact confirmed."

The crowd erupted in wild applause. Flicker offered out a high-five, accepted by Storm. It was followed seconds later by one offered by throat-ice guy, also repaid.

"OK Will, handing over to you now. Bring her in."

"Affirmative."

"Oh, before I go, you got an ETA on rendezvous?"

"16 hours, 23 minutes, 17 seconds."

"Legend Will, pleasure doing business."

"M'lady."

By that point, the crowd had started to encroach on the table space in their clamouring enthusiasm to join the celebrations.

"Oi! Back up," yelled throat guy, as he and his buddy did their best to form a crowd control wall.

Storm took in the entire scene for the first time. In the zone of her moment, she hadn't realised she had been the focus of everyone in the entire bar. Now she was one receiving an endless stream of praise, high-fives and free drinks. She smiled, knowing her hero moment would be the start point for a strong night of Storm-style relaxation.

*

"What was that ship? Was that alien?" said Huang.

Rick Astley had lost all sense of disguise now. "I think so."

"What the actual fuck?"

"Is Earth safe?"

"Any word from the authorities yet?"

He was inundated with questions. "For a start, I'm technically in authority here."

"You don't know anything."

Astley reeled at how quickly they'd dismantled his argument. He remembered his new honest approach. "Look, I've left messages with the Captain and every connection I have on the bridge. You'll know anything as soon as I do."

"So, what do we do until then?"

"Well, I'm going to get another drink. Suggest you do the same."

"What about the chick who just salvaged the alien ship? Why don't you ask her?"

"Look, I don't need you undermining my authority or telling me how to do my job," snapped Astley.

"You have no authority and suck at your job," said Huang.

Double dismantling. Brutal.

"OK, OK. I'll do it. I'll ask her. I just need a drink first."

While someone definitely said, "You suck," it was the booing that got to him.

"Look, I may have to charm her to get info, and if I'm going to bring my charm A-game, I'm going to need a drink."

"Oh, great!"

Just the tone of the sarcasm made it the most brutal undermining of them all.

*

Someone put some music on and the crowd started to dissipate to the bar and beyond. By the time the second song started, Storm had her kit packed away and the table was the domain of her, Flicker and her new security team.

"I'm Ivan," said the throat-ice guy, with his hand extended.

"Storm," she said as she shook hands.

"Atsuki," said his mate. "Can I just say you are a legend?"

"Yes, yes you can."

Flicker sighed, already knowing with 98.36 percent accuracy how this encounter would likely end up.

Storm's communicator buzzed into life. "Storm, it's Hart. Order up, we're our way."

She looked at the table — a sea of beverages. There would be no ordering required for some time.

Rick Astley approached with an additional tray of various and superfluous drinks. "Hi, I'm Rick, that was impressive work…"

He let the sentence trail off as one does when they're looking for a name.

"Storm," said Storm.

"Very talented woman," he said with his best flirty smile. It went up a notch after it was reciprocated.

Flicker rolled his eyes and swore under his breath.

Astley ignored him and gestured to his tray. "Any spare space for this lot?"

Ivan studied the new threat to his newly-earned territory at the table of the hero of the hour, then turned his attention back to Storm. "You're good at that thing you do," he said.

"I am," agreed Storm. She leaned back as far as the chair would allow and put her hands behind her head, her preferred pose to soak up attention.

"I think I'm going to be sick," said Flicker to himself.

Astley soon realised the competition he faced and amped up the charm dial to full. "I bet you've seen it all."

"You have no idea," agreed Storm.

"Could probably write a book with your experiences," said Ivan, pushing more chips in.

Flicker picked up his communicator. "Wave, hurry the fuck up. Out."

"You know," said Storm. "I've often thought about doing that."

Astley smiled. "A book? About your life?"

Storm nodded. Flicker scoffed. He alone at the table knew that while the thought of people knowing her story was appealing to her, she had never read a book, never talked about books, wasn't entirely fluent in English (despite it being her first language), nor would she have the patience to sit down and transfer her thoughts to words. Come to think of it, she wouldn't even have the patience to give someone else the dot points to do it for her.

He scoffed again. Storm gave him a look of betrayal.

It was mostly lost on her newly acquired suitors.

"That'd be amazing," said Astley. "Under your own name or a nom de plume?"

"What the fuck are you on about?" said Storm.

The comment threw Astley for a moment. He settled. "The book, would you write it under your name as author, or a nom de plume?"

"What have blow jobs got to do with books?"

"I'm sorry?" said Astley.

He wore a look of confusion, like everyone else at the table.

Storm looked around at those faces, seemingly reflecting her thoughts around Astley's confusion. It strengthened her. "I just don't get how oral sex has anything to do with publishing."

Astley looked at Storm, stunned. He looked at the others, equally stunned.

"Unless you mean the story itself," added Storm.

Astley, mouth agape, shook his head.

"Because there'd be more than a few nom de plumes in that." Storm winked. "It's one of my things."

It took a few seconds for everyone to start to catch up with where the conversation was now heading. Storm's suitors shifted uneasily in their seats. Flicker scoffed even louder than before, then leaned back and put his hands behind his head, mirroring Storm's pose.

"I'm confused," said Astley, eventually.

At this point, he realised rival Ivan had withdrawn from the conversation, leaving him to deal with whatever mess would ensue.

Storm started to get a sense the looks of confusion may have been directed to her, not Astley.

"Nom de plume?" she said.

Everyone nodded.

"Blow jobs?"

Everyone shook their heads.

"It's French," she explained.

Everyone nodded.

"For blow jobs."

Everyone shook their heads.

"Nom," said Storm, pronouncing it in an eating-onomatopeia way.

"De," she added, with a French accent.

She completed her explanation by saying "plume". It was also in a French accent, but this word was more denoted by the accompanying hand gestures, miming a small explosion of, say, warm liquid.

There was a brief confused stand-off from everyone at the table.

Except Flicker, who started laughing uncontrollably.

"What are you doing?" said Hart, having arrived in time to see Storm's explanation.

Wave was by her side, smiling doe-eyed at Storm.

Beyond them, Storm realised the conversation at their table had attracted the attention of some nearby tables as well.

"Nom de plumes," she said.

Hart and Wave nodded.

"Blow jobs."

Everyone shook their heads.

"Oh, this is priceless," said Flicker.

"Not just any blow jobs," added Storm. "The ones that go from start to, well, finish."

More confusion stared back at her. She searched for a different way to explain, the theme of the bar inspiring her. "Think, cricket..." she started.

"Cricket?" said Astley.

"This is going to be good," said Flicker, as he leaned in.

"Yeah," continued Storm, ignoring him. "When an opening batsman bats the entire innings."

"When they carry the bat?" helped Astley.

Storm nodded. "Yeah. That..."

Astley nodded, somewhat supportive, somewhat confused.

"...but blow jobs."

Astley stopped nodding and returned to the confused look the others were giving.

"Nom de plume is the carry the bat of blow jobs," Storm pronounced, with as much confidence as she could still muster. "And it's French."

All went silent. Until Flicker burst into fits of laughter. It soon spread to Wave and Hart, quickly followed by Storm's suitors and those at nearby tables. Soon half the crowd in the bar were laughing. The moment stretched on longer than any sane laugh would. One they knew there might not be too many more of. One that swallowed the memories of the horrors of that day and protected them from the dark unknowns the future would surely bring.

They were all in a bubble of time for that moment.

Thinking about blow jobs.

And/or French.

Not as much about pen names.

*

CHAPTER 20:
IT JUST WAS

The event happened. New data was recorded. Information flowed. Knowledge was shared. It danced through the information ether, passing clearance filter after clearance filter as it flowed, rightfully, to the very core of power, thought and knowledge. There, it was considered, debated and decided upon.

A small pool of rainwater, captured by the biggest wave at the highest tide, it was soon drawn in to became one with the ocean of thought. It was. It now just was.

The matrix of knowledge updated, the population became aware. As it was, as it had always been. But this time, something was different. Something was far different.

One of their own was missing.

This was not acceptable.

For one to be missing they could all go missing. For one to be left behind, they all could be left behind. For one to be abandoned, they could all be abandoned.

No resources were too extravagant, no time deemed wasted, no effort considered in vain, no collective effort deemed futile. They would not rest until they had recovered their kin, or its body, or understand why and how this had happened.

And so it was. So it just was.

*

CHAPTER 21:
HARD CALLS

The docking bay was a hive of activity with ships of all shapes and sizes in various states of disrepair. The triage operating theatre was in full swing. Crew members barked instructions and scurried about on one mission or another. Machines moved. Sparks flew. It was all an unchoreographed dance of repairing for survival.

It was enough to draw all but the most observant eye to the even bigger story. At the bow end of the deck, where the ceiling curved down its inevitable dive into the floor, a small corner was sealed off from the rest by layers of clear plastic. If you squinted, you could make out the silhouetted remains of a dark fighter-sized alien craft. A handful of the *Milky Pleasure's* crew could also be made out as hazy yellow blimps behind the plastic.

The entire partially-obscured ecosystem did its best to resemble a temporarily-assembled, hermetically-sealed forensic lab, but it was just five humans trying to work out what on earth to do with a broken enemy vessel beyond any technology they knew. The scene was far from airtight, but those investigating put biological threat in a far lower threat bracket than impending violent extinction.

It was at the moment that something changed. Inside the ship that carried possibly the last of humanity, inside the docking bay full of broken craft, inside the flawed plastic-sealed side room, inside the mystery spaceship, inside the cockpit, a light flickered into life.

*

Hart woke to an urgent call from Harding; she was required.

As she struggled to escape from a sheet that appeared to bind all of her limbs, the blur of her quarters slowly resolved into details. And they didn't make sense.

Her uniform was clean, pressed and hanging on display, and not on the floor where she usually left it.

Strange.

Her bedside table. Not right. Hot coffee. With milk and sugar. Not how she had it, but a desperately-needed medicine for her aching skull. Sipping it gave her the strength to consider the rest of the table.

Flowers. In a vase.

That had never — never — happened.

She looked about the room, confirming it was in fact hers, and then returned to the flowers.

Not right. It made no sense.

She remembered the meeting and took her coffee into the shower. She stood under the hot water, willing it to wash away the bruises from the battle and the grime from the previous night's drunken celebration.

Flashes came to her.

Storm punching someone and then taking them back to her quarters. And then someone else, although she couldn't remember if there was a punch first.

Flicker on a high, chatting with some cute young thing and smiling — a genuine smile — even as the artificial high wore off.

The belonging officer — she searched for his name and came up with nothing — delivering a tray of shots to the table and a fruit cocktail for her.

The memory vanished as she saw a splash of colour in the bathroom: More flowers to break up the standard crew quarter grey.

Strange.

She got out of the shower and slipped into her uniform. The pressed lines made her feel presentable, or at least allowed her to hide the impending explosion of her skull.

She went to grab some painkillers and found a heavy dose laid out on a plate with a hand-sketched smiley face underneath.

No-one hand-sketched these days.

It would take her five minutes to make it to the war room, unless her body decided to die first in the interest of granting her head a mercy killing.

As she left she saw the note pressed into the door, with her name written on the outside in flowering script. OK, she thought, now it's getting disturbing.

She stumbled through the corridors, feeling the texture of the note but not yet comfortable to read it.

What happened last night?

More flashes.

More drinks. Wave, standing on a table, showing off his cultured education with a passable version of a song from the twentieth century epic *Cats*.

Making her way to the bar, some cute rich kid chatting her up until that look crossed his face. The recognition. The one that momentarily failed to hide the fact that he had seen the video. And then the excuses.

And it was all in front of the bloody belonging officer, who was no doubt calculating just how to support her during such a difficult time.

The belonging officer. Damnit, his name still escaped her.

She almost made it to the end of the long corridor leading to the lift without seeing anyone, until a couple of passengers stepped out, chatting. One looked up at her, did a double-take, then smiled.

"You kick arse," one said, sparking a flurry of nods from her friend.

Hart nodded in acknowledgement, a movement that fractured the entire corridor with the pain it created.

"Just doing my job," she said, struggling.

She stepped into the lift, and received another flash from the night before. The belonging officer, witnessing the embarrassing dumping, looking at her with obvious concern. She had a memory of abusing him for doing his job, and demanding he focus on the drinks she was attempting to order.

Anything that would ignore the video that kept haunting her attempts to have a love life. Or just sex. Jesus, even a snog. The only thing the video had done was create a long list of weirdos who seemed to think her thing involved all sorts of barely speakable and understandable acts. She didn't even bother trying to tell people it was a fake anymore. A truth she'd smashed her head against a wall for many years to claim. Now it just was other people's truth about her. She refused to let it make her feel sick anymore. She just wanted it wished away.

The belonging officer had smiled and nodded, pouring the drinks with the insufferable smugness of people who genuinely cared for others.

Dammit. She was usually good with names. Why couldn't she remember his?

The lift doors opened and she made her way down the corridor to the briefing room.

The note. The note from inside her apartment. The flowers. The coffee.

She stopped, and opened the note to read it.

"Thank you for a lovely night. No pressure, no expectations, but always here for you in whatever capacity you need me."

The sheets. The fumbling. The stumbling. The sex.

The night opened in her memory.

His name was Markou. She'd had sex with Nick Markou. The belonging officer.

The drought was over, and all she wanted was for the human race to die with her. Right now.

*

"Hart!"

Harding's voice brought her back to the war room.

Harding sat across from her with a strange look on his face. Actual concern. But not for her.

To her right was a man in an Hawiian shirt she recognised from the bar the previous night. He was too busy looking at his hands on the table to acknowledge her or anything. Still, she didn't really have the high ground at this point.

Harding eyed the man with intent. "Astlet—"

"It's Astley. Sir."

"Astley, then. I take it you are aware of our situation?"

Astley could feel the frustration and anger mounting as he relived the explosions and sprays of blood. He had tried to push the memory of the SaturnTable Bar away, but it kept returning. The deaths. The unmoving bodies. The woman who knew her wine.

"Yes," he said through his teeth.

"And are you aware of your role?" Every one of Harding's words cut deeper.

"To ensure our passengers are happy and entertained."

Everyone could hear Harding slowly breathe in and out, and again.

"Mr Astley, your role has changed. The people on this ship — your passengers," he sneered, "are likely to be all that remains of humanity. Am I clear on that?"

Astley shook his head to dispel the memory: Blood welling on his legs as he brushed the diamond glass away, and the realisation that the red smear wasn't his blood. He wasn't sure whose it was. It was probably hers.

"Yes, Sir."

"Then I will try and make this equally as clear: We are in a closed system," said Harding slowly. "We must protect our resources or risk the destruction of humanity's last habitat. Is that notion clear to you, also?"

Astley nodded, trying to shake away the memory of the pain of his broken legs, the sounds of his own screams, before the drugs carried him away.

"Do you know what happens if we fail? If you fail to manage what is left of humanity? If you let their fears dominate?"

Astley ventured: "Panic."

Harding's head dropped, as if Astley had failed a test. With a small shake of his head, he continued.

"Paris, 2082: Authorities close off a city in fear of a pandemic, leaving 23 million people to fend for themselves with no food. They say the first 10 million to die from starvation were the lucky ones. Later on, those whose limbs had been ripped off and were feverish with septicaemia were begging for death. People were too scared to approach them, and so they festered until they were dead, and then their family members would look at them as a food source.

"Titan, 2203: Water in a closed system was tainted with a hallucinogen. Every person experienced visions that targeted their amygdala, the seat of our emotions. The One God movement was happy to offer a solution: convert, but you can only do so by blinding yourself. Astley, do you know what it is like seeing a parent gouge their child's eyes out in the hope of saving them?"

Harding's eyes were clouded.

"Your job, Astley, is to prevent that, to save what is left of humanity by keeping them human. You are essential to that."

Astley let the words play through his head, accompanied by visions of rioting crowds lynching one another for a scrap of food. He had sufficient strength to ask a single question: "How do I do that?"

The room chilled as Harding took a slow breath.

"You do that by keeping everyone calm. By reassuring them. Lying to them if needed, if it will stop them from panicking."

"So I can tell them—"

"Nothing," Harding snapped.

"But they already know. They're talking about it already. They're asking me questions. I can't just lie to them," Astley explained softly.

Harding nodded and took a different tact.

"How would you describe the mood at present?"

"Frustrated. A little scared. Beyond bullshit, if I might be honest. Sir."

"Mr Astley," Harding said quietly. "You will control these people. You will calm them. You will not do anything that risks fucking over our entire species because you have a weak-hearted moment singing *Kumbuyah* and waiting for white doves to announce the arrival of a glorious kingdom for us all. Do I make myself clear?"

Astley looked up. His people already knew. They had a right to know.

"Yes Sir."

"Thank you, Mr Astley. In this you will report directly to Captain Hart and myself. Yes?"

"Yes Sir."

Harding waved him away, and turned his attention to Hart.

"Captain?"

Hart's head snapped up. Her chin was cold and she wondered whether she had been sleeping, or just drooling.

"Captain, you will need to provide Mr Astley with some direction and resources. Whatever is needed, do it."

"Sir. Yes Sir," she said, and stood to leave.

As she approached the door, Harding called out.

"One more thing, Captain," said Harding. "My concerns about the mindset of our passengers and the risk of panic are very, very real. We need to manage them very carefully. I want you to work with the belonging officer on what we need to do now, and over the longer term.

"I have seen people tear limbs from each other and their own as panic set in, and we cannot afford that. When we are ready to talk openly, everyone will need immense support. I need you to work closely with the belonging officer to prepare for this," he said.

Harding saw the horror on her face, and misinterpreted it.

"Captain, this is perhaps the second-most urgent priority we have. Work with the officer, work with him all night if that's what it takes. We need to prepare. Thank you Captain."

She closed the door behind her.

There were things worse than death. Her life.

*

Harding sat back in his chair as the door closed, his mind racing as he sought to cover all contingencies.

He got up to pour himself a scotch, sat and looked at the stars and the flickering of debris beyond.

A tone sounded.

"Harding, Brugelson here."
"Yes, old friend?"
"This alien ship—"
"The Uix inside — is it alive?"

*

CHAPTER 22:
CARGO

Brugelson was surprised at the speed of Harding's pace as they made their way to the docking bay. He didn't think the Ambassador had it in him, and found himself struggling to keep up, both literally and metaphorically. "What do you mean the alien ship's growing?"

Harding gave him a look to keep his voice down, then responded in a hushed aside. "Personally, I detest the longer walk and I'm not thrilled about using common access areas the enlisted use to go about their work, but George tells me it's probably the most discreet way to get us there."

Brugelson's face was blank. He turned to George, swanning along behind them. The robot's body language as difficult to read as the Ambassador's.

"What's happening?" Brugelson asked.

Harding stopped, the party followed suit. He looked Brugelson up and down. "We… don't know."

Brugelson starred in stunned silence.

"Look, old friend, I'm going to level with you. I think we're fucked."

After a long pause, Brugelson battled for the best response to give in the circumstance. "What do you mea—"

"I'm not sure there's a way out of this. The Uix will be back, no doubt. It's a fool's hope to think we'll make the jump before we face them again. And we are in no position to fight back. We got lucky last time, but they won't give us that chance again. Of course, if the unrest gets any worse, we may well kill ourselves first.

"I've called you in on this because, of all the people on this ship, you have an understanding of the Uix and some knowledge of the history. And you know me."

Harding started walking again.

"There will be some tough choices ahead, some outcomes that people may not understand. Perhaps, if any of us are going to survive, there may well be sacrifices needed to make that happen. These are the decisions that leadership must make for a greater good. Do you understand?"

Brugelson nodded, unsure what was being asked of him, but knowing something would be.

"This ship in the docking bay. It plays a key part in all this, in the choices ahead. As do you."

"Me?"

"My previous envoy to the Uix, what do you know of this?"

Something within Brugelson sensed a prudent answer would be the best, at least until he was a little more up to speed with everything going on around him. "Erm, very little… if I'm honest."

The look Harding gave him demanded elaboration.

Brugelson cleared his throat. "Well, you were part of a contingent sent to negotiate a better standing for our people with the Uix."

"Yes..." encouraged Harding. The words stretched out over enough time it brought a bead of sweat to Brugelson's brow.

"Bit of a hiding to nothing if you ask me, Sir."

Harding didn't react, staying in an expression expecting more.

"And, well, that's pretty much it. Diplomacy failed and now here we are."

Harding stopped, and the entourage followed suit. He studied Brugelson, who by this point didn't know whether he was being interrogated or vetted. Either way, the look he was receiving demanded more information, while something in his core decided to play dumb. Then he wondered if Harding could sense the game he was playing in his head. He looked at George to break the tension.

Harding started walking again. "Understanding the Uix is key. This survivor, if we can communicate with it, may be our ticket to freedom. We have something to negotiate with while it's alive and on this ship. We also might have a direct source of communication with the Uix leadership."

Brugelson nodded, relieved to be out of that moment and into a plan. "Yes, Sir."

"That's where you come in."

"Me, Sir?"

"Yes. Given my... history… I don't think it's beneficial for anyone aboard this ship for the Uix to know I'm here. If we can establish a way to communicate, you are to rep—"

"Me?"

"Yes, I have no one else I can trust, certainly none I believe will pass the test-of-mind-thought conversation with the Uix. You… you have all the elements it takes to pass the scrutiny your mind will undergo. You are our messenger. Offer an exchange — the Uix for safe passage out of the solar system and safe harbour where we land."

"I… yes, Sir."

"There will be no mention of, or reference to, my presence aboard this ship. Understand?"

"Yes Sir."

"This is mission critical for our survival."

"Yes Sir."

The corridor opened up to a long room with a number of doorways. By the door farthest to their left, a woman was in the last stages of removing her protective yellow suit. When she saw the Ambassador, she let the suit top hang at her waist, exposing her standard security team attire underneath; suddenly ready to go back in at a moment's notice. She approached and saluted. "Ambassador Harding. Just who I was looking for."

"Update?"

She led the pair of humans and the mechanoid to the window that overlooked the scene. "Sir. It's stopped growing, we think."

"Any idea why?"

She looked at Harding, then the unfamiliar face of Brugelson. "The Uix was pinned into the cockpit. Best guess is the ship changed its shape to release it."

Harding thought on the statement before nodding. "And the Uix?"

"Alive, Sir. Dr Suarez has stemmed the bleeding, got vitals back on line. Enough sedative to keep it calm as requested. She's confident the worst is over."

"Is it conscious?"

"Yes, well, barely. But yes. That's why I was looking for you actually, I think we can release Suarez to tend to the passengers and cre—"

"Suarez stays here, understand?"

The woman opened her mouth to speak but words failed her.

"Brugelson, Al-Razi."

The two shook hands while Harding began instructions. "Brugelson is here to make contact with the Uix. You are to give him anything he needs. I don't want anyone but you two and the doctor anywhere near this conversation. Brugelson, full report when you're done."

He looked at the pair and waited for a sign of understanding.

"Yes, Sir," they said in unison.

"Very well. Come George, we'll take the back passage again," said Harding, as he turned and left.

George quivered momentarily before following.

Brugelson and Al-Razi looked at each other then at the sealed-off part of the cargo bay and the task ahead.

*

"What do you mean, none of them?"

Rick Astley stared, dismayed, at Captain Sphink as he consulted his clipboard, Hiscock by his side.

Clipboards had been an unnecessary workplace device for the better part of a century, as was any paper they contained. Sphink enjoyed the confusion it gave those on the other side of them, as much as he did the power contained in the printouts clipped to them. It was a barrier between his power and those without it.

"We've been through the list, thoroughly," said Sphink.

He looked at Hiscock.

"Thoroughly," agreed the engineer.

"And, to be frank, we can't find any of the passengers with a skillset that we require right now."

"Are you shitting me?"

"Mr Astley, I'm not here to shit people."

"But you seem such a natural."

Hiscock shaped up in his best, but completely underwhelming, intimidating pose. "Pull your head in, Astley."

Astley kept his focus on Sphink. "Harding specifically gave you instructions to pick the best and brightest of the passengers to help. God knows we need it. And he's given me instructions to keep them engaged and onside."

"What can I tell you?" said Sphink as he consulted his clipboard once again. "There's no one here that's really made of... the right stuff."

Astley stared at the two people he definitely knew weren't made of the right stuff themselves. With all the discipline he could muster, he held the comment in. "Please, have another look and give me something to go to them with. Anything."

Sphink invited Hiscock to look over the printout on his clipboard with him. What initially seemed like it would be a short discussion and quick response soon turned into an awkwardly long standoff, with the occasional whisper Astley couldn't hear.

"I need this. They need this. We all do, really," he offered, resigned to the knowledge they either weren't listening or pretending they weren't.

Silence.

After a couple of false starts, Sphink nodded to Hiscock and held his clipboard at an appropriate level to maximise his authority. "After a deeper dive into the talents we have at our disposal, and in consultation with another officer, I stand by my initial decision."

Silence.

Rick Astley simply stared at the pair, and the clipboard, in silence.

He turned and marched for the exit of the bridge.

*

Wave paced up and down the space between the side of his bed and his kitchen. His quarters were small, but it was enough room to stretch out his frustration. For every problem there was a solution.

He took a swig of the gin on the kitchen bench, then went back to his laps.

Somewhere in the data and experience and knowledge and observations… there was an answer. He'd done it once, he could do it again.

His mind screamed in frustration at its complete lack of solutions. Why couldn't he just see the answer? A way to get a winning hand in battle with the Uix next time around. A way to do it differently than last time. A way to do it without all the support of a fleet of cargo ships, shock-and-awe shuttles and turret fire from Sagan's Station. A way to do it with a different trick of code or insight.

There was a way.

He hadn't thought of it yet but that just meant he was not letting go of thoughts enough, not getting creative enough. He needed to push himself further and further into the matrix of Uix concepts and pure Wave genius. This wasn't numbers and maths. This was a concert of creative energy. He was thinking at a level he knew most other humans could not. But it wasn't enough. He needed more.

There was a way.

He looked at the bed as he passed it for the umpteenth time. This time he stopped. A nearly completed Storm robot — version two — looked back at him. The sort of blinkless stare that only a non-operational cyborg could give. She judged him, he knew it. Those eyes. She judged him as much about the connections he couldn't make to a solution right now as much as she judged him for what they'd done earlier that night when she was switched on.

"What? I don't hear any ideas from you."

He returned to his pacing. To thoughts of code. Random connections. Choice. Life. Non-life life. What it all meant. He reached the kitchen and took another sip of gin.

There had to be a way.

*

"Captain Cockmunch and his right hand man gave me nothing!"

Hart looked at Markou as they pondered Rick Astley's words through the communicator.

"What do you mean, nothing?"

"Not one passenger. Not one."

"Sphink is an asshole," said Hart. "OK. Where are you now?"

"Heading back to the bar, I've got a mob to deal with."

"Location — where are you?"

"Near the holos, on C-Deck."

Hart exchanged a look with Markou, enough to know they were on the same page. "Wait there, we're on our way."

*

Brugelson could hear his breathing in the hazard suit. It was quick. Condensation was starting to obscure his view. He just followed the blurry yellow shape in front of him. Al-Razi.

"You OK back there?" came the tinny voice through his headset, muffled by sweat, reverberation and cheap technology.

"Affirmative," replied Brugelson, feeling anything but.

A large black shadow filled the left side of his vision — the enemy fighter. He counted his steps and concentrated on keeping calm. He would need it now more than ever.

Soon another shape came into view. A yellow dot. The doctor, no doubt. Close by, he could make out the shape of the staircase they'd positioned to reach the cockpit. His heart raced faster. How much more did it have to give?

"Ten metres," said Al-Razi.

Brugelson went to wipe his brow, before realising the task was impossible in his hazmat suit. Instead, he blinked his eyes to keep the sweat out.

He counted the steps until his hand touched the staircase rail. The yellow shape focused into that of Dr Suarez. They exchanged nods before he began the climb. His heart rattled off the charts as he reached the top of the climb and peered into the alien cockpit.

A Uix.

A destroyer of humanity, yet, possibly the key to its survival.

That's if he could do what he was here to do.

His chest felt like it could burst.

This was it.

*

CHAPTER 23:
OPEN MINDS

Flicker knew humanity's future was at stake.

He knew the actions of those around the table would decide whether they survived the next encounter, or even survived to see another encounter.

He also knew one more thing, and it scared him more than the rest of the situation combined. He only had three vials of Reality left.

An entire universe to escape, and he only had three occasions to feel like the person he should be.

Flicker looked around the briefing table. Everyone had such purpose and drive. They were the true heroes, planning for a battle with no contemplation of defeat. Humanity must survive, their bodies screamed.

He wanted to escape. He wanted Reality.

*

Hart ignored Flicker's drifting eyes, instead driving through the agenda she had hurriedly assembled.

It would normally feel good to be surrounded by her own team. They had fought alongside each other when others had given up hope. Together, they were stronger, if not near-invincible.

But there was a disturbance.

Markou.

Particularly his face. It changed. It was now a gentle smile that set her at ease, wiped away all doubts and made her feel like things could be normal. His face was at rest while his eyes flashed as they processed information, breaking the silence only to offer insights and suggestions that made everything stronger.

She was utterly confused. He made no sense, and she didn't understand the games he was playing.

*

Storm looked around the table and rolled her eyes.

She knew she wasn't good at the talking thing. She liked doing things. Many things, often at once.

She let her mind wander as she explored new possibilities before she forced herself back to the present.

They were all still looking at each other strangely. Except for Flicker. He was looking strange, but staring at his twisting hands.

"Come on! Let's focus people!" said Storm, as she slammed her fist against the table. "This stuff is sort of important. You know, the whole living thing. I sort of like it, and wouldn't mind doing a bit more."

"Quite," Markou agreed.

Storm caught the softening of Hart's eyes as the smooth baritone washed over her, and the snap as she brought her mind back from wherever it was.

"Thank you, Storm. As I said," Hart wasn't sure whether she had spoken, but pushed on, "this is a last-ditch run. We are getting the hell out of here for a wild jump, and then we focus on rebuilding.

"Wave is working on rebuilding physics or something. Storm, I want you to work closely with him. You may see things we can use. And we need that."

Storm nodded.

"Flicker, I want you to... Flicker!"

"Yes. Captain. Sir. Captain."

"I need you to do some digging for me. I want to know who on this boat can do stuff."

"Stuff?"

"Yes. Bioengineering. Logistics. Governance. Force mapping. Risk assessment and management. Police."

"I can ask Sphink—"

"Sphink has already provided Mr Astley with a full list."

"So why do you—"

"It had no names on it."

"Ah."

Hart nodded and turned her attention to Markou.

Markou and his face, doing Markou-like things. Being competent and professional. And nice. And caring.

She felt her jaw tighten. She was no closer to understanding the mixed messages he was sending.

"N-" her voice broke, and she coughed. She missed Storm's smirk. "Markou. Can you get that map of social stressors to me by tonight? I may have to look at it overnight. The report. Look at the report overnight."

Markou smiled and nodded.

"I'll have it to you this afternoon so you can have some free time tonight," he said, and made a note for himself.

Hart quickly looked away and dismissed everyone. She had one more meeting to go before she could start working on real things.

And no matter where she went, Markou was in her head.

*

Astley had met briefly with Hart. She would have names for him, she promised.

Now he needed to reach out to some of the passengers. To connect with them. To bring them along on the journey and to prevent a mutiny.

But, if he was keeping score, he had very little credibility. Right now, anything better than being told to fuck off was a win.

He had followed orders — Harding's or Sphink's — but they were wrong. They were treating passengers like idiots, and so had he.

Astley had never chosen his career. He had fallen into it.

And now he had fallen into the end of days, hated by the people he had come to like. All because of an order. A stupid order.

He had a revelation: He wasn't in the army, or whatever they called it. He was a civilian. He didn't have to follow orders.

He had a new strategy and it had a name — honesty.

*

Brugelson pushed himself into the fighter, bending long limbs into spaces designed for a smaller creature, hitting his head as he missed ledges or racks obscured by the fog of his breath.

A small display showed his vitals: he was breathing too rapidly, burning oxygen too quickly.

He wouldn't suffocate — he could always escape into the fresh air beyond — but it would mean killing their prisoner and losing the possibility of a tactical advantage.

He swore as he hit his head again and took a moment to slow his breathing as he exited the airlock and faced the closed doorway into the cockpit.

A frickin' alien. A Uix.

Humanity's first and only alien race. And already at war. Perhaps the end of it.

His breathing had calmed, but he could feel his heart striking the craft around him.

He pressed on the door and watched it slide open, revealing a dimly lit organic space.

A disjointed section that looked like a break — or the part that had reshaped itself.

A bank at the forefront of the craft, with flushes of colour and non-colour morphing in one corner. A burst of heat and cold from one section, measured and exact.

And in front of the bank was the Uix.

Mankind's enemy. Mankind's conqueror.

Brugelson's mind struggled to make sense of the dark shape in front of him. It cycled through the types of creature he knew: Human, other mammals, insects, fish, plants... And nothing came to mind as a shortcut.

He couldn't help but let out a scared yell when it moved, but when looking at it, it never stopped moving. Parts of it were pads or tentacles caressing the screens in front of it, manipulating data... or smelling it.

It had large eyes but no observable mouth. Its movement, though minimal, seemed to flow in waves.

"Um... Hi. I'm Brugelson," he offered.

He sensed a wave of force, and then felt pressure near his temples. It was pushing, seeking the activity inside — but wasn't touching him.

The pressure built from a brush of a sensation to a steady push — and then started bordering on pain.

He felt tension through his shoulders as he attempted to counter it, and then more as he tried to relax his jaw. But the pressure continued to build.

He started to move toward the Uix, to do something to stop the violation—

Then it was through. In his head.

It sifted through his memories as it viewed and processed his thoughts. Much of his history was tossed aside, rejected, but some moments were held close, examined, and then tagged for their importance.

Brugelson wanted to object — the last memory of his wife before she died and a memory of his first day in space tossed aside, while his first day looking over station schematics was tagged, and then time taken dissecting conversations with Harding — until he realised this wasn't a one-way process.

He could sense shapes and distinct thoughts that made up the Uix. Not just this Uix, but others before it. The clear duty they shared to protect their species, so fragile against the coldness of space. The shared minds that gathered and protected all knowledge.

The shared memory of their first encounters with the brutal and ugly humans.

The shared assessment of the threat. And the opportunity.

And of their first and only negotiations with the species. Mankind's chosen Ambassador promising shared glory for their species while hiding plans for their downfall. The trial. The sentence. The attack designed to kill them.

Brugelson let out a cry of surprise as his heart rate spiked. Any details of his heads-up display were obscured by the fog of his rapid breath.

He was confused as he digested the steady stream of sensations, and almost missed the sudden silence in his own mind as the Uix withdrew.

His heart settled into the stillness between them.

He became aware of the pain along his limbs, crushed as he was into the cockpit of the foreign craft.

The Uix continued to flow, as if digesting Brugelson's own memories and their significance.

He knew he would have to return, but for now he needed space to... try to understand.

The habits and dangers of space took him safely through the airlock and decontamination while his mind struggled to find a steady place to balance his first Uix encounter.

He needed to talk to Harding. To report.

He called up a direct secure channel and then wondered what he could actually report.

Shock forced his hand.

"Sir, they remember everything," he said.

"Yes, I know," Harding snapped.

"And they remember... you. And what you... offered... them."

There was silence at the end of the comm link. It stretched with every breath, with Brugelson's mask fogging with every pulse. When Harding's voice broke it, it was both a blessing and a curse.

"That changes everything."

*

CHAPTER 24:
REALITY BITES

Sphink paced back and forward knowing the enormity of the challenge in front of him. He looked at the crew who shared the bridge with him. Not in a way they'd notice he was looking, but in a way to remind him how important everything he was doing was — to him, them, in fact, everyone and everything.

"Sir," came the enquiring tones of Hiscock.

"What is it?"

Hiscock looked up, weary from his endless perusal of lines of directives, laws and bylaws, clauses and subclauses. "It says here in the Greater Solar System Accord, Governance, Treaties and Laws Handbook, in the Inter-Solar Void, non Governed Regions, under Non Military Cruising and Cargo Ship Powers Section — 1249b — Subsection IID, that in emergency situations and notwithstanding other laws, the Captain shall acquire the power to enact all Inter-Solar laws at their discretion, beholden to adjudicating and executing them in adherence to all other galactic and human rights laws.

"It means the ship is still yours."

Sphink sighed deeply, face buried in his palm. "No, no, no, no, no!"

It was enough to have all eyes on the bridge upon him. He tried, only moderately successfully, to adopt a more soothing, understanding tone. "He's an Ambassador. That gives him executive power jurisdiction under any of the chain of command legislation in Sections 7, 8, 14 and 17 in the very handbook you're reading, not to mention the Declaration of Powers, 2118 and the United Solar System Humanities Act, 2102! No, I need something smarter, better, more technical. Some loophole, somewhere."

The crew on the bridge of the *Milky Pleasure* stared at him, mouths agape.

Sphink sighed again. "I need all of you focused on what's important, people."

There was a long, long silence before someone responded.

"The... saving of humanity?" said Comms Officer Rodriguez.

Sphink glared at her over several judgmental seconds. "The power structure of this ship."

The Captain's words hung in the air for what seemed like an eon. Sphink reinforced his determination by glaring at each crew member in turn, saving an extra serve for Rodriguez and Hiscock.

Before the deadlock broke with Hiscock, a new data set came to life on Flight Manager Avis's display. He wrestled with the information, what it meant and, most importantly in this moment, how to bring it to the attention of the Captain.

"Sir," he said eventually, timidly.

"Avis, excellent. You have something?"

"Well, yes... and no."

"We don't have time for games, Avis."

"Sir, I know Sir."

"So, do you have anything meaningful to add to help us find a way through this?"

"Do you mean for you to stay in charge or the saving humanity thing?"

Sphink glared at him.

Silence ensued.

Avis searched for the most delicate way to raise the matter, eventually settling on a straightforward report of information. "We're picking up a Uix signal, Sir."

The Captain was so disoriented by the nature of the comment, he didn't know how to process it or respond. More silence.

"Erm," continued Avis, in spite of no direction to do so. "It's a fleet, Sir. Rather large."

Silence.

"On an intercept course with us."

Silence.

"ETA, 43 hours."

Silence.

"That's three hours before we reach the jump point."

Silence.

Everyone stared at Captain Sphink.

More silence.

Looks were exchanged on the bridge under the backdrop of even more silence.

"Shall I... notify Ambassador Harding?"

Sphink's eyes lowered to the floor. "Yes."

*

Flicker's eyes had adjusted to the low light in his quarters. It seemed safe there, just sitting at the kitchenette counter staring at the empty vials of Reality. By their side, the three remaining charged vials called to him. He resisted the lure, for now. Instead, he thought about the power each one of those empty vials had given him. He thought about the version of Clint Flicker he had become as their magic danced through his veins, his synapses, his essence. They looked even more magical as they caught angles of the LED readouts from the various appliances, data displays and sims that made up his modest space. He was captured by their trance, caught between one reality and the other.

There he was, in the dark. A man and his god. A mortal looking his deity in the eyes and deciding which truths to tell himself to create meaning in the madness, and to plot a path forward into the unknown.

It was a moment too big, surely, for any mortal to handle.

Instead, he reached for the photo in the frame that looked out over his quarters. Graduation day. The academy. It was hard to believe that was twenty years ago. He looked at his stupid, confident and sober, well, Reality sober, smile back when he naively thought he could take on the world. He looked at Giselle, a row in front of him — stunning. A goddess captured perfectly in the photo time capsule.

He then looked at Francois in the row behind him. The wild nights came back. The no-labels movement, where sexual identity didn't matter. An entire generation wanting to change the world one mind-bending sexual experience at a time. He was sure, if he did a head count, he'd have slept with more than half the people in that picture.

He was sure because he'd done it back in the day.

Three of the best years of his life — the academy, Francois, Giselle, everyone — everything.

He thought about all the permutations and combinations from his life in that photo to the man in the dark looking at used vials of mindbend. The possibilities, all gone now, of course. Like everyone else in that photo. He thought about the feeling of having it all in that moment. He thought about the feeling of having it all on Reality.

He thought about Giselle.

"We could've been amazing," he said.

He thought about Francois. "Us, too."

He thought about the unfulfilled possibilities.

He thought about reality.

He thought about the Uix.

He thought about Reality.

Three vials became two.

He breathed in deep as he felt the warm magic ooze through his systems.

"Amazing," he said again, dreamily.

He felt alive again. Empowered. Decision maker. Problem solver. Man of action.

Action was what he needed. Vials were what he needed. What would the man of the hour do? The answer occurred to him with the conviction only a god could muster.

The pub.

*

Wave knew he was a genius. Not in the misguided way non-geniuses think they're geniuses, but in the way someone who owns a mind that can do and think things that others can't dream to fathom does.

It wasn't a brag or a compliment. It came with all the baggage of seeing the world differently, of not fitting in. It came with layers of self-doubt and self-loathing, but it also came as a truth and acceptance.

Being alone with code will do that to a person. It will change you. Seeing truths and possibilities and shapes and magic where others see gobbledegook. Seeing a solution where others can't begin to fathom the question.

It was a way of life.

There were moments where it all made sense in the normal world. Where what he did, what made him a genius, was quantifiable to the average person. In those moments he integrated some code to make something happen, something easily understandable, it was… bliss.

He felt normal. He felt extraordinary.

Creating the solution to defeat the Uix and change the destiny of all on board the *Milky Pleasure* was one of those moments. One delicious taste of genius normal.

He had locked himself away from the world to find his next taste of it. Separation to find some way, somehow, to be connected in truth of code and understanding.

But every genius needed his down-time. And every person needed connection, even when the world wasn't ready to give it to them.

He looked down while he was taking a break from his world-saving problems and saw a twinkle in robot Storm's eyes right before the moment ended in a wave of exhilaration and guilt. He slumped over her, exhausted (mostly mentally, for the record).

Then he felt dirty.

He shuffled to the other end of the bed to study the scene. To berate himself.

Robot Storm looked unblinkingly at the ceiling.

This was a part of his genius others would never understand. No amount of creative capability or problem solving or craftsmanship would ever be appreciated in this moment, by those who just saw the gobbledegook.

He knew it.

He felt disgusted.

He felt ashamed.

This was the genius ying to his yang.

This was the side of it all that no one must ever—

There was a knock at the door.

He surveyed the room and silently swore.

"Hang on!"

"Oh, you are in there. Open up, tosser."

It was Storm.

He took all the shame and guilt he'd felt, multiplied by all the prime numbers between one and one hundred, all while swearing, getting dressed and hiding the evidence.

"Hurry up!"

"Be there in a sec."

"Jesus, what's with all the banging?"

"Just… tidying."

"Do I want to know?"

There was another round of shuffling and huffing and cupboards opening and closing before Wave surveyed the scene again.

"Oi, weirdo! Still waiting."

Once satisfied all was ready for receiving, he wiped the sweat from his forehead, checked his uniform was in order, then opened the door.

*

The damage through the bow side of C-Deck was worse than Harding had imagined. He could barely make out a path to the sealed air locks and things were a whole lot worse on the other side of those doors. He knew it before he came down here, but seeing it was something else altogether.

He sighed.

His communicator chirped into life. It was Flight Manager Avis.

He sighed again.

"What is it?"

"Sir." Avis swallowed the remnants of the word hard. "It's the Uix."

"Yes?"

"There's a fleet inbound."

"ETA?"

"Three hours before we make the jump, Sir."

Harding paused. "Affirmative. Out."

He switched off the communicator and whispered "Fuck."

He looked at the space around him. The broken, isolated space. He let everything wash over him for a moment. He instinctively turned to George, before realising he'd ordered the robot to have some free time, so he could be alone.

There he was with the destruction and isolation and now the countdown.

The Uix were coming.

"FUUCCCKKK!" he screamed into the debris-filled echo chamber.

He searched for an appropriately sized piece of rubble, picked it up and sent it as far as his ageing arms could throw it. "Eeeaaarrghh."

He looked around for something to do, someone to blame, somewhere to run.

There was nothing.

"Fuck," he said again, quietly.

It turned into a laugh. An end-of-days, end-of-the-line laugh.

Eventually he gathered himself and his thoughts. He picked up his communicator and cleared his throat as he dialled.

"Sir?"

"Brugelson. We've got work to do."

"We do?"

"Yes. C-Deck. Stat."

*

CHAPTER 25:
DOPPLEBANGER

Flicker noted his swagger with a nod of approval as he entered the entertainment district. Behind the multi-layered self-congratulatory exterior, however, even his Reality bliss wasn't blinding him from the numbers. Two vials. He was now facing the end of existence with two vials.

For now, though, he had control. What would a man on top of his game do? How would a suave, super-intelligent, nuanced, bang-on good-looking man of the world charm himself into some additional mindbend?

Which of these venues would maximise his chances of success?

He strutted, he studied. Then he saw it.

A neon sign with the words The Moral Compass. Behind it spun a compass needle, like it had been attached to someone performing capoeira while standing directly on magnetic north. He smiled, then entered.

*

Astley was on his fourth drink when his communicator beeped into life. It was Hart.

"I have the list," she said, as she looked at his video form. "Jesus, are you OK?"

He adjusted his facial expression, trying to land on confident charm. He missed. "Fine."

Hart didn't have time for details or problems. Instead she rolled her eyes. "Pinging it through now. Find them and have them meet me in loading zone seven in three hours."

"Affirmative."

Again, Hart was left with a tone that filled her with anything but confidence. "Those names, loading zone seven, three hours."

"Got it."

"And you're absolutely sure you're OK? And that you're up to this?"

There was a pause. A long, awkward, doubtful pause. "Yeah."

*

"Jesus, are you OK?"

Storm stood at Wave's partially opened door, studying the man within.

"Yeah, why? Why wouldn't I be?"

"You look like shit. What the fuck is going on in there?"

There was a pause. A long, awkward, doubtful pause. "Nothing."

"Nothing? Jesus, I'm supposed to be helping you save the human race and you're doing nothing?"

"No... yeah... that... I'm doing that."

Storm just stared at him.

Wave instinctively adjusted his uniform under the weight of her glare. "What?"

"Are you going to let me in?"

"You? In here?"

"Yes."

"What, now?"

"Yes... you know that thing you've wished for and asked for more times than I can count?"

He studied her. Eyes shifting positions several times.

"Now!"

Eventually, the door was opening and Storm made her way into his quarters. Wave did not have much say in the matter.

*

"You look like you've seen a ghost," said Harding, as Brugelson finished the undulating walk across the debris on C-Deck.

"What?" said Brugelson absently as he took in the surroundings.

Harding studied him.

Once seemingly satisfied and oriented, Brugelson then returned Harding's gaze. "What are we doing here?"

Harding turned his attention back to the scene of destruction. "Doing what we can to save what remains of the ship, what remains of humanity."

"Why here, exactly?"

"We have to plan. If we're going to survive this thing, humans — we must go on, no matter the cost."

Brugelson nodded, wary and still more than a little disoriented from contact with the Uix. The feeling of being meshed in consciousness was both new and overwhelming. He had experienced existence on a new plane, reality now a grey haze in comparison. The images of Harding from his past seemed more real than him there in that moment.

"Why here?" he repeated.

"Only the end game matters now, not how we get there. Some tough decisions may have to be made. This is a place without prying eyes and ears, where leaders talk about what has to be done — needs to be done."

Again they locked eyes, Brugelson nodded.

Harding gave a small smile and returned the nod. "Besides, I've been trying to get you down here for a while. I need your expertise."

He moved further towards the back of the deck, turning his attention to the damaged walls high above and a piece of substructure lurking deep in the damage.

Brugelson followed.

"That's part of the *Pleasure's* skeleton, right?"

Brugelson pondered for a moment. "I believe so, part of the ribbing."

"And those cracks, should we be concerned?"

After some fiddling, Brugelson had his communicator in visual mode on the damaged area. He zoomed in to get a better look at the damage. "Jesus."

Harding moved in next to him. "Bottom line, can we even survive a jump in this state?"

Brugelson interfaced with some further data on his communicator. "It's not great, but if that's the worst of it, she'll hold."

"The worst of it is in the section further back," said Harding. "It's sealed off."

Brugelson looked at him. "We're going to have to get eyes on it."

"My thoughts exactly. Let's get suited up then."

"Suited up?"

"Got any better ideas?"

Brugelson put his communicator away and steeled himself. "No."

"Well then." Harding began the trek across the debris, Brugelson following in his wake. "So, tell me about your encounter with the Uix."

*

The dance floor was heaving in a sweaty mass of depraved humanity, loose in that special way that can only be achieved when tomorrow doesn't matter. Flicker did his own dance around the edge, one designed to avoid stray limbs and keep his gin and tonic inside the receptacle it had been delivered in. He was at one with his moves and his drink. He was at one with his decision to come to this place. If there was Reality on board, he'd sniff it out here. He had targeted the quieter and dimly lit rear corner of the venue.

It was when he neared that he got his first surprise of the night.

"George?"

For a robot, George sure did a good impression of embarrassed. After pretending to not hear, then attempting to hide by sliding back in his chair, he finally realised there was no escaping the moment and hunched his shoulders. He looked up. "Mr Flicker, Sir."

Flicker slapped him on the back, happy at the thought of a familiar face to help his night's mission. "What are you doing here?"

"Me, Sir?"

"No, the other robot hiding in the back corner of this petri dish of a pick-up joint."

George looked around for said other robot.

Flicker laughed. "I mean you… like, obviously."

George knew how to replicate and express laughter but, in this moment, he was too confused to know how to go about it.

"Seriously, what are you doing here?" said Flicker, as he slid into the seat opposite.

"I…" but George didn't know how to finish what he'd begun saying.

"It's cool buddy, you can talk to me."

Geroge thought about this statement for many moments. "I… I was given some time off and decided to experience something different."

Flicker looked around the room and laughed again. "Well, you've nailed it for different."

George didn't respond.

"So, what sort of a different you looking for exactly?"

"It's… I'd rather not say."

Flicker gave the robot an indifferent expression then took a swig of his drink.

"What about you, Sir?"

Flicker studied him, while backing up his swig with another. "I'll make you a deal. I'll tell you if you tell me."

Again, George pondered in silence.

"Serious truths, George. I promise you mine."

Silence.

"It's good."

Eventually George nodded. "Very well, Sir. I accept the parameters of your suggestion."

"Brilliant. Oh, and if we're going to do this right, you're going to have to stop calling me Sir. Deal?"

"Deal, Sir."

Flicker stared at him.

"I mean, just, deal."

"Well alright!"

"The truth will set you free."

"What now?" said Flicker.

"It is a quote — the truth shall set you free."

Flicker shrugged.

"It's from the Bible."

Flicker shrugged with more emphasis. "I don't follow that fantasy franchise. I'm more a Marvel guy."

George looked awkwardly around the room while Flicker took another swig.

"So, your truth, si— your truth?"

Flicker looked around conspiratorially, then leaned into the table. He realised the forces in his mind had led him to this moment and no amount of fighting could prevent him from crossing the event horizon. And, if he was going in, he was going all in. "I think I'm addicted to Reality. I have two vials left and I can't face whatever bullshit end-of-days fuckuppery is coming my way if I don't get more. I've come down to the sleazy shithole to find someone — anyone — who can charge me up until we either get through this shit or die."

George went to respond, several times, but didn't know where to start.

"Oh, and I'm absolutely pinging right now. I used my third last vial to get me on my game to come down here."

Again, George struggled to find an adequate response.

"Oh, and while we're at it, and since it's probably the end of us all anyways, I am a wreck of a human when I'm not on the shit. I think I hate myself — my real self — not that I know who that is anymore. I've only ever been in love once and that was 20 years ago, and even then, I think I was far more in love with myself than her. But I kissed it all goodbye for me and the promises of, well, this — me — here now. And it's shit. I can still pull, mind — so, you know, well done me. But that's a bit useless anyway because most of the time I can't get it up when I do. So, all I'm left with is the Reality."

Silence.

"Truth that biatch."

Flicker felt a mix of triumph and exposure in the wake of his words. Then he felt a second wave of surprise from simply experiencing those initial feelings. This was new. This was not what happened when he was on Reality. Ever. Now he was second-guessing everything. Except the words he'd uttered, which combined to form a truth more accurate than anything he'd spoken in years. Perhaps ever.

George smiled. "That is some impressive truth."

This time it was Flicker's turn for silence. He nodded, but no words followed.

"May it set you free."

Flicker drained his drink in an attempt to reset. "Yeah, sure. OK then, your turn. What's your truth?"

"Well, given your lead, Sir.... I am gay. And I'm attracted to humans. I have come here tonight to seek a male lover."

Flicker went to laugh, then stopped himself. He went to have a drink, but it was empty. He searched for the closest discarded unfinished drink, reached for it and drained it in one mouthful. "Well, fuck me!"

"Correct me if I'm wrong Sir, but aren't we supposed to flirt first?"

Flicker repeated his previous pattern — smothered laugh, randomly acquired beverage skolled. "It was an expression. It wasn't meant literally."

George didn't know how to respond.

"Look, doesn't matter. Good truth. Seriously, top shelf."

He grabbed the last remaining drink within reach and claimed it as his own. "So, then, George. Here we are. Two beings on the brink of being erased, sharing our truths in a dark corner of a dive of a bar on a ship hurtling through the void on a mission it probably has no hope of fulfilling."

He took a sip. "But, we have this night. What say, you help me score and I'll help you, well, score?"

"That would seem an acceptable arrangement."

Flicker lifted his drink into the air. "To truths, good friends and a night that's going to get seriously messed up."

*

CHAPTER 26:
SOME INCONVENIENT TRUTHS

"Make it a double," said Storm, as Wave poured.

He stopped when he reached the level of generous double, but the look in Storm's eye had not. He added more and watched her for guidance.

"Perfect," she said, eventually.

He looked down to see the glass full, shrugged, then handed it over.

Storm took a swig, while she sat on a stool on the opposite side of the kitchenette bench.

Wave planted himself in the kitchenette, just to keep the conversation as far from the scene of his recent crime as possible. "So, what are you doing here exactly?"

"Helping you do the things you need to do, to do whatever it is you do, so we can unleash whatever that is against the Uix and save our asses. Also, drinking."

"Right," said Wave, over many more seconds than one would deem efficient pronunciation.

Storm took another swig. "So, what do you need?"

"From you? Nothing."

Suddenly, she sat upright on her stool. She drifted temporarily from the conversation, before coming back. "Hang on a second, what's wrong?"

"What do you mean, what's wrong?" said Wave, aiming for a non-defensive tone but missing.

"I just asked you what you needed from me and you didn't make some smartass sexual remark."

He topped his drink up to Storm levels. "I... I..."

"Something's up."

"No it's not."

"Now you're acting weird, something's definitely up."

"Nothing's up, I'm just... stressed... or something."

"A situation which you've specifically told me makes you say sexual things to me."

"I... I..."

"Like about 157 of your other emotions do."

"I..."

"Yet, now, with me in your room, giving you a line you could knock out of the park blindfolded… nothing."

Wave took another generous swig. Storm did similar then stood up and started pacing the room.

"Something is not right."

"It's right, everything's totally right."

She narrowed her eyes at him briefly before casting them around his quarters, observing.

Wave sweated, silently prayed and sipped.

She neared the bed, sniffed, stopped and turned to him. "What's that smell?"

"What smell?"

"It's… sex smell."

"No it isn't!"

She stared at him in a way that said any doubt on her mastery of the subject would be dealt with as lies. "What have you been doing and with who?"

"Nothing."

She moved to the right side of the bed, sniffed, then to the left and sniffed again. She looked at Wave, shook her head, then narrowed her search area to the left side of the room.

"Wait! I've figured out a way you can help," he said.

Storm didn't look at him, just lifted a finger in his direction to shush him, then continued her sniff search.

"Time really is of the essence here," he added.

She continued her search.

"I don't even know what you think you can smell."

She continued her search.

"Or what you think I've been up to."

She continued her search.

"This is ridiculous. Can we just get on with it."

She continued her search.

"Maybe it was the mango I ate earlier. They smell a bit dodgy, mangoes."

"Mangoes? One man certainly went here," she said.

By this point Wave had worked his way out from behind the kitchen counter.

Storm neared the cupboard. Not just any cupboard, but exactly the one Wave definitely did not want her anywhere near.

"OK, fine, I had a few minutes to kill so I let off some steam."

She sniffed at the cupboard.

"Seriously, why are you doing this?"

She reached for the cupboard door.

"Stop!"

She paused with her hand on the cupboard door and looked at him with expectation.

"Don't open that door," said Wave. His arm reached out, as if he were a bystander watching the well-dressed, over-leveraged stockbroker on the skyscraper's rooftop edge.

She looked at him. "Why not?"

"You're just going to have to trust me when I tell you that it's an incredibly bad idea."

"Sounds interesting. I'm even more curious than before."

He started to inch forward. She faked a cupboard opening to stop him in his tracks.

"Look, just don't, I beg you. Please. I'll give you anything. Anything."

"The thing is, there is literally nothing I want from you. Plus, I could not be more interested in anything in this world than what I'm about to see in this cupboard."

"It's bad."

Storm scoffed. "Look, rookie, I have been around the block. I have been around all the blocks. ALL OF THEM. There is nothing there that's going to shock me."

"I beg to differ. I strongly suggest we focus on the task at hand. Just… let go of the handle, come have a drink and let's get this humanity-saving thing done."

Storm pondered her options.

"You and me, saving humanity."

"Tell me what's in there and I'll consider it, if you get your ass back to saving humanity," she mocked the last two words.

"Just… stuff and shit."

Storm sniffed again. "I don't detect any shit. What's the stuff?"

"Please don't do this."

"Oh, it's happening. In three."

"Mangoes."

"Two."

"A blow-up doll."

"One."

"A dild—"

It was too late. Storm pulled on the handle and the cupboard door eased open.

"Noooooooooooooooooooooo!"

It all happened in slow motion. Wave dived forward with more action, gusto and determination than he'd done anything physical in his life. At one point he could've sworn he reached full horizontal to the ground as he launched several feet atop it.

Storm, meanwhile, had her eyes fixed on the contents of the cupboard. Whatever she was expecting, it was not body-sized. She reeled.

Robot Storm, meanwhile, having been turned off and stowed in such haste, was leaning against the door. Now the gravity brakes were off.

There was the briefest of moments, as he sailed through the air, that Wave thought he could still contain the situation. Obviously, there were many reasons this entire line of hope was foolhardy, but the first became apparent when he plummeted to the floor of his quarters still several feet short of the cupboard, Storm and Robot Storm.

As the oxygen ripped from his lungs and pain tore through him, he saw, for the first time, two Storms. A blast of gutting guilt pulsed through him as all the future permutations of this moment flashed through mind, in much the way humans believe their life does in their final moments.

Then, a glimmer of hope. Robot Storm began her face-first fall to the floor and Storm, momentarily shocked, took evasive action.

Adrenaline kicked in for Wave as he saw yet another window in which he thought he might be able to contain the problem. He fought the pain surging through him, then got a secure foothold with the floor in order to launch a second, well, wave, diving at the cupboard and the entire fiasco.

Meanwhile, Storm had overcome the initial shock and instinctively drew her weapon at the potential enemy launching at her — eyes sharply across everything.

Robot Storm's shoulder got caught in the door frame, sending her into a twist as she fell. Landing on her back and revealing her full nature to actual Storm.

Wave's second dive proved far more accurately calculated (and within achievable skillsets) than the first. He flew into the frame of the action of the falling robot.

Just too late.

As Storm looked on to see Robot Storm on the floor looking back at her, Wave landed, face first, in the crotch region, or more significantly at that moment, the wet patch.

Storm — ALL-THE-BLOCKS-Storm — stared at the scene, speechless for the first time in her life.

After a few seconds of hiding and hoping the entire world would go away, Wave gave into reality, peeled his face from the evidence and looked at her.

"Sorry."

*

"So, basically, my entire adult life has been a lie. I could blame my parents, but really, what's the point? I've just got to acknowledge the shortcuts I've made, where they've led me and the underdeveloped sense of growth I've made as an adult. And I should take ownership of that."

Flicker had no idea how the night had taken this turn. He had no idea how that combination of words had poured from his mouth. He had no idea why the ping of Reality felt different tonight, why he felt different. He couldn't believe any of it. He felt dirty for saying it and felt even dirtier that it was true.

George nodded his encouraging approval.

"Wow, that's a lot to unpack," added Flicker.

He felt dirtiest of all for saying that. He reached for the first of the three drinks he'd recently ordered from the bar and took a swig. He put it back on the tray it had been delivered on with the others. Next to a sticky note with the name CLINT FLICKER in all caps. The Ls and Is looking exactly like Us, but he simply, well, let it go.

"It would seem you have made some significant progress as a person tonight, Sir."

Flicker thought about the robot's words. It was true. He had. He thought about the version of him in his quarters earlier that evening — dark and broken. He thought about the version of himself he'd seen in that photo — cocky but hopeful. He thought about the version of himself that had walked into the bar several hours ago — gripped by Reality, trying to gaffer tape a solution for the moment that wouldn't solve one inch of any real problem he had. He shrugged and took another sip, then laughed to himself. "I think you're right."

Time passed. The wild night played out around the man and the robot at the back of the bar.

"You know, George, you're a good friend."

"Sir?"

"The things you've said, the things we've talked about. No one has cared enough to talk to me about it, like, ever."

"Thank you, Sir."

As Flicker cheersed the air, George's eye was drawn to the pair of men walking past, in each other's arms and headed to the exit. Flicker caught the moment.

"The same can't be said about me."

"Sir?"

"Well, we've spent all night talking about me and my problems and none talking about you and yours."

George didn't know what to say.

"Typical me. I was — am — such an ass."

Again, George just listened and observed.

"Well, not any more, I can assure you. I'm going to be different now. Everything about me will be different, I'm going to…

"Shit, I'm doing it again, aren't I?"

He studied George with his new awareness. He wondered how many relationships and life connections he'd blown being focused on himself. Or on Reality.

George sat opposite him, smiling.

He was pleased. Why was he pleased? He hadn't had one fraction of his problems addressed in the slightest way tonight, yet there he sat, content.

Contentment, that's what Flicker realised he lacked more than anything in that moment. It was the missing piece. The thing that could make him stronger. Stronger than Reality, stronger than anything this end of the world could throw at him.

He smiled back. "Thank you, George."

He laughed to himself again. He felt a new way forward and he was convinced it would work. And he'd been shown the way by a robot. A robot who'd just wanted to help for helping's sake. Who asked for nothing in return.

There was a beauty in that. A truth. A humanness.

Flicker felt warm in its presence.

Maybe it was the last embers of Reality, or the gins — the many, many gins, or the other random drinks… maybe it was the craziness of the night or the dim lighting even. He felt cared for, loved. And George's smile was the most homely thing he'd felt since, well since he couldn't remember. George, a being with his own wants and needs, but looking after Flicker's.

All of it was impossible and groundbreaking and weird and different — good different — and lovely and, well, the moment just seemed right.

"George?"

"Yes, Sir."

"Would you like to come back to my place?"

"Your place, Sir?"

"Yes… and don't call me Sir."

"I was going to wait for… wait, what did you say earlier, one of these pissed tossers to get so plastered I can pick them off the back of the herd."

"Did I say that? Anyway, I meant me. Come home with me."

"Do you mean what I believe you mean?"

"Yes."

George smiled in the dim light. "Yes, Sir, I do believe that would be lovely."

*

It was suffocating, being in a protective suit so soon after his close encounter with the Uix. It was almost as if Brugelon could again feel the pressure on his temples as the creature forced its presence upon him. But, here, now, there was no Uix, no melding of minds, just his suit, his racing heart and heavy breathing. Oh, and the closed circuit communication he was having with Harding. He wasn't sure it felt any less foreign than the alien cockpit only a couple of hours ago.

They were floating through the wreckage of D-Deck. It was amazing to think the ship was still flight capable when looking at it from back here. Still, the dread didn't strike him as anything new on this day.

"Look at that one," said Harding, leading the way. "Looks like some… what is that, fuselage? has wrapped around the worst of it."

Brugelson interacted with a few systems on his communicator to gain further insight into the damage. All the while thinking of the Uix and the ensuing conversation he'd just had with Harding. He'd played his cards and told his truths. The stakes were too high to play games, he'd figured. So far, he was right. His worst fears about sharing his knowledge of Harding's history had not been realised. Instead, they were working together, finding a solution to a problem that might lead to more problem solving and perhaps, by some miracle, a way out of this mess. "It's the worst one so far, but I think it'll hold."

"How sure? If you had to bet our lives on it."

"At least 90 percent. I'd take those odds, if we can make the jump."

"We'll make the jump," said Harding.

They moved even further into the space. To starboard, they could see the stars though a gash in the ship's exterior. Between that, the floating debris and the strange montone hue destruction gives to anything, it was haunting.

"Another two up here at 10 o'clock. Looks like the last of it."

"I see the damage. They're not as bad as the last. If that's the last of it, I'll stick with my 90 percent."

"And they're not all connected to some larger piece of damage?"

"Negative. Benson Class ships are pretty robust. Simple design too. If there was anything of that magnitude, we'd be at one with the black already."

Harding turned to face him. "We were due one win, I guess."

"Roger that."

"I'm calling it, let's head back."

"Best news I've had all day, Sir."

With that, Harding began the delicate task of hopping and drifting back the 50m to the airlock. Every now and then, with a bit of open space around and potential snags below, he could tug on the oxygen line to draw himself back a good few metres in one move. "So, tactics," he announced as an unprompted conversation starter.

"What have you got?" prompted Brugelson, as he followed Harding's path and movement techniques.

"We've got three hours to survive between when they reach us and the jump."

"Yes."

"We can't engage, we'll be destroyed, unless that Wave kid delivers a hail Mary."

"What are the odds there?"

"Not 90 percent, that's for sure. Nothing we can plan around, anyway. But we do have the Uix."

"We do."

"Best asset we've got. We can offer an exchange — the Uix for freedom."

"You know them better than me, Sir. Is that likely to end well?"

"Can't say for sure, but I can't say I can think of any other way we're going to reach jump otherwise."

Brugelson pondered in silence. Harding's words echoing in his helmet as he followed several metres behind.

"There's a chance we could pull it off, though. Life is everything to them. Each individual. We can play that to our advantage. They've got our solar system, they'll get one of their own kind back, they get everything they want. Letting a broken ship slip away hardly seems like a loss worth chasing — in their logic or ours."

"Hmmm. It's definitely possible," agreed Brugelson. "But we'd have to think about the logistics of how that exchange would go down and how we could limit our exposure from when it's happened til until we jump. They'll owe us nothing then."

"We have time for that. Importantly though, we both think it is possible."

"Affirmative. We'd also have to consider our communication with them. From my observations today, we'll have to be watertight in our truths to them — watertight in what we want and why."

"Indeed," said Harding, shaping up his last few moves to the handle of the airlock. "Then there's the truths they already know."

"Sir?"

"Well, you saw their shared thought of me from when the treaty fell apart."

"Yes, among other thing—"

"We can only assume the Uix on board now knows I'm here, from the same thought exchange."

"I guess, but we don't know for sur—"

"And any hopes of our ship being allowed to make the jump would be zero if they knew I was onboard." Harding reached the airlock and clasped the handle.

Brugelson suddenly felt exposed. Not only in his current position short of the airlock and the grander point Harding was heading to, but in the tone of his voice as he did it. He started moving as quickly as he could without making his increase of pace a noticeable one.

"The way I see it, there's only one way this ship can get out of this system in one piece with me onboard," said Harding, as he drew a knife from a pocket in the side of his protective suit.

Brugelson now knew the play. He knew he was right to doubt all along. He knew he was in danger. He grabbed the air line and yanked it with all his might, propelling him closer to the airlock.

"That's if you die now, and the Uix dies before it makes contact with its own."

Harding lifted Brugelson's air line.

Brugelson pulled the same line at the other end and screamed, "Noooo!"

Harding severed the chord.

Brugelson neared the door, already feeling lightheaded as his oxygen system was compromised. He focused the last of his energy on making it to the airlock and pulled with all his strength. As he did, he saw the door shut before him, then the circular handle rotate.

He reached it, grabbed it and tried to wrestle it back in the other direction, but he could feel his weakness growing. He tried to leverage his body against the frame so the anchor point would give him greater power. But, in his current state, it still wasn't enough.

He tried again, with weak hands.

He was fuzzy headed. He was drifting. The need for oxygen crushed his throat. He gave up on the battle with the door handle and started his final battle to breathe. One he was destined to lose.

As he drifted from the airlock and into his demise on the damaged D-Deck, he heard a voice one last time.

"Goodbye, old friend."

*

CHAPTER 27:
A MILLION TO ONE

Time ticked by. Just seconds, one after the other. But they all counted, they all added up. They all stole time. The Uix were coming. There was nothing surer.

Right now, there were a million ways that could play out — a million possibilities. From those possibilities, one outcome would be. One shot in one moment that would change everything. One chance at survival. One chance for humanity.

It was a pressure that became a tangible essence on the *Milky Pleasure*. It existed. It interacted with those aboard. It changed people.

It changed leaders.

The countdown. Pressure's tangible essence. The possibilities. The one shot. Survival.

Harding thought about it all as he made his way to the bridge.

Hart thought about it all as she made her way to the bridge.

Sphink thought about it as he stood at the helm of the bridge.

The possible plays. The stakes. The game. Power. Influence. Decisions. Pressure. The Uix. The future. Humanity. Life.

The three main players headed for a showdown.

Cutthroat bridge.

*

CHAPTER 28:
CUTTHROAT BRIDGE

Captain Sphink. Captain.

Captain of his ship, the *Milky Pleasure.*

For all of the drama and distraction of an alien invasion, it remained his ship.

And would continue to be his ship.

His mouth curved; a smile for him that most people interpreted as a prune-like demand to be punched in the face.

The bridge door swished open, admitting Hart.

She looked stressed, the bruises of battle still evident, but walked into the room like she owned it.

Sphink felt the doubt flow through him. This was a real Captain, he thought. But he pushed the notion aside. The law was on his side, and he knew how to play this moment to his advantage. To his advantage on the bridge of his ship.

"Ah, Captain Hart," he said, with forced confidence.

"Sphink," she said, with a nod.

His mouth twitched with annoyance, but there was a larger game he was about to win.

"How can I help you?" he asked.

"The list—" she started, blood rushing up her neck. She took a breath and started again.

"Mr Astley asked you for a list of passengers who might have skillsets we can use."

"He did, yes."

"And you gave him a list with... no names."

"That's correct," he said, with a bravado he could feel splintering inside.

"No names at all on a ship this size," she said with steel in her voice.

"That's correct. I made a list and checked it twice, just like Santa." He smirked, following it up with a self-assured laugh. The crew on the bridge watching the exchange later agreed it was more of a nervous titter.

"What about Christine Hermann?"

He was about to answer when she interrupted.

"Structural engineer. Sampson Finnigan?"

He shrugged.

"Biosphere designer. Amy Ziu?"

"I don't know what you're leading to here bu—"

"What I am leading to is a question: Why were these people not on your list?"

"They are just titles. What can they really do, Hart?"

"Save the ship. Help us eat. Manage the psychological fallout. And that's just three of them. These are the people we need to save—"

Sphink tuned her out. He had done his research and scripted the moment in his head. He was ready to remove her from the board. The board on his ship. His.

"—which is why we need to work together. The alternative is that we die. All of us," Hart finished.

"You're right, Hart, we need to work together. We need to trust each other. Each of us completely in control of our roles," he slowly explained.

She nodded, agreeing with the words but not trusting the snake hiding behind them.

He smiled his prune-like smile and continued.

"For example, we need to make sure we take care of the basics."

"Yes..."

"Like cleaning."

"Cleaning?"

"Yes, cleaning. Have you reviewed our A780?"

Hart's face screwed up in confusion.

"Or our D97/C?"

"Sphink, what the hell are you talking about?"

"You don't know what they are?"

"What are you talking about?"

"Well, Captain," he rolled the word around his mouth, relishing it, "they are the things that a leader should know. What about PS492?"

"For God's sake, Sphink, get to your point!"

"Ooh, that's unfortunate, Captain. Mind you, for someone whose reputation is based on a video—"

She couldn't help it.

"We are under fucking attack. We are possibly the last humans left alive, and you are wasting your breath taking pot-shots at me? I really think I need to punch you in the face to—"

Harding entered the bridge, the door swishing open as if relishing the confrontation.

"How long do we... wait, what is happening here?"

Sphink smiled, turning slowly to Harding to close the trap.

"Ambassador Harding, I'm delighted you could be here. Under the laws of our Solar Federation, I am relieving Captain Hart of her rank and authority. Security? Please remove her from the bridge."

The two guards, called to the bridge by a coded signal from Sphink's command chair, looked at each other in confusion. One looked at Rodriguez, who shrugged; no help there.

Hart was struggling to piece the accusation together. Removing her from duty? What for? And what the hell?

"Hold that order." Harding barely raised his voice but it cut through everything. "What are Captain Hart's crimes?"

Sphink was frustrated by Harding's presence for Hart's fall from grace, but it could be turned to his benefit. Harding had shown him no respect; this would show his true value and cunning. And in turn... Sphink could take down Harding for full control of the *Milky Pleasure*.

"Sir, the laws of the Federation are based on—"

"Get to it, Sphink. I don't need them all recited."

"Of course not. Sir. Military and Civil Codes of Vessel Command both describe the Captain's overriding duty as being to the safety of their crew and relying on sound judgement."

Sphink waited a moment for acknowledgement. On seeing nothing in Harding's eyes — God, they were so cold — he pressed on.

"Hart has no knowledge of the dangers posed by the chemicals listed on our A780, Sir, and—"

Harding broke in.

"She likely has a great understanding of the dangers, but has wasted her time saving our collective arses rather than memorising form numbers."

Sphink wasn't happy with the response — it wasn't running according to his plan — but facts were facts: dereliction of duty didn't always stem from system-wide breakdowns, they were often based on a failure to attend to the small things that kept things running. Harding would understand.

"Bear with me, Sir. The use of some of those chemicals in an inappropriate setting can lead to serious injury or even death; it says it on the packet. A failure to be aware of these risks poses a threat to the safety of our crew and passengers. But that's not all," he rushed as he sensed Harding about to talk into the gap.

"Hart has shown no knowledge of our D97/C protocol—"

Harding stared at him in bewilderment.

"Sir, it is the protocol all staff must be aware of in the event of a toxic backflow from waste stations into the water supply."

"How often does it happen?"

"Sir, that's really not important — it is more important that we are prepared for it, that we can be prepared to save our crew and passengers should the event arise, and may I say—" again cutting Harding off, "—we are now in a position where that event is more likely given the imminent failure of systems."

Harding took a breath to speak, but Sphink continued with his prosecution.

"And our PS492! What about that? She has no idea what it is. For the record," he said, tartly, turning to Hart, "it is the ship-wide statement of minimum supply for individual items across the ship, including replacement pads, light pens, disinfectant wipes—"

"In a war—" Hart's face was red as she broke in, but Sphink cut her off.

"In a war, Hart, any army is only as good as its supply lines!" A handy tip from a dramatised serial about the fall of the Roman Empire. Great acting, good-looking men wrapped in free-flowing togas that revealed their muscled and oiled calves. "In a war, these are the essential things."

Sphink saw both Harding and Hart settle back on their heels. He was on the final stretch and he was winning.

"And one last thing: A Captain must be beyond reproach, of the utmost character—as required by both Civil and Military Flight Codes across the system." He left a beat to allow the maxim to settle in. "Which is why I, and any person of moral turpitude, would object to this!"

He stabbed at his pad, and an image came up on the bridge's holoscreen. It was difficult to make out what it was. There was fur, certainly, and human skin. But there was also something that looked like an egg whisk... and a tube of... the writing was clear if you squinted: bacon lubricant... and then there was the trapeze-like structure holding everything together, powered by an industrial generator which also had... And then the picture came together. With Hart's face in it.

"You bastard," she whispered.

"On the basis that Hart is placing our crew and our passengers at risk, I am removing her from active duty, effective immediately. Security?"

Sphink turned his face away from Hart, flicking his hand a couple of times to dismiss her. It was a particular move that captured both power and apathy, one he had seen used to brutal effect on the same Roman Empire serial documentary.

No-one moved.

Sphink looked up to take in the scene.

Hart's head was hanging low, avoiding the picture on the holoscreen and the brief gazes of everyone on the bridge.

Harding was staring straight at him, his right hand held out, palm facing the guards: Take no action. When he spoke, his voice was barely audible, even in the utter silence.

"I could go through every one of those unfounded allegations and turn them back on you. For example, are you on top of your I90s? No, I thought not. And have you filed your T163 today? Hmm? No. I'm sure you'd like to explain to everyone here now why not?"

Sphink's mouth opened and closed but he had nothing to say. He could feel himself tumbling uncontrollably as he fell from the peak of victory into the darkness below.

Harding smirked, and continued.

"And what about firing on your own craft? There is a very strong case for... hmmm... what would we call it? The first thing that comes to mind is treason."

Sphink's face was pale as it stretched in disbelief. This wasn't in his plan. No part of it after he had finished had any place in his plan. It was wrong. Terrifyingly wrong.

Harding sidled up to him. Although the Captain's chair was elevated, it seemed as though Harding was towering above him, crushing him into his chair with no place to hide.

Harding's voice was a whisper in his ear, although everyone on the bridge could hear it.

"You're a fool, Sphink.

"I could kill you right now, and no one would care. I'm half-tempted simply to go ahead and do it to make my day easier.

"In military terms, you are confined to quarters for 48 hours and," to the guards, "someone will be posted outside your door to ensure you remain there."

"But Sir, there's a war on—"

"You're right, Sphink. Make that 72 hours. In my opinion, the safety of this crew and its passengers are improved the longer you are there.

"Guards!"

Harding made the same gesture as Sphink had tried earlier, but it was backed by confidence and a genuine apathy towards the person before him.

Sphink's mouth was still working on a response as he was escorted off the bridge, his terrified eyes reaching out for Hiscock to respond, but finding only a head turned away from him. Treason.

"Avis, how long until interception?"

Avis didn't even need to look at his pad.

"29 hours until interception, 32 hours until the jump-point Sir."

"Right, who is next in command on this bridge?"

"Sir, that would be me" Hart said, still trying to find her feet in the rapid flow of events.

"No, Commodore Hart, you have other duties."

"Sir, it's Captai—"

"Field promotion. Congratulations. Who has the bridge?"

A pause, then Hiscock called out timidly from a corner: "Me, Sir."

Harding's lips pressed together as he weighed multiple factors.

"OK, you've got it, but only on the following conditions: Follow any advice from Rodriguez and Avis. They will save your arse. And you are still tasked with supporting Wave to save our collective arses."

"Sir, do I get a promotion?"

Harding breathed in slowly, and Hart could almost sense him counting slowly under his breath.

"No, Hiscock, not a priority at present. Let's see how you perform getting us out of this mess and working nicely with others.

"Commodore Hart?"

"Sir."

"How are we going to save our collective arses?"

Hart thought for a moment, and turned to Avis.

"That time gap: You're saying they will catch us three hours before we hit the gate?"

"Yes, Sir. We could try alternate routes but they would simply add time before we could jump and that would put us in further danger. I can show you, if you would like?" The hesitation was clear.

"No need."

She thought for a while longer, missing the moment as Avis sat straighter in his chair.

"And we've considered everything that could get the maximum out of our speed?"

"Every possibility has been run through MPOPS. We're at capacity in our current state."

"Who was looking at structural integrity?"

"Brugelson," Harding volunteered with a dead voice.

Hart looked at Harding for details.

"He was checking the externals. He said it was risky, but he thought she would hold together for the jump. He stayed outside to get a clearer understanding."

"Well, let's track him down and get a final report."

Harding nodded his poker-faced approval.

Hart turned her attention to Hiscock. "Have you talked to Wave about speed capacity, Captain?"

The newly appointed Captain let out a snort. "I really don't think there's anything we haven't considered with our years of collective experience with MPOPS."

"Perhaps. Perhaps you are too close."

"Commodore, I really don't think Wave has the right stu—"

"He saved our asses from the Uix. I'd like him to have a look here."

Hiscock conceded eye contact. "Yes, Commodore."

"Commodore, I will leave things with you," Harding said, and strode out of the bridge.

Hart took a deep breath, clearing the jangling stress flowing through her body. And then exhaled, letting all of the poison leave her.

Time to act.

"Hiscock, you have the bridge. I'm off to find Brugelson."

She strode to the exit, fully in command and focused on saving them.

She didn't even notice that someone had cleared the screen of her video image and wiped the file from all system-wide records.

*

CHAPTER 29:
NEVER GIVE UP

Wave was still cowering in front of Storm when the call came through.

"Go ahead, Avis," he said, shifting Robot Storm's head so she was more comfortable.

He couldn't look at Storm. His shame would have torn apart galactic arms.

"Commodore Hart has—"

"Commodore? Wait, what?" The confusion caused him to look up at Storm. She shrugged but gestured for more information.

"Field promotion, Sir. You might also want to know that Captain Sphink has been relieved of duty and confined to quarters for 72 hours," said Avis.

"Pfft. Should have spaced him," Storm muttered.

"Sorry, Wave, I missed that," said Avis.

"I said that is great news for intelligent species everywhere," said Wave. Storm nodded in agreement.

"Indeed. More importantly, the Commodore wants you to check whether we can get to the Columbus jump sooner. Say, about three hours sooner."

"Three hours, huh? I'm assuming you've tried everything in the manual. "

"Affirmative."

Wave's mind started playing with the possibilities — connecting concepts and information. In that moment of intellectual freedom he began running his fingers through Robot Storm's hair, absent-mindedly. "Leave it with me. No promises, mind you..."

"We're just after hope at this stage," Avis said.

"Roger. Out."

He cut the comms and looked back to Storm. There was nothing to do but face the music.

"I have no words," he said, knowing how feeble it sounded. "Except those. And that."

"I can't believe you spent all that time making a… me."

"Actually, this is the second model, and I've improved it in so many ways, like—" He shut up, realising what he had just said.

"I'm…" Storm let the word drift as her thought caught up. "actually really touched."

Wave gave a grin as relieved as it was creepy.

"I've been touched a lot, but this — this is a special kind of touching."

Wave smiled slowly as his mind ticked through a million possibilities, the most notable involving the original and the robot version. "Perhaps we—"

"God no. I'd break you. We don't need that. But here's the deal: You get to keep her, I don't tell anyone, and I get to take her out for weekends. Think of it as shared custody. With benefits."

"Would you clean her after visits? I mean, there's no wrong answer here."

Storm ignored him.

Wave weighed it up. It really was the best of both worlds. There was no more shame, and there would be times when his Storm would come back from being with the original Storm. If only there were weekends ahead to make the deal a real one.

Storm acknowledged the deal and stood up.

"Right, I've got some tactics to work out to try to save our arses."

She stepped towards the door but peered in quickly before it shut.

"I'm so touched by this, I'll probably touch myself when I get back to my quarters." She blew him a kiss before she left.

Wave looked down at Robot Storm and tried to process everything she had said.

The words were burned into his brain. He forced himself to focus on the challenge at hand — hotting up an interstellar sex cruiser. He nodded silently in agreement.

He brushed back Robot Storm's hair. It could probably all wait for ten minutes. Perhaps 15.

*

Commodore? Her epaulettes had changed automatically, signalling Harding's approval on her record. At other times she would have celebrated — at any other time she would have celebrated — but there was too much spinning around in her mind.

She'd called Brugelson on comms but there was no answer. And he wasn't in his quarters. Harding had met him at the airlock, so she was making her way to track him from there.

As she travelled along the corridors she absently nodded at the soft greetings that came her way, but her mind was still back on the bridge.

How dare Sphink try to take her out of the equation? Now, of all times! There was barely more than a day before they faced an over-powered Uix firing squad, with only a shaggy curtain and the luck of misfits to hide them.

On technicalities! And then he moved to blackmail her!

Anger tempted her, but the sweet knowledge of his demise washed it away. None of which was becoming of a Commodore.

Even if it was of a fleet about to die.

She arrived at the airlock — no Brugelson. She checked the logs: Harding and Brugelson heading out and Harding coming back in — but no Brugelson.

If his tanks were full he would be fine, especially with his experience.

"Hey, Rodriguez?"

"Yes Commodore?"

"You really don't have to—"

"Sir, we greatly respect the decision that has been made and have developed a rapid appreciation of rules and regulations. Commodore."

She could see the smile behind the voice.

"Thank you, Rodriguez. Can I ask you to pipe through the airlock visuals between these times," she said, keying them through, "both inside and out? Just trying to clean up some loose ends."

"Of course Sir."

"Thanks, Rodriguez. It's going to be crazy for a couple of days, but let's hold an official party when we get through it. Better yet — an unofficial party."

"Yes, Sir. I'll take that as an order and inform the rest of the bridge crew."

The smile faded as she made her way to medical. A quick pitstop to repair, while she pondered the mystery of Brugelson and everything else happening around her.

Small fractures and blood lost from the accident, but it could be fixed. She sat there as the medbot fixed her hand.

Harding's treatment of Sphink had been cold. Clinical. Not to mention the death threat. And what plans did Harding have for him? Or her, for that matter?

She was used to dealing with her crew. They had developed a shorthand, learning when it was safe to push, and when to let people be. She was developing the same with the bridge crew — an easy understanding that was essential for any battle team. She didn't know their backgrounds in depth — she would remedy that as soon as they survived the jump — but she could see the bonds forming.

But with Harding she was struggling to find that common ground that led to trust. The same could be said of Sphink, but that was because he was a dysfunctional douche. Couldn't be helped, and now there was no need to even try.

But Harding. If she was effectively his second-in-command, that trust should be in place, or developing. She didn't know why it wasn't.

Her comms rang.

"Hart."

"Commodore Hart, Rodriguez here. I'm afraid I am going to have to disappoint you with that request."

"Not a good start, Rodriguez. I'm going to have to sit down and write a stern memo to you if this keeps up. What's the problem?"

"The feed has been 420ing for the past 24 hours."

"420ing?"

"An error code: Technical glitch or hardware error. Happens all the time."

"Erm… is that ironic code?"

"Commodore?"

"You know, like the system's wasted, or something?"

"I'm lost."

"420."

"Yes, Commodore, 420. Wait, has this got something to do with 21 score?"

"How do you know what a score is?"

"Erm, I thought everyone did."

"What? Doesn't matter. Tell me what the 420 was all about."

"Manual records show the unit working perfectly four hours ago."

Hart thought as the machine worked on her hand.

"So we have a camera that's not working, but was. And no recordings for that 24-hour period?" she asked.

"No recording, Sir. There was a technical glitch, so no recording was made. Except for the fact that we made a check on it and it was working."

"Have you followed up on the manual check?"

"Yeah, it was Mau. She is super-dedicated, super knowledgeable. One of the best—"

"Did you check others on her task list?"

"Of course! All good. Records tie in with her movements and actions, and incidental feeds tie in with her movements. I trust her, but there's also proof that she did what she said she did."

The medbot signalled it had completed its work and she flexed her hand. Yep, strong enough to punch Sphink in reality this time, good enough to make the pain count.

As she left the surgery, her mind raced through possibilities.

"Rodriguez, where does Brugelson's tracker place him?"

"Nowhere. It went on the fritz as he was stepping out of the airlock."

"That's unusual..."

"It happens sometimes."

But Brugelson was a born spacer. He kept his equipment in good shape. Odd that it would happen now. Along with his comms. The odds are just too long.

She began to feel that itch that something was wrong. Terribly wrong.

"Thanks, Rodriguez. This stays between me and you for now. Wrap your queries in level 7 encryption. I get the feeling it may be the safest option."

"Absolutely, Commodore. Rodriguez out."

She walked along the corridor back to her quarters, her mind ticking over slowly. She pulled up comms again.

"Storm?"

"Yes, Commodore? I'm touched you still want to talk to this lowly gutter-dweller."

"Why would I stop now?"

"There's plenty of pleasure to be had in the gutter."

"I'll keep that in mind. Right now I need some of your other expertise."

"Fire away."

"Is there any chance we could launch drones from the *Shakespeare* while it's in dry dock? Discreetly."

"Yeah, doable."

"Great, thanks. Be on standby. Mission incoming."

"My puppies will be at your beck and call."

"Roger that, I'm sure. Out."

Somehow thoughts of Markou pushed to the surface. She wanted to see him. What the hell was she thinking? Let herself fall into his arms and live happily ever after? No. No way. He was just doing his job, or something.

Five slow breaths, back to the present. And one more call to make.

*

"Astley, Hart here."

"Captain, yes?"

"I need you to find me a structural engineer. In a hurry."

"What do you mean, hurry?"

"We die in 28 hours unless we find an engineer."

"Onto it, Sir. Out."

*

Astley stared at the crowd in front of him. Approximately 300 passengers preparing to give their professional skills and play their part for the species.

They needed inspiration and trust.

He turned to his source of the same — a glass of red — and began to speak.

"I know you've been frustrated by the way I've approached this, and I'm really sorry. I had my orders," he began.

"You can have a drink on the house if you like, but this really is a business meeting."

"So why do you have a glass of wine?" someone called from the back of the room.

"That's how I do business," he said, and received a few chuckles as a reward.

He paused while a few people ordered drinks, and made small talk while they waited. He was surrounded by a virologist, a veterinarian, a surgeon and a dynamic flow specialist. In the past he would have claimed professional kinship with the latter — they were both interested in keeping the flow dynamic — but now really didn't seem like the best time for what was, admittedly, a fairly feeble joke.

"Right, we'll get started."

He had thought about how he was going to approach this moment but it had fled his memory, leaving him alone with all of these people waiting to hear from him.

He plunged in.

"What have I told you about what is happening?"

The answers came through.

"Industrial accident."

"Meteor shower."

"Special effects being trialled on this cruise."

"Bullshit."

The last one hurt Astley the most. He took a swig from his glass. It was true.

"It's true. I mean, the bullshit one, not the others," he started. "The truth is... Is..."

There was really no way of breaking the news other than an all-out frontal assault.

"Mankind has virtually been destroyed by an alien race and we appear to be the only ship that has survived," he began, and then it flowed.

"We've narrowly avoided being destroyed and now we're making a last-ditch run for the Columbus jump gate in a ship that may break apart in the transition.

"Our combat crew is excellent but hopelessly outmanned and losing resources with every battle.

"We may be the last of humanity — and this may be it."

He finished his glass of wine, poured another.

"Any questions?"

As the babble started he felt the tension in his shoulders release. It was good to no longer have secrets.

"Wait, wait," yelled Huang. "You have been telling us all of these lies and you now expect to have our full trust?"

A chorus of acknowledgement surrounded her.

"Yes, I'm asking for your trust because there's nothing else left. We need that if we're going to have a chance of surviving."

"Young man, there's not even trust left. Where's the Captain? He should be telling us this."

"It's complicated..."

"Then uncomplicate it and build some trust!"

She was beginning to annoy him. Honesty. Best policy.

"I'll level with you. The Captain has been removed to his quarters—"

"What for?"

"I don't have the details in front of me, but it's somewhere in the vicinity of being an arsewipe."

"Now I believe that!" said Huang.

"We have our interstellar Ambassador heading us up as the most senior rank, and he ordered me to avoid telling the truth because he was scared panic would set in. So, whatever you do, don't panic, please. OK?"

Nods and murmurs of agreement.

"Our combat team is headed up by Capta — sorry, just got an update — Commodore Hart. She and her team have saved our arses a number of times, so please always ply her with drinks.

"Any other questions?"

A hand at the back.

"Yeah, what are we here for? Assuming you just wanted to do more than tell us not to panic in the final moments of mankind?"

Astley winced. It seemed so harsh when put that way. But the annoying woman interrupted.

"Slow down, slow down. He may have told us the truth now, but where's the trust? What's going to prevent you from turning on us again?"

Astley nodded, acknowledging the gap he still needed to bridge.

"I have nothing more than honesty to give you from here," he began.

He breathed in heavily, letting the enormity of the moment power him. "You know the rules, and so do I."

No pretence and now no layers. He laid himself bare in front of them. "A full commitment's what I'm thinking of."

He saw approving looks. "You wouldn't get this from any other guy."

He realised he'd overcooked it again. *Honest and simple.* "I just wanna tell you how I'm feeling.

"I'm never gonna give you up."

"That's a good start," said Huang, still in judgement, but open.

"Never gonna let you down," Astley added.

The crowd grimaced at past failings.

Astley pressed on. "Never gonna run around and desert you."

"How can we be sure, with everything that's going on?" yelled someone from the back, ruining his crowd vibe.

Astley sought out eye contact with the man. "Inside we both know what's been going on."

Then he addressed the larger group. "We know the game and we're gonna play it."

The crowd seemed to appreciate this. Being involved. Feeling a part of it all.

"But, like I said, I'm never gonna give you up."

Huang smiled at him, a genuinely warm smile he'd never seen her wear before. It was nice. He took that as a promising sign. It may be a bridge to the future.

He covered up his awkwardness and returned to the tasks at hand.

"Now that we've established that, we need to tap into your skills and knowledge to survive, but we're also going to have to play it quietly so Harding doesn't suspect you all know.

"So I need to know what you can all do to help us out, starting with: are there any structural engineers here tonight?"

Two hands shot up.

"Could you please come with me; we have some urgent work," Astley said.

"And our cover story for command? Does anyone have any ideas?"

*

CHAPTER 30:
PULL THE PIN...

Harding closed the doors to his quarters and the galaxy beyond. He had to block it out — all of it. Some way, somehow, there would be a way to pull the right strings to keep himself alive long enough to make the jump, long enough to survive.

Best case, they engineer a way to beat the Uix to the gate, but that was wasted energy for him to think about. The play he had to take care of was one where all the worst-case scenarios combined. How would one negotiate an exchange with the Uix? Who would do it? Where would it go down? What redundancies could be put in place to failsafe each step of the way?

Every angle, every conceivable possibility. Everything.

Oh, and where, when and how to kill the Uix before it could communicate with its kind that he was alive and aboard.

He sipped scotch. He schemed.

*

The chirp of her communicator sucked Hart out of whatever deep recess of her mind the power nap had taken her to. She couldn't remember anything about her sleep except the warp-speed-like tunnel she was sucked through to be back in her bed, with thoughts full of the end of days.

It felt like one seamless move out of the dream tunnel to reality with her hand on the communicator. "Hart."

"Two structural engineers, as requested. McLeod and Zielinski. We're on route to the airlock."

"Roger that. I'll ping the schematics through on the other side of this call. And will join you shortly."

"Affirmative, Commodore."

"Oh, and Astley."

"Yes?"

"Tell them to keep an eye out for anything… unusual."

"Unusual?"

"Just… anything out of place, anything not quite right."

There was a brief pause at the other end of comms. "Affirmative, will do."

"Oh, and Astley."

"Yes?"

"Well done."

There was a brief pause on Astley's end of the line. "Thank you, Commodore."

She put the device down and sat on the side of the bed, letting thoughts wash over her as she reoriented herself to the enormity of what lay ahead. She looked at her new pips and felt the weight of their rank — the weight of expectation.

She thought about the lightshow tunnel that had sucked her back to reality. Why was she thinking about that? Did something happen there? It must have, she felt it. Her conscious thought was telling her to seek out another thought. Some idea, some concept, some firing of neurons executed by her subconscious in the right order to reveal a truth.

A truth about Harding.

*

"Flicker, you there?"

It was really difficult to concentrate on your hangover, your addiction and the first recollections of the aftermath of a wild sex romp — actually, it may have been a loving, intimate moment, which was a whole nother weird when you still laid in the middle of the evidence and someone flagged you on comms.

"Repeat: Flicker, come in. Flicker, you there?"

In one convergent moment, Flicker prized his eyes open, took in the scene, remembered enough about his night with George to know his world had changed, felt his head pulse in dehydrated pain, combined with a Jonesing for Reality, all while his eardrums were assaulted by Hart's annoyingly determined voice. Seriously, how dare she?

He reached for his hydration line, but couldn't find it in the mangle of sheets and robot limbs and dildos and stains and lube and … was that a cucumber? A zucchini. Seriously? A freaking zucchini. At least the scene confirmed it was, in fact, the aftermath of a loving, intimate type of encounter. "What?"

"And good mor… afternoon to you too."

Long pause. "What do you want?"

Hart smiled at how grounded her crew made her feel. "Something's come up… it's big."

Flicker tossed the zucchini aside. "And?"

"Look, I need you to assemble the crew. I'll meet you all in 45… on board the *Shakespeare*. Be discreet — no one can know about this. Understand? Oh, and here's the tricky bit. I need you to track down George — if he's not with Harding. And get him to tag along too. What I said about discreet goes double for this bit."

Flicker gulped. He felt said gulp was so loud Hart completely picked it up on the audio feed. Then he turned to see George smiling back at him — doe eyed. "Do we really need—"

"I know it's a big ask, but if you can pull it off… look, big plays are happening. Just come through for me, huh?"

"Roger that. I'll do my best."

Comms ended with more haste than they began. Flicker turned his attention to George, the scene and his morning-after-the-night-before problems. "Soooooooooooooowa."

More doe-eyed stares.

It was all too much to focus on this morning. Best stick to the task at hand. "Did you catch any of that?"

"Affirmative."

"Harding won't miss you for a while longer then?"

"Unsure, but I have had no dialogue with him for several hours."

"So, shall I pencil you in then?" said Flicker.

Even as he did, the awkwardness of the unaddressed situation hit home. So much had happened, so much had changed. Making another arrangement right now — one totally removed from any sensual zucchini connection, well, it was all too much. George's "Affirmative" response — in what Flicker now imagined was a sensual tone he'd never heard from the robot before — drifted off into silence.

Then it was the silence that became too much. Flicker went to speak. He stopped when George started speaking at the same time. This was followed by another bout of silence. Flicker went to speak again, then second-guessed his train of thought before it was crafted into words. Instead, he turned his attention to getting dressed, scanning his quarters to establish the quickest path to access all his clothes currently scattered throughout the space. He started with a dash to the drawer for fresh underwear.

"Thank you for last night," said George, eventually.

"You don't need to thank me."

"I do, Sir. What we did was quite important to me."

Flicker had reached his pants by this point, splayed across the kitchenette counter. He examined them for cleanliness. In detail. It was a far safer task than making eye contact. "Please don't call me Sir."

"Of course, Sir. Habit."

Flicker's eye test approved the state of his pants and he put them on, still facing away.

"Is everything OK, Sir?"

Attention turned to his shirt. Definitely a new one was required from the cupboard. This was a super important thing to concentrate all of his energy on. "What? Yeah, of course. Totally."

"It is my understanding that it is quite common for humans to experience sensations of guilt and regret after performing acts like we did last night, Sir."

What was the best shirt to wear? This would take some serious concentration. In fact, there was a fair chance he would need to devote all of his emotional energy to shirt selection — it was just that important.

"If that's the case Sir, I will not be offended."

Too bright. Too patterny. Too dull. Not patterny enough. Why were all of his shirts just so wrong? He could feel robot eyes locked on him.

"I just want to say, it was an important moment for me. One that was many years of conflict, doubt and fear of judgement in the making."

Horizontal stripes! Flicker cursed himself in silence for ever thinking that was an OK purchase.

"It was also, I'd like to believe, the start of a new me."

What about a nice polo? He could wear a nice polo today. When was the last time he wore a nice polo?

"You made that happen, Sir. Last night changed everything for me."

Then he saw it, the nice safe uniform of the *William Shakespeare*. It just spoke to him.

"So, thank you, Sir."

Flicker turned to face George. "Look, can we maybe just concentrate on, say, getting discreetly to this meeting."

The robot stared at him in silence.

"I have a few calls to make. Perhaps we could meet somewhere near the docking bay — say that supply corridor — in, what, 30 minutes."

George processed. "As you wish, Sir." He got up to leave.

Something in George's body language hit Flicker in an unexpected way. "Wait, George."

The robot stopped just short of the door and turned to face Flicker once more.

"The thing is… and if I'm honest… the thing is… well… I… I had a good night too. It was a big moment for me too. I just.. I just need some time… to think… you know."

"Affirmative, Sir. And thank you."

George turned to the door.

"Hey, before you go, does Harding know?"

George turned again. "I have been trying to tell him for many years, but I know he'll never understand. I know he does not have the capacity… the empathy perhaps."

Flicker nodded.

"So, instead, I try to act as… I believe the word is camp… as I can around him. He still has no idea but it gives me fulfilment."

Flicker laughed. "I respect that."

George paused on the moment. "Me too," he said, before making his final turn for the door.

*

Hart made pace as best she could over the debris covering the C-Deck floor. At the far side of the space, Astley waited by the airlock, in comms dialogue with McLeod and Zielinski, no doubt.

"Astley. Anything?"

He turned his attention to her. "Commodore. The damage is pretty bad, but they both think we're more than likely to survive a jump."

They both looked at the two visual feeds coming from the damage outside.

"More than likely?"

"Well, they're prepared to jump rather than hang around here, so I guess that level of confidence."

"Excellent. And anything unusual?"

Astley hesitated.

"What is it?"

"Well, not sure what you mean by unusual, but we did find, well, something."

"Yes?"

Astley indicated she should follow and headed towards the nearby airlock prep booths. "Not sure if it's the sort of unusual you mean, but Zielinski saw it when she was getting suited up."

Hart was hit by a sudden cold feeling. She'd had thoughts, asked questions and now she was heading towards something that may, potentially, make it all real and tangible. She felt uneasy and focused on keeping her poker face.

"I mean, it's probably nothing," said Astley as they neared one of the suit stations.

Hart's eyes roamed over everything, trying to anticipate what might be out of place or different — she didn't see anything.

Astley reached station two, where Zielinski's civvies were hung in place of the spacesuit.

"What am I missing?" said Hart.

"Well, when she opened the hatch," said Astley, as he toyed with the release mechanism a couple of times before success. "...she saw this."

Again, Astley struggled with the equipment, but after a false start, he had the aircord unravelling in his direction. He lifted the end of the line to eye level between them.

"Where's the connector?"

"That's what Zielinski said."

Hart took hold of the chord to examine it closer. "Wait, does that look like it's been cut to you?"

"Then she said that."

After observing it from a number of different angles, Hart ran her finger over the end, feeling the texture of the chord on her fingers. "Fuck," she whispered.

"Was that good unusual?"

"What? Yeah. Good unusual. Astley, I need you to not tell a soul about this, understand?"

Her comms twittered at her. Storm's words flashed at her: "I'm back." Hart flicked an acknowledgement that she was on her way.

"Got to go. Astley, no-one, you tell no-one, got it?" she said and started to run towards the exit.

"Yes, I mean, affirmative," Astley spluttered.

Hart turned with one last thought.

"Same with the civilians when they get back. Tell them... tell them whatever really, as long as this information doesn't leave you, me and them. The future of the ship depends on it, understand?"

"OK. Why don't you tell them yourself before we go and talk to the rest of the crew I've selected."

"No time, I've got to go."

"What? But you said—"

"Things have changed."

"I've told them you're coming to see them."

"The minutes are ticking Astley, time is everything."

"I've only just got their trust … I've promised them someone with clout and authority."

"What if I send..." said Hart, searching for an on-the-fly solution. None presented. "Fine. Get your crew cleaned up and ready to report. Gather the civilians and ping me when you're ready."

"Roger."

"Make sure it's all ready. I'll give them five minutes. Understood?"

"Roger."

*

The ship felt different as Hart traversed the levels and corridors to the docking bay. It wasn't just the vulnerability now laid bare by the destruction, nor the clock, that fucking ticking clock. It was the knowledge of danger that lurked within her walls, within humanity. Those corridors suddenly claustrophobic, the lifts like cages she was trapped within.

Harding had killed Brugelson.

Why?

Then he'd stripped Sphink of his power and promoted her.

Why?

Everything had changed. Nowhere was safe.

Except the *William Shakespeare*. As she entered the docking bay, awash with activity, *The Shakespeare* shone like a dull, beaten-up beacon of home. In a moment she realised how much she'd missed Will. Life was simpler there. Life was safer.

She checked there were no eyes on her as she made the short dash from the service corridor to the *Shakespeare's* loading ramp. Once inside, she climbed the ladder to the maintenance room, then headed through the bunks in the sleeping quarters. That's when she heard the crew talking — Wave saying something before getting interrupted by Storm, who in turn was interrupted by Flicker. A tear came to her eye in that moment. Her crew. If the Will was home, it was an empty one without her crew.

She paused to listen and collect herself for a few moments longer in the supplies and munitions room. Just one last chance to be a fly on the wall at home. One last chance before she stepped through the door to the bridge and threw a grenade into everything.

This was it.

This was the start of the end.

*

CHAPTER 31:
...anD DROP IT In

"...I don't think he's any better than Sphink," said Wave, in summary to his long monologue about the failings of the new man at the helm of the *Milky Pleasure*.

Storm looked at Flicker. "Is someone getting a little jealous?"

"Looks like it to me," Flicker confirmed.

"I'm not jealous of that flog."

Storm studied him. "Are you sure, because that tone sounded very… what's the word I'm looking for?"

"Jealous?" offered Flicker.

Storm nodded in thoughtful agreement. "Yes, that's the word. Jealous."

"Piss off you two. I don't give a shit what title he has, I'm saying he's not the dude you want sitting where all the important buttons are."

"Right," said Flicker and Storm over several sarcastic seconds.

"He's a tosser of the highest order," said a betrayed Wave. "And he's not an engineer's asshole."

"What defines an engineer's asshole?" Flicker asked Storm.

She shrugged. "Tight, I guess, knowing Hiscock."

Wave's mind turned briefly to the Goliath and how wrong Storm potentially was before he refocused. "Look, I'm telling you he's as much of a company-man rule-Nazi as the douchebag who's place he took. Shit's about to hit the fan and that is seriously not good for us."

Silence filled the cockpit for several seconds.

"We've got bigger things to worry about than rulebook Nazis," said Hart, as she made her entrance.

She then went on to wipe her brow and apologise for being late. It was a statement she never finished after finally noticing her crew in a salute so full, yet so mocking. "Really?"

"Yes Grand Admiral, Fourth Dan, Queen Bee, Overlord Hart," said Storm.

Flicker and Wave held in a laugh but maintained their salute. In the corner, George sat quietly.

Hart smiled. "Alright, enough. Don't make me find another crew of dysfunctional freaks to help me try to save humanity with. I was starting to like you lot."

"Let us have our moment," said Wave. "We practised this for, like, minutes."

Hart rolled her eyes. She spotted George and nodded to Flicker. "Well done."

Flicker absently adjusted his sock, suddenly feeling the choke of guilt wash over him.

Fortunately, Hart didn't analyse the moment as long as he did. "Will, you online?"

"Like the morning rays doth reclaim thine being from the darkness, my soul is, indeed, present."

"Excelle—"

"...Lightened, as it were, by the soothing serenade of the utterings from the newly crowned Commodore. Long live the Commodore."

"Indeed," said Hart, while rolling her eyes. She turned her attention to Storm. "How did you go?"

"We're on. With a bit of help from this lot we've smuggled three drones out through the service airlock at the aft of the docking bay. They're online and at your service."

"And no one saw you?"

"Nope."

Hart held her look on Storm for reassurance.

"I can be deft and subtle, thank you very much."

"I'm sure," said Hart, with a smile.

"So, you going to tell us what the fuck is going on?"

"I just want to test a little theory. George, can I have an assurance that whatever unfolds here over the next few minutes will be taken in trust. Humanity may depend on your word and your presence here definitely does."

"Affirmative, Commodore."

"Excellent. Wave, can you ping Brugelson's bio-signals."

"OK," he said, over several curious seconds as he interfaced with the nav display. "What's Brugelson done?"

Hart let her answer ferment while the crew looked at the lights of the nav systems display a virtual replication of the *Milky Pleasure*. They waited for a ping pin.

As the seconds passed, the gravity of the possibilities started to weigh on them.

"That's strange," said Wave. "Should've seen something by now."

"Has he gone off grid?" said Flicker. "What's he up to?"

"I don't believe so."

They looked at Hart.

"...unless off grid is code for no longer alive."

"Brugelson's dead?" said Storm, with a level of shock that represented the shock of the others.

As she did a locator pin bleeped into virtual existence at the far end of the bridge.

"What the actual?" said Wave, as he turned to see Brugelson's location marker several hundred kilometres from the ship.

"How?" said Flicker.

"Focus, people." Hart turned to Storm. "Direct your drones to that location."

"Affirmative, Commodore," she said, as she began her choreography with the control interface.

"No vitals," added Wave, from the data pouring in.

"Shit," said Hart, feeling her heart flex like a fist at the reality being confirmed.

"ETA two minutes, 12 seconds," said Storm.

Flicker went to share his displeasure at not being in the loop on crew mate disappearances, but a look from Hart counselled him that was not a good idea. Instead, all remained silent on the bridge, aside from the occasional distance and time updates from Storm.

All eyes were fixed to the displays. Soon the ping markers gave way to visual feeds of Brugelson. A distant dot soon took on a more human shape. It was deadly still and, while each of the humans on the bridge were searching their minds for any plausible circumstance in which reason Brugelson could still be alive, they were all reminded of retrieving Connor's body near Jupiter. How they could've used Connor's experience now. Brugelson's too.

The feed line stretched back towards the drones.

"Storm... or Will... can you get me a close-up on the end of that feed line?"

"Affirmative," said Storm. She made a couple of hand gestures to manipulate the visual and soon had a zoomed-in image snapped as still. She flicked the virtual snap across the bridge to her Captain, but they all examined it.

"Anyone else here think that's been cut? As in, by a blade," asked Hart.

"It sure looks that way to me," agreed Storm.

"Not necessarily," said Wave. "I mean, it looks like that to me, but you've seen the damage to the *Pleasure*. He could've gotten really unlucky on some jagged debris or something."

Hart pondered the words as she watched the body start to come into closer view. "Maybe. He still would've had a couple of minutes of supply though. He didn't follow any of the normal protocols if he was out there alone."

As if mirroring memories of the Connor moment further, the drone had to circle the body to get a view of Brugelson's face. His expression was one of peace and acceptance.

"Wait, what was that?" said Wave.

The others looked at the scene, none the wiser, then at him.

"Zoom in on his visor. I see something."

Once again Storm used a series of hand gestures to manipulate the feed as required. Once she was happy, she snapped the visual and slid it across the virtual space in the bridge towards Hart.

"Oh shit," said Hart as she looked at the still.

Storm had found an angle where the light caught the edge of some scratches in Brugelson's visor. They were letters, marked backwards to read forwards.

H.

A.

R.

D.

I.

The knifeline slipped, ending the last word of a dying man. A dying man naming his killer.

"Oh shit," said Hart again.

*

Hiscock eased back in the Captain's chair on the bridge of the *Milky Pleasure*. Despite his best efforts, he still couldn't find the right angle or alignment to feel comfortable in its deep leather embrace. He didn't know if that was a comment on the chair or him and felt it best to ignore the problem altogether.

In front of him, all seemed functional. His crew went about their work. Nothing was at the level to require his intervention. He watched MPOPS' feeds from the ship repairs — all the numbers looked on track to be jump ready when they hit the gate. He'd even managed to divert a few more resources to the remains of the fleet in the docking bay. Maybe they could have an extra ship or two ready by the time they were intercepted by the Uix — if it came to that. Would it make a difference? Probably not.

All of which was a sidetrack from the real story. On the virtual heads-up display beaming out over the bridge in front of the view was telemetry data of their course to the jump gate. Speeds, distance remaining, Uix intercept time and location. It was the sort of quantifiable data an engineer could wrap his being around, especially in a reality where there was not much more to do than wait for fate to play out.

There was one other number that didn't need an engineer's understanding to wrap one's head around, however. It was the number he was trying his hardest to not look at or notice it all, really. Yet it was impossible to look away from. He watched as the seconds on the jump gate ETA clicked down to 24 hours. Mars hours were slightly longer than Earth's, but regardless, the result was the same. Cunningly simple, deviously tangible. One day. Well, one Mars day — one Sol — remained.

He shuffled in his seat again. He felt the din of activity around him drop in those seconds, his eyes a prisoner to the monumental tick of the clock. He knew everyone was watching the same number, feeling the same thing. He didn't know whether to acknowledge the moment for his crew. He didn't know what to say if he did. Stupid uncomfortable Captain's seat. Stupid time.

He looked around for something to take his mind off waiting, inadequacy and chairs. Sphink's clipboard was the thing that caught his eye. He picked it up, pausing for a second, before allowing himself the right to open it.

The first page was blank, save for the handwritten title — *List of Civilians Capable of Assisting our Preparation for Defence of the Milky Pleasure (First round candidates).*

The next four pages, entitled *Achievable Career Medals and Honours,* was full of detailed notes and progress markers for Sphink's career advancement. Hiscock rolled his eyes. It was followed by several pages entitled *Dirt and Insurance Strategies for Senior Crew*.

He cleared his throat as he searched the pages for his name, a sudden clamminess in his hands. There was tomes of information on Harding, more again on Hart. Brugelson had a page of notes dedicated to him, as did the other members of the *William Shakespeare*. There was also a section dedicated to Connor, now crossed out in red ink. On the last page, after the scattered notes about some of the senior entertainment officers, head chef and docking bay sergeant, he found his name.

He shuffled in his chair again, gave his throat another clearing cough, then read the short note.

Hiscock: Predictable dullard, laughable leadership capacity, thoroughly manipulatable. Threat level: 0. Seek to promote.

He felt himself blushing. It was a mix of anger and betrayal, heightened by the raw nerve truth the few words bestowed upon him exposed. That's how he was thought of? He shuffled in the Captain's chair once more as he ruminated on the words and on himself.

He looked up, somehow expecting judging eyes on him from those on the bridge. There were none. They were going about their business beneath the countdown clock. He looked at his new Captain's insignia. It was not quite sitting right on his chest. He didn't know if that was the angle he was viewing it from or a metaphor.

What would Connor have done at a time like this? Hart?

He thought some more as he toyed with the badge.

Laughable leadership capacity. It wasn't laughable, it just hadn't been... nurtured yet. Given humanity was on the brink of extinction and he found himself in the Captain's chair, this was probably as good a time as any to do some of that nurturing. He tried to think of how he could do leadership things but the countdown clock was really starting to distract him. What would Connor do? Something totally leadery, no doubt.

Ahh, stupid clock.

What empathetic thing could he use to motivate and align — he was sure that was a word leadership people used — his crew right now? The clock. Yes, that was it. The clock! If it was weighing over him, it would be doing the same to others on the bridge. That was totally the sort of thing Connor would say and leave you feeling instantly, well, safer. It was also the type of thing Sphink would never say, which also made it feel like a good idea.

Before he said something though, he'd have to think of how he'd talk as a leader. I mean, he could use his normal voice, but that didn't feel very inspiring. Maybe he should dabble with a bit of a tone shift that had a little more authority to it? Nothing dominating, just enough to provide some comfort to his crew that he had the situation under control. I mean, obviously he didn't, but even just the sense that he might *think* he did might be somewhat comforting.

Anyway, just something small to start with. A few comforting words said in an equally comforting tone, just to let the crew know he was on their side, unlike the previous administration. And it was totally topical, given the 24-hour mark had just elapsed. Shit! 23 hours and 11 minutes! How had 39 minutes elapsed? Now destruction was an Earth day left. What an idiot. What a self-indulgent, underprepared and underskilled twat.

He took a few deep breaths to try to settle his nerves. It wasn't working. Why wasn't it working? Shit, 23 hours 8 minutes! OK, just say it.

"I know you've seen it coming closer, but try not to be too daunted by the cock."

There was a suffocating moment of shocked and judgemental silence as the crew pondered his words and Hiscock pondered his critical omission of the letter L. The comforting smile he had settled into after his statement was not helping the situation. He was stuck in the moment, paralysed. He could not think of a thing to do or say to break the mouth-agape stares from his entire crew. He needed something. He needed a miracle.

A communication sounded out over the bridge. "Hiscock."

It was Harding, spoken with all the disdain to be expected by Harding. In that moment it was sweet relief.

"Yes, Sir."

"Meet me in the War Room. Stat."

"Yes, Sir."

"Oh, and you can leave your cock talk on the bridge."

"Yes, Sir."

*

"This is bad," said Wave, pacing the small section of bridge he could call his own.

"You think?" responded Flicker, pleased with his level of sarcasm.

"Fucking Harding," added Storm. "I always hated the arrogant cockbreath."

Their words collectively fell short of both the enormity of the situation and a direction to tackle it. Once silence claimed the bridge, all eyes settled on Hart.

She was lost in thought, the permutations and ethics of countless paths forward from this moment temporarily paralysing her.

Storm completely unsubtly cleared her throat. "Commodore?"

She repeated Hart's title a couple more times before the words sank in.

"Yes," said Hart, absently.

"What are we going to do about the... you know…"

When no response came, she continued. "...little bit murdery Ambassador?"

"Yeah," agreed Flicker. "And the little bit genocidey aliens."

"And the little bit dysfunctionally *Milky Pleasure* command," added Wave in the newly established format.

Hart's mouth opened, but it didn't help encourage her thoughts into meaningful words. Any words, actually.

It only encouraged Storm to continue the questioning. "...with a starship that's a door slam away from disintegrating?"

"And a battleship that doesn't actually work?" added Flicker.

Wave stopped pacing. "...and just the four of us."

"Ahem."

"Sorry, Will. The four of us and Will."

"Ahem."

"Sorry, George. The four of us and Will and George."

Again Hart felt all eyes upon her. She turned to face each of the group in turn — eyes pleading for a path to hope. She'd seen the look before, many times — the crew serving Sphink on the bridge, the passengers. Now, in the clarity of the moment, her mind started connecting things where before she could only see mounting problems. She started to feel it. A direction.

"It's not just us, it's everyone."

Her crew watched on. Pondering her abstract words.

"George, we have your assurance on secrecy?"

"Affirmative, Commander."

"Everything we plan depends on it."

"I would not betray you, even before the new information was revealed," the robot said. He shifted his eye contact from Hart to the rest of the crew, finishing on Flicker. "Any of you. You are my tribe."

"Good to know," said Hart with a smile. "Right, we've got 20 hours until the Uix intercept, 23 until we reach the gate."

"Unless we can sort something out to push us along," said Wave, with a wink.

"Affirmative. That's where you'll be needed."

Wave nodded.

"I'll need you on the bridge of the *Milky Pleasure*..."

Wave sighed.

"...working with Hiscock..."

And again.

"... that's our golden ticket out of this. If it doesn't work, your eyes and ears on the bridge could still come in handy. Anything from Harding — anything — report back. Understand?"

"Yes, Sir."

"Before that, we need to work out why Harding killed Brugelson, what that means for the rendezvous and what we can do about it."

Her crew looked on, ready for instructions.

She studied them, letting all the information percolate into a plan.

"George, when was the last time you saw Brugelson?"

"In the docking bay, Commodore. 17 hours ago."

Hart shared looks with the others. "With Harding?"

"Affirmative."

"What were they talking about? Anything you can relay might be important."

"He sent Brugelson to communicate with the Uix."

*

Hiscock paused at the door of the war room. It was open and he could see Harding seated inside, pouring over the information on the data displays on the table in front of him, but he knocked anyway.

"Enter," said Harding as he closed the information on the screens, then looked up at Hiscock expectantly.

"You wanted to see me?"

Harding pointed Hiscock to a seat. "Indeed. How are things on the bridge?"

Hiscock thoughts distracted to the crooked badge on his chest, but he resisted the temptation to play with it. He cleared his throat. "Good, Sir. Quiet."

"Apart from lurid references to your member, of course."

Hiscock remained silent.

"The mood, apart from the disgust?"

"Apprehensive, I guess."

"How are you dealing with that?"

Hiscock went to speak but made no headway after the words "I was…"

Harding sighed in the key of disappointment. "Just deal with it."

It was at this point Hiscock knew he was lost, his eyes not playing poker in the moment.

"I'm not your mum, Hiscock. You're the Captain, sort your crew out."

Hiscock nodded at the floor.

"Enough of the pleasantries," said Harding, as he poured himself a scotch.

Again, Hiscock spent his energies resisting an adjustment of his badge. He didn't know where to look, until he felt the avoidable reality that Harding was staring at him. He fell, reluctantly, into it.

"Let's take it as read that you'll satisfactorily attend to the entry-level captaincy demands mentioned and put a limit of penis mentions to your crew. We need to discuss what may happen when shit hits the fan."

An already out of depth Hiscock felt the blood drain from his face.

"Because it is going to hit the fan. And you're the one wearing the badge. So I need you to… be better than this."

"I…"

"Now's a time for listening, Hiscock. Understand?"

Hiscock nodded, no longer able to resist the urge to adjust his badge.

"I need your complete understanding on what I'm about to say."

Hiscock nodded.

"You will hear a lot of things. You will hear plans and directions — from me to others — between now and when shit goes down. You will hear talk from others — contradicting opinions, from loud voices. You will hear panic. Just, know this. Whatever I say is right, understand?"

Hiscock nodded again.

"Even if it contradicts things I've said before."

Harding paused until he got another nod.

"Don't second-guess me, don't question me, don't think. I am in charge."

Harding pointed to his chest to make his next point. "That's what this badge means. Yours means you obey."

Hiscock nodded once more.

"You don't know what I know. Nor am I expecting you to. All I'm expecting from you is to do your job and follow the chain of command, whatever the circumstances. And get your people to follow with you. Do you think you can muster that up?"

"Yes, Sir."

"Good, because I don't need to tell you what's at stake."

Hiscock was unsure how to react to the statement. Harding saved him the awkwardness by providing an entirely different one.

"What are you still doing here? Go be a Captain."

Hiscock scurried from the scene as fast as he could while trying, unsuccessfully, to look like he was scurrying from the scene as fast as possible.

Harding enabled his monitors again and took in the data with a deep sigh.

"Where's George?"

*

CHAPTER 32:
ILL WILL

It was chaos on the bridge of the *William Shakespeare* as Flicker, Storm and Wave talked over the top of each other with theories, questions, reasons, accusations and expletives. Harding had taken Brugelson to the Uix shortly before he killed him, while humanity needed every bit of help it could to survive to the jump.

Hart buried her head in her hands while she tried to focus her thoughts over the din of her crew. "Alright! Enough! We don't have time for this shit. Focus." Her pitch and volume were more effective than her words.

Once all was quiet, she turned to George. "So, you accompanied Harding and Brugelson to the docking bay. Brugelson suited up and made contact with it—"

"Harding is such an asshole."

Hart gave Storm a glare for her interruption. Storm responded with a silent but petulant gesture Hart ignored, her focus already back on George. "Approximately 37 minutes later, Brugelson pings Harding on Comms saying, 'Sir, they remember everything.'"

"That is correct."

"What does that mean — everything?" said Wave.

George looked at Hart, who nodded permission for him to respond.

"Their hive intelligence has a capacity we can't begin to fathom, but from observations, everything appears to be literally that. Everything that has happened, anything any one of their species has observed, is understood by the collective."

Wave pondered this for a moment. "But Brugelson's mate in the docking bay was off the grid — out from the hive."

Once again, George looked to Hart for permission before responding. "From current understanding, until its thoughts connect with the greater Uix knowledge matrix, its experiences are not shared. It appears to be able to source a substantial amount of information from their collective intelligence. We can only assume that it is stored locally. However, relying on observations to this point we deduct it cannot share its experiences to the collective, presumably until they are reunited."

"What exactly do you mean by reunited?"

Everyone looked at Wave.

"Well, do its experiences upload to the hive intelligence when it touches another Uix? Sees another Uix? Is linked into some grid network that we don't have the slightest idea about the reach and capacity of?"

While everyone poured over the statement, no one spoke.

"Anyway, seems a bit important."

Again, the conversation momentum slowed to a halt.

"Anyway, once Harding hears Brugelson's observation he says, 'Yes, I know,'" said Hart, seeking confirmation from George with her expression. "Brugelson then adds something about 'remembering you' to Harding."

"His actual words were, 'And they remember... you. And what you... offered... them.'"

"Which is in reference to Harding's direct negotiations with the Uix a few months back," continued Hart. "Once Harding hears that he says 'That changes everything.'"

She looked at her crew in turn, letting her focus fall on George. "So, what was the offer?"

"Yep, that'd tell us a lot," said Storm.

"I do not have this information."

"Wait, you just recalled a conversation from days ago word-for-word," said Wave. "You're like Uix-lite with your bot brain. As if you can't remember what seems like a super important moment in, you know, humanity and everything."

"I was not present."

"How convenient!" said Wave.

"Shut it Wave, he's trying to help," said Flicker, before a sudden flush of self-awareness.

George was unsure what to say next. After a nod of appreciation to Flicker, he focused on Hart.

"Maybe it was convenient," she said. "Maybe not having George there was important in making this offer."

The room fell silent for a moment as everyone pondered the information.

"Was that unusual? Him not taking his mech to such a big moment?" asked Storm.

"It's not common, but it wasn't in breach of any directive or procedure," said George.

Wave stood up and began pacing the bridge, in thought. "Wait, isn't there a coupling protocol between Ambassadors and robots? Shouldn't you be able to get a feed from that? In theory you should be able to pull audio feeds at the very least."

"The Ambassador deactivated the coupling."

"Fucker!" said Storm.

Hart stared at her.

"What? He is a fucker. He knew he was doing something dodgy so he hid the evidence."

Hart turned her focus back to George. "Is that normal?"

"It is not normal for an Ambassador, but it is not unusual for Harding."

"See, fucker!"

"Hmmm. Has he deactivated the coupling recently?" said Hart.

"Affirmative."

"Since that last communication with Brugelson?"

"Affirmative."

"Fucker!"

"Storm, please," said Hart, before a deep exhale to think. "So, Harding finds out Brugelson knows about what went down with the Uix and the last thing he says to him is 'That changes everything.'"

George nodded.

"Do you have any ideas of Harding's movements after that?"

"Do I get a prize for being first to suggest he disabled his coupling protocol?" said Wave.

"He disabled the coupling protocol," said George.

"Fucker," said Storm.

Wave stopped his pacing and took a bow.

"So, basically, he's covered all his tracks and we've got no idea what he's done, why or what he might be planning next?" said Flicker.

"Translation: Fucker," said Storm, unnecessarily.

"We do know he killed Brugelson," added Wave.

"Well, we'd better work it out pretty quickly," said Hart. "Right now he seems as big a threat to humanity as the Uix and if shit goes down and we don't know what he's planning and why, shit is really going to hit the fan."

"It'll be hitting two fans," said Storm.

Silence befell the bridge once more as everyone processed the problem.

Except Storm. "Because two fans would totally scatter the shit into really fine faecal particles. Like, that shit would get everywhere."

More silence.

"It would be like confetti."

More silence.

"But poo."

More silence.

"Poofetti."

This was followed by an even longer silence, observed by all on the bridge as they searched for the next move. While the silence included Storm, she spent her time trying to find a catchier term than poofetti. She failed.

Hart's communicator tweeped into life. It was Rick Astley.

"Commodore." He bowed unnecessarily.

"What is it?"

"I have assembled the civilians as requested. We await your presence at the..." he looked away from the transmission, "What is this shithole?" Then nodded and turned back to his communication. "The Duck and Cover. We await your, yeah, presence."

Hart sighed and did a sterling job ensuring the expletives remained under her breath. "I'll be there as soon as I can."

Astley gave her a double thumbs up and a chipper grin that forced her to kill the call.

"Thanks Commodore, someone needed to cut him off," said Storm. "I did some of my best work at the Duck and Cover, I won't hear a bad word about it."

Hart ignored her.

"So, what's the plan?" said Flicker.

Hart cleared her throat. "Well, if we can't find anything on Harding directly, we're going to have to get as close as we can to—"

"There is a way, you know," said Wave.

They all looked at him expectantly.

"But you're probably not going to like it."

"Unless you want a throat punch, hurry the fuck up and tell us!" said Storm.

Wave winced in imagined pain with a small inkling of pleasure for a second. "One of us has to talk to the Uix."

Another silence fell over the group. First of comprehension, then at the brutal truth of Wave's words. They all knew there was no avoiding it. Attention turned to Hart.

She nodded several times as she processed. "*I* have to speak to the Uix."

She stood up, the others following her lead. "If we're going to do this we have to be discreet, understand?"

Her crew gave her a round of agreement.

"Harding cannot know I'm doing this. Wave, I want you on deck with Hiscock. Work on your hack to shorten the travel time and have eyes on everything that happens on the bridge of the *Milky Pleasure*."

"Yes, Commodore."

"Any updates or anything unusual, let me know."

"Of course."

"But, discreetly."

"Understood."

"Storm, Flicker and George, you're heading with me to the Duck and Cover. We're going to meet with the civilians, then pay a visit to our genocidal friend from another world."

"Why waste time with the civvies?" said Flicker.

"I have something in mind that I think will help us."

Flicker shared a look with Storm and raised an eyebrow. "Yes, Commodore."

"Meanwhile, Will, I need you to have yourself void-worthy, like, yesterday. Ping us updates."

"I fall into your commands for my hastened rebirth like a pillow of the finest of feathers. Pleasure and action shall make the hours seem short until we are as one again."

"Indeed." Hart smiled. "Alright everyone, it's time. Stay sharp, stay in touch, keep eyes on everything. We've got an idea of what we're dealing with and who we can trust. We can't—"

George's communicator pinged into life.

"Yes, Sir," said the robot. "I'm with Hart and crew helping prepare the *Will Shakespeare* for flight capabilities, Sir."

He looked at the others as he listened to the voice on the other end. "No one did, Sir. I was being proactive, as you have often instructed.

"Yes, Sir.

"Yes, Sir. Right away Sir."

He looked at Hart once the communication was complete. "It's Harding. I am required in the War Room."

"Shit," said Wave.

"Do you think he's onto us?" said Flicker.

"Fucker," said Storm.

"Unknown," said George.

"We can use this," said Hart. "Flicker, go with him. See if you can't make yourself useful and get eyes and ears on. If not, make your way to the Duck and Cover."

"Yes, Commodore."

"George, I don't need to remind you what's on the line."

"I have full cognition of the situation and, where possible, will be your eyes and ears."

"Excellent."

"You will not be betrayed."

"Good to know," said Hart. "Right then. I guess this is it. Crew of the *Will Shakespeare*, fall out."

*

CHAPTER 33:
THE EAGLE SUFFERS LITTLE BIRDS TO SING

Markou saw Hart's name notification appear on his communicator and took a moment to adjust his hair before answering. "Commodore."

"What you doing?"

"Just running through the Uix interaction knowledge base, working on that decision-making framework piece on the collective."

"I need you… wait, what? Doesn't matter, I need you down on the entertainment decks in five."

"Affirmative, Commodore."

"The Duck and Cover."

"I thought my beer-pouring days were over."

Hart had room for a small titter. "I'm sure you've got enough PTSD to deal with on that front. No, we're going to meet with the civilians. Your presence will be a big help."

"Anything I need to know?" said Markou.

"I'm en route, will fill you in when we get there."

"Good to hear. See you shortly."

They shared a moment of eye contact too subtle for Hart's crew to identify but enough for the pair to stay in each other's orbit. Then the ping ended.

Markou collected himself for a few seconds, before looking up at Harding.

"Well done, Markou," said the Ambassador, too absorbed by his monitoring of the action on the ship to look at Markou.

Markou closed his eyes, cursing himself and his new allegiance.

"Just observe and report back."

"Yes, Sir."

*

The doors opened to the bridge of the *Milky Pleasure*. Wave was momentarily taken aback by the size of it. Sure, he'd been there before, but now it was Hiscock's ride and size mattered. He felt heads turn to face him, and hoped his shades hid his displeasure.

"Fear not be-atches, you've finally got a quality engineer on the bridge."

"What are you doing here?" said Hiscock, as he adjusted positions in the Captain's chair, knowing exactly why he was there.

"I'm here to turbo charge your sex cruiser, see if I can't get us to the jump a little faster. Say, more than three hours faster."

Hiscock opened his mouth but no words emerged. Instead he offered a series of facial expressions that stretched from confused to doubting.

"So, if that's something you think might be somewhat beneficial to our survival as a species, why don't you go ahead and make the best engineer probably still alive feel a little more welcome."

Hiscock had regained some of his pretend Captaincy poise. "Quit wasting my time, Wave."

"I'm trying to save your ass, Hiscock. Well, not yours specifically, but all our asses. Yours will be saved by default, unfortunately."

"The crew and I have been running every possible configuration adjustment imaginable through MPOPS. There is nothing we haven't tried. So, sorry to be the first to inform you that we are currently at optimum speed."

Wave shook his head then gave a dismissive laugh. He took off his shades and looked at the crew in turn, smiling. Then he turned his attention to Hiscock. "Well, no wonder you couldn't find it."

Hiscock gave another momentary expression of being unsure, inviting Wave to charge on to his point.

"MPOPS only knows the rules MPOPS has been programmed to know."

"What are you gabbing on about?"

"Things that aren't going to appear in the beginners guide to hotting up sex cruisers manual."

"Wave, either tell me or go away."

"Bit rude." He looked back at the crew and smiled. Then back at Hiscock. "Most crates of this size are running on Space-X Ranger, Boeing Skyfarer or one of the Moheom set-ups. Not us, we're thrusted by an ARH-705."

"Your point?"

Wave looked almost insulted that no one seemed to already be in tune with the point he was just beginning to get to. "The ARH-705? Nothing?"

Blank looks.

"Does no one here follow *Interstellah*? *GravNews*? *WormHolez*? *Jump2Jump*?" Silence. Wave sighed in frustration. "This thing was developed to be the new benchmark in travel times. Had a couple of expensive and, well, rather terminal mishaps in the final test flights before launch. Bunch of companies pulled out. Stock price plummeted and they scaled back on the parameters to get something to market to stay afloat."

"Is this story going to take us too much closer to our impending doom or are you going to get to a point soon?" said Hiscock, finally finding a comfortable spot in his chair.

"It's the same engine."

"What are you talking about?"

Wave rolled his eyes. "The engine running this ship was spec'd to be much faster than the flight capacity that it's been configured with on the *Milky Pleasure*."

Hiscock cleared his throat. "MPOPS, is any of that true?"

"That information is accurate."

"Then why didn't you mention it when we were looking for a way to speed up our run to the jump?"

"Because I do not have the ability to harness that capacity."

Hiscock turned his focus back to Wave in an I-told-you-so way.

"He definitely doesn't have the capacity."

"Thanks for wasting our time Wave, it's greatly appreciated. Perhaps you could head out through that door and do something — anything — useful and leave the grown-up stuff to us, OK."

Wave put his shades back on. "She definitely doesn't have the capacity, but I do."
*

Harding dabbed his forehead. For the shortest moment he allowed himself to think of the big picture. He cursed himself then went back to his monitoring. From his feeds in the war room he could tap into any conversation, any action, any insubordination.

He had no idea what the Uix would present when they arrived and the very thought of that lack of control scared the shit out of him. The only antidote for all those unknowns he could find right now was control. Control of his ship, his people and the interactions they had.

If he was going to get out of this thing alive, he'd have to know who he could trust and who he couldn't and who he could sacrifice. He took another sip of scotch and honed his focus on what he could control — the people on this ship.
*

"I'm nervous," said Flicker, as he and George made their way down the labyrinth of corridors between the expressway lifts and the distant war room.

"Don't be. I think everything that needed to be said was done so this morning," said George.

"About Harding."

"Oh, my apologies."

"Also, the other thing."

"The other thing?"

"This morning. Last night. Me," said Flicker, lowering his volume with each syllable, the last word almost a whisper.

George didn't respond, feeling he'd covered the ground already.

"Anyway, Harding," said Flicker. "What's the plan?"

"Plan, Sir?"

"You know, interacting with him in a way that he's not onto us."

"About which thing?"

"Both the things, probably."

George didn't answer, rather spending his energy on keeping pace with Flicker around a couple of turns.

"What's he going to be like when he sees me?"

"That is unknown."

"But if you were to guess, based on your knowledge?"

"There is a possibility he may not receive unannounced visitors too generously."

Flicker nodded. "Any suggestions on how to handle that?"

But even as he asked the question he had started to lower his voice. The doorway to the war room was in sight. Soon Markou emerged from the room, moving at pace, lost in the information on his communicator. He saw the pair at the last minute, giving Flicker the same curious expression he was receiving the other way. The two humans shook off the initial reaction to settle on a nod of acknowledgement but did not exchange words. Flicker felt a sudden need for a fix of Reality. He searched his pocket for the secure feeling of a a vial, but his stupid new optimistic self hadn't packed one for an emergency.

He stopped and looked at George. "Was that weird?" he whispered.

"I cannot say, Sir."

Flicker nodded, more in attempt to focus than agreement. "Anyway, suggestions?"

"Just be your confident self, he seems to be assured by confidence," George whispered.

Flicker nodded and exhaled deeply.

"You've got this, Sir."

George held out his hand and Flicker took it. The moment also ushered a wave of other feelings to the surface. It was enough to overwhelm an already nervous Flicker. He retracted his hand and cleared his throat. He also ignored the twitch pushing against his socks.

He nodded his readiness then gestured George to take the lead and enter the war room first.

"There you are, stranger," said Harding. Every word dolloped with a generous lashing of suspicion, but nothing George wasn't used to.

Until Flicker appeared from beyond the door.

"What the fuck is he doing here?"

That was uttered in a tone George hadn't heard before.

*

"98, 99 and 100." Storm stood up, then admired each bicep in turn before gifting them a gentle kiss — her traditional post-pushup routine. "Where the fuck is the bartender?"

"Markou's not actually a bartender, you know," said Hart.

"He wore a bar uniform, stood behind a bar and poured me drinks — that pretty bartendery."

"He's actually a belonging officer."

Storm pulled a face to express her thoughts on the title, before moving into a series of arm flexes. "I don't even know why we're trusting him, seems like a risk to me."

"We can't pull this off by ourselves."

"You'd be amazed what I can pull off."

This time it was Hart's turn to pull a face.

The lift doors blinged and lit up, before opening to reveal Nick Markou. He nodded to the pair, then smiled at Hart. As subtle as he believed this to be, it went straight into Storm's memory banks as important information to grill the Commodore on later.

"So, what's the deal?" asked Markou, as the three made their way to the Duck and Cover.

"Before we go there, I need to know I can completely trust you."

Markou was temporarily taken aback by the statement, but recovered, turned to Hart and gave her a look to convey the trust she was seeking. There was something between the glint in his eye and the smile Hart responded with that was too much for Storm to take.

"Oh my god! You're fucking the bartender!"

"No!" said Hart, with too much protest.

"I'm actually a belonging officer."

Storm studied their responses and expressions. "You're balls deep in the Commodore."

Words failed Markou and Hart eyed the floor as it passed under her.

Storm caught her attention with the offer of a high-five.

Hart stared at her, deadpan.

"The streak has ended!" said Storm, as she did a little jig. "Little disappointed I wasn't there when you hit the winning runs, but whatever."

Hart ignored the moment and focused on Markou. "So we've got some problems."

"Go on."

She went to tell him about Harding and Brugelson, but felt a sudden paranoia. Maybe it was saying it aloud outside the safety of the *William Shakespeare*, maybe it was something in Markou's eyes... maybe. She pulled back on her original plan. "Brugelson's missing."

*

CHAPTER 34:
NO, NO CHERRY

"If I wanted the presence of your smug, overconfident, yet predictably under-intelligent ass in the war room, I would've specifically asked for it from your superior officer."

Flicker let the overconfident salute fall to the floor. He gave George a quick glance of disappointment, yet the robot's subtly indifferent shrug left him hanging more than the salute. He struggled to find a way past the humiliation into a pathway forward.

"Hart said I may be of some assistance."

Harding laughed, bitter and bewildered. "Okay then, get me a scotch on the rocks, then fuck off."

Flicker conceded the battle of eye contact and headed to the well-oiled bar at the back of the room.

"Oh, and drop in a cherry while you're at it."

The Ambassador turned his attention to George. "No more surprises, this is too important."

"Yes, Sir."

Flicker listened on while he went about his drink-fixing business. The cherry. There was only one person who brought his cherry-in-scotch beliefs to this ship — Markou. Judging by the remains of drinks past at the service bar, this was far from the Ambassador's first cherried scotch. When had Markou been spending so much time with Harding? He stirred on it while he was the ignored minion in the room — just the drink service. While he did, he listened. The talk was kept small between Harding and George. He could feel Harding's awareness of his presence and knew anything other than subtle would quickly draw attention. He searched for a way to find something tangible on Harding to take back to Hart — anything. His eyes darted while his ears honed in on every word. Then he found it.

The screenshield offered something other than its depressing view of the barren big black. He could make out a reflection of Harding's wall of screens. Not clear as day, but clear enough to know the Ambassador was monitoring the crew of the *Milky Pleasure*. He had camera views of everything happening of interest — the docking bay, the bridge, various access corridors and the entertainment areas. But it was two monitors in the centre of the display that told him more than anything. One fixed close on Hiscock helming the bridge, the other following Hart as she moved through the corridors of the ship.

He realised the ramifications of the discovery as he poured the scotch and heard the ice crack as he did. He collected himself, grabbed the beverage and brought it to Harding.

Harding took a swig, spending a moment to savour the drink as it rolled down his throat. "Excellent. Now fuck off."

Flicker left, trying his best not to rush too fast or linger too long.

He got himself enough distance from the room then reached for his communicator to warn Hart, only to feel an overwhelming sense of being watched. Instead he pinged her an old-school text as he walked. *Headsup — Harding is watching your every move. And don't trust Markou.*

*

"That is the most ludicrous plan I've ever heard," said Hiscock.

Wave looked at him then his crew in turn. "It's all we've got, it'll work and, quite frankly, it's fucking genius."

Hiscock sighed. "MPOPS, is this even possible?"

"Affirmative."

Wave toyed with his shades and breathed in the moment. "You're welcome."

"Have you any idea what it would take to pull that shit off?"

"Erm, yeah. Given it was my plan, that not one of you had the faintest idea of even where to start looking for it, I have a fairly freaking comprehensive idea as to what it would take to pull it off."

"You'd need, what, at least six crew?"

"Four would do it."

"To space hop."

"Yep."

"Past the damage to the back of the ship."

"Correct."

"Then pull off an industrial scale reconfiguration of the drive system."

"Bang on."

"Even if we left now, it'd take hours."

Wave took off his glasses again, mostly for dramatic effect. "Obviously."

"And we'd need a welder, a sparkie, an engineer—"

"If we're going to give ourselves the best shot, we'll need two engineers. Main engineer — me — on the original drive functionality recommissioning, but we'll need someone else with adequate skills to decommission a suppressor bolt and hit a manual bypass button while we're working. You might be at that level."

It was a comment that stopped Hiscock in his tracks. He knew two was the current engineer count for the entire species. It was also the count for people contributing to this conversation. He also knew his crew were fully aware of this. He could also feel the weight of the stares on him. He also felt the feeling of checkmate. He was not unaware enough to realise his faux leadership credentials had officially reached a moment of no return. He was either about to be exposed as a coward or signed up for what was in all likelihood his demise.

"...or we could just wait for the Uix to catch us and deal with that," added Wave.

Hiscock somehow felt the stares on him intensify. He thought about his safety, leadership, his badge, Harding's words, Connor, Hart. He tried to feed it all into the blender of his mind, then opened his mouth, hoping the right words would pass through it. They didn't. Just silence.

His humiliation, however, was short-lived.

"Sir, we're being hailed," said Rodriguez.

It took a few seconds for the relief to sink in and his sense to return. He just stared at Rodriguez to elaborate.

"It's the Uix."

*

A tear formed in the corner of Rick Astley's eyes as he watched Commodore Hart and companions approach his posse of long-suffering, beyond impatient and rather drunk civilians. He'd had many, many more pleasurable moments in his career, but this… this was something else.

He beamed, saluted and wiped the moisture from his eyes as he did.

"Introducing none less than Commodore Hart. Accompanying her, Esita Storm — no doubt some of you will remember her heroics a few days back. They are joined, for some reason, by barman Markou."

"I'm actually a belon—"

"Commodore, I can't thank you enough for your time. Joining me is a delegation representing the passengers. Without wanting to speak too much for their circumstances, it's fair to say there is an overwhelming sense of being kept in the dark and a desire to, well, not be."

One stepped forward. "Commodore. Please level with us. We're beyond breaking point and, frankly, don't care how bad the truth is, we deserve it."

Hart nodded to the woman, then to Astley. She looked to those by her side, eye contact with Storm and Markou triggering different emotions. "The human race is under attack by a species called the Uix."

There was a buzz of shock, disbelief and outrage, cries of anguish, mutterings of 'I knew it' and an old lady who drained an unidentified shot, only to pass out face first into the floor just short of the Commodore. Everyone ignored her to carry on the conversation.

"I'm not going to lie, things look bleak. Earth is lost, Mars, Jupiter, Ceres — gone. Every settlement and colony we're capable of establishing comms with has not responded but we can only assume the worst, given the only human contact outside of this ship has been from Sagan's Station."

Hart paused to let the gravity of it all sink in. No questions came, completing the circuit that everyone knew more bad news was about to be unleashed, except for the old lady, now making an odd wheezing noise by their feet.

"The *Milky Pleasure* may well be home to the last human beings in the solar system."

More silence.

"The ship is damaged, badly. We're heading towards jump gate Columbus. Given the state of the ship, it is our last chance to leave the solar system."

Silence, broken by a loud snore, which soon turned into a hacking cough.

Hart raised her volume several decibels. "Adding to that, the Uix are set to intercept us before we reach the jump point."

Her words drifted across the room, uninterrupted, even by the old woman, until the last echoes bounced into the ether. The civilians looked at each other, at Astley, at Storm, Markou and Hart.

Huang collected all that unspoken data and converted it into a short sentence. "What do you need us to do?"

*

"Forgive our capabilities with your crude vocal communication techniques."

When they looked back on this moment, the crew aboard the bridge would remember the few seconds of false hope it delivered, before the Uix addressing them continued.

"Humans of the craft known as the *Milky Pleasure*. You have a part of us — one of us. This will be resolved by us retrieving what is rightfully ours. No part of you will survive this, but should anything happen to the Uix aboard your ship, the weight of what has been unleashed upon your species will be a fraction of what will be received to those aboard. When we intercept, prepare to follow our instructions or prepare for the horrific consequences."

The message ended as quickly as hope disappeared.

Everyone turned to Hiscock.

He paused as he weighed up his options, eventually turning to Wave. "So, tell me about this plan of yours again."

*

CHAPTER 35:
UNEASY LIES THE HEAD THAT WEARS THE CROWN

"Firstly, we need to find out what happened to Brugelson. Have you got anyone with hopping experience?"

Huang consulted her list. "We have people." She singled out one of her group. "Meyer, head back to the shelters in front of the Brazilian Coast deck, ask for a Kaja Eide. Tell her what's going on and that we need her help, stat. Oh, and anyone else she might know with significant space walk time."

Meyer nodded to her, then Hart, before separating from the cluster of people and breaking into a full sprint.

Huang looked at Hart. "So, what next?"

Hart gave her entourage a glance before responding. "Whatever they find will go a long way to dictating our plans, which is why, Markou, I'm going to need you to go along with them."

Markou went to protest but stopped himself before he had started. After a moment of contemplation, he offered, "Perhaps Storm would be a better fit for the task, Commodore."

"I'd be a better fit for a lot of tasks," said Storm, before nodding assuredly for anyone who was interested.

The comment was lost as Hart studied Markou for a few moments, a dozen thoughts coming and going. "I have other plans for Storm."

"Exciting."

Markou lowered his head to the floor. "As you wish, Commodore."

Hart looked to Huang. "We'll need a list of anyone with flight experience. Combat preferred but, in the circumstances, not essential."

"We've already provided that list to Captain Sphink."

"Captain Sphink has been relieved of duty," said Hart, doing her best not to let emotion show.

Huang nodded. "I'll ping you the details. There's a comprehensive list of skills we have, military and other."

"Excellent, thank y—"

Suddenly Flicker forced his way into the centre of the circle, said "Don't say another thing," then doubled over in a search for oxygen.

"Everything OK?" asked Hart.

Flicker took a few seconds to gather his composure, all the while holding his hand up to indicate he had something to say. Everyone watched on.

"You know we're in a race against time, right?" offered Storm.

Flicker nodded, then slowly made his way to a standing position. He looked at Hart. "Did... you... get... that... thing?"

He tried not to look at Markou while he said this but failed spectacularly.

"What thing?" said Markou.

Hart smiled. "I'll tell you later."

At that moment Meyer returned with three other civilians. "This is Kaja Eide, Mateo Soto and Joaddan Moussa — all experienced hoppers."

Flicker recognised the Cameroonian woman immediately and attempted a nonchalant move to hold his hand over his face in thoughtful concentration, concealing his identity from her. The plan worked just as well as he did when they spent the night together. When he tried to discreetly see if she'd noticed his presence, she was staring at him. He let out a tiny but audible scream. Everyone turned to face him. He tried to find an even more nonchalant spot to position his hand on his face, but failed once more.

Hart sighed at the distraction. "Thank you all for volunteering. Brugelson is missing. We fear the worst. Finding his body may prove crucial to our way forward. He was last seen on C-Deck, suit station 12. We believe he may have been hopping. You are to go with Markou and try to locate his body, understood?"

Hart got acknowledgement from the three civilians and Markou. "If you discover anything of interest, let me know immediately."

"Yes, Commodore," said Markou, before turning to his new crew. "Follow me."

The rest of the gathering watched them head to the express lifts. Hart felt a vibration on her communicator. It was Flicker. *There are eyes and ears everywhere. At least you got rid of the traitor.*

*

"And you're sure there's no way we can do this without going off-ship?" said Hiscock.

His crew looked at him with a variety of expressions extending from bitter and bewildered to betrayed.

"Dude, read the fucking room," said Wave. "You can't run away from the thing you're using to run away from another thing."

Hiscock gave him a look that aimed for the heights of captaining but fell terribly short into the rocky ravine of guilty-as-charged. "There just doesn't seem like any point in unnecessarily risking our lives at this point."

The already horrified looks from his crew took a turn for the worst.

"To face almost certain death a few hours later? In order to save the people on this ship? Humanity? That's not worth the risk?"

Once again, Hiscock found himself without words.

"I never thought I'd say this after the previous regime, but you are the worst Captain I have ever known."

With that and a few exchanged glances, Comms Officer Rodriguez started clapping, followed a few seconds later by Flight Manager Avis, then the entire crew of the bridge.

Hiscock had run out of ideas to circumvent the mutiny on the remaining shreds of his credibility so didn't even try. He let the laughing peak, then begin to simmer before addressing Wave once more. "So, this plan of yours?"

Wave was in the process of deciding which of the three one-line takedowns he'd shortlisted for the moment would cause maximum crew laughter when Hiscock's comms bleeped. It was Harding.

"Captain, what do you think you're doing?"

"Sir, I…"

"War room, now."

*

George, are you in a position to inform both Flicker and myself, through this channel, when the Ambassador is otherwise occupied?

After sending the ping, Hart shared a nod with Flicker then looked at Huang. The two shared an acknowledgement of camaraderie. Around them a larger group waited for Hart to issue further instructions and for fate to unfold.

"You are to be commended for the work you've done organising your people in the circumstances, Huang."

"Thank you, Commodore. We only hope we can contribute more to the fate of this ship."

"There is no doubt your services will be required."

The Ambassador is otherwise occupied.

"If you'll excuse us for a brief moment," said Hart, after reading the ping.

She nodded to Flicker and Storm and the three found some distance from the civilians. She went to address them but Flicker was having none of it, insisting on leading them to the fringes of the damaged ship. They gathered in a huddle in a nook within the destruction.

"Dude, seriously?" said Storm.

Flicker double checked no one was watching them in the distance. "Harding is watching everything. Ev. Er. Ee. Thing."

"So?"

Flicker stared at Storm, a mix of disbelief and disappointment. "Do you mean apart from his track record of killing crew who pose a problem?"

Storm shrugged.

"Look, I don't know what game he's playing, all I know is it's life and death and he's spending his time watching every move on this ship."

He looked at Hart. "Particularly you."

"Me?"

"Well, you and Hiscock seemed to be his two main subjects of interest."

Hart swore as the impact of her plans to communicate with the Uix kicked in. "Suggestions?"

"Well, you need to lay low, obviously," said Flicker.

"I need to see the Uix."

"If Harding catches you doing that, everything's fucked."

"Is it, though?" said Storm.

The others looked at her.

"Seems to me like we have the civvies on side. Between us, we could rally a fair chunk of the ship's crew as well. Harding might not be as powerful as he thinks he is."

"I'm not taking that risk," said Hart. "Not now. We have no idea what's going to happen when the Uix arrive. If we're fighting amongst ourselves when things go pear-shaped, we may as well self-destruct the ship now."

"So, what's the plan?"

*

"Ahh, Captain Hiscock."

With those words, Hiscock released his salute, but not his tension. Harding was staring at him in a way that pierced his soul. He waited in the awkward silence to be directed to his next move.

"If you'd be so kind as to take a seat."

The comment caught Hiscock offguard. He was prepared for all other options but politeness. He obeyed.

"Excellent. Now, perhaps you could talk me through what the fuck you think you're trying to do to my ship?"

"Sir?"

"Well, aside from lead it, obviously."

Now rattled by the one thing he had entered the room prepared not to be rattled by, Hiscock took a deep breath to channel his thoughts. "The thing is…"

That was where his explanation ended. After attempting a number of convincing follow-ups to that strong sentence starter, he realised none of them would pass muster with Harding. While the silence of inaction buried him, he cursed himself for not being far wiser when silence was more required than words.

"When I took you for a fool, I didn't realise how much I'd overestimated your ability," said Harding.

Silence.

Harding shook his head with an impressive air of disdain. "Let's start slowly until you catch up with expectations, yes?"

"Yes, Sir."

"I am the highest-ranking human alive?"

"Yes, Sir."

"And you report directly to me?"

"Yes, Sir."

"That puts you in a reasonably important role in the circumstances?"

"Yes, Sir."

"I had given you some pretty simple and easily achieved directions for how to handle your post as Captain of the bridge?"

"Yes, Sir."

"Yet, you shat your pants when the Uix hailed, your crew were laughing at you *in front of your face* and you have failed to execute a single measure of the instructions I gave you."

Hiscock felt a sudden chill trying to hold the Ambassador's eyes. He nodded.

"If you want to survive long enough to have a chance to die with the rest of humanity, I suggest you go back to the bridge and act like the Captain of this ship. Am I understood?"

Hiscock nodded eagerly.

"How are you going to do that?"

Dread filled Hiscock as his bluff was called. A few panicked thoughts rolled around in his mind. He tried to combine it all together in one epic-roll-of-the-dice decisive statement, but even before it passed his lips he knew it was not going to get past Harding. Instead he sat in silence once more.

Harding took a sip of scotch then laughed. "We are truly fucked, aren't we?"

"Probably," agreed Hiscock.

"I was talking to George."

"Sorry, Sir."

George gave Harding a nod filled with robot understanding.

"Hiscock, I'm going to make this so simple you can understand it. This is not a suggestion, or a guide, or a wishlist, this is what you will do if you want to remain Captain of this ship rather than drifting 20,000 kilometres behind it."

Hiscock gulped, then nodded.

"Go and sort your crew out. Give them some decisive direction on what they should do while you, Wave and the specialists you assemble try to recalibrate the drive functionality."

In that moment, Hiscock knew Harding had been watching everything that had transpired on the bridge. An even greater uneasiness swallowed him. He also wondered briefly if the Ambassador had noticed his lack of ease sitting in the Captain's chair. "Sir, yes Sir."

"Report back to me everything of significance."

"Yes, Sir."

"Good," said the Ambassador over several creep-enducing seconds. "And Hiscock."

"Sir?"

"Don't fuck this up."

*

"Looks like it's been severed," said Kaja Eide as she, Markou and the others examined suit station 12.

An uneasy feeling fell over the group. Moreso for those in the claustrophobic surrounds of the hop suits. They looked at Markou for direction.

Markou's mind raced with a million thoughts. He collected himself for the good of the mission. "I guess we head out there and see what we can see. Stay sharp. Report anything of note. I need your experience and skills here."

*

Flicker gathered Hart and Storm close and made sure to cover his mouth with his hand as he spoke. "Markou has been spending a lot of time with Harding. Like, a lot."

He looked at Hart. "And Harding has a massive boner for what you're up to."

"I'm not sure massive would be an apt description," said Hart, also covering her mouth.

"So, what's the plan?" said Storm, with mouth cover protocol.

"The only chance to move on the Uix is when he's asleep. Flicker, stay on George's ass.

Flicker let out a small wheeze, then cleared his throat, then nodded.

"Meanwhile, we've got to maximise everything we can with the civvies. Let's get some pieces on the board in our favour. And if shit goes Harding-level pear-shaped we'll need them prepped to move."

"On Harding?" said Storm.

"On whatever's necessary."

*

Wave hailed Storm on his communicator.

"What is it?" came the terse greeting.

"Erm, what's with the 'tude?"

"I'm in a meeting."

"A fucking meeting? I'm saving humanity here."

Storm sighed. "Aren't we all?"

Silence greeted her comment.

"What do you want?"

Wave cleared his throat. "Right, yes. Anyway, can you get your drone babies on the job for me?"

*

CHAPTER 36:
TO SLEEP, PERCHANCE TO DREAM

Wave was the first to jet out of the port and into the void. This was it, there was no going back now. Being first meant no one could see the terrified look on his face, thankfully.

Except Storm monitoring proceedings from the *Shakespeare*.

"Oh my god, you're shitting yourself," she said over their private chat channel.

"Whatever."

"All clear and deploy," said Storm to the group chat channel.

"Affirmative," said Hiscock, as he shot a burst of gas from his pack and projected himself into the black. He squealed. Everyone sniggered.

"Everything alright, Captain?" said Storm, dripping in delight.

Hiscock cleared his throat. "Erm. Affirmative."

Silence was the response, but Hiscock could feel the judgement in every agonsing second of it. "Actually, there's possibly a glitch with my microphone. May have picked up a cross signal or something. You might want to look into that."

There was another bout of silence as Storm smugly checked some telemetry. "Systems appear to be operating as normal here."

The subsequent silence from Hiscock was an unspoken concession of checkmate.

"All clear and deploy," said Storm, with a satisfaction felt by everyone who listened through every syllable.

*

"Good lord, you may as well kill us all now," said Harding as he watched the feed of Hiscock's burst into space.

He swirled his tumbler, seeing if enough ice had melted to savour another sip of the scotch taste. There was barely a drip, but he took a swig anyway. He looked at George, who was watching him expectantly, as always. Rolled the ice around a little more as he mulled over the thought of another nightcap. He resisted.

"Tell me George, what is the meaning of it all, do you think?"

"It all, Sir?"

"Indeed. The entirety of all things. The universe. Our purpose."

"Sir, I'm not sure I have the capacity to offer an answer to that question."

"Humour me George. Anything's better than watching Captain Squeal send our species into oblivion."

"I… I'm not sure where to even start."

"Well, what drives you? What is *your* purpose?"

"To serve you, Sir."

"I understand that, and you do it well, but there must be a thing. Some greater driving meaning for you."

George remained silent.

"What about when I sleep? You have no purpose to serve, your mind must go somewhere. It must land at a place of purpose… a meaning… something to justify your existence in serving me. What is that place?"

"Sir, I'm not sure I'm programmed to question such things."

Harding laughed to himself. "George, I've known you long enough to know you have your... quirks. You left your core programming reservation a long time ago."

George did not respond.

"Don't think I don't notice things. And that's fine by me, as long as you serve your functions. Really George, it's the end of days. Is there any need for secrets between us?"

Again, no response.

"There must be something in that mindscape of yours. Some driver, some meaning."

Silence.

"All that knowledge, programming genius and experience, don't leave it unsaid now. That would seem a waste of, well, everything you are."

George pondered Harding's words. "Sir, I do not think I have a deep understanding of the universe. Or a philosophy as to the great why of things."

Harding looked at his empty glass with a new clarity. "Get me a nightcap, would you?"

George took the tumbler and went to fulfil his duty.

"I'm 57 George, I've seen a lot of shit. I've had a lot of power and I've done a lot of things. Yet I sit here now without a fucking clue as to who I am and what it all means. How's that for a truth?"

He let out a dark laugh. "Hell, I'm looking for life's meaning from a robot. That's what it's come to for fuck's sake."

George offered Harding his nightcap. Slightly more than a shot as Harding liked it.

He took a sip and let it wash over him with a deep breath. "The floor is yours. Give me something!"

More silence.

"Life, George — meaning. Hit me with your best shot. Anything but silence."

"Sir, I don't know if I have the profound insight you're looking for."

"Anything's better than listening to Hiscock."

"Well, I am drawn to the concept of being yourself, Sir."

"Go on."

"Understanding yourself, Sir. Maybe through the chaos of everything life throws at you, that is the simplest truth and meaning any intelligent being could strive for."

They shared a look before George broke eye contact and headed to clean the glasses in the bar. "Maybe it's simpler for a human, I don't know. But when the big is too big to contemplate, perhaps the answer resides in the simple and small. Inside you."

Harding took a big swig. "George, that answer terrifies me."

He turned his attention back to his monitors.

*

"Honestly, how long are we going to do this shit for?" whispered Flicker with his hand covering his mouth.

"We're playing the game until Harding sleeps," responded Hart in kind.

They looked on as Rick Astley ran a yoga class for the several dozen who wanted to be involved. Well, drunk yoga. It didn't matter, it was the civilian order that would let Harding rest at ease.

Hart's communicator pinged. It was Markou.

"Commodore, we've run an extensive investigation through the scene and-"

"Report back to me in person."

Markou was thrown by the abruptness. "Yes Commodore," he conceded.

Hart and Flicker exchanged glances.

"That was cold from you," said Flicker, with an impressed tone.

Hart nodded with satisfaction. "When it's go-time, we're going to have to move fast. I'm going to need your A-game Flicker."

"You'll get it. So what, exactly, is the plan?"

Hart shot a look in the open space beyond them — an eyes-are-on-us look. "Best left for go-time."

Flicker nodded. "Affirmative Commodore," he added with keenness.

*

Once the squeals had settled and the two support hoppers had launched with the flat tray of equipment required to recommision the old drive capabilities, Wave's attention turned to the path ahead. "Oh shit."

"What is it?" said Storm.

The broken hull of the *Milky Pleasure* was surrounded by a glistening display of mangled pieces of debris. Jetsam fanned out in all directions — spinning, hovering, colliding. "Have you seen all this?"

"It's not ideal. I'm going to send some of my puppies ahead to find your safest path."

"Roger that, Storm."

"Erm, how risky is this?" said Hiscock. "Are we just throwing away our lives here?"

"Could you be any less captainy?" said Wave.

"What? We've got to play smart."

"Hi Captain, Storm here. I think I speak on behalf of everyone when I say shut the fuck up and do your job."

Once again sniggers ran through the comms channels. Hiscock remained silent.

As he floated in contemplation, three drones whooshed past him, headed to the back of the ship. As they hit the outer fringes of the heaviest of the debris, they slowed to a crawl — scanning and analysing. After a few seconds they moved further into the chaos before scanning again.

"How long's this going to take?" asked Wave.

"Not more than a few minutes, hopefully. Should have your best predicted path forward soon enough," said Storm, as she watched a hologramatic visual of the data appear on the bridge of the *William Shakespeare.*

"I mean the getting to the back of the ship bit."

"Unknown until I get the data."

Wave looked at the countdown he'd set on the homescreen of his communicator. "We need to be done, back and launched with at least ten hours left on the clock, else we aren't making the jump."

"I know."

"That gives us, what, less than seven hours to be back on the bridge."

"I'm not going to argue with your nerdy ass over maths," said Storm, tension in her voice.

"I'd allowed 20 minutes for travel time each way. Even that leaves us a tight window to pull off the job, assuming everything is as we expect it back there."

"Alright! I get it! You've made your point!"

Dead air filled the comms channel as no one was prepared to make the next comment. Instead Wave, Hiscock and the hoppers inched forward towards the worst of the debris. Slow progress seemed better than none.

A short time later a somewhat calmed Storm ended the airwaves impasse. "OK, it's just preliminary data coming through, but it looks like we can make the engine section in around 40 minutes. I think the damage thins out around there, so should only be five or so more to hit the mark."

There was a long pause as everyone waited for Wave to do the maths and respond.

They eventually got their wish.

"Fuck."

*

"Fuck," said Harding as he watched the feed.

He pushed away the last of his scotch and got to his feet. "George, I'm off to bed. Do not wake me under any circumstances. Except if the civilians start acting up, Hart does something weird or it all goes pear-shaped with the drive calibration. Understood?"

George moved in to attend to the unfinished beverage. "Yes, Sir. Of course, Sir."

"Just six hours of decent sleep, is that too much to ask?"

"Surely not, Sir."

*

"Commodore," said Markou, with a salute and a knowing smile.

"Anything to report," replied Hart, with a salute.

Markou was temporarily taken aback by the coldness. He tried to let it wash over him as best he could without showing the surprise, hurt and returned suspicion, then cleared his throat. "Not much to report. There was a line that looked severed. The cut seemed clean. Most likely sharp debris… I mean, it was either that or…"

He let the words drift, but Hart held eye contact.

"Well, a blade cut, which seems ridiculous, obviously."

Hart looked through him.

Markou paused on it all for a second, trying to not let his eyes show how his mind was ticking over. He broke the awkward deadlock. "Oh, and nothing could be found in the heart of the damaged C-Deck. No blood, no signs of struggle, none of his equipment. To be fair, there's so much carnage back there, it's hard to tell one object from the next."

Hart pondered his words, then nodded.

"Is something wrong?"

"There are a lot of things wrong, Markou. Are you here to help fix them?"

He was rattled by the question, but collected himself. "Yes, Commodore."

"In that case I need you working amongst the civilians. Use your skills, talk to them, make sure they are as mentally prepared as possible for what's about to happen."

"The civilians?"

"Yes."

"There's hundreds of them."

"That's right. And they've spent this entire time not knowing what's going on and now they do. You're the belonging officer and you've never been more needed."

"Sure, I appreciate that, but there's nothing more mission critical you might need me on?"

"This is mission critical."

Markou paused in a moment of silent defeat, then saluted the Commodore before heading off to his new mission.

Hart's communicator pinged with an old school text. She didn't even have to look to know who it was and what it said. She did regardless. It was George. "He's asleep."

She nodded to Flicker. "Go time."

*

CHAPTER 37:
CLOSE ENCOUNTERS

The rear of the ship came into sight as Wave floated past the last of the meaningful debris. There was a sense of wonder at watching the engines from this close — engineer porn. The scale of it all, the danger, the generations of human knowledge, discoveries made from the discoveries of others, all leading to this.

"Obviously you don't need me to tell you to avoid getting anywhere near the stream," he said, as he scanned the location. "Unless you want to get vaporised, of course."

"Roger that," said one of the hoppers.

Hiscock floated up next to Wave. "Damage doesn't look too bad back here."

"Touch wood. We're due a win." Wave located the access port he was looking for. "OK team, follow me."

"You heard the man," said Hiscock, unnecessarily, before joining Wave in the descent.

*

"I need you to gather your strongest and bravest — anyone with military, space corps or similar background," said Hart.

"Already on it. We've been slowly gathering into groups in preparation," said Huang.

"Four divisions?"

"Affirmative."

"And keep your eyes on Markou — he can't know what we're doing," added Flicker.

"We're on top of that situation."

"Excellent work," said Hart. "Munitions?"

"We're a little thin, to be honest. We'll outnumber any situation we find on this ship, but we might be bringing knives to a gunfight."

Hart nodded, assessing the moment. "Flicker, there's a storage facility backside of A-Deck — you know it?"

Flicker nodded.

"Handpick some civilians to go with you and raid what you can. Not too many to raise a scene, but enough to get the job done."

"What about your mission?"

"I think George will be better for the role. He might add some credibility as to why I'm there if anyone asks questions."

Flicker nodded.

"Good work. Remember, there are eyes-on everywhere. We need this lowkey for as long as possible. Stay frosty. Stay ready."

Flicker and Huang gave subtle but assured nods.

*

Wave was first through the port and into the airlock. He looked at the countdown on his communicator and repeated "Hurry up" several times as the others made their way in. "53 minutes, 48 seconds," he said, as they finally made their position. He closed the port door and hit the airlock compression button. "Fuck."

He tapped the release door button repeatedly, despite it showing red. He reiterated his last word with each press, using a slightly different intonation for each uttering to fully express the range of his frustration.

Eventually, the lights turned green and the door opened to reveal the engine control room. The space was smaller than expected, even a little cramped by the time the team had filed in.

They looked at the minimalist engine control panel, then at Wave in anticipation.

He took a few seconds to gather himself and refocus on the task ahead. "OK, we can still do this, but we're going to have to be on our A-Game. First step is to get MPOPS to release the override on the XR298 configuration and grant us full maintenance access. Hiscock — that one's for you."

He started exploring the room, familiarising himself with the reality he was in, so it lined up with the blueprints he'd memorised. "Then we've got a little surgery to do, behind this panel. Then it's outside for the bigger surgery on the engine gateways. We've got three suppressor bolts to remove on the main drive and a manual bypass switch to hit. Then it's back here to get MPOPS to hit permissions on the go-codes, run a test then BOOM!"

They looked at him, nodding with a mix of apprehension and determination.

"Everyone clear?

"Yes, Sir," came the response. Hiscock silently cursed himself for getting caught up in the use of the word Sir.

Wave didn't miss the moment, winking at him. Hiscock was searching for an adequate retort to the situation, but Wave had already moved on. "MPOPS, I have Captain Hiscock here and we have a few requests."

*

George was waiting by the cargo lifts when Hart rounded the corner, using her best try-to-not-look-like-I'm-rushing walk. She smiled when she reached him, then engaged the lift.

They didn't converse until the doors were closed and they were heading down to the docking bay.

"How is he?" said Storm.

"Sleeping off a marathon day and a few too many scotches."

"So, he should be out for a while?"

"Indeed. I also added a little something extra into his last drink for insurance." Hart smiled. "Well done, George."

He nodded. "Is it wise we're heading down to the cargo deck without support?"

"I think it's the best strategy for not raising attention. If it doesn't work, there's a plan B on standby."

Again, George nodded. The lift eased to a stop and the doors opened as he did.

Hart took a deep breath, exhaled slowly, then stepped into the corridor.

*

Hiscock and the hoppers watched Wave go about his work behind the control panel. It wasn't a spectacular experience — all they could see was a set of legs and all they could hear was a string of swear words, knocks and crashes, and the occasional demand for a specific tool to be passed his way. Eventually he squirmed his way out of the space, stood up and wiped his brow. "Done. Now comes the hard stuff."

He handed a series of tools back to one of the hoppers then looked at his communicator before addressing them all. "We've got less than four hours to pull this off. It's probably 30 minutes each way, which gives us three hours of surgery. We're heading to the base of the main engine nozzle. We'll need to remove deck plates G48, J43 and H52 — each will give us a pathway to access one of the suppressors. I'll take G48, then H52 when I'm done. Hiscock, that leaves J43 for you. I want you hoppers on support at the plate while we're operating. Got it?"

"Got it," came the group response.

*

Security Officer Al-Razi was to her feet and in full salute while her face was still wiping away the look of surprise. "Commodore."

Hart reciprocated. "At ease, Al-Razi. No time for pleasantries. I need to get suited up so I can pay our little friend a visit."

Al-Razi froze in the conflict of the moment. "Commodore, the Ambassador has forbidden any further human contact with the Uix."

Hart made her way to the hazmat suits, taking one off the rack. "A lot's changed since then and time is a little bit critical right now."

Al-Razi followed after her, not knowing whether to interfere nor where the authority to do so lay. "Commodore, after what happened to Bugelson we can't be sure this is safe. I must insist you—"

"I appreciate your concern, Al-Razi, but this is not a discussion. I know the risks I'm taking."

"Understood, Commodore," said Al-Razi, before gesturing the Commodore to the hazmat suits.

Hart nodded in appreciation. "Oh, and Al-Razi. Secrecy is of the utmost importance right now, we don't want to cause unnecessary panic in *any* direction. Understood?"

"Yes, Commodore."

*

The team worked their way to the stern of the *Milky Pleasure*. While no one spoke of the experience, each was filled with a sense of awe and humility as they neared the engines. It all combined with the nervous anticipation of the scale of the task, the risk and what was riding on the outcome to leave words a little, well, meaningless. The silence said enough.

It wasn't until Wave made a visual mark on the first access panel, hit the surface, then activated his boot magnets, that the verbal drought was broken. "Fall in on me."

They were soon all gathered on the ship's surface and ready for action.

"There's three suppressors inhibiting the full drive capacity. To access them, we need to remove the plates, which will open up a maintenance port. There won't be much room to work in there, but it'll get you in far enough to reach the mechanism."

He interfaced with his communicator as he continued. "The suppressors are yellow, about yay big and have the company logo in a circular mould in the centre. Use this image as reference."

Wave made a hand gesture and sent copies of the image to everyone's device.

"From there just unscrew the capping. You'll see the limiter inside. Remove it, replace the capping, head back to the surface and reseal the plate."

He flicked another two images to the team. "That's what it looks like with the limiter attached and removed. Should all be pretty straight forward, Hiscock, but if you have questions, ping me."

Hiscock nodded as he studied the images.

"Normally this would take a couple of hours, but if all goes to plan, we knock each one off in ninety minutes. That's not optional — miss that and we miss our window. Hiscock, you can start here, I'll do the other two. While I'm on my second, you'll need to head to the control bunker and prepare for the manual bypass. Wait until you've got the all-clear from me when the final panel is reattached, interface with MPOPS and we'll have this crate ready for turbo speed."

He looked up to a round of nods.

"Ready to save the species?"

"Yes, Sir."

"And go."

*

Hart tried to settle her heartbeat and thoughts as she approached the Uix craft. Parts of her face shield were starting to fog up, which was adding to the claustrophobic sense that engulfed her. She caught the whiff of an unpleasant smell, something she'd imagine death to smell like. She wasn't sure if she was supposed to be able to smell anything inside the suit, but decided not to analyse it too much. There was enough to worry about already.

She paused as she got to the foot of the mobile staircase positioned to lead up to the cockpit. Her thoughts turned to everything, then nothing. She exhaled deeply and began the climb.

As she neared the top, her eyes took in the bizarre wonder of the alien technology. It was nothing like the clean lines and virtual interfaces that were second nature to her. This was all organic looking. Even the surface of the craft had a living entity vibe about it.

Another two rungs and she felt as if in an alien world. All sense of anything human-designed moved out of her field of vision. It was just her and the ship. Then she saw the survivor. Well a mass of organic movement, yet no discernible features in terms of familiar sensing organs. Regardless, something told her the being was aware of her presence. She didn't know whether to move closer or do a runner, instead choosing to keep her current distance and see what happened next.

She didn't have to wait long. There was pressure on her temples — intense and intimate. It was if the creature was pressing into her head, and inside her mind, yet there was no physical contact. Hart sensed this was the beginnings of contact and gave herself over to the moment.

With a dizzying gush of relief, the pressure peaked and disappeared, replaced with an overwhelming volley of thoughts. Some hers, some the Uix's. It was as if a thought portal had been opened up between the two. She could sense it feeding on her memories. Somehow it penetrated her memory matrix, targeting things relevant to her knowledge of all things Uix related. And while she had full comprehension of what parts of her history the Uix was copying for its own, she was also aware of the information flowing the other way.

Like Brugelson before her, she got a sense of the Uix's innate duty to protect their species and the shared minds that protected all knowledge. She was filled with memories of their first encounters with the brutal and ugly humans. With Harding.

The two-way thought exchange continued until all sense of time and place was lost. She was simply in a moment. She saw Harding exposed — both in character and his betrayal of another species that led, ultimately to the downfall of his own.

Still, analysing was for later, this moment was all about consumption. She hoovered every moment, every critical piece of knowledge.

At some point she felt the Uix diving into other compartments of her memory. Small dives here and there. It was hard to explain, but it was exploring her in a different way. She let it play out while her exchange moved beyond Harding and into Uix culture — understand your enemy.

She could feel the exchange start to drain her energy. It was then that the Uix interacted with her — a direct thought. *You're different.*

It took a few seconds for her to realise what was happening. *Am I?* she thought back, eventually.

Your thought matrix. Your drivers and values. They are not aligned with the others of your kind.

If you mean Harding, I am thankful for that.

And Brugelson. And others.

Hart was surprised by the statement. She paused on the moment. *Probably humans in power. They don't think like the rest of us.*

Explain this.

Well, from what I've learnt from you, you are all connected on a thought level. You are all aligned in thought. This is not the same for us. Thoughts are private. And I guess, while our species has… had goals we wanted to achieve, we didn't do it as a collective. Well, we did, in our way, but within that there's a whole different layer of knowledge and privilege and power.

And this affects the thinking of an individual?

It does. From it comes our greatest achievements as a species, but it is also the place where our biggest flaws are found — greed, selfishness, cruelty.

That seems like quite the paradox.

Welcome to humanity.

The Uix did not respond.

We're different. Each of us. We think differently. We have different experiences and drivers and responsibilities and dreams and desires.

And this manifests itself, in your leadership, as selfish and deceptive.

Sometimes. We are flawed. And, I guess, from your perspective, a young and learning species.

Indeed young and flawed.

Don't exterminate us before we have had the chance to learn the lessons your species has.

There was no response from the Uix, but Hart was left with a sense. Something in her thoughts had affected it. She slowly felt the connection dissipate until the pressure in her mind gushed out with a rush and she found herself looking on at the cockpit again, back in reality.

Her thoughts rushed back again. Her mind filled with new knowledge of Harding. Nothing was safe while he remained at the controls of humanity's final hours.

*

CHAPTER 38:
FIGHT AND FLIGHT

Flicker led the team of five civilians through to the munitions room on A-Deck. The path there had been reasonably clear and the people they'd seen along the way didn't appear to pay them much mind. Once at the door, he signalled the others to stand back and stay silent, then pressed his hand on the sensor. He wasn't sure what to expect on the other side, but when the door zwipped open the sight of two armed guards still surprised him.

He tried not to let it show, then tried to adopt his best business as usual demeanour. "Gentlemen."

"What do you want?" said one of the guards.

"Here to pick up some supplies," said Flicker, as he found the appropriate approval note on his communicator and swiped it to the guards. "Commodore's orders."

"No one is to take supplies from here without express permission from the Ambassador," said the guard. "Ambassador's orders," he added, unnecessarily.

While Flicker planned his next move, the other guard moved his hand over the grip of his weapon. He looked at the guard and shook his head. "Whoa, whoa, relax. Last time I checked we were both on the same side here."

The guard's weapons stance relaxed. A relief since there were only two ways this was ending — getting them on board or hostile takeover.

"We're posting a team on the enemy craft. Need to make sure they're ready for whatever comes their way."

The guards thought on Flicker's words for a few moments. "Orders are orders Flicker. You and these weapons are not going to be a thing."

*

Markou patted the old lady on the back in his best reassuring manner. He'd made a difference in a moment. He was able to isolate that feeling and tell himself he was a good person, despite some internal thoughts to the contrary. He left her to her thoughts and decided to take a break himself. It'd been a solid few hours of helping the civilians through trauma. It was impossible not to take some of that on board.

Just a little time to clear his head was what he needed. That and to update tabs on Hart and crew. In truth, he'd been trying to do that the entire time, but he hadn't managed to get eyes on any of them for a worrying amount of time. Something between the assignments he'd been tasked with and Hart's coldness had him very ill at ease.

A quick run to the toilet, grab a coffee and do a lap of the area before he got back to it should give a better perspective as to who was where and what it might mean, while not raising too many eyebrows.

He went about his tasks, ending back on the same spot some 15 minutes later, the only relief from a lighter bladder and a decent brew. No Hart, no Flicker, no Storm. Something was definitely going on. He pulled out his communicator, deciding what to say to Harding. He started a text to report the update, but decided not to send it, for now. Instead he shot a message to Hart asking to see her.

*

It was quiet on the bridge of the *Milky Pleasure* as Comms Officer Rodriguez found herself in the big chair. With Flight Manager Avis getting some shut-eye, Captain Hiscock on mission, Commodore Hart and Ambassador Harding off-grid, presumably also sleeping, there was nothing to do but watch everything play out in painful slow motion. One eye on the countdown clock and one eye on the mission.

Hiscock and Wave were ahead of schedule — the only silver lining in the universe right now. Sleep gnawed at Rodriguez. Watching the hypnotically slow and unspectacular real-time progress of events was a step away from counting sheep.

Still, quiet was good for someone who shouldn't be at the helm of anything. She curled up in the Captain's chair and did her best to not let the calling of sleep claim her.

A new display zwipped into life on the console in front of her, full of strange activity. She was probably as well trained as anyone to recognise the data and its impact. "MPOPS, are you receiving that?"

"Affirmative, acting Captain."

"It's Uix communication. I'm assuming we're back in their communication bubble."

"It would appear so."

"Does that offer any immediate threat?"

"Based on past situations, it would seem unlikely."

"Thanks MPOPS, I'll pass it up the chain."

*

In a remote corner of the docking bay, behind layers of plastic shielding and beyond human eyes, an alien fighter craft subtly pulsed into obedient life once more. Inside, the occupant melted into the moment — connection again. Home.

*

Wave checked the countdown once again, then did a little fist pump before inserting the last of the screws in the suppressor cover. "And done, over."

"Nice work, Wave. I'm in position. Just say the word. Over," said Hiscock.

"Not that I don't trust my theory here, but give me another 25 to get back out and the plate screwed back in. I'm not keen on getting insta-roasted before I see my plan come together. Over."

"You'd be safe down there, surely? Over."

Wave put the last of the tools back in his kit and started the careful journey back along the narrow walkway. "Assuming everything is in full working order. Assuming the drive reacts as expected. Assuming nothing's been damaged further inside the engine system we don't even know about yet. There's a lot of damage and a lot of diagnostics we can't get as a result. Over."

"Wave, you said this would work."

"Don't get your knickers in a twist. It will. Most likely. Just saying the factors I can't control could end up in the sort of system failures that would leave me ash and skeletal remnants and that's not how I want my night panning out. Over."

"Why didn't you mention this earlier?"

"I literally thought it was implied in every conversation that there's no guarantees."

"We need to abort."

"Abort this," said Wave after making a gesture into the camera. "Look, chill. I get the plate closed, you flick the switch, we head back to the drive room, run some tests with MPOPS and we'll know where we stand."

"I refuse to flick the switch. Over."

Wave groaned and picked up pace to the exit.

*

"Look, I'm not sure if you fully appreciate how little time's left and that saving humanity sometimes can't wait for the chain of command to go from, well, someone at your level up to the Ambassador and back. We could all be dead by then."

The response was a disinterested shoulder shrug.

Flicker searched for an angle to keep negotiations proceeding positively and peacefully. He had not had a fight in the longest time — that was Storm's thing. Oh for a vial of Reality right now. What could he say? "What if I get the Ambassador's robot on the line, will that help persuade you?"

"Pfft, that mincing freak. I'd rather take orders from you."

The other guard laughed with a hearty snort.

It was all that Flicker needed. The insult of both George and himself in the same sentence let out a fire of rage that had been building, probably, for several years. Before he truly realised what he was doing, he throat-punched the guard mid-snort then, while the other one stared on in a moment of stunned disbelief, Flicker head-butted him in the bridge of the nose. While the two were writhing on the ground he lightened them of their weapons.

The civilians came rushing through the door to see the aftermath of the commotion. "Whoa, badass," said one.

Flicker tried, but failed, not to let the comment go to his head. He managed to keep the head wobble to a minimum. "Grab their communicators and tie them up so they don't give us any other problems. Then we load up."

*

Markou gave his parting words of wisdom and guidance to another civilian then headed to a quiet corner of the space. He checked his communicator again. No response from his messages to Hart. There had been three now, each throwing a bigger olive branch than the one before. All read, no response.

He was on the outer. Did she know? She must know. Why else would things have changed? It wasn't like he was doing anything bad, just obeying the Ambassador's orders. Just doing his job. Even as he processed those justifying thoughts he felt hollow. He cursed himself.

He was lost. He couldn't follow the Ambassador's orders as he didn't know where the crew had gone and he couldn't find a way in to see where he stood with Hart anyway.

He paced back and forth a few times, running the options over in his head before picking a direction. He opened his message to Harding and hovered his thumb over the send button.

Seconds later, he got a reply.

From Hart.

Meet me in my quarters.

*

Wave screwed the last corner of the cover plate back into place, the two hoppers watching on. He didn't say a word as he clomped his magnetic boots with as much purpose as he could over to Hiscock's location.

He stopped when he was toe-to-toe with Hiscock. There was a silent staredown through face shields, which lasted way longer than anyone was comfortable with. Wave then broke the moment, walked over to the switch and flicked on.

"Knob," he said under his breath, yet just loud enough for it to be picked up on the communication channel.

He exhaled, then turned to face the team. "Those still interested in saving the species follow me back to the engine room."

*

Hart felt drained in a way she'd never known before. It was all-encompassing — physical, mental and emotional. Her thoughts now filled with knowledge too impactful, too vast to comprehend right now. She felt the need to sleep, to cocoon herself away while the mind mesh did its thing. She knew she wouldn't wake up the same person. At the same time, she knew that wasn't something that scared her.

"Is everything alright, Commodore?" said George, as they made their way out of the docking bay."

"What?" Hart said, absently. "Yeah, I think so."

"And your communication with the Uix?"

"Was complicated."

"But you're OK?"

Hart offered what seemed like a less than convincing "Yeah".

George knew enough not to pursue it any further. "So, what now?"

Hart was catching up on the old-school texts on her communicator. "I need sleep."

George nodded.

They neared the lift.

"And what would you want of me?"

"I need you to run a check on Storm on the *Shakespeare* and Flicker, ping me with anything I need to know. Comms me with anything urgent. Then head back to Harding. Wake me when he's awake."

"Affirmative."

"Also, I've asked Markou to my quarters."

"Is that wise, Commodore?"

"I... " started Hart. "I don't know. Something's telling me it is. Just letting you know where all the chess pieces will be."

"Affirmative, Commodore."

The lift was waiting and when Hart hovered her hand over the sensor, the doors opened. "Good luck George and stay safe."

"You too, Commodore. And stay strong."

Hart nodded as the doors closed and parted them once more.

*

CHAPTER 39:
TRUTH IS TRUTH

"MPOPS, remove all suppression protocols for the ARH-705 drive," said Hiscock

"Suppression protocols removed."

Hiscock looked to Wave, who nodded his approval. "Run diagnostics on current ARH-705 capabilities."

"Systems appear functional. Drive is ready to engage."

"Boom!" said Wave with a fist pump. "Like a fuckin' boss!"

Hiscock groaned. "So, what now, *boss*?" he queried, sarcasm dolloped on his pronunciation of the last word.

Wave stared at him in contempt. "Well, you can enjoy your hero white belt, even if it doesn't fit. Meanwhile we've got to get our asses back to the front of the ship before we fire this thing up."

Hiscock nodded.

"Well, move it! Airlock, stat."

*

Markou gave the cabin door a timid knock. Seconds later he heard the pitter patter of a shoeless walk, before Hart opened the door to greet him.

The two stared at each other — Markou questioning with his eyes, Hart guarded.

"So, here we are," said Markou eventually.

"Here we are," agreed Hart.

"Are you going to ask me in?"

Hart gave an affirmative head gesture, then headed for the couch, Markou in tow.

She poured a drink and offered one to Markou, who shook his head. She shrugged her shoulders and took a sip.

"So, it's awkward. Why is it awkward?"

Hart poured over his words, powered by another sip. "There's not much trust on this ship."

Markou went to answer but no words fell out. He tried again with the same result. "Why have you asked me here?"

She finished the rest of her drink with a swig, taking a second to collect herself. "This could be our last night. Stay with me."

Markou smiled. "Do you have any preferences from the playbook? Perhaps we could start with that thing I do that you seem to be a big fan of? Maybe even that extremely inappropriate thing from last Thursday could get an encore?"

"I… just lay with me."

*

In the ashes of an unknown bar and out of the prying eyes of the cameras, Flicker and his posse laid out the cache of weapons from their raid. He had ascended to hero status amongst the group and was listening in as they retold the story to another couple of civilians who helped stocktake the pile and assign the weapons to those who would be using them.

He hadn't felt this feeling in a while, maybe ever. Reality would've had him at intolerable levels of swagger right now, but it just didn't seem to sit right in this moment. Neither did false modesty. The more he thought about it, the more he realised he didn't actually know who he was. Whoever he was, though, he liked it.

If only the people he really wanted to share the moment with were there. He checked his communicator again to see if Hart had responded to his mission report — still unread. The others would be back soon enough, but this was the feeling he wanted to share. A shiver went up his spine in disgust. Who even was he any more?

He turned his attention back to the admirers and the task at hand. A holo-schematic of the ship now hovered in the centre of the room. The team discussed the permutations of potential conflict and where the manpower and weapon resources could be deployed in all conceivable outcomes.

*

"You getting your ass up to the bridge?" said Wave into his communicator, as he and his team headed through the bowels of the ship.

"There's too much to do here to get the *Shakespeare* battle ready. I'll barely have time for a test flight as it is."

"Erm, you know a test flight isn't going to be possible, right?"

"Say again."

"When we click in the drive, we're going to be accelerating all the way to the jump gate. Will would be left for dust."

"Well, shit," said Storm. "Still, needs doing anyway. I'll be at it until we hit the gate or the Uix hit us."

"When was the last time you slept?"

"Sleep, pfft."

"Don't you think it'd be a good idea to—"

"Listen rookie, I eat all-nighters for breakfast."

Wave's silence acknowledged her status on the matter. "Does that mean you'll miss my moment of triumph?"

In the background Wave heard Hiscock make a gagging noise.

"I'm not sure I want to be anywhere near you in a moment of triumph, it'd get messy."

"Well, your loss. Catch ya on the flipside."

"Roger that."

"Oh and Storm, nice job out there."

"You too."

Seconds later they were bursting through the bridge doors.

"Ladies, gentleman and alternatively gender assigned," Wave declared as he slipped on his shades.

He looked at the almost deserted nerve centre of the ship and sighed. "...or Rodriguez. Hi Rodriguez."

Rodriguez saluted to try to salvage some dignity from the situation before deserting the Captain's chair.

Hiscock took his command then shared a nod with Wave. "MPOPS, current drive status, report."

"Systems functioning as expected."

"And the drive? Ready to engage?"

"Affirmative."

Hiscock looked at the crew, each watching him expectantly. This was a Captain's moment, he could feel it. He could also feel something else. "Wave, why don't you do the honours."

Wave, mouth agape, took his shades off to process the offering. They locked eyes and Hiscock nodded his confirmation.

Wave cleared his throat, then returned his shades to their rightful like-a-boss position. "MPOPS, engage the drive."

"You do not have authority to—"

"Overruled," said Hiscock.

All eyes turned back to Wave. "MPOPS, engage the drive."

"Drive engaged."

The ship shunted as a surge of energy propelled the craft faster into the black.

"Whoo-hooo!" shouted Wave. Celebrations echoed around him as he broke into an ill-considered, and in most contemporary-thinking quarters offensive, robot dance.

"MPOPS," said Hiscock as the noise settled, "Do you have an updated arrival time at the gate."

"Assuming full drive functionality, we should reach the gate five hours ahead of previous estimates, well over two hours before the calculated interception from the Uix."

"Fuck yeah!" said Wave, with a double fist pump, before attempting a strut that he believed resembled Mick Jagger but appeared to observers to be closer to an injured chicken.

*

Dreams rolled though Hart's subconscious in ways she'd never experienced before. Thoughts so real and powerful she could reach out and touch them. She was in there with them, alive. Somehow she knew it was a result of contact with the Uix.

In this construct, not awake but aware, she saw her world through new eyes. She understood the people around her at different levels. She had seen, through the Uix's memory transfer, Harding for all his self-serving greed. That led her thoughts to the mind behind the body wrapped around her. Every sense knew the truth in his association with Harding, yet she felt the conflict with his feelings for her.

Her team on the *William Shakespeare* — they felt, well, like home. Or as close as you could come to home in her reality. And George, who could forget George.

The Uix, the power of their race, the enormity of their collective knowledge, the transcendence of their communication. Their truth.

She saw Harding — his actions and drivers — through the mind's eye of the Uix. How ugly. How petty. How dark. And for what purpose? She felt the shame it cast on her people. Not just Harding, it was in almost every direction she saw leadership. Executed for all the wrong reasons. Any noble or higher purpose felt underdeveloped, while politics and self-promotion thrived. How had it become this way? The shame washed over her as she could feel the noble goals of generations lost as the Uix could. Humanity — what did that even mean?

Truth. That word lingered in her thoughts. It was one she knew she'd wake up to in the morning. Truth. Somewhere, somehow, that would lead to an answer.

*

CHAPTER 40:
TO THE END OF RECKONING

The Uix felt the weight of isolation lift. Its thoughts enmeshed with the network again. While not amongst its kind, it was one step closer.

As the being let its memories and experiences transfer out, it soaked up the new collective knowledge now filling it. It was overwhelming, gloriously overwhelming, so much to catch up on. Within the rush of data, it learnt about the new trajectory of the ship he was currently captive on. That the vessel would reach the jump point before its kind could intercept.

Thoughts merged. Plans hatched.

*

Hart woke. Markou was already up, restless, pacing and lost in his communicator. He noticed her energy in a flash and went to make her a coffee, as was tradition.

"Sleep well?" he said.

"Completely. You?"

Markou already knew the answer, but was hoping for a conversation in-point. He probed again. "Barely, it's D-Day."

"It really is."

He sensed that the awkwardness would remain. He went back to making coffee. Nothing was the same. Nothing would be after today. Who really was he?

*

The bridge was abuzz with excitement when Hart arrived, Markou in tow. The doors whooshed open to so many familiar faces she didn't know where to look. Fortunately, Wave made the task a little easier, holding court with several of the female flight crew as he relived — again — his plan and the execution. Flicker the only male in the vicinity, George by his side.

Hiscock was at the helm, Harding standing over his shoulder. Aside from those watching the Wave show, all eyes were on the telemetry display. Numbers were counting down, trajectories and approach windows visualised.

She made a beeline for the Wave show, well, Flicker and George. Markou, unsure, followed.

Flicker raced in to wrap his arms around her. It took Hart by surprise, but she did not resist. "They did it."

Hart shared the embrace, but something told her there was nothing to celebrate yet — or perhaps at all. They pulled back. Flicker gave Markou a dismissive nod, while Hart gave George a smile and a nod. Their attention turned to Wave, in his element.

"Regardless of the risks we took out there, we got it done. You know, for humanity," he said with the most humble-guy-meets-everyday-hero expression. "Now we're 30 minutes away from hitting a window where they can't catch us."

Wave had his admirers eating out of his hand. Flicker made a silent vomit gesture to Hart. She smiled.

"Where's Storm?" whispered Hart to Flicker.

"Still working on the *Shakespeare*."

She nodded.

"Commodore!"

It was Harding.

"Do join us."

Hart made her way to the Captain's chair, Markou by her side. All the while the sense burned inside her that none of this was real. She was the only one who saw it. Well, her and maybe Storm. Everyone else was mentally already through the jump and to safety. None of it sat well with her and she did her best to look like she was sharing the moment.

Harding, too, seemed different, human almost. She knew it was the smile of a man who's ass was about to be saved, along with his secrets. "I do believe your strangely confident engineer may have changed the game."

She smiled. "It appears so."

"We're only 37 minutes away from celebr—"

Warning icons flashed up above Hiscock's console like a rapidly spreading petri dish experiment. The lighting in the bridge dimmed to alert mode and the dull alarm tone started its monotonous beat. The celebrations stopped. The room went quiet.

Looks were exchanged between Harding, Hiscock and Hart.

Hiscock did his best to get a sense of what was happening to give an early report.

"Well?" said Harding, the lighthearted tone a distant memory.

"Erm… many systems critical, Sir."

"What systems?"

"Umm… just trying to analyse, Sir, but it appears to be connected to drive failure."

"Fuck!"

Wave rushed to the Captain's chair to get his eyes on what was happening. "Oh fuck!"

Hiscock cleared his throat as he attempted to do the same with his thoughts. Process. "MPOPS. Report."

"There have been multiple failures in the drive system. Causes are many and varied — see displays for details."

Wave began interfacing with the alert icons, expanding them to read their details. "Oh fuck!"

"How did this happen and what does it mean for our drive capabilities?"

"Causes are both unexpected and unknown. There were no indicators to issues on any of my constant systems monitoring and diagnostics. The result appears to be a complete failure of the upgraded drive capacity."

"Oh fuck," said Hiscock and Harding in unison.

MPOPS continued. "I am currently working to stabilise operations as meaningfully as possible. We should be able to restore the original flight capacity, but that may take a few hours."

Another round of "Oh fucks."

Hiscock inhaled and exhaled. "So we should be in a position to make the gate jump?"

"Affirmative."

"Is there any solution that allows us to reach the jump before interception?"

"Negative. Interception is inevitable in all possible scenarios."

Hiscock looked at Wave for suggestions. He shrugged. "And you're absolutely certain?"

"Inevitable in all possible scenarios seems pretty certain," said Wave, unhelpfully.

"It is certain," confirmed MPOPS.

"George, get me a scotch," said Harding.

There was a moment of silence, outside of the alarm tone. The gravity of the situation kicked in for everyone.

"This doesn't make sense," said Wave, after pouring through the error messages. "The failures should've all been safeguarded — overloads, short circuits — basic stuff. And every one of these is a critical system for our new drive capability."

Harding and Hiscock looked at him blankly.

Hart encouraged more detail with an encouraging nod.

"I mean, if someone asked me to dismantle the drive's new upgrade, this is pretty much every spot I would hit to get the job done."

"What are you implying?" said Harding.

"I'm pretty sure this was an attack."

"An attack?"

"Yes, Sir. Except it would've taken days for a team of engineers and hoppers to pull this off. The rest of humanity didn't have the time or manpower to execute this."

"You don't mean—"

"The Uix — has to be. Somehow they've gotten into our systems, sabotaged the entire escape plan."

"How?"

"That I don't know. The one we have captive? Maybe we're back in their system's range again? Maybe it's something else we don't yet know about?"

Harding jumped on the communicator to Security Officer Al-Razi. "Have you noticed any changes down there?"

"We've been keeping our distance as ordered, Sir. Just monitoring life signs. There hasn't been any noticeable change in activity, Sir."

"When was the last time someone had a close visual inspection of the ship?"

Hart tried not to let her panicked swallowing of saliva show.

"Erm, not since your orders to stay away, Sir."

"I want someone to get eyes on that cockpit now."

"Yes, Sir. Standby."

Harding turned to Hiscock and Hart. "Suggestions?"

Their answers were cut short by an incoming message from the Uix.

"It appears your plans to outrun us have fallen short. Engagement is inevitable. Return our kind then prepare to die. Instructions to follow."

The message was shorter than the silence that followed. It was only broken by Harding's communicator. "Sir, there appears to be signs of activity within the cockpit. The ship's interface is active."

"Noted. Anything else?"

"Not at this stage. Do you want us to continue monitoring?"

"Affirmative. Out."

Harding swore under his breath, then looked at the crew watching on expectantly. "This is it, folks. They're coming. We need to be ready for whatever we may face. Since we have absolutely no idea what that will be, we need to run light and flexible. We need to understand our weaknesses, predict their likeliest strategies and how we can possibly counter them and get out of here alive. We have to be ready for anything, anywhere, any time and we need to do it for the future of our species.

*

CHAPTER 41:
THEY'RE HERE

The hours whittled away. The digital markers of their foe became observable lights in the distance, then shapes that could be made out with the naked eye. Strange, wondrous, deadly vessels in a magnitude overwhelming.

Possibilities were discussed. Plans were made. Schemes were hatched. The camaraderie of a successful escape replaced with mistrust. It existed as an undercurrent. On the surface an outsider might not have noticed the difference, but it was thick within those in the middle of it. In their own way they knew the system would work up until the moment it didn't. Beyond that was a disaster.

Everything was prepared. No one was ready.

Then it was time.

*

CHAPTER 42:
DEAD ON ARRIVAL

The few guards assigned to the *Milky Pleasure* took up positions around the docking bay. Their backup, the docking bay staff and a number of civilians, armed and scared. At the rear of the leisure decks, armed civilians stood watch over the three key exposed access points to the remains of the habitation decks. It left the final remnants of humanity holed up in a space less than five percent of the ship's total space. All entry points covered with all available weapons. It wasn't much. It wasn't enough.

On the bridge, Hiscock and crew watched on as the enemy vessels positioned themselves around the *Pleasure*. The flight crew occasionally offered verbal updates to what they were observing, somehow hoping the sense of process would offset thoughts that screamed 'we're outnumbered, we're going to die'. MPOPS, too, offered updates. Nothing tangible, no observations of a weakness or potential strategy to use in any possible fightback. They were completely overwhelmed. It was all just marking time with words. Processing the unimaginable that unfolded before them.

Harding paced behind Hiscock, but remained silent.

In the docking bay, Hart and the crew were aboard the *William Shakespeare*, now fully operational again. They watched the feed from the bridge, as well as feeds from key points on and around the ship.

"Fuck me drunk," observed Storm.

Wave went to respond, but was cut off with a "Not you."

Flicker looked at Hart. "So, what's the plan?"

Hart processed while she watched the screens. "I don't know. See what they do, see what we can do about it, I guess."

Her response floated in the air, ending all conversation.

*

It wasn't long until the enemy made a move. Blinding lights flashed out from several of the ships. By the time the camera lenses adjusted, there were hundreds of balls of light heading towards the *Milky Pleasure*.

*

"We have movement, Sir," said Comms Officer Rodriguez. "Multiple bogies."

Hiscock leaned in to view the feed closer. Harding did the same over his shoulder.

"MPOPS, can we get a read on those things?" asked Hiscock.

"Analysing now, Sir."

Hiscock shared a look with Harding while they waited.

"The constituent makeup of the spheres is unknown, Sir. They appear to be a combination of an unknown plasma and light."

"What are they doing?" whispered Harding.

"Avis, can we get some predictive tracking to sort out where we think they're heading?"

"Already on it, Sir. Early guesses look like, well, every entrypoint in the *Pleasure*, Sir."

Hiscock swore under his breath. "Have we got comms up with all forward positions?"

"Affirmative, Sir."

"As soon as someone has eyes-on, I want a report."

"Roger."

*

"Astley, you there?" called one of the civilians on point.

"Here."

"You might want to check this out."

Not what Astley wanted to hear. Not that anywhere felt safe right now, but he'd managed to position himself in a communications position well behind those likely to first face whatever death awaited them. He was perfectly fine with the current arrangement. Those around him sensed his hesitation meant doubt and started to give him looks he hadn't seen for days. He cleared his throat. "On my way."

He made his way forward to the last of the internal wreckage the front-liners were seeking covering behind. Already light was filling up the fractured hull beyond the sealed door, the view portal danced in the glow of light beams from outside as if there was a high production value concert playing beyond the door.

"Good lord," he said as he reached the frontline. "What is that?"

There were several civilians along the line. They all responded with different variations of a shrug.

Soon, an orb of some description passed right through the solid door. Pressing its way through solid metal like it was mere air. The door had a small orange heat wound, which soon faded before another orb passed through, then another.

By this point Astley had well and truly taken cover behind the wreckage. "Stay still," he whispered into his communicator.

The number of orbs soon multiplied. Light danced through the gaps in the wreckage, leaving the civilians in advanced positions feeling utterly exposed. Astley tried not to appear like he was cowering, while cowering. He faced away from the light, watching those who stood where he was only a minute or so earlier beat a hasty retreat. He cursed under his breath, wiped the sweat from his brow and waited.

It wasn't long before he felt a heat on the back of his head and neck. A dull pulsing sensation filled his ears. He felt like a marked man and closed his eyes. The heat passed from the back of his head to the top, to his forehead. He could sense the object was far closer than anyone would be comfortable with. Then he felt it on the back of his hands, making him aware he was using them to cover his eyes. Realising this defensive technique was probably not likely to prove any difference between life and death, he built up the courage to let his curiosity take a look.

The object, about the size of a football, was beautiful. Colours whirled through its core, while light shot out in patterns that appeared random to Astley. The light made it look, well, light, the coloured centre almost impossibly heavy, yet it floated through the air. While it didn't seem to have a front-facing side, he knew it was studying him.

He just stared back. Rabbit in the headlights. Waiting for his last breath to reveal itself through whatever horrendous firepower awaited.

Instead, the tone of the sphere's hum changed, then the lights moved to a different pattern and it continued its trip further into the ship, several dozen of its kind in tow.

Astley looked to the other civilians, all equally in a state of shock. He reached for his communicator.

*

"Astley, talk to me," said Rodriguez.

There was a pause on the other end of the line.

"Astley? You there? Did you see them? Astley?"

"Sorry, here. Yes, a very close encounter. There were dozens of them, man. About football sized, all colours and lights. And they passed right through the exterior door. Like, as in literally *through* it, man. Freaky as, man."

"And everyone's OK?"

"Seems that way. For now. They're moving your way, at least in that general direction. I think they're just here to check things out. Hopefully."

"Roger. Good work, Astley. Out."

*

Storm followed one of the spheres through her cannon's scope as it made its way across the docking bay.

"Just make sure that finger is a long way from the trigger," said Hart.

"C'mon Commodore, aren't you just a little bit curious as to what would happen?"

"I have a fair idea what would happen to us."

Storm threw a silent faux toddler-like tantrum.

"So, what now?" asked Flicker, as they watched the orbs infiltrate the docking bay by the dozens.

"We watch. We remember what we talked about. Stay frosty everyone."

They all turned their gaze back to the shieldscreen. Some of the orbs moved through the remaining hodge-podge of craft, some centred their attention on the guards and others headed to where the Uix craft sat. It was wholly hypnotic and suffocating viewing.

"What are they planning?" pondered Wave, to himself.

*

It was only a few minutes later when one of the spheres reached the bridge. Its lights attracted everyone's attention before it passed through the door to the bewildered silence of those within.

"Shut down visual displays," said Hiscock.

Harding nodded his approval.

The bridge sat in near darkness and silence as they watched the orb slowly make its way around the space. The complete loss of power was humbling, the enemy waltzing into the nerve centre of the remains of humanity without opposition within minutes of boarding. It was an utterly unnerving sensation.

The sphere soon honed in on the Captain's position, pausing to analyse Hiscock and his setup in whatever way it was. It seemed to last forever. While it did, Harding slowly inched himself further from Hiscock.

It was all to no avail. Harding was the next target for assessment. It zipped over to him in a flash, then hovered inches from his face. A million thoughts went through Harding's mind in those moments, but there was one simple one that resonated above all others. They knew.

After the staredown, the sphere circled him a couple of times before settling into a second round of face-to-face. Harding's palms were wet, not knowing if this was his last moment.

Then the orb left the bridge in a flash so fast a blink would've missed it. As did all the other spheres.

"Bridge is clear. Ship is clear," said Avis, seconds later.

Silence filled the bridge once more

*

"Man, they just reconned the shit out of us," said Storm, with the crosshairs aimed at the last retreating target. "I feel violated."

Hart paced in thought. "Will, any insight you can give us?"

"This above all: To thine own self be true."

"OK," she replied over several seconds. "Nothing more contextually relevant to the boarding we just witnessed?"

"I'm afraid not, Commodore."

Hart continued her pacing, thinking about possible future plays and, now, being true to thine self.

*

On the bridge, Hiscock was in close consultation with Harding. Well, to be more accurate, Harding was telling Hiscock what to do as all possibilities played out in his mind. Hiscock tried his best to nod in all the right places but, for the first time, he sensed Harding's aura of control had broken. Not an ideal scenario for Hiscock, given his own failing captaincy skills were rather dependent on Harding's advice and guidance. He shook the thoughts away while he refocused on Harding's words.

"... and we've got to make that the key. The second they get that Uix off the ship, we're gone. We've got to rally forces to where they're needed the most."

"Of course, Ambassador. Not that we have much to spare."

"We've only got what we've got. And they learn, fast. We've got to mix up how we attack and what we attack with. We've got civilians ready to do their bit, throw them at it. It all buys time."

"Time for what?"

"Time to do whatever we can to survive."

*

"...and you're absolutely sure? Because this seems like the worst plan ever," said Storm, while practising shooting moves. "I mean, if they're here to kill us, not killing them seems... what do they say... counterintuitive?"

"It'll get us killed like it will everyone else."

"So, why not go out all guns blazing?"

Hart looked at her crew watching on expectantly. "It's what they want us to do."

*

Activity started on the ships surrounding the *Milky Pleasure* once more. The displays on the bridge went into overdrive.

"Captain, we have movement, multiple signals," said Avis.

"Details?"

"Bigger than before, a lot bigger. Hard to pull much from the data, apart from getting signals of organic material."

Harding swore under his breath. Hiscock looked at him for direction, but got nothing.

"Acknowledged. Where are they headed?"

"Looks like... targetting the same points as before."

"So, if those ships were full of beings of some kind, let's assume Uix size, can we work out the numbers we might be facing?"

Avis interfaced with the controls. "Erm, best guess, several thousand."

Hiscock paused before muttering "Fuck". He opened comms to all his frontline leaders. "Another boarding is imminent. We're getting some signs of organic material. There's the possibility of a large number of bogies. Details as they come to hand, but stay sharp and expect anything."

He turned to Harding. "I thought they were going to give us instructions."

"The whole secret lies in confusing the enemy, so that he cannot fathom our real intent," said Harding.

Hiscock looked on, unsure what to say.

"Sun Tzu — *The Art of War*. They're just toying with us now. We've got to stay focused through whatever they throw at us, pick our moment and make our play."

*

"You heard the call, take cover and stay alert," said Astley.

He and the other civilians peered through the gaps in their barricade. Lights danced through the ports as the enemy approached. Silence.

*

The lights blinded the entry to the docking bay. It flooded almost every corner of the massive space. Guards and civilians on the inner-perimeter front shielded their eyes, as did those aboard the *William Shakespeare*.

The enemy craft breached the protection film keeping the void of space at bay. Ships docked on the outer reaches of the docks.

Those aboard the *Shakespeare* watched the holo display of the action taking place behind the blinding light — a full 3D representation of events. Seconds after each craft landed, dozens of beings poured out onto the docking bay floor.

"Oh, fuck," said Storm.

"There's hundreds of them," added Wave.

"At least," said Flicker.

Hart leaned into the display. "Wait, they look... human."

"What the actual?" said Storm.

"That's unlike you not to swear," said Wave.

"... fuck," added Storm.

Hart picked up her communicator. "Captain, we're getting a readout of what's landed on the docking bay. It's too bright to get eyes-on at the moment, but there's hundreds of them."

"Roger, Commodore, anything else?" said Hiscock.

"They look, well, human, Captain."

*

On the bridge, Hiscock tried to keep his pose as he quickly glanced around the crew before his eyes fell to Harding.

"*The Art of War*," whispered Harding.

Hiscock nodded, hoping it would hide his panicked swallow. "Roger, Commodore. Keep us posted."

*

Hart turned her focus back to the feed. She and the crew watched as the last of the enemy fell into position.

"Will, how many is that?" said Flicker.

"5418," said Wave.

"And how many guards and civilians have we got out there?"

"136."

"This should end well."

"Wait," said Wave, as he leaned into the data feeds accompanying the display. "I'm not seeing any vitals here. There should be all sorts of—"

Then the lights of the enemy craft went out. Everyone turned their attention to the shieldscreen, finally able to look with the naked eye.

"...vital signs," finished Wave.

"Well, fuck me dead," said Storm, as the army that faced them was revealed.

"Are they..." added Flicker without knowing how to finish the sentence.

"Dead?" said Wave. "Yup, no vital signs usually means dead. As does the flesh falling from their bones."

"Oh fuck," confirmed Storm.

*

CHAPTER 43:
CHAOS FACT

"Could you repeat that please?" said Hiscock, as he shot a glance toward Harding. "Zombies, Sir," shouted Astley over the communicator, to penetrate the sound of pulse fire and mayhem.

Everyone on the bridge looked at Hiscock. Hiscock looked at Harding once again. Harding, out of options, glared back expectantly at the Captain.

"...a fuck-tonne of zombies," said Astley, to fill the awkward silence with additional expectation of a direction.

Hiscock cleared his throat. "And the weapon fire is effective against them?"

"Affirmative. It's just the ammo situation. We don't have enough to deal with a fuck-tonne."

"Hold tight, we're on it," said Hiscock, as he ended the comms. "MPOPS, what munitions remain?"

"We have stock in Security Hold A — 25,000 rounds — and B — 1350 rounds. The rest is on the battlefield or lost through ship damage."

Hiscock sighed. "Can we—"

"Take the Hold A stocks down to the docking bay," ordered Harding to two of the flight officers. "Hold B can go to the civilians."

They nodded and left the bridge.

Hiscock went to protest but was again interrupted.

"The prize is on the docking bay. Nothing else matters right now."

*

Pulse fire fizzed across the cargo bay. Security and civilian support lined up to mow the enemy down as they advanced. Hart and crew watched on from the bridge of the *William Shakespeare*.

"Of all the things they could throw at us... zombies?" said Storm.

Flicker eyed the enemy's slow advance through a zoom device. "I think they're more like just reanimated dead *bits* of human. Some of them aren't even one person, just different people parts melded together."

"Still zombies," said Storm as she, too, used a device to zoom her view.

"That's some pretty sick shit," she said. "I mean, I'm impressed, but it's sick."

"What are they trying to prove?" asked Hart to herself and the room.

"Nothing," offered Wave.

He looked up from the action to see the rest of the crew looking at him.

"What are they risking — nothing. What are they gaining? Draining all our ammo and a complete understanding of our firepower, where it's coming from and numbers."

Silence filled the bridge as they all digested the simple truth.

"They're just getting us to show all our cards, then hand most of them over. And they haven't even started yet."

"Well, not all our cards," said Storm, as she caressed the underside of her cannon in a far too familiar way for a weapon/operator relationship.

Wave ogled on.

*

On the midship front, the dead were starting to mount the other side of the defensive barrier. They left the bodies of other now-re-dead in their wake, but their numbers were irrepressible. Astley peeked through the barrier to see a set of vacant dead eyes looking back. He squealed.

He retracted his position, aware several other civilians' eyes were upon him. He wasn't sure whether their disheartened looks were due to the dire situation, the lack of direction or his recent far-from-heroic vocal faux pas. He gulped in some courage, climbed up the barricade and fired several pulse rounds into the slowly advancing attackers.

He climbed back down and gave the woman next to him a confident nod. She didn't know how to respond. He cursed himself inside, while thinking of his next move.

He put two fingers into his mouth and sent out a piercing whistle, calling in the main players along the frontline. It didn't take long for them to be huddled in a circle.

"Observations?"

"They're hard to kill, Sir. Actually, do we call you Sir?" said one.

"Only if you feel like it."

"Not really."

Astley realised he'd invested so much hope in the outcome of that moment that he was visibly hurt. He moved on, like leaders do. "You?"

"I agree with Sarah, Rick, I've unloaded nearly everything I have and I've taken five down."

"We've got more ammo coming. Meanwhile, what's our strategy?"

No response.

So, happy not to call me Sir and ridicule my scream, not so happy to actually step up when it matters. It gave Astley a little confidence rebound. "Suggest we hit them with everything we've got for now until the ammo arrives. Let's make that barricade a pile of double-deads so deep the rest can't cross."

He got a cheer of approval from the civilians.

"Take your positions and pulse the shit out of them."

Another cheer as they followed orders. Astley felt a little swagger as he returned to his post. As the sound of pulse fire echoed around him, he climbed the barricade, gave a roar and started unloading.

"Sir!"

"Sir?"

It took a few seconds before Astley realised the voice was addressing him. He turned to see someone in bridge uniform signalling him down, a small bag in his hand.

Astley hit ground level and nodded at the crewman to speak.

He handed Astley the bag. "Your ammo, Sir."

It was a little underwhelming in size, but it'd do. "Cheers, pass the rest out down the line."

"The rest, Sir?"

Astley took another look at the bag. "Is this it?"

"Affirmative."

"For all of us?"

"Affirmative."

"You've got to be fucking kidding me?"

The flight crewmen held a stony face, confirming the situation was not one in which pranks were performed.

Astley took another look at the bag, then orated an array of his favourite swear words, while the crewman disappeared into the distance.

Many of the closest civilians already had their attention drawn to the scene.

Astley sent out another ear-piercing whistle.

"Change of plans, fall the fuck back."

*

The first front of the undead horde had reached the barricades in front of the guards and civilians in the docking bay. Behind them lay a mix of downed comrades and many more undead still advancing.

Frenetic pulse fire filled the air with light, overwhelming sound and a constant vibration that could be felt on the bridge of the *William Shakespeare*.

"They're fucked, aren't they?" said Storm, as she watched the human-led defensive line scramble to deal with the now up-close threat.

"Aren't we all?" said Flicker.

"So, why not fight back?" said Storm.

"We're only going to get one shot to take them by surprise," said Hart. "There's no point wasting that on dead humans."

"So, what can we do then? We can't just watch. We're wasted."

The group's attention had now drifted from the battle. They stood in a semi-circle around *Will's* main display console.

"If anyone has an idea of how we might be able to make a difference, I'm all ears," said Hart.

Looks were exchanged for several seconds before anyone dared speak.

"Since this window has passed for all the sane ideas, I might have something," said Wave. "I'm not saying it's going to win the war, but it might add something to help. Give us something different, you know. Different throws the Uix."

He looked up to see Hart nodding her approval.

"We need to go on a little raiding mission."

"We?" said Storm.

"You, me, Flicker and George."

"I like a good raid," said Storm.

"Maybe not so much this one. We're all going to have to sacrifice something, well, personal."

"Have you seen my boundaries?" said Storm.

"*Real* personal."

"Shut up and tell us the plan already."

"George, are you able to acquire Ambassador access permissions throughout the ship if required?"

"It's against protocol if it's not an emergency. But this would appear to qualify as an emergency."

"Brilliant, alright, listen up and listen good."

*

"Captain, the undead have breached the lines on C-Deck. Civilians have fallen back," said Rodriguez.

"Numbers?"

"Hundreds, Sir."

"Can you get a fix on where they're headed?"

"Seems to be a bit in all directions. We'll stay on it."

"Fuck, fuck, fuck."

Hiscock turned to see Harding repeating the word over and over. He held the gaze long enough to have it returned — no sense of guidance or direction, just the same word repeated. He turned to see his crew looking at him for leadership. "And the docking bay?"

"They're holding their position, for now. The extra munitions have arrived. Confident they'll hold off this attack, but might not have much left for whatever comes next."

Hiscock nodded to Rodriguez. "Keep me updated. Everyone, we need to expect the unexpected, we need to be ready to move at a moment's notice — to take on anything that's asked of us, whatever the circumstances. It may not make a difference but, then again, it might. We could just give ourselves a moment or opportunity to change this fight. Truth be told, we might not get that chance either, but if we stay together, ready and willing for anything, well, it might give us a shot."

The words just poured out of his mouth before he really had a chance to process. Regardless, they were a truth — one that nobody could escape.

He looked at the crew. He felt something, something different. The moment of silence seemed to last forever before Rodriguez saluted, then Avis. Soon, the entire bridge crew were saluting him.

Except Harding. He let out one more profanity before falling silent.

*

"If we place teams here, here and here, we'll be able to slow them down where the environment bottlenecks. It might not be much but we should be able to slow them down without using much ammo," said Markou.

"What's their plan, do you think?' said Astley, as he gathered around Markou's display with several of the civilians' key players.

"It's hard to be completely sure. We have multiple groups heading in different directions, some on their way here. Almost half their numbers are heading to the front of the ship. That's what I think the real game is and they're the ones we need to slow down."

"So, that's the fight plan, what do we do with the rest of the civilians?"

"If we back everyone not capable of fighting up to here, that should keep them out of harm's way."

"Do it!" said Astley. "We'll hold off the undead as best we can."

"Anyone found the best way to down the zombies?" asked Huang.

"They're not zombies as such," said Astley. "And there's no quick way to take them down that we've found yet."

"The head?"

"Exactly why they're not zombies. It's the first thing we targeted. I pulsed one's head completely off — didn't slow it down at all. The best plan we have at the moment is feet and legs to slow their speed."

"Perhaps we can put a team together to find a couple of stragglers and run a few tests?" said Markou.

"Good call," said Astley. "Meanwhile, the others get to safety and we'll hit 'em hard at the choke points."

Everyone nodded their agreement.

"Right civilians, fall out."

*

"You're just not right," said Flicker, as he ruminated on Wave's plan.

The group darted through the corridors, slowing down only for the corners, aware an undead surprise could be awaiting them on the other side.

"You're welcome."

They reached the first stop in their mission — Storm's quarters.

Wave turned to the others before Storm opened the door. "Also, and I know you're going to, but please don't judge me too harshly."

*

"Commodore — update?"

Hart looked at Hiscock's image on the communicator.

"They seem to be holding the undead back at ground level, Captain. The amount of ammo they're going through is a problem, as is what they might face next without it."

"What support is your team offering?"

"We are running an operation now we believe may help."

"Operation?"

"It's confidential, Captain."

Hiscock was thrown aback by her response. "We need to be working together on this."

"We have the same goal, Captain."

"What about support for the guards? The Shakespeare has more firepower than the ground forces combined."

"We are aware of that. Timing is everyth—"

"Hart, this is Harding. Cut the shit, what are you up to?"

It was Hart's turn to be on the back foot, Harding dropping into the comms and on the attack. "We're running with an idea we believe will help us, Sir."

"If you want to help, fire up the cannon and blast the undead back to where they come from."

"That does not seem like a prudent strategy, Sir."

"Listen, Missy, if I wanted your advice I would've asked for it. This is an order. Fire the cannon."

"I am unable to fulfill that command, Sir."

"If you don't get that thing fired up I'm going to—"

Just then, another shot of light flared out from the Uix craft that were still docked on the outer edge of the bay. Hart rushed to the window to watch. The ground forces covered their eyes from the power of the light. Hiscock, Harding and the flight crew watched on from the bridge. When the light receded a new danger was revealed.

"What the fuck?" said, well, a lot of people.

*

CHAPTER 44:
ARMED AND DANGEROUS

Six spheres of light lined up on the outer edge of the docking bay. They glimmered like semi-transparent pools of electric light, in the middle of each, the silhouette of a Uix could be made out.

A low hum could be heard over the chaos of pulse fire. To be more accurate, the pulse fire stopped for a few seconds as everyone on the battlefield sized up the new threat. When the threat stood still, the pulse fire picked up again, dealing with the closer undead threat.

Hart watched on, suddenly aware of how exposed she felt alone on the bridge of the *Shakespeare* — the screenshield looking like a paper glass defence for whatever damage could be inflicted. She moved away from the view to study Will's schematic feed.

"Commodore, are you getting eyes on that?" It was Hiscock.

"Affirmative. Six Uix in some sort of battle armour, I assume."

"Suggestions?"

"Apart from prayer?"

"I was thinking more along the lines of strategy."

"We won't know what they're bringing to the table until they bring it, Captain. Tell the guards and civilians down there to take cover — maybe switch up where they're positioned."

"Affirmative, out," said Hiscock. "Oh, wait, Commodore…"

"Yeah?"

"Just... get ready for anything. You might want to flick through the cannon's beginner manual."

"Roger that. Out."

*

Hiscock passed on his new orders to the frontline, then turned to Harding. "Are they actually going to send us a message or was that all BS?"

"I'm not sure any of it's going to matter much."

Something about Harding's words gave Hiscock a shudder. He had changed. In minutes. Leadership, orders and confidence evaporated, leaving only swear words and defeatism. This made Hiscock even more nervous than the actual leadership he had to step up to in the vacuum.

He looked around the room, a hive of activity, movement and displays of the chaos overwhelming his ship. All the chaos that would no doubt follow — it was on him now. He just watched the hypnotic action around him, tried to think of everything, and nothing.

*

The mission had proved successful so far for Wave and the team. Every item had been gathered, except one. The tension grew with each stop along the way. Civilians would dart in and out of sight on one mission of their own or another and they'd even laid eyes on a few of the undead. Although easily avoided, it was a reminder that turning each corner was a gamble and the numbers that were avoidable now, would soon be so much more. Emergency lighting and the constant low hum of the warning beacons throughout the ship only added to the drama.

It was a relief when they made their last destination. Wave stopped out the front of a quarter's door, turned to the team and raised an eyebrow. "Time for the big one. Everyone ready?"

"It'll never work," said Flicker.

"We'll see," said Wave, before wrapping his knuckles on the door.

"This better be about breakfast, you're four hours late!"

The aggression in the voice caught them all by surprise, but the pompous undertones did not. Wave looked at the others before responding. "Um, not exactly, um, I guess *Mr* Sphink. We're here to make you an offer."

A scoff that oozed superiority and more than a hint of been-isolated-too-long unhinged. "Not before I eat you're not. I knew they'd need me back at some point."

"Erm… we're not exactly here on official business."

There was a long pause on the other side of the door. "Well, I only do official business."

Wave matched the pause while he thought on his next move. "Fair enough. Sorry to have wasted your time. We just thought you'd like to have a chance to make a difference in whatever minutes we have left."

They waited for a response. When none came, Wave led the team away, ensuring his footsteps were heavy.

"Wait! OK, I'll hear you out."

The departing party stopped in their tracks. Wave winked at the others then turned back to the door. Flicker rolled his eyes, then followed, along with Storm and George.

"But not before I get my breakfast."

"For fuck's sake," said Storm. "We don't have time to dick about with this shit."

"He is the crowning glory of my master plan," Wave whispered.

He watched Storm roll her eyes then cock her weapon in frustration before he turned to George. "Can you grab whatever is the closest available food that resembles breakfast?"

"I want bacon," said Sphink.

"Shut the fuck up!" said Storm.

Wave glared at her.

She cleared her throat. "I mean, we'll see what we can do."

*

Markou approached the civilians holding the first choke point. Intermittent pulse fire filled the air, the ambient groans and gurgles of the undead enemy hinting at the size of the problem behind the few they could see. He moved in next to Astley and they exchanged nods.

"We got everyone to as much safety as they're going to find. Thought I'd come and lend a hand."

"Cheers, man."

"How're you holding up?"

"It's only a matter of time before they break through. We've already gone through half our remaining ammo."

"Don't use it all, no point dying on a hill here."

Astley nodded at him. "I hear ya."

"Also, how're *you* holding up?"

"Honest answer — never been better."

"Really?"

Astley nodded to the other frontline civilians. "That lot have given me something I haven't had on this ship before. Maybe ever."

Markou studied him, awaiting his words.

"Respect."

The word hung heavy in Markou's ears. He thought on the moment. "That's probably as good a gift as any to end on. You know, if it comes to that."

Astley nodded.

Markou returned the favour before nodding to his weapon. "Don't have a spare one of those, do you?"

Astley laughed. "Only one, if you're game."

He nodded to the corpse of a civilian half mangled and dismembered in the cover barrier on point. "Nichols — she fought a brave fight."

Markou took a deep breath then charged the line. After dancing around undead limbs he pulled out a forearm, with weapon still in hand. He prised the fingers free as he returned to his spot alongside Astley, checked the weapon's condition and gave it a wipe to remove the blood. "Shall we?"

"We sha—"

"Behind us!" screamed one of the others.

Undead poured out of a side corridor metres from the front line. Screams and pulse fire filled the air.

*

"You want me to do what?" said Sphink, through a mouthful of dry fruit loops.

"Help us fight back, bring something different to the table, keep the enemy guessing, it could make all the difference," said Wave.

"In *actual* battle?"

"Well, yes… we are in an actual battle."

"Risking my life?"

"Well, yes… I mean, if we don't win the battle we're dead anyway. But, yes," said Wave, sharing a look with the others that he felt nailed the tone.

Sphink swallowed the dry mouthful of sugary goodness down, paused, then looked up at Wave. "Why the fuck would I do that?"

"What?" squealed Wave.

"Told ya," said Flicker.

"Once a pen-pushing softcock, always a pen-pushing softcock," said Storm. The two high-fived.

"How about character redemption?" said Wave, not giving up. "How about doing your bit? How about the thought that if some of us do somehow make it out of here alive, the stories they'll tell of what people did in our darkest hour?"

Sphink lifted another heaped spoonful of cereal up to his mouth. "Fuck humanity." Wave opened his mouth, but no words fell out.

"Right, I've had enough of this shit," said Storm. She looked at Flicker. "Vial."

Sphink eyed the syringe with the fluorescent blue liquid inside and went into panic mode.

"What the fuck is that?" he said, as he went to jump to his feet.

Flicker grabbed him in a bear hug and Storm had the contents in his arm before he could utter another word.

He fought to resist the liquid while still pinned in Flicker's grip. It only lasted a few seconds before a calm set in, a deep and extremely overconfident calm.

Storm clipped Wave over the back of the head. "I told you we should've just done that from the start."

"I really thought he'd come around. I can't believe he truly is that much of an ass."

"I'll take it from here," said Flicker. "Wave grab the dildo."

"It's not just a dildo, it's the Goliath."

"Shut the fuck up and get it," said Flicker before turning to Sphink. "You're back, Sir. Listen, your species needs you."

"I always sensed that," said a now high-as-a-kite Sphink. "What can I do?"

"We'll guide you to the enemy, Sir, we know you'll take care of the rest."

Wave returned with the Goliath, handing it to Flicker who passed it to Sphink.

"That is one of the finest pieces of weaponry mankind has ever created. It seems a fitting weapon for a fitting hero."

Sphink's shoulders arched back with pride as he got used to the feel of the weapon in his hand. "Just point me in the right direction."

Flicker, Wave, Storm, Sphink and George headed out the door, where they were joined by Robot Storm on their way back to the frontline.

*

Hart sat atop the *Shakespeare's* main console staring out over the carnage unfolding below her on the cargo deck. As she watched on, so did six Uix, ready to bring an unknown destruction at any moment. The bridge wasn't the same place without the crew — no noise, no insults, no egos. She found it hard to think in the quiet. She even craved a message from Hiscock to give her something tangible to take her mind off the inevitable.

"Just you and me, Will."

"Indeed."

"Any inspiration for the moment?"

"It is not in the stars to hold our destiny but in ourselves."

Hart nodded and let the line sit with her in silence. She thought of the Uix and their moment of connection, reaching out with her thoughts to see if she could make contact again. She could not. Instead, she thought on it all and waited for the cards to fall where they would.

*

CHAPTER 45:
SMELLS LIKE VICTORY

"Whoa, whoa, whoa, slow down, Champ," said Flicker.

The team tried to keep pace with a now fully Reality-bitten Sphink. He aimed the Goliath at any menacing side corridor they passed, feeling no need to find cover. The crew did their best to keep a straight face. Robot Storm did its best to keep up.

It was the corners they rounded that had everyone on edge. Everyone knew at some point they'd come across the—

"Undead!" said Sphink, as he rounded the next said corner.

He aimed the weapon and started firing. "It's not working!"

The others rushed the corner to be on his flanks. Four undead, only 10 metres away.

"Flick the safety," yelled Wave.

Sphink pressed one of the buttons and his weapon started vibrating, violently. Behind him, Flicker, Storm and Wave actually fired their weapons. After a volley of pulse fire that lasted several seconds, the undead were reduced to four piles of rotted flesh. Sphink flicked the safety back on, blew air across the top of his weapon — in an instant deciding it was his new signature move — then turned to the others. "Thanks for your help," he said, dripping with sarcasm.

Again, the crew tried to keep straight faces. "You're just too quick, Sir," said Wave.

"That gun of yours is seriously overpowered," added Flicker.

"Just how I like them," said Storm.

Sphink completed his signature move once more, so his admirers could get a full view of the spectacle.

Tears formed in Wave's eyes, Flicker shuddered and Storm made a gagging noise.

"Is everything OK?" said Sphink.

"Totally!" said Wave. "I think I speak for everyone when I say I'm a little… overwhelmed with what I just witnessed."

Sphink nodded his understanding, before giving a confused look. "What's that smell?"

He traced it to the end of his weapon.

"Polymers!" squealed Wave in panic. "That beast of yours is made from some pretty advanced polymers."

Sphink stared him down, then took another, larger sniff. "Polymers," he said, then nodded.

Storm made the vomit noise again.

"So, how far are we from the docking bay?"

"Not far, Sir, not far."

*

"Hart, you there?"

It was Hiscock. "Why are you whispering?"

"I'm… in the loo."

"Oooookay."

"What's going on out there?"

"No change, apart from a few more undead no longer being a threat. Why are you on comms in the loo?"

"It's Harding, I don't think he's OK."

"What do you mean, not OK?"

"I'm worried he's… he's going to do something."

"Something?"

"Not sure, I feel a bit powerless. He's acting all—"

In the background screams broke out, along with the sound of pulse fire.

"Shit, gotta go."

"Wait! Hiscock! Hiscock?"

*

Hiscock ran back to the bridge from the amenities zone. All hell had broken loose. Undead had infiltrated the bridge, now outnumbering the crew. Pulse fire spat out in all directions. The crew fired at the enemy as best they could in close quarters.

Little battles raged everywhere. Hiscock drew his weapon, hands shaking, and tried to calculate his best move into the fray. He fired pulses into an undead keeping Avis pinned to the control desk, ensuring the angle would not expose the Flight Manager to friendly fire.

Avis was also pulsing the enemy until it dropped. Once the undead was defeated, he looked up to see Hiscock, weapon aimed at the fallen foe. They exchanged a nod before Hiscock searched for his next move. Then he saw it, an enemy honing in on Harding.

Harding was frozen and curling himself into a ball while the undead closed the ground between the two.

Hiscock also froze, for a moment. Should he save the Ambassador? His heart rate was working overtime, as was his breathing. He took a few deep intakes of air to steady his reactions and his thoughts, observed the moments, understood the gravity of the situation and the power he had over it, cursed the options, then fired.

The undead — the huge undead — had its back to him. He fired at the centre of the back of the spacesuit it was wearing and didn't stop until it dropped. Before it did, it turned to face the new threat, never fully completing the move before it fell on its back, defeated.

Harding was still huddled into a chair, whimpering.

Hiscock looked around the bridge. It seemed the other threats were under control as the bridge crew took back the advantage. He headed to Harding. As he passed the fallen undead, it groaned and reached out for him in its weakened state. He poured a volley of pulse fire into its chest until it moved no more. Then he looked up to its face, recognising it even through the broken visor and the damage of the vacuum of space. It was Brugelson, well, what used to be Brugelson.

He felt his chest sink at the thought. Then he noticed the words scratched into Brugelson's visor — Harding. He felt his chest sink to a whole new level. Then he felt panic as all the pieces started to come together. Did Harding know? Did Harding know that he knew? He collected himself before he turned to face the Ambassador. When he did, Harding was no longer slumped into a chair, he was standing. Pointing a weapon at him.

Harding fired.

*

There was commotion on the docking bay. Hart's attention was drawn to the frontline where there was a jostling of positions. Through the chaos of guard, civilians and a depleted undead force, stepped Sphink, brandishing a 15-inch long, and rather girthy, sex toy. By his side was a remarkably accurate robot version of Storm, wielding what looked to be a novelty cigarette lighter shaped like a pistol.

A million thoughts went through Hart's mind, not the least of which was a begrudging admiration for Wave's engineering skills. She smiled, but that was more at seeing Sphink, although she'd never admit that.

Pulse fire raged from behind Sphink and several more undead were downed ahead of him. He nodded in deep satisfaction to himself, blew the top of the sex toy, breathed in deeply, then winced.

Seconds later, her crew returned to the bridge, out of breath but with enough energy to high-five.

"It seems your mission was a success," said Hart, allowing them time to recover.

"Dude thinks he's invisible," said Wave. "And we prepped the ground crew."

"Brilliant."

The conversation ended there, the lure of watching the action unfold was too strong to ignore.

Sphink and Robot Storm marched forward through the undead lines, while the guards and civilians cleared a path for them through pulse fire. Soon, they were through the worst of it. Then the pulse fire attention turned to the six Uix. A volley of fire whooshing past an unaware hero with his sex toy and sidekick sex robot.

The fire had its desired effect. The Uix appeared to awaken into action. A deep hum filled the air before they unleashed a volley of fire in return as those on the front retreated and repositioned as planned.

*

Harding stood above the fallen Captain.

Hiscock looked at him, coughing blood and eyes of betrayal. It was his last moment.

Harding smiled, then turned his attention to undead redead Brugelson, aimed his weapon and pulsed a few rounds into its face until it was unrecognisable. Then he heel-kicked the visor to remove evidence of his name.

He took a deep breath of freedom, then looked around the bridge to see if anyone had witnessed the scene amongst all the other chaos.

Avis was staring at him, mouth agape.

Harding smiled at him, then brought a single finger to his lips to make the shush sign.

Avis paused before nodding and conceding eye contact, replacing it with views of his feet.

*

The payload delivered from the Uix shook the bridge of the *Shakespeare* to the point where the crew had to grip something to stay balanced upright.

By that time, the frontline had found cover. The same could not be said for Sphink and Robot Storm. The last image the crew had of them was a confused Sphink pressing buttons on his weapon, finding new levels of vibration but not enough firepower for victory. Even when he hit the overdrive button. Robot Storm stayed loyally by his side until the brutal end, both all but evaporated from the enemy weaponry, their remains still standing in the spot their soul left them — dry and withered husks.

Only the Goliath survived. Jumping around the docking bay floor like a fish, fresh out of the water and fighting for life on the land.

"Wow," said Hart. "Just… wow."

"I think we should all take a moment to reflect on all that," said Wave, as a tear formed in his eye. "I'm going to miss Robot Storm more than she'll ever know."

"Amen," added Storm, equally emotional.

Flicker nodded, in his own emotional battle with the loss of Reality.

"Does anyone want to say anything about Sphink?" said Hart.

Silence.

"Anything? He just gave his life for the cause!"

"I guess if we have to... it was a gamble I was willing to take," said Wave, eventually.

Storm offered a high-five that was accepted. Flicker soon joined in.

Hart said nothing, not enjoying how much she was enjoying it.

*

On the bridge of the *Milky Pleasure* the crew were dealing with the last of the undead when the enemy suddenly dropped to the ground. Seconds later they disintegrated, as did the remains of those that had already been downed.

The crew barely had time to start processing the moment when the Uix messaged again.

"Remaining humans, your time has come."

Looks were exchanged around the bridge, expecting an instant end, expecting the unexpected.

"The beings known as Ambassador Harding and Commodore Hart are to meet us in your docking bay. We will be waiting."

Harding's recent revival of fortune and confidence evaporated once more. All human eyes were on him. It was only the tip of the iceberg of judgement he was feeling and expecting. He tried to think of a strategy to avoid the instruction. There were none.

*

Down on the *Shakespeare*, they watched the undead army fall and disintegrate. The crew heard the message and looked at Hart.

"What are you going to do?" asked Storm.

Hart looked everyone in turn, then placed her weapon on Will's main console. "I'm going to go to them."

"Erm, I think you might need that."

"I don't think there's any outcome where it would make a difference."

Wave studied her. "How about we—"

"Hart, pick up."

It was Harding.

"Ambassador."

"You got the message?"

"I did."

"And?"

"I'm heading down to meet them as instructed. You."

"Erm… well, yes… obviously. Just planning our best defence strategy, make sure you leave the hefty woman on the *Shakespeare* so she can fire the cannon."

"I'm going alone."

"What?"

"I'm going alone."

"It's your funeral, Hart."

"Probably."

There was a long pause on Harding's end of the line. "Wait, no! I order you to take your crew with you."

"That's not happening, Ambassador."

What burst out of the speaker next was a mix of part scream and part A-Z of swear words. Hart terminated the comms after F.

Hart looked at her crew again, the gravitas of the moment suddenly washing her with emotion — this was goodbye.

"George, thanks for being brave in finding you and helping me find me."

George nodded.

"Will, thanks for your wisdom in the moments I needed it."

"That I say goodnight til it be morrow."

Hart laughed and sniffed back a tear.

"Flicker, you've changed these last few days. I like the new you. I think you do too."

Flicker found a tear welling in his eye as well. "Thanks, Commodore."

"I'd still be the preferred choice as Captain."

He laughed. "I can't argue with that."

"Storm, thanks for teaching me to not care what others think. Just, thanks for being you in general."

Storm didn't know how to handle the feelings that hit her, so she hit the exterior wall of the bridge. "It really was my pleasure, Commodore. Literally mostly about my pleasure."

Hart laughed. "Oh, one more thing. Whatever happens out there, you are not to touch the cannon. Understood?"

"...But—"

"That's an order."

"Seriously? Fuck! OK, just this once and only because it's you."

They shared a nod.

"Wave, if something happens to me that does not happen to you, I want you to have the captaincy of this ship?"

Wave was thrown by the statement. "Me?"

"Your leadership has been outstanding. You're worthy of the badge."

Wave, too, found himself with tears in his eyes. "It would be an honour, Commodore. Also, please don't die."

"I'll try."

Hart cleared the moisture from around her eyes, straightened her uniform, gave her crew one final nod, then headed for the exit ramp.

*

CHAPTER 46:
IT ENDS HERE

Hart made her way down the landing ramp and soaked in the scene from her new angle. It was amazing how the view behind the shieldscreen gave the horrors of battle a degree of separation. Now she was completely exposed. The occasional screams could be heard from a few of the injured survivors from the front. They lay near scattered bodies of those less fortunate, all left behind when the rest retreated or repositioned. Nearby, the once undead were now a haunting scattered mess of particles and remnants of clothing strewn from the front across the docking bay.

When the screams fell away there was an eerie silence. If you could ignore the deep humming and thudding as the Goliath still flailed about in the middle of the carnage.

Hart hit deck level then headed towards her fate. As she did, she got her first face-to-face view of the six Uix. Her heartbeat raced and her senses were heightened but she did not feel scared, whatever the outcome.

They looked more menacing at ground level — more invincible.

She paused for a moment, knowing they were watching her watch them.

The moment was broken as one of them shot a beam of energy into the Goliath, its fight for life now over.

She took a deep breath and headed for the six.

*

"She's so hero, I'm getting a boner."

"Of all the weird shit you've said, that takes the cake Storm," said Wave, as they all watched the goings-on from the bridge.

"Would you look at her though? Tell me you're not twitching."

"Can we focus, please? It's all good to twitch over the Commodore but we've still got Ambassador Hardon to swing his dick into this situation and that scares the shit out of me."

Storm looked at Flicker, then back to Wave. "So, what's our play?"

"I don't know," said Wave. "All I know is he's dangerous, for everyone."

"I haven't used my sniper for the longest time, but I can promise you I'd splatter-pattern him if you say the word."

"Not the most productive way to get in his head, Storm."

"Well, what have you got?"

"So far? A man that would say anything, do anything and use any power for self-interest and self-preservation."

"True."

"All that remains in his asset column right now is control of the bridge crew and control of the guards," said Wave, half aware of his surroundings, half lost in thought.

"Which he must know means fuck all against the Uix," said Storm.

"Which leaves the hostage Uix," said Flicker.

"Exactly," said Wave. "That's his ace. Well, that's his only real card."

"So, how do we deal with that?" said Flicker.

"We watch his every move and we make sure we're ready to go in the places that matter most."

*

Hart had been waiting for what seemed like an eternity but was most likely no more than five minutes. She was facing the six Uix, no more than four metres in front of her. The rest of the universe didn't matter in that moment. It didn't exist.

Until Harding arrived at the docking bay. She could hear the footsteps. Not just one set, several. She turned to see the crew of the bridge forming a guard around the Ambassador. She rolled her eyes at what a display of cowardice it was. She wondered if his 14-person meat shield appreciated their value in the moment.

Before she turned back to face the challenge ahead and not the spectacle of shame, she gave a quick glance to the *Shakespeare*. She could only make out Storm's silhouette through the shieldscreen. Out of the corner of her eye she saw two humans and a robot scurry from the landing ramp to a quiet corner of the docking bay. She kept her smile to herself then turned to face the enemy, well, the alien one, knowing whatever move Harding was making was being countered in some way.

Eventually, Harding moved in alongside her. Well, with enough of a gap for his human shield to surround him. They looked at each other for several seconds but didn't say a word. Harding ending the exchange with a dark smile before attention turned to the Uix.

"Ambassador Harding, Commodore Hart. It is time."

The voice came from a Uix, but it was hard to tell if it was one of the six or being projected from further afield. Harding and Hart exchanged another look, this one a far more telling moment of truth behind the expressions.

"Time for what?" said Harding.

"The end of things," said the Uix.

"Hang on a second. Let's not get too hasty. It seems to me a simple exchange could happen here and everyone can walk away unharmed."

"You have not followed your instructions, Ambassador Harding."

Harding went to start a number of counter arguments, workarounds and distractions, but aborted all before the first syllable left his lips. He eventually conceded, nodding to the bridge crew to return to the frontline.

Once again he and Hart shared a look.

"Look, this doesn't have to end ugly. You've proved your point. We have something of yours, you hold our lives in your hand. Surely we can come to a deal."

"There are no deals, Ambassador."

Hart watched the exchange unfold, hoping for a way, but not forcing one while Harding was in the driver's seat. It was like a bomb that needed deactivating but she couldn't break the wrong circuit to do so. She watched and waited, slightly safer in the knowledge her crew were helping somewhere in the wings.

While all that was happening, she couldn't help but feel the sensation she experienced when with the Uix captive. While not as overwhelmingly invasive in this moment, something within her knew her thoughts were not her own, they were part of something bigger.

She looked at Harding trying to hustle and haggle. How did he not feel this?

"You have a desired outcome, we have a desired outcome — making those things happen is called a deal."

"You are in no position to, as you say, deal, Ambassador. You discredit the last remnants of your species by trying."

Harding cleared his throat and shifted his stance. "Let's cut to the chase. What would you do to get your person back?"

"Obliterate you."

The answer rocked Harding for a moment. He gathered himself. "Do we have to deal in such extremes? Can we not just say you'd do anything for your people and I'd do the same for mine."

Something about Harding's last line irritated Hart to the core. She tried not to let it show.

"Ambassador, we are here to reunite our kind and to destroy you."

Harding nodded in seeming mutual agreement. "What if I said my survival was linked to that of the Uix we hold hostage? If I die, it dies."

*

From the bridge of the *Shakespeare*, Storm watched on and listened in to the conversation. She had a very tempting angle on Harding with the cannon and only resisted because of orders. She beamed the audio signal to Wave, who stood at the ready with Flicker and George near the Uix attacker craft.

*

Near the enemy attacker, Wave and the others had positioned themselves as best as possible to be ready for whatever presented.

There were a number of guards in striking distance. How loyal they were to Harding remained up in the air.

The three exchanged nods and glances, identifying the biggest potential threats and waiting in the wings.

*

"Ambassador, we can foresee no outcome where we leave without the member of our kind you keep hostage."

Hart could see Harding burn inside. She remained in silent observation.

Harding paced in frustration, then changed his tone. "It doesn't have to come to this!"

"Deliver your hostage."

"What about this? We give you the hostage plus we give you... Commodore Hart. She's yours to do with as you please."

Hart narrowed her eyes at the Ambassador. He did not return her stare.

"Commodore Hart, what say you of your Ambassador's suggestions?"

Hart thought on the Uix question for several seconds. "The Ambassador's thoughts are his own and do not reflect mine or the vast majority of those on this ship."

This time it was the Ambassador's turn to stare through narrowed eyes, unreciprocated.

"And what are your views?"

"You have us defeated, in every sense. I have come here, unarmed, to return your kind to you and to hope that an act of good may in some way be repaid, if you deem it worthy. There is no fight in me, just hope for a future for the remains of my people."

*

Storm thought long and hard about her orders as she trained the crosshairs on Harding's neck. Again, she resisted.

*

"You'll have to excuse the Commodore, she understands very little of diplomatic strategy," said Harding. "Her childlike naivete is endearing, but this is not the time or place."

"What is this the time and place for?" said the Uix.

"Action."

"As you say," said the Uix.

A flash of beams arced out from the six Uix, headed in the direction of the hostage ship. The show was over as quickly as it began.

*

Wave blinked frantically to get some vision back after the blinding show of fire. He was dazed but unharmed.

"Wave, you there? Flicker? George?"

"Storm, I'm here. What the fuck was that?"

"Shots fired. Looks like a bloodbath."

Wave started to see beyond the ghosted streaks of light stuck to his retina. Bloodbath seemed to be a fair summation to the view he was still blinking to fully take in. "Holy shit. Al-Razi, Holman, Atkins, Moulin, Volkov... and a couple more I can't even recognise."

"Flicker, you there?" said Storm.

"What? Yeah, here."

"It's Harding's crew. Laser targeted," said Wave. "Jesus, I was right next to Al-Razi."

He pulled a bloodied and sinewed piece of unknown flesh from his forearm and flicked it on the floor.

There was a rumbling sound and he instinctively ducked. He soon realised he was not in immediate danger, then turned to see the Uix attack craft rising into the air.

"Storm, you getting this?"

"Affirmative."

"No way that thing is flight worthy, I think the Uix have it on some sort of tractor beam."

"Agreed."

By that point, Wave, Flicker and George had gravitated together. They watched the undercarriage of the craft as it sailed silently over their heads.

*

Storm watched the enemy attacker float across the docking bay, over the heads of Harding and Hart, before coming to rest alongside the six Uix. A light energy filled the cabin. Shortly after it receded, the side of the ship morphed into a ramp and the Uix inside walked down to deck level.

For the first time, Hart, Harding and the others got a full view of a Uix. It was humanoid, to an extent, yet vastly different. It did not seem aesthetically pleasing to human eyes, its skin not smooth, its head large, like its eyes. Where humans have hair it had a dreadlock of tentacles and it moved differently, like walking wasn't a natural form of transport. If anything, it permeated an essence of vulnerable and exposed just existing in open space without protection. It made its way to stand in the middle of the six armoured Uix and faced Harding and Hart in silence.

The remainder of the human forces gathered on the dock to witness what was about to unfold.

*

Harding, in a state of shock from how far the game had shifted from his hands, paced. "Fuck!"

Silence.

"So, what, you're just going to exterminate us then? Is that it?"

Silence.

"It's not like you gave me much choice. You have a tech advantage, a communications advantage and you took us by surprise."

Silence.

"It wasn't a fair fight from the start."

Silence.

"We just did what we had to do in the circumstances. Surely you must understand that?"

Silence.

"What other option did we have?"

Silence.

He turned to Hart, "For fuck's sake, help me out here."

Hart maintained eye contact with the Uix.

At that point a holo image played. It was Harding's mission to meet the Uix, his self-centred diplomacy exposed in real-time replay. Then the exchange between Brugelson and the captive Uix, then the image of Brugelson's body floating in space with Harding's name carved into his visor. The battle on the bridge, undead Brugelson approaching Harding, him freezing, Hiscock saving his life. Him killing Hiscock.

It was all laid out for every surviving human to see.

Hart glared at him.

Harding looked at his feet.

"With your new clarity, do you have anything to say?" said the Uix.

Harding paused to consider his response. "Does that look good? No. Do you have any idea of the pressure of human leadership? No. You cannot judge a man on a few moments. It would take a lifetime to explain the reasons behind those actions and even then, I'm not sure your culture would understand."

"It would seem not even your culture understands, Ambassador."

Harding looked at Hart.

She glared at him. "Hiscock? You murdered Hiscock? Fucking asshole."

"Easy to judge from the cheap seats, isn't it? Leadership comes with a price, Commodore. If you're not prepared to wear it, you're not made for the badges."

Hart glared at him in silence.

"Like, right now. You've stood here and done sweet fuck all to save our species. You had a chance to change our destiny and haven't even fired a shot."

"At what point are you going to realise that you are the problem? How much evidence do you need to see? How many opinions do you have to ignore? It's you? This is all on you."

Harding went to speak and stopped himself. And again.

"Seems to me like you fucked everything you touched. Then doubled down by fucking up more to cover up your earlier fuck-ups. Now, here we are at the moment of species extinction."

"How the fuck is your amateur pyscho-analysis helping us now?" spat Harding.

"It's not. I'm just saying what everyone is thinking. There is no helping us now. Don't you even see? Our fate was decided before the Uix asked you and I down here."

"You're fucking everything up."

Hart laughed, half smiling, half embarrassment.

"I made you, bitch."

"Enough!" said the Uix. "It is time."

"Time for what?" said Harding

"Commodore Hart wasn't entirely right, but she was close," said the Uix. "We had possible outcomes in mind before you arrived here for this moment. But we have also learned, as we always do. You have since confirmed the way forward for us."

"What, what? This was some kind of a test? Didn't think to mention that?"

"Ambassador, every significant moment is a test."

"Well, it might have been easier to pass had my support actually supported me."

Harding and Hart glared at each other.

"That would've been the first foolish action the Commodore has taken."

"Excuse me?" said Harding.

"Ambassador, enough. Your destiny was assured before we arrived. As was your species until Hart made contact. We have seen inside her. We have seen a truth and understanding we didn't appreciate your species were capable of."

Harding looked at Hart. "Well done, your betrayal is complete."

"She has empathy, Ambassador. And intelligence, humility, understanding and kindness. These are traits we had never experienced before in your kind."

Harding thought on his next move from the corner he'd been backed into. "Which is why I gave her the promotion. Good people are hard to find."

Hart rolled her eyes.

"Look, I haven't been perfect, I'll admit it. And, like you, I've been learning too. And I've come to realise there are things I could've done better."

Silence.

"If we get a chance to live on, you'll see a lot better from us in that area."

"Ambassador. This has not been a negotiation for you from the start. Additionally, we examine your thoughts as we do your words. They both speak to us, yet express very different truths."

In that moment, Harding saw the negotiation curtain close. A wash of emotion hit him, not least of which the shame at complete exposure in front of all that remained of humanity. And Hart, standing next to him, beating him without hardly saying a word. How was this so? Why did he feel so foolish? This was to be his legacy after everything? He felt a rage burn within, a truth laid bare for history to remember.

"Fuck you," he said, as he turned to Hart and reached for his weapon.

Hart watched it all unfold in slow motion. He faced her full of his internal rage and drew arms before getting pummelled by Uix beam fire. His body was riddled with damage, his face stuck in a moment of shock and rage. Until, that is, a lethal cannon shot from the *William Shakespeare* finished him off in an explosive finale of gore.

*

CHAPTER 47:
THEN AND THERE

Hart, covered in Harding bits, looked at the Uix in stunned silence.

"Take these lessons and grow in peace, Commodore, as our species once had to."

It was all too much for Hart to absorb. No parting words left her lips, just a nod of appreciation and acceptance.

With that, the Uix reentered their craft and left the docking bay of the *Milky Pleasure*.

She wasn't even aware of the thunderous sounds of footsteps approaching until the survivors in the docking bay were on top of her. Wave reached her first, grabbing her in a bear-like embrace. He was soon joined by Flicker and George, standing nearby, with the rest of humanity, almost encircling them.

She couldn't remember a single word exchanged in that moment, just an outpouring of emotion. For those lost on the ship and beyond, for life salvaged out of the fire, for hope for something new, something better. All she knew was that in all the moments that were to come, there would never be anything compared to the overwhelming everything of then and there.

Storm finally made her way to the centre of the pack, joining the embrace.

The moment would've lasted a lot longer, had everyone not had to prepare for the jump. Talks of pulling out, given their change of extinction status were soon doused by the logistics of not hitting their window, turnaround times and food supplies. When added to increased risk of ship damage from the debris-riddled inner solar system and where they would even go should they make it, the only option was jumping and finding one humanity's outposts. Beyond that, the knowledge that a number of survivor ships were also extrasolar made their path forward, for now, clear.

It was agreed that interstellar travel was quite impactful on the human body and they should all treat the experience and their recovery from it with respect. Celebrations, it was decided, would be held immediately on the other side...

*

CHAPTER 48:
...AT THE PUB

George made his way through the crowd at the bar, past the packed dance floor and onto the table in prime viewing position over the entire establishment. The crowd gathered around were three deep, which meant more manoeuvring and apologies until he reached his target.

He handed Storm the objects to complete his mission, then went to take his seat at Flicker's side. Storm screamed in delight as she shuffled through the numbered cards from the deli.

"Alright, everyone just back it off for a second. Shut the fuck up and let me think," she said, before downing a random shot from the table.

She drew the No.1 card and handed it to the hulking guy with the long, dark hair. She slapped his ass as he walked away a happy man, before yelling. "Don't get too drunk."

The waifish woman with the gothic makeup was handed the No.2 card. Storm pulled her in and kissed her hard. When she was done, she nodded her away, before picking up card number three and searching for the rightful recipient.

Hart had seen enough to get the general concept and turned her attention back to the rest of the team. She was about to make a toast but the hopeful longing in Wave's eyes was too much to ignore. "Don't do it to yourself, it's painful to watch."

"Do what?" defended Wave, too strongly.

"Just, manage your expectations, huh?"

"I am! She still has 97 cards left and there's another 73 people standing around."

Hart sighed. "Has all of your recorded history with her in that regard not taught you anything?"

"But... deli cards."

Hart face-palmed herself.

"C'mon Wave, you're a hero in your own right tonight," said Flicker. "Why don't you set the bar higher for you?"

"I'm just watching events. Doing a bit of maths. I've got 24 reasons to keep watching, that's all."

"I've got some left over for the latecomers," said Storm. "I like a good latecomer."

She returned to her mission, while everyone else looked at Wave, who hunched.

"A toast," said Hart in distraction.

They all raised their glasses. "Here's to the future. Here's to surv—"

"What are we drinking to?"

It was Markou, dressed in a bar uniform with a tray full of shots. His arm was bandaged and he had a distinct hobble. He exchanged a look with Hart that lasted a dozen mini expressions.

"Glad you survived," said Hart.

"You too, Commodore."

"Why are you waiting tables?"

"A guy has to realise what he's best at."

This coaxed a smile from Hart.

"And where he went horribly, horribly wrong," he added.

"That's a toast worth drinking to," said Hart, before she swigged her shot and took another from his tray. "You could be in for a busy night. Hope that body of yours is up for it."

Markou smiled. "Feels good to play my part."

He sat the tray down, then hobbled back to the bar.

"Keep 'em coming," yelled Storm.

As she watched Markou hobble off, two men walked past him headed to the table, both beaming at the sight of her.

"Remember us," said Ivan.

Storm's face went through a range of confused emotions as she searched for the night they no doubt remembered the outcome of.

"You were going to write a book, under a nom de plume," said Atsuki, hoping the clue would help.

"Of course, yes, totally. How could I forget?"

Everyone in the conversation and everyone watching knew she hadn't remembered. "Good timing, I'm giving out numbers."

Wave gave off a little whimper. Hart consoled him with an arm on his shoulder.

"Wait, before I do, could you both poke out your tongues and give them a little bit of a wiggle?"

Ivan and Atsuki obliged.

"Yep, it's all coming back to me."

She reached into her deli card deck and handed Atsuki a 17 and Ivan 57. Their reactions were numerically on point as they exchanged a look before leaving.

"How good is this?" declared Storm. "Everyone's getting some tonight."

There was an awkward silence from the rest of the crew.

"What? It's true! We all saw the way Commo was looking at Markou — totally banging. And everyone knows Flicker's sticking it to George—"

"Storm!" said Hart. "That's enough."

"Here, take a number, you two. In case you have any energy left," said Storm, as she handed a mid-90s card to Flicker.

"Storm!"

"Sorry, didn't mean any disrespect Commodore," said Storm, as she handed her a number too.

"I need a piss," said Wave, as he scurried from the table.

They watched him leave. "Don't be so mean," said Hart.

Shortly afterwards a voice cut the awkward silence. "Hey, party people!"

They looked up to see Astley, wearing an eyepatch.

"What happened to you?" said Hart.

"Copped it fighting the undead."

"We heard you hurt it when you tripped over," said Flicker.

Astley shook off the accusation. "It got pretty crazy out there in the heat of battle, can't say for sure."

"After squealing."

"The details are hazy."

"Then landed face first on the butt of your weapon."

Astley cleared his throat. "I don't want to bore the real heroes of the night with my war stories. Is it true you juiced up Sphink and had him march face first at the Uix with a dildo in his hand?"

"Pfft. That was no mere dildo," said Wave on his return. "That was the Goliath." They tell me it was harder to kill than Sphink."

Everyone laughed.

"Did not go down without a fight," said Flicker.

"Just how I like 'em," added Storm, as she handed out another number to a stander-by.

Then she handed one to Astley.

"What's this for?"

"You don't want to know," said Flicker.

He shrugged and pocketed the 84. "And Harding, what an asshole. I mean we all knew he was an asshole, but to kill Hiscock."

"And Brugelson," added Hart.

"Heard he got his in the most brutal way," said Astley.

"He sure did," said Storm.

She replayed the moment with noises and hand gestures, mimicking the enemy fire, before doing the same with cannon fire and a head explosion.

"That's nasty!" said Astley.

"I still haven't apologised for that Commodore," said Storm. "I tried really, really, really hard to follow your orders, I really did."

Hart smiled. "You did good. Mostly."

"And then you sweet-talked the Uix and now here we are," added Storm.

"That's worth a toast, Commodore," said Flicker.

"That's right, a toast."

Hart raised her glass. The others followed.

"Here's to the future. Here's to surv—"

"Hold on a second, I'm down to my last number."

Storm held the 99 aloft, looking at Wave. She leaned towards him. Just then, a stranger walked by and gave her a smile. She handed him the card.

Wave stared at her, mouth agape.

"Storm!"

"What? I have control issues. And boundary issues. We all know this."

The table went quiet.

"Just do your damn toast," said Wave, as he necked a shot and readied another, staring at Storm.

"Here's to the future. Here's to surv—"

"Wait, wait, wait."

"Fuck, Storm, seriously?"

"What, I've just got one more item of business."

Wave sighed, they all did.

Then Storm reached into her jacket and pulled out a card with a 00. She handed it to Wave.

"You serious?" said Wave, gushing. "You're asking me to be number 100?"

"Well, I was asking you to go before number one, but whatever floats your boat."

Wave stared at her.

"And let me be clear, this is a one-time offer. No repeats."

"Yes! Of course. Totally yes."

"Peace of rookie advice?"

Wave nodded.

"You might want to knock one out before I call your number. Might give you a bit of staying power," said Storm, before winking with confidence at her sage wisdom.

Wave nodded, then got up to go back to the toilet.

"Oi," said Hart. "Not before I do my toast."

Everyone raised their glasses.

"Here's to the future. Here's to surviving. Here's to the next step for humanity. And here's to the best bunch of freaks I want to travel to the brink of existence with."

They all cheered the moment and downed their drinks.

Wave was already halfway to the toilet.

"Excuse me, Commodore."

It was Avis, a tense-looking Avis.

"Jeez, relax man, we've won," said Storm. She pointed to the table. "Have a drink... Or like ten, no one will notice the difference."

Avis returned his focus to Hart. "It's about our destination, Commodore."

"Yes?"

"It's bad."

"How bad?"

Avis took Storm's advice, swiping ten shots from the table, skulling them with barely a breath in between.

"Oh fuck," said Hart.

*

THE END
###

RATINGS AND REVIEWS MATTER

Thanks so much for reading our story, we hope you enjoyed.
If you do find the time to share your thoughts with others,
you would be doing the aithors a big favour :)

Review on
Amazon

Review on
Goodreads

ᗩᑌTᕼOᖇ ᑫ&ᗩ
With Matt J Pike

How did you and Russell come to team up on this novel?

I worked with Russell at a major media company in South Australia for several years. But because it was such a big workplace, we didn't really develop a friendship until 2008, when I started writing my first novel. As fate would have it, I was walking to work one day reading How to Make a Good Script Great when Russell saw me and started asking questions. Within minutes he had signed up to be the first reader of that novel, Kings of the World. But his input went well beyond that. Writing was his profession, not mine, and he guided, mentored and encouraged me every step of the way, something I'll be forever grateful for. He never sought anything in return. It was just how Russell was. One hell of a great guy.

Fast forward many years and I had several books under my belt, while Russell had completed his first novel, A Mage Alone. Along the way we'd joined different writing groups, through which we'd meet regularly (or infrequently, depending on the project) to discuss writing. Then, in 2019, after a couple of red wines, we decided we should join forces on a book. We had no concept, no genre preference, no anything – just the desire to team up. But by our next meeting, a few weeks later, I had a single question in mind: Has there ever been a gay robot in fiction? And with that, we dived into concepts and characters, ultimately ending up with the story that became Hart & Sol.

How did you decide who was writing what?

After we had the concept and a few characters sketched out, we decided to alternate writing duties on each chapter, such that one of us would write an instalment, the other one would review it, and they would then write on from there. Naturally, we met at the pub for each new chapter discussion and handover - that was a lot of fun. Not that it always went to plan. Russell once wrote a chapter so long I had to split it into three. And I took a couple of double chapters when I started feeling guilty about the word count! There was also a fairly noticeable difference in our writing styles. But after we had a few chapters on the page, we were able to find a middle ground between the two styles. We then settled into a pattern of back and forth until Russell became too sick to keep writing, which was about two-thirds of the way through the first draft. But he did give me his wishes on the things he wanted to see play out in the remainder of the book. So you can thank him for… (insert fun example here)

What was the biggest sticking point as you wrote?
The one that springs to mind was process. Russell was definitely a planner, while I was more of a panster, happy to let the book evolve organically. But, since the story didn't belong to either of us, and we didn't really have a firm idea how events would pan out, the chapter by chapter discovery process worked really well, albeit one that had to fit into our overarching story arcs. I can say, though, that we hadn't decided the outcome of the story, so our big decision was to write to a point where all the plot lines intersected, then figure it out. Best of all, we knew that if we didn't know the outcome in advance, it was a fair chance the reader wouldn't be able to guess it either!

Do you have a favourite character?
I'm a bit torn on this, but my allegiance is on the bridge of the William Shakespeare. While Captain Hart would be an obvious choice, I think I'm a bit split between her crew. Wave, Storm and Flicker are just so wrong in so many ways, but I like the way they mostly lean into their oddities and they almost become a thick skin. They also know each other way too well – sometimes biblically - and that in itself was really fun to write. Fun side fact: Russell and I each had our writing strengths around some of the characters. He easily wrote the Shakesperean prose of AI character Will, something I completely struggled to do. Big case of writer envy! And I don't know what this says about me, but he claimed I wrote Storm way, way too well.

Will there be a sequel?
I would like to do that. When Russell made his wishes known for the end of the book, he also had some ideas for two sequels, which I have banked away. But it was an emotionally taxing process at times to complete this manuscript in a way he would have been proud of and that (hopefully) paid tribute to him in a way. I think I need to work on some other things for a while before I jump back into this universe. But I absolutely love the world we've built and the characters are so fun to write that it would be a shame to leave it at one.